BEWARE

Book Four of Quarter Life

Adrian J. Smith

Supposed Crimes LLC • Matthews, North Carolina

This book is a work of fiction. Names, characters, places, and incidents are products of the author's imagination or are used fictitiously. Any resemblance to actual events or locales or persons, living or dead, is entirely coincidental.

All Rights Reserved
Copyright © 2022 Adrian J. Smith

Published in the United States.

ISBN: 978-1-952150-35-7

www.supposedcrimes.com

This book is typeset in Goudy Old Style.

Beware

CHAPTER ONE

THE HEAVY beat of the music pounded in Faye's chest making her heart thrum right along with it. The lights had all been changed since the last time she was down there, the ethereal glow no longer. The bar had become dingy and harder, less sanctuary and more club. It had been a long time since she'd been in a proper club, but it was freeing.

Faye stepped out onto the moss-covered floor, dragging Joel with her. She'd insisted on dressing him, shucking his normal plaid over-shirt in favor of an edgier look. She herself had gone to the nines to blend in that night. Faye gripped Joel's hips and dragged his front to her ass, grinding against him like she had not a care in the world.

The last few months had been the best in her life. She and Molly had figured some of their shit out, and she was back on the friendship wagon with Joel and Ben, making an effort to get to know Joel better and outside of his normal duties at the house.

Faye lifted her arms over her head, rocking her hips back and forth against Joel, who finally loosened up enough to move with her. The beat of the music thrummed through her to the point that she was pretty sure if Joel bent his head to speak, she wouldn't hear him.

The light changed. It became harsher and more vibrant. It was like a high without the drugs, and Faye reveled in it. They had changed so much since she'd been in there last. The entire atmosphere of the bar in the sewers had become something else, Faye was pretty sure she would have enjoyed it either way—she had multiple times—but this new ambiance was far more to her style than it had been before.

Wrapping her arms behind Joel's neck, Faye gave over to the beat of the bass. She closed her eyes, feeling everything as it moved through her. She wished Molly would have joined, just to see her dancing like this, but Faye knew that would never happen. Molly was far too uptight for something like that.

Faye turned in Joel's arms and slid one thigh between his, grinding against his leg. Pleasure shot through her body, and she bit her lip as she looked up at him with a hooded gaze. In another time and in another place, she may have once thought about it, may have once debated whether or not to entice him out the door and into the back room somewhere where she could sink her teeth into him. Joel was cute, he was young, he had a mess of dirty blond hair and bright blue eyes that stared into everyone's soul. Empaths often had that look about them, she'd found, but Joel was more than just a quick fuck or an energy feed. He was fast becoming one of her best friends.

The songs never stopped. Her head spun, and she needed more liquor to bolster herself for the upcoming night, not that liquor made too much of a dent in her life lately. No, she was too well juiced up on pure witch blood for that.

When Faye felt she couldn't take grinding against him any longer, she dug her dull nails into his side and moved up to whisper into his ear at a scream level. "Let's take a break."

Joel nodded at her and followed when she took his hand and headed for the bar area. There were no stools to sit on, so Faye leaned into the edge of the hard, gnarly wood that clearly an elf had made. It was smooth from years of use, but sturdy and perfect for what was needed.

"Aliya," Faye whispered. "Give us your pleasure."

Aliya, a young and spritely bartender and most likely a faerie of some sort, though Faye wasn't quite sure, smiled at her. Faye's heart melted a little more, and she wondered briefly when she had become so soft. Joel squeezed her hand, sending her comfort through their physical connection. Swallowing, Faye turned on him and grinned.

"Who would have ever thought I could get you to come down here?"

He chuckled. "Who would have thought you'd want to come

with me?"

Faye trailed a finger up Joel's chest. "I've always liked you."

Leaning in, Joel's lips were against her ear. "Not true, but I'll let it slide."

Aliya handed them both over a drink and pressed her forearms into the hard wood of the counter and stared Faye down. "Did you want anything else?"

Normal Faye would have asked for something a little harder than alcohol, but she'd been sober from heroin since she'd returned from Colorado with Molly. Months without the stuff and only Molly's blood to sustain her had been a surprise but her blood was a much better drug anyway. Faye shook her head. It would take so much for her to get high anyway with the blood coursing through her veins that it wouldn't be worth it.

"We've got something new to try," Aliya's voice lowered.

"Oh?" Faye leaned in, curious as to where this was going. Drugs weren't strictly forbidden from the establishment, but they also weren't normally doled out so freely. While Faye had been sober for the better part of four months, she was still interested, as she always was, in new drugs out there. "What's it like?"

"I haven't tried it yet." Aliya traced a finger on the table. "I just got some in tonight, but I know you have a preference for the harder stuff."

Faye slid a glance to Joel who shook his head at her, reminding her why she hadn't done drugs in forever and a day, but Faye was still curious. But more than curious, she was tempted. Joel put a hand on her back, the pressure enough to bring her focus to him and off Aliya.

"Faye, let's dance again."

"Sure." She chugged her drink, glad for its sour flavor as it hit the back of her tongue. When Joel didn't touch his, she downed it as well and went out to the moss-covered dance floor with him again, the music far louder in that area of the club than over by Aliya—done magically no doubt.

As Faye turned and grinded her ass into Joel's front, she stared at Aliya, her mind spinning about the drug. She'd get some. If only to have on hand for when she had a moment to try it. It was her first night off in months, her first night out without Molly insisting on being with her, and she wanted to relax, wanted to be free, wanted time to lose herself in whatever escape she could find.

Joel's lips against her ear startled her. "Remember, Faye, I'm an empath. I know what you're feeling."

She smiled seductively, twisting to face him and wrapping her arms around his neck as she danced with him. "Then you know why we're here instead of out on the creature capture with Molly and Ben."

He nodded. "Yes, but no drugs."

"Spoilsport," she said with a chuckle. Sliding her hand down his side in a forward movement, she knew they would never do anything, but she could push her limits with him. She always pushed with him. "What harm would a little dip do?"

"It could do a lot. Remember last year?"

How could Faye forget. Nearly a year before she'd been so intoxicated with getting high and escaping she had done anything for heroin. Stealing thousands of dollars from Molly, not that it'd made a dent in Molly's fortunes, and sneaking heroin at all times of the day and night just to find release and escape. It had been necessary then. She hadn't wanted to think about what had happened in Colombia and Molly had been useless in helping her come to terms with rape and kidnapping.

Faye pressed her lips against Joel's neck, smelling the blood flowing through his veins. Blood was her true sustainer, and Molly's blood far more than anyone else's. It had taken two years for Molly to finally admit why Faye craved her blood more than anyone else's, why they would likely be forever linked together. Faye still wasn't sure how she felt about fate's twist there, but she could live with it if the sex was hot and the blood sustaining.

Faye caught sight of her two favorite bouncers coming toward her. They would give Joel a good lesson in what it meant to be a lover. Smirking and waving them over behind Joel's back, the snake-like twins caught sight of her and joined on the dance floor. Faye spun around, the three of them paying her body as much attention as she could possibly stand before the twins no doubt became far more interested in Joel himself.

Slipping away, Faye made her way back to Aliya. She leaned onto the bar, her lips brushing Aliya's cheek like they had many times as she whispered, "Give me some to try."

"Anything for you." Aliya's mouth pressed against Faye's, dragging her in close. Her hand skimmed the front of Faye's body, dipping below the line of Faye's clothes. The small plastic baggie of whatever it was was deposited right where no one would see it. Aliya pulled back with a smirk. "First is free."

"And the second? You know it takes a lot for me."

"This should do it."

Faye hummed and carded her thumb across Aliya's high cheekbone that had either a natural shimmer to it or some kind of makeup she slathered on—Faye could never tell. "And the second?"

"Tell me what you think of this first."

"All right."

Joel was at her back, hands on her hips. "Don't leave me with them again."

Laughing, Faye rolled her eyes at Aliya and dragged Joel back to the dance floor with the snake-twins, making sure to give everyone as good at time as they were willing to have.

Molly breathed heavily, her back against the stone wall of the bridge. She stared across the way at the troll frozen in time in front of her, the torturous prison she had put him in. He didn't move to speak to her, although she was fairly sure he was amused by the scenario she found herself in. Molly turned to look down at her youngest employee, Benjamin, the man she had partially raised and was still working on some of that as he came into his own Tainted side.

"Where is it, boss?"

She let out a sigh and glanced around the small bridge with the road running right through it. "I don't know."

They'd tracked the creature there that night and risked going out to get it just the two of them. Benjamin had barely any experience in the field, although the last few months he had stepped up his game in that area. Molly adored watching him grow and explore everything he could and would be.

Listening carefully, Molly waited to see if she could find it. The tranquilizer gun was pressed firmly into her hand and Ben had one with a net on it. Their goal was for her to shoot first and put the beast to sleep and then Ben to finish the capture, but they had yet to find it in a state where Molly could get a proper shot off.

The tension in her chest rose as she waited for it to show face again, but she had a feeling it was already gone. The creature was unlike anything she had ever seen before, which was odd considering she had lived nearly three hundred years and had been ensconced in the creature capturing world for the better part of that.

This one, however, looked like a cross between a centipede and a scorpion, with a man's head covered in a fine layer of sheer slimy material. Every muscle in her body tensed as a vehicle drove under the bridge and she had to press herself to the wall to not be seen by the headlights.

She had promised Faye and Joel the night off, and she wanted to stick to that. They both deserved the break—Joel for everything he had done while Molly was under the curse and Faye because she needed to learn how to be a part of their team again and rekindle those connections after being thrust from the house.

"Any signs of it?" she asked Ben, risking a glance to where he stood next to her before she made sure to look around again.

"None."

"Your tracker?"

"Oh right." Ben pulled out a small sleek device and stared down at it.

Once again, Molly looked down at it and knew before Ben said anything that it was gone. They were going to have to do some research on what kind of creature it was and how best to capture it once they had more information because with the way it looked, Molly was sure the damage it had done was going to be catastrophic if they didn't put an end to its reign.

"It's gone."

"All right," she whispered. "Let's get home, and see if we can find some other ways to track it down or perhaps it'll resurface in that time."

Molly stared at the troll across from them under the other half of the bridge, anger burning in her chest. She'd seen him since that fated night over twenty-five years before, yet none of the anger and hate she had felt for him had subsided since that twisted and cruel night.

"Molly?"

"Yeah?" She turned to Benjamin, surely with a look of utter disdain before she corrected it so he could know she wasn't mad at him.

"We going?"

"Yes." Straightening her back and pushing off the wall, Molly stepped out toward the troll. His features looked exactly the same, but she had frozen him in time in a prison that could only be released by herself—perhaps her entire fold. The pain it caused him every second he was in there was no substitute for the pain he caused her.

"Molly?"

Once again she had been caught lost to her own memories. Shaking her head, Molly put the weapon down to her side and focused on Ben as best she could. "My apologies, Benjamin. I have seem to have lost my concentration."

"It's okay." He reached up and brushed fingers down the side of her arm before walking in front of her. "We'll catch him next time."

"Right."

Molly followed Ben to their van they had parked six blocks away when they'd originally tried to capture the creature. Molly wasn't sure if it was her failure or not, but it certainly wasn't Ben's. He was so new into embracing his Tainted side that he still hadn't worked out how to be in tune with all of his abilities.

Ben drove them home, and as soon as they entered the iron gates to the small white-washed house that had been her main home for the better part of a century, relief washed over her. Calm seeped into her bones, and she relaxed as he drove the long winding driveway to the garage. As soon as they were parked, she cleaned up their equipment after sending him to do some research and put everything in its proper spot. The rhythm of cleaning eased her left-over nerves of standing there with the troll, wondering just what he saw when he looked at her other than an old wretched crow who had put him in a prison. He'd probably think rather unjustly, but Molly knew better.

Molly walked through the upper floors of the house, checking on the rooms. Faye and Joel were still gone, which was no surprise to her, but everything else was quiet and just as it should be. Still unable to ease the ache in her heart, Molly took the elevator to the lower floors of her house, those underground, that housed every creature she had captured and more, those that were hidden from the public eye above who only saw a small white-washed house with large grounds in the middle of the old downtown area which was run down and hardly worth a second look.

She'd owned the property for two centuries, and when she'd bought it, she'd never thought it would become as much a home as it had, but Molly wouldn't give up the memories the halls held for her. She walked through the long hallways of the lower levels, checking on each of the creatures she had living with her. Her heart stopped when she saw him standing at the other end of the hall, staring at her.

For whatever reason, Molly could not understand why Malek was still there, still living in her house, why he hadn't up and run and left already as he was best at doing. Clenching her jaw, she walked toward him, his shock of blond hair perfectly combed on his head, the preppy polo shirt he always seemed to wear perfectly pressed and without a wrinkle. She felt like a dirty whore standing next to him covered in soot from under the bridge, her hair a mess.

"Malek," she stated, hoping he would open the floor to the conversation for the questions she had yet to ask him in the four months since he'd taken up residence in one of the rooms on the lower levels of her house.

He smiled at her, eyes lighting as he raked his gaze up and down her body. No matter what she did, Molly couldn't stop the swell in her chest and the shiver down her spine every time he did that, but she had zero desire to rekindle their liaison.

"I take it you failed."

The word hit her hard. Molly refused to move her gaze from him as she stepped in closer, daring him to try and put her down. Staring in his eyes, she saw the lust in them she knew would be there. "A failed capture is never a complete failure."

Without another word, Molly spun on her toes and left him standing there in the wake of her anger.

CHAPTER TWO

BEN'S HEART ached. He'd been the one to lose the centivalk, not Molly. She'd been on top of it until he had failed to help her keep track. Sitting at his work bench in the basement of the house, where he spent the majority of his time, Ben shoved his hands through his hair and let out a sigh. He felt awful.

The cool metal of the table against his elbows reminded him where he was, why he was there, but he'd never been able to master that side of himself. He'd always avoided it, to the point of taking medication to make sure he didn't shift into something he didn't want to be, someone who wasn't him. But Ben wasn't going to lie, that skill would have been massively helpful when trying to track the centivalk.

Rubbing his hands over his face, Ben turned up to look at his computers. Well, he'd been off his medication for a total of two months now after weaning off it and nothing had happened yet. Not even an inkling of shifting or feeling like he could shift.

He clenched his jaw and opened up his computer, transferring the data from the tracking device he'd brought with him on the capture. He wanted to work through the last chunk of their capture and see if he could figure out where the centivalk had gone. Then perhaps he could right his wrong.

He was deep into the data when the door to his workspace opened and shut. When he turned, he almost expected Faye to be there, but then he remembered she and Joel had gone out for the night, which only irked him even more. He wanted to be out with them. He understood the split of duties, that since he was going on more captures and doing more field work, he and Joel wouldn't always have time together, but he wanted to be with them, sharing in the time together, having fun, letting off steam. He was after all Faye's best friend, not Joel.

"Find anything?" Molly's smooth British tones floated over him.

Ben shook his head and focused to the computer, his heart fluttering and his stomach tightening. He had to find something to make everything better compared to what he had done. He'd really fucked it all up.

Molly's hand against his shoulder was warm and just what he needed to be grounded. She bent down and pressed a light kiss to his cheek. "It's not your fault."

"It is." He snorted when he spat those words out.

"Benjamin…" Molly turned him on the stool, grabbing his cheeks and holding him so they stared at each other. "It is not your fault. The creature is incredibly smart and adept at hiding."

"I could have found it if I could have shifted."

"You haven't been able to explore your Tainted side yet." She gave him a pitying smile. "The medication isn't fully out of your system."

Rolling his eyes, Ben twisted back to his computer and effectively broke her hold on him. "I haven't been on it for two months. It's out of my system, Molly."

"Perhaps it did permanent damage then. We never knew what the long term consequences were."

Ben let out a breath, tears stinging at his eyes. That would just be perfect, wouldn't it? He would have to be permanently human and his birthright forsaken. He should have done more thinking on taking the small white pills Molly had made for him when he was younger, but then again, he hadn't wanted anything but to be normal. He was so afraid of what his Tainted side would do to others.

"Benjamin," Molly pleaded again. "This isn't your fault."

He ignored her. Nothing Molly said was going to make him feel better, so he wasn't even sure why she was bothering. He just wanted to pick up the trail of the centivalk while it was still hot and maybe get out there for a second chance at capturing it that night.

She stuck around for another minute before dropping a kiss to his hair and walking out of his work area, shutting the door behind her. Once again alone, Ben let out a sigh. He sent Joel a text, telling him he was having a shitty night, but he knew Joel likely wouldn't get it any time soon and definitely wouldn't be able to answer. He didn't want to ruin Joel's and Faye's night off either. One night ruined was plenty.

Focusing back on his computer, Ben finished transferring the information into his desktop and then filtered through it. When the door opened again, he was going to turn and glare at Molly and kick her out again, but he was surprised to see Malek standing somewhat sheepishly just to the side.

"Need something?" Ben asked. Malek rubbed him the wrong way from the start. It was odd finding someone who knew so much about Molly but who was unwilling to share any of that information, and in fact, someone who seemed to lord that knowledge over everyone in the house. Faye really got annoyed with him quickly because of it.

"I thought I could help."

"With that?"

Malek's plump lips thinned, and he stepped in, the door closing behind him. "With the centivalk."

"Do you know much about it? Because we know jack shit."

Malek gave a wan smile. "I know some. I've at least encountered one before, although I never was stupid enough to try and catch it."

"You've seen one before?"

Malek nodded. "When I was very young, still in training myself."

Ben's throat constricted. That would have been close to three hundred fifty years before. If it had been that long since the last centivalk had been seen, no wonder Molly was shocked to find it lurking in their city.

"Are you going to share more than that or just stare at me like I'm psychic?" Ben hadn't meant his tone to come out so brash, but he was exhausted after a long day of work and then a failed capture. If Malek had information for him, he wanted it sooner rather than later, and he wanted to be able to do something with it.

Malek stepped farther into the room but still maintained his distance. "All I remember are rumors about how they could vanish at the snap of someone's fingers."

Ben cocked his head to the side. "Go on."

"It had terrorized that town for near a decade, and they hadn't been able to capture it or kill it. One person had managed to attack it, but the outer shell was very tough."

"Is that why you were called in?"

Malek shook his head. "No, I happened upon there by accident."

"What happened?"

"Eventually the town died."

Ben stiffened. "What do you mean died?"

"The centivalk killed them all, and I presume, moved on to the next place."

"Great," Ben muttered. "Do you remember anything else?"

Malek shook his head.

"Okay, well, thanks. I guess." Ben knew Molly was likely holed up in her office with books strewn about as she tried to research the damn thing and find some way to track it better, but Ben was just as much at a loss for how to do that now than he was before. Malek took the dismissal for what it was and left Ben to his own devices. Ben tried his best to keep his mind off his own failure to shift and track the centivalk and instead focused as much of his energy as possible on finding the creature again.

Faye grabbed Joel's hand as they stepped out of the underground club in the sewers. The fresh damp air hit her face as she drew in a deep breath. Pressing her head to Joel's shoulder as she walked with him along the sidewalk, her body thrummed from the beat of the club as it left her.

"Let's go visit my friend."

"The troll?" he asked.

"Yeah. It's been so long since I've visited him."

"Sure. We can do that."

Faye smiled and squeezed his arm lightly. "I want to get something for him. I promise you, it's not for me."

"Get what?"

Looking into Joel's blue eyes, Faye let out a breath. Of course he wouldn't know. She was pretty sure she was the only person who knew anything about her troll as she'd come to think of him. Most people just thought he was a tourist attraction staple in their fair city.

"I promise you, it's not for me."

Joel narrowed his gaze at her, no doubt feeling her nerves at even bringing the topic up but also her excitement from it. It had been so many months since she'd been high, and while she didn't plan on using the heroin she bought, the two small pills shoved into the edge of her bra were enough cause of excitement, and she did plan on trying them.

"My friend is imprisoned, you know that."

"Yeah," Joel answered.

"It's painful for him to be stuck frozen in place. Usually when I can visit him, I bring him something that can help ease his pain for a little, give him some relief."

Joel's lips thinned, but he nodded. Faye grabbed his hand, and she turned away from the bridge and walked down toward the pier where the man in the red hat was. She purchased just a small amount for her friend, bartering for a needle since she hadn't brought one with her.

On the walk back toward, Faye wrapped her arm around Joel's and pressed her head into his shoulder. "Thank you for coming out tonight. I know it's more my scene than yours."

He snorted. "As much as it is, Faye, I still enjoyed it."

"Good." She gave a sad smile. "Molly would never be caught dead there."

"You might be surprised," Joel muttered.

"Really?"

He shrugged. "She's been there before, though from my understanding it's been a long time since she's returned."

"How long has the club been operational?"

"About a century, or something like that. It's changed since then, but it's kind of always been a safe haven for Tainted."

Faye processed that information. She'd known it'd been there since she'd moved to their fair city but hadn't realized it'd been quite so long. Finally they reached the bridge. Faye let go of Joel's arm and smiled at her troll friend. He looked scary in some ways. Half his body above ground while the other half remained underneath.

Most humans thought he was just a statue and nothing more. A tourist site for those who visited. His face was elongated, looking almost as if his skin was drooping off with his age. Faye knew better. He would come alive, and his skin would turn to be like leather, shifting around as he barely moved what he could in order to visit with her.

Crawling up his hand to his arm then his shoulder, Faye patted his cheek. "Care for a visit, my friend?"

It took time for him to move, the rattling of stone moving against stone as he came alive. Faye waited patiently, knowing this was the most painful part of the prison for him. As soon as his eyes lit up on her, she smiled at him.

"I brought relief."

"Then don't wait." His voice was deep, and he spoke slowly, his entire body frozen in time slowing down Faye's world every time they spoke.

"I won't." Faye went to work mixing the heroin powder she'd bought with some water. "I brought a friend with me today, hope you don't mind."

"He's young."

She snorted. "We've had this conversation before, my dear friend. Everyone is young compared to me and you."

"Who is he?"

"Joel!" Faye called, beckoning him to join her from his place on the sidewalk under the bridge.

He gave her a wary look but did follow the path she'd made, climbing up to sit next to her on the troll's oversized shoulder.

"Good to meet you, properly," Joel added.

"Likewise. You work for the witch?"

Joel nodded sharply. "I do."

"Be careful with your life," the troll answered until he hissed when Faye dipped the needle into his tough skin and depressed the drug into his body. She watched his features change as relief flooded him.

Tossing the needle behind her troll, Faye brushed her fingers over his skin then dipped her fingers below her bra line. She couldn't wait any longer. She wanted to try out the two small pills she'd acquired at the club and see how they would affect her, what kind of high she would get. Worrying that only two pills wouldn't be enough, Faye popped them in her mouth and swallowed before turning to Joel who still had his eyes riveted on the troll.

"We were out tonight," Faye stated. "I convinced Joel here to visit you because it has been far too long, my friend."

"Yes, too long," her troll answered. "Your witch was here earlier."

"Was she?" Faye leaned forward to catch his eye and smiled at him. "With Ben?"

"Yes." He held out the last consonant, hissing.

"Are you feeling better, friend?"

The troll nodded. Faye shifted a glance to Joel. She wondered briefly how long it would take for her own indulgence to hit. Pills took longer than injection, but even though, she'd only had two pills and with her body makeup, her metabolism, her healing abilities, it often took her a whole lot more to get high than the average person—like insane amounts. She wondered if she'd feel it at all.

Faye pressed her cheek to her troll and stared at Joel. "I took Joel here down to the club tonight."

Her troll snorted. "He does not fit in."

Faye smirked as she looked the silent Joel over. "He doesn't, but he enjoyed it. So did I."

Joel scrunched his nose at her. "It was a good break from the usual."

"Yes. Exactly." Faye chuckled. She patted her troll's cheek and shifted from where she leaned against him. "We must get back, my friend."

"I understand."

"I wanted to give you some relief since we were out here."

"Visit again."

"Soon. I promise." Getting on her hands and knees, Faye pressed her lips to her troll's cheek and grinned at him as she pulled back. "I won't wait as long."

He nodded and then morphed back into stone. Faye stood up and walked precariously back down her troll's arm to the sidewalk below. Joel followed her, and as soon as they were on even footing, she once again wrapped her arms around his and pressed her head to his shoulder.

"We should head back."

"Probably," Joel whispered. "It's late, and we have to be up in the morning."

Faye groaned. "Don't remind me."

They walked toward the motorcycle they'd taken to get there. Faye had driven while Joel held tightly to her back. She saw it in the distance under a streetlamp when Joel's cellphone buzzed in his pocket. Faye's superior hearing picked it up immediately as Joel fumbled around and reached for it.

He pressed it to his ear, and Faye heard every word of the conversation.

"What's wrong?" Joel asked.

"I need your help." Molly's sweet voice filled the other end of the line, but there was an edge of worry and frustration in it.

"We're mostly sober."

"Good. Meet me at the docks. This thing likes water."

"What thing?"

"I'll fill you in when you get here."

Molly hung up. Joel turned to Faye, and Faye shrugged. "Adventure number two?"

"Yeah. Let's get going. She sounded…"

"Distracted?"

"That might be the word for it." Joel drew in a deep breath. "I'm sure you're sober because you suck at getting drunk. I, however, am not as sober as you."

"Hang on tight, then." Smirking, Faye grabbed Joel's hand and dragged him forward. She jumped on the bike and waited for him to sit behind her, his arms circling her waist as she revved the engine and headed off toward the docks.

CHAPTER THREE

MOLLY'S HEART raced. She glanced to Benjamin, making sure he was safer than she was. They dashed around old buildings, broken trashcans kicked onto their side, junk left all around the edge of the docks. She remembered when this was once the prime place to be, the prime real estate to have, but that wasn't the case anymore. It hadn't been for decades.

Swallowing, Molly readjusted her fingers on the weapon in her hands. She was going to tranquilize the creature, and Ben was supposed to net it, but she doubted his concentration and his abilities. She always had, as much as she didn't want to. It wasn't that she didn't believe he couldn't do it but that he would get in the way of himself and stop himself from accomplishing all that he could. She'd seen him do it so many times over the eighteen or nineteen years she'd known him.

The echo of the motorcycle washed a sense of relief over her. She hated to call them in for assistance, but she needed the help. She did not want to lose track of the centivalk again. Faye parked her bike next to the van. Joel was off the back in two seconds flat, coming toward Molly. Faye, however, stopped at the van and grabbed her own weapon before standing opposite of Molly on the other side of the shipping container near Ben.

It was how they always worked. Joel with her and Faye with Ben. Falling into the rhythm of the capture, finally, Molly let out a breath and nodded toward the edge of the water. "See it?" she whispered to Joel.

He squinted and then nodded. "Yeah."

"There is no way to surround it since it faces the water."

"Can it swim?" Joel asked.

Molly shrugged. She knew it liked water, but it hadn't actually tried to go into the river yet, which was something she definitely did not want to test out because if it did, she knew their second attempt that night was going to be a loss.

Faye, without warning, stepped out from behind the container. She shoved her handgun into the back of her tight pleather pants and walked boldly toward the creature. "What is she doing?"

"I have no idea," Joel whispered.

Ben stuck his head out to make eye contact with Molly and shook it, shrugging.

"Ben's just as lost."

Molly gripped her gun tighter, sweat forming on her skin and making it cold and clammy as she watched Faye's hips sway as she stepped closer to the centivalk. "Does she even know what it is?"

"Doubt it. But you know Faye, she's reckless."

"Not lately. This is...new." Molly swallowed. She was going to have to come up with a backup plan.

Faye walked closer, her boots quiet on the cement of the pier. Molly's heart was in her throat.

"She can't—"

"She might," Joel answered. "I can't...her feelings are odd."

"Odd?" Molly turned on him with accusation before focusing back on Faye. "What do you mean odd?"

"I can't...I can't get a read on them. I can't tell what she's feeling at all."

Molly's gaze caught sight of Faye's nails elongating, her shoulders hunching, and her neck cracking. "Bloody hell, she's changed."

"What?"

Without hesitating, Molly moved out from behind the shipping container and ran as fast as she could toward Faye, hoping to catch her before she got to the centivalk, but in her vampiric form, there would be no contest. Faye would be so fast Molly would stand no chance of keeping up with her.

Power tingled in her fingertips, but she ignored it. She didn't want to use magic that night, and she definitely did not want to use it on Faye, though she may have no other option. The centivalk must have heard Molly because it turned sharply, it's white domelike head spinning in their direction. The hundred legs under its body shifting to tighten, but it didn't jump into the water.

Molly breathed heavily, hoping Faye would turn to face her, but she didn't. Joel and Ben followed. She was only feet away from Faye when she reached out, but Faye was faster. She spun around, her eyes completely black compared to their normal slate-gray, her face pale and set as she focused all her energy on Molly.

Molly stopped short, her boots skidding her to a halt. She glanced at the centivalk, who still hadn't moved. Raising her weapon, she aimed it at the creature and fired, hoping she hit it because Faye was on her in two seconds flat as soon as the gun went off.

Faye had a hand against her throat, fingers pressing down and cutting off Molly's airway so she struggled to breathe. She kept her gun clenched in her fingers, intuitively knowing Faye wouldn't injure her, she never did. They were rough together. But this time...Molly drew in a sharp breath. Faye's eyes were wild.

"Faye stop. I think I know what's wrong." Molly whispered, barely able to speak through the force of Faye's hand.

Faye's eyes blinked, briefly flashing to their normal slate-gray before going back to completely black, the entirety of the eye, not just the iris and color vanishing. Faye drew in sharp breaths, her chest rising and falling in an uneven rhythm.

"Faye. It's too much."

Before Molly could finish speaking, Faye's lips were against her ear, her tongue curling over the edge of her earlobe. Molly tried to glance around and find where Ben and Joel had gone off to, see if she'd managed to take down the centivalk for them, but she could see nothing but Faye.

"Faye—"

"Bloooood." Faye's voice was deep, but it was slow as well, like she had to work hard to get the word out. Her fingers twitched against Molly's neck, and Molly knew she was going to have a bruise from it.

Bringing her own hand up, Molly cupped Faye's cheek to try and distract her from whatever was going through her head. "Faye."

"Bloooood."

"You can have some when we get home."

Faye snorted. "Now."

"Why? You shouldn't need any yet."

Faye's long teeth scraped down the tender and soft skin of Molly's neck from just under her ear to the top of her collarbone.

Molly couldn't help the shiver than ran through her body, settling in the base of her spine. Something was very wrong—this was so unlike her. Faye hated being a vampire, and she certainly wouldn't beg for energy, as Faye called it, in the middle of a capture without good reason.

Nearly giving in, since it was her one weakness, Molly focused everything she had on Faye. "What's wrong?"

"Bloooood."

Molly moved her hand down to the one Faye had wrapped around her throat and attempted to loosen her fingers. It worked momentarily, and once again Faye's eyes flashed back to their slate-gray before morphing into their vampiric black.

"So you keep saying," Molly whispered. "Now is neither the time nor the place."

Faye drew in a deep breath through her nose, the hiss of air surprising in the dark of the night. Her forehead pressed into Molly's shoulder as her hand skimmed down to Molly's side. Faye clenched her fist while holding Molly's hip, her sharp and long nails breaking through the fabric and skin at Molly's side.

Molly cried out from the pain, white flashing in her vision as she tried to focus on what was happening. What shouldn't be happening. Something was wrong, and she had no idea what it was.

"Faye, you're hurting me," Molly spoke through clenched teeth, tears stinging at her eyes. "Faye, stop, please."

Shouts could be heard from the edge of the pier, but Molly couldn't focus on them. Faye had hold of her, her nails piercing so deeply into her waist that Molly worried if she moved the damage done to her side would be irreparable. Molly panicked. For the first time in decades, she full-out panicked.

"Let go of me."

"Bloooood," Faye repeated.

Molly whimpered. "Then take it already."

Faye's teeth plunged into Molly's neck, but this time, it wasn't pleasurable like it had been every other time they had done this. Pain surged through Molly's body, rocking her to her core. She could barely focus as Faye's tongue lapped against her skin, feeling like it had spikes on every taste bud as it dragged along her flesh.

The power that had been working into Molly's fingers intensified. It was a protective reaction, and she knew it was one she was going to have to follow as much as she didn't want to. Blinking tears from her pain, Molly called on her power, building it in her chest before she blew it out at Faye, ripping her strong body from

Molly's and flinging her back at least twenty feet. Faye's form bounced against the cement of the pier, skidding as she came to a halt.

Molly dropped down to her knees, blood pouring form her side where Faye had no doubt ripped a chunk of flesh. Whipping her head around, Molly stared at Joel and Ben, who were struggling with the centivalk in its net as they tried to get the situation under control. Molly closed her eyes and called on the power she had left, the nature around her. Thunder rocked the pier, loudly booming.

When she opened her eyes, Faye was coming back to her, stalking her like a prey ready to be consumed. Molly could help with the centivalk, but Joel and Ben would be helpless against Faye. Pulling down two fingers of electricity, Molly aimed them. One hit her target completely, rendering the centivalk motionless so Ben and Joel could take care of it, but Faye dodged the second finger of lightening.

"Faye, please," Molly pleaded. She wasn't sure she had the focus to cast another spell. Not to mention the will to do it.

Faye's jaw was set as she moved forward. Molly lifted up her hand from her side, putting both out in front of her as she focused everything she had. Faye's body once again flung back, but Molly hadn't done it. Looking around wildly, Molly cursed as she slumped to the ground. Malek stood near the shipping container, his eyes glowing with light as he used his own magic, holding her in place.

Molly's shoulders pressed into the cold cement as she pushed her hand back into her side, fruitlessly trying to stop the bleeding. She tasted iron in the back of her throat as Faye stood up again. Something was wrong, seriously wrong. Faye shouldn't be able to break hold of Malek's holding spell.

Twisting her head, Molly watched Malek walk closer as he put all his energy into holding her back. Molly was going to have to help him. There was no other option at that point. With a mutter of words on the whisper of a breath, Molly cast the spell, binding Faye unto herself. Faye dropped to the pier, her body writhing as she tried to break loose. Molly kept the spell in place as Malek ran toward her along with Joel and Ben.

They crowded around her, Malek's hand against her side. Ben looked like he was going to run from fear, and Joel looked flat-out confused. Blood moved into Molly's mouth. She didn't have much time. Malek said something, but she couldn't hear him. Joel and Ben backed up, stepping away as they watched. Molly turned to look down at Malek, their eyes locking.

"This is going to hurt."

She nodded sharply, knowing exactly what was about to happen, and it wasn't going to hurt her near as much as it was going to hurt him, but once again, her injuries were severe, and he would need her magical assistance in order to seal the wound while also maintaining the spell to keep Faye bound.

"Quickly," Molly whisper, her voice so far off she wasn't even sure she had spoken.

Malek's hand was hot against her side, and she knew blood still spilled from her. Molly turned toward Faye, who struggled to get loose from the invisible bonds. While Malek worked a second spell, Molly began a third. She mimicked his words, adding her magic to his. The wound was bad. Malek closed his eyes to concentrate. Molly joined their magic, briefly, and Malek's head rose back in pain as her injury seared across his body before it vanished completely.

Before he had a chance to step back, Molly doubled her magic on the bonds that held Faye, keeping her completely still. Malek's thumb brushed against her cheek, just under her eye, as he stared down at her. She said nothing as she rolled away from him and pushed to her knees. Joel and Ben still stared wide-eyed, but she nodded at the centivalk.

"Finish containing the creature." Her voice still didn't sound like hers. It sounded far off, and Molly was certain Malek's magic hadn't been able to penetrate all of her injuries. She would have to deal with that later.

As she stood, the sticky feel of blood rubbed against her leg and side, the battered fabric of her shirt showing the true amount of blood she'd lost. Malek held her arm to steady her, and as much as Molly didn't want to hold on, she needed to in order to stay upright.

She stalked toward Faye, and then once again dropped to her knees. Faye's form kept morphing into her human form from her Tainted form and then back again. She was unable to control it. Molly brushed fingers through Faye's dirty-blonde shoulder-length hair.

"What did you do?" she whispered.

"Bloooood. Please."

"Let me," Malek whispered.

Molly shook her head immediately. No. She and Faye had agreed that if Faye were to need blood it would be from Molly, not to mention, she didn't want Faye to get a taste of Malek's purer blood, the stronger blood. It might pull Faye away from her. Even though she was weak, Molly extended her wrist over Faye's lips, waiting for the pierce of her teeth into her skin.

Faye drank freely, pain once again showering Molly's body. She winced but bit her cheek to keep the scream threatening inside. Faye couldn't stop. Molly realized it too late. Whatever Faye had done, she couldn't control herself, and Molly's blood wasn't helping to heal her. Malek ripped Molly's arm away, obviously realizing the same thing. He wrapped her wrist with his hand as blood continued to pool along her skin and held tight to stop the flow of it.

"What's wrong with her?" Malek asked.

"No idea. We need get back."

He grunted, helping Molly to stand. She swayed into his side, barely able to keep her feet steady on the ground. Closing her eyes, Molly turned into Malek as much as she didn't want to. Everything around her spun in circles, and she felt weaker than she had in so long she couldn't even remember the last time.

Joel and Ben finished wrangling the centivalk into the van, and then Joel came back to her, helping her to stand and move while Ben helped Malek with Faye. As soon as she was pressed inside her Tesla, which Malek had obviously taken from her garage, Molly closed her eyes.

It was almost too much. Everything had been going so well for the past months since Faye had come back into her life. She had shared with Faye all about the combined histories of vampires and witches, how they needed to join together to be strong and powerful, how witches had been weakened significantly since the genocide of vampires.

Faye had been rooted, even-keeled since then. They had worked together as a team. She'd banished drugs from her house, and Molly knew Faye hadn't imbibed, but even then, when Faye was high, she'd never been like this. This was...Molly had no idea what had happened, but she intended to find out.

She watched out the front windshield as they shoved Faye into the back of the van with the centivalk, Malek still holding the spell with Molly's help. They wouldn't be able to get too far from them as they drove home, but Molly was sure both Joel and Malek were aware of that.

Sighing, Molly closed her eyes, whispering, "Faye...what have you done this time?"

CHAPTER FOUR

FAYE HAD been pliant on the hospital bed in Amachon's medical bay for hours. Molly had been in the next section on her own bed, watching Faye through the glass windows that afforded her a view in. Amachon had given Faye something to make her sleep and then panicked when her heart stopped briefly and he had to shock her back to life.

Whatever Faye had done, it rendered her body human. Not even Molly's blood that Faye had insisted on taking and Amachon had given even more of could help her come back around to her normal strength and healing. Molly's lips pressed together, nearly disappearing as her mind worked through everything that could have happened.

She'd allowed Faye and Joel to go out that night, hoping they would have a night out on the town—which they did. It wasn't solely for the purpose of letting them relax, Molly had hoped they'd glean some information from the local Tainted crowd. There were rumors running amok, and Molly wanted to know if they were true or not, and if they were, how much weight they had to them. She'd done it on purpose, though neither Faye nor Joel had known that at the time.

She wished she could get up off the bed, but she knew she had to reserve her strength. Malek would have expected her to expend a lot of her magical energy, but she still had some in store. Faye's bloodletting wasn't helping anything, not to mention the internal bleeding Malek had failed to heal which had landed her in the medical bay with Amachon to begin with.

Groaning as she shifted on the thin mattress, Molly turned as best as she could to look at Faye through the glass. In all their years together, there were only two times she had seen Faye in a bed like this, completely out. When they'd first met and Faye had been weak from feeding only on dead animals for years instead of humans or Tainted and injured. Faye had extreme base jumped from one of the skyscrapers near her house and landed rather spectacularly in the maple tree in the front yard. Molly's suspicions had been up since then.

The only other time Faye had been in a bed like this was after she'd done a self-abortion, a baby that had been the product of a month-long kidnapping, torture, and rape. She'd been this pale then too, though not as weak, and Molly's blood would have healed her right up. This time, however, Molly feared she'd never be back to her usual vampiric self.

The door shutting alerted her to the fact she wasn't alone. Molly hadn't realized how lost she'd become in her thoughts. Turning toward the door, she was glad to see Joel instead of Malek, though she had no doubt Malek would join her soon enough.

"How's the centivalk?"

"Fine. Hanging out in a habitat for now. Joel is fixing it up to be more pleasant and specific."

"No attacks?"

Joel shook his head. "No, that lightning bolt you hit him with seemed to take everything out of him. He's slowly coming around. A lot easier to handle for now."

"Good." Molly relaxed, her gaze moving straight back to Faye through the open window. "Tell me what happened tonight."

Joel shrugged and shoved his hands into his pockets, rocking back on his heels. "We captured the creature you'd been hunting all night. I'd say that was a success."

Molly's lips pulled into a slight smile. Joel was good at avoiding what she really wanted to know when he didn't want to talk about it. She was also very good at waiting him out to convince him to speak.

"Whatever happened with Faye and you…"

"What happened before you got to the docks?"

"Not much." Joel shrugged. "We went to the sewers. Had some drinks. Did a lot of dancing—she likes to dance, by the way."

"I didn't know that."

"Well, you should. Anyway, we did a lot of dancing, and then finally we went for a walk."

"Where'd you go?" Molly wanted to know if Faye was high on something or if another witch had cursed her. Faye had been anything but normal when they'd gotten to the docks.

Joel blanched. "We went down to the pier and then to visit her troll friend."

Molly stiffened. "I didn't realize she still visited him."

"They're friends."

Snorting, Molly glared at Faye through the glass. "No one is friends with him. He uses people and then he kills them."

"Molly—"

"Did she do anything else?"

"No. No drugs. I swear."

Molly pursed her lips. "All right. See if you can find anything else. Amachon's running some tests."

"Molly." Joel's voice nearly broke, and he sat on the edge of the bed to get her full attention. "How are you?"

"Fine."

"No, really."

"I'm fine, Joel. Thank you for asking." She reached up and cupped his cheek. They had been close too long for her to fool him. "I'll be fine shortly, as soon as Faye wakes up and my power is restored."

At his nod, Joel stood and smirked at the door. "You have another visitor."

"Malek?"

"Yeah."

"Go check on Benjamin, would you?"

"Absolutely."

As Joel left, Malek came in. Malek didn't waste any time, sitting on the edge of the mattress and running a hand up and down Molly's arm. His eyes looked so soft and concerned for her, and she knew she could easily lose herself in him again, but she wouldn't. She would never risk herself like that.

"How are you?" Malek's accent almost matched her own, but it held a hint of otherness to it.

"Well enough," Molly answered, not wanting to show any weakness to him. It would be the death of her if he saw her weaker than she already was.

"She near killed you."

Molly turned back to Faye, lying prone still. "She did. What the hell were you doing there? How did you know where to find us?"

"I'm not immune to the workings of your house, Molly. I saw you and Ben leave. I thought I could help."

"So instead of offering it outright, you stalked us until you could come in and be the hero. Typical." Rolling her eyes, she snorted out a breath. "Never would a man glean to offer help instead of just giving it."

"Why are you so angry? I saved your life."

"You didn't need to."

"Obviously I did."

Molly was very close to letting it slip, but she held back and shook her head. "Your presence in this house is at my discretion only. You are not to interfere with how operations occur here."

"Noted." Malek glared at her. "Would you like me to leave?"

"Yes. And don't think about joining in on our work again. You are not welcome."

"Such hostility." Malek leaned down close to her, nose to nose. "I wonder, Molly, if that hostility is because you may have feelings still."

"Nonsense."

"Hmm," Malek whispered, his breath against her cheek. "What is your repulsion for rejoining the fold, Molly? We can only help you achieve greater power."

"I don't want more power." Molly stared directly into his eyes. "And I certainly don't want you."

"You say that, but I feel your body betraying you. You need me."

"I need nothing but a good night's rest and some peace and quiet, none of which I am getting with you here."

His lips were so close. She wondered if he would try to kiss her. Malek had never been one to be so forward in advances. He always let her make the final decision of how far they would take it, but it had been nearly a century since she'd seen him properly, and he'd just shown up at the door like a lost boy needing a bed and food. She'd regretted every moment allowing him into her house, and the fact he hadn't left yet only irked her more.

"I'll see you in the morning then." Malek pressed a kiss to her cheek and then stood up straight, still staring at her. "Until then."

Molly wisely didn't answer him. As soon as he was out of her sight, she turned back to watch Faye in the room opposite, expecting to find her still asleep. Instead, Faye stared directly at her through the glass. Molly's heart raced. Once she was sure Malek was gone, Molly pushed herself up from the bed and hobbled through to Faye's room.

"Hey there."

"Hey back," Faye answered. "What the hell happened?"

Molly smirked. "You went off the rails."

"I...I what?"

"You really don't remember?"

Faye shook her head.

"Did you take something tonight?"

At Faye's silence, Molly had her answer.

"What was it?"

"Something new. I haven't...I swear I haven't done drugs since we came back here."

"I know." Molly stroked the back of her fingers against Faye's cheek then twined their fingers. "Malek thinks he's the big hero of the night."

"Is he?"

Molly sighed. "Probably, though I could have handled it."

"I have no doubt of that."

"What did you take?"

"Don't know."

"Faye—"

"I swear. I have no idea what it was. I just got it and thought I'd try it."

"Where'd you get it?"

"Downtown." Faye licked her lips. "Do you mind? I'm awfully hungry."

Molly cocked her head to the side. "You want blood?"

"Yeah. I just...I don't know. I feel weird."

"Faye, you fed already, twice over, and we gave you some when we returned, and it made no difference."

"Really?" Faye's slate-gray eyes widened. "Can we try again?"

Bending down, Molly pressed her lips softly to Faye's. Faye didn't wait as she curled her fingers into Molly's hair, holding the back of her head as they continued to kiss. At some point the embrace moved from soft to sharp. Faye's teeth had elongated and scraped at Molly's lips exactly as she liked it.

Moaning into the embrace, Molly pushed into Faye and hoped beyond hope that her blood would at least do something. She opened her power to the moment as it was happening, twining her magic with the blood sacrifice Faye was taking. Drawing in a sharp breath, Molly carded a hand down Faye's front, over her breast and settled it on her hip. She had no energy beyond anything except what they were doing, but she wanted to make sure Faye could get what she needed and that she herself got something in return.

Faye's sharp nails dug into her tender side, and Molly gasped as pain coursed through her. Faye didn't stop though. She just barreled forward right like Molly expected her to. They liked pain, the both of them, and although this was different, they needed it.

Molly shifted, offering her neck, the same place Faye had taken from her earlier. Faye didn't wait as she plunged her teeth into Molly's skin. This time, instead of hurt like it had been down at the docks, it was pure pleasure like it was meant to be. Faye's tongue soothed the burn Molly had come to love and crave. Faye's hand moved back up, cupping Molly's breast and carding her thumb over her nipple through the thin fabric of the scrubs Amachon had given her to wear.

They stayed that way for some time before Faye gasped and jerked back. Then she licked along Molly's neck after a moment's hesitation and sealed the wound so it wouldn't bleed. When she moved away again, Faye traced her thumb over Molly's lips and shook her head.

"You didn't tell me I nearly killed you."

"I'm harder to kill than most people think."

"Yet, also easier than you think." Faye smirked. "In my head, everything was wonderful and perfect."

"What do you mean?" Molly shifted back up and took Faye's hand in hers, folding their fingers together again.

"I mean, what I remember is the polar opposite of what you remember."

"How do you know what I remember?"

Faye raised a thin eyebrow at her. "You just...I just...I don't know. I just saw it, when we were kissing."

"Interesting. I didn't share it with you."

"Then who did?"

"Perhaps it was your latent memory coming back."

Faye shook her head. "I think you shared."

"I promise you, Faye, I didn't."

"Malek certainly did come to the rescue."

"I suppose he did."

"You still don't trust him?"

Leave it to Faye to avoid the one subject they should be talking about and switch it to another. "I don't. He's here for a reason, and in four months, I still haven't figure out what that reason is."

"Want to tag team this?"

"What do you mean?"

Faye grinned. "Well, he's a witch, Molly, like you, so I can get out of him the same I do you, minus the beauties of a woman which I have come to be near addicted to. But perhaps I can get some information from him that you're struggling with because of your own hesitation."

"What are you thinking?" Molly curled her hair that had fallen forward behind her ear. She knew what Faye was suggesting. She'd even thought of it at one point and then dismissed it because she didn't want to share, and she certainly didn't want Faye to get a taste of his blood in comparison to hers.

"I will seduce him. Men always share their secrets in the throes of sex." Faye looked damned pleased with herself. "Unlike you, it should be easy to get something out of him."

Molly laughed, genuinely. "All right. You work your magic there, though I suspect he'll be harder to fuck than I am."

"What do you mean?"

"I know one reason Malek is here is to try and get me to rejoin the fold. The only way for that to happen is for me to make the final commitment to him."

"Final commitment?"

Molly trailed a finger down Faye's cheek again. "Yes, to become his mate, his pair, his partner. Whatever it is you want to call it. I was about to make the final commitment when I left the fold and never looked back. He obviously still wants me back."

"They'd be stronger with you."

"Yes, they would." Molly smiled down at her. "And I would be weaker."

"O...kay?" Faye looked confused, but Molly didn't want to explain any further.

"Right, so he wants me in the fold, meaning he's less likely to fuck you since he knows it would piss me off."

Faye grinned. "Then give permission. Come on, Molly, I want to know why he's here, and I don't think it's just to get you back into the fold."

"I agree with you." Faye's hand squeezing hers drew her back to the moment. "So let's do this. You work from one direction, and I'll work from the other. We'll hopefully meet in the middle and have some information to share with each other."

"Yes, let's."

"How are you feeling now?"

Faye grinned broadly, and Molly knew in an instant Faye was much better off than she had been before. "Fantastic. You?"

"Better."

Molly was surprised by Faye's hand at the back of her head again dragging her down until their lips connected. This time Faye was far more insistent than she had been before. Molly lost herself in the moment, like she always did. Faye was the one person who had been able to do that for her since she'd first met Malek, but even then, she'd found herself eventually.

"Do you think we should take this somewhere else?" Faye whispered into Molly's ear, her breath heavy.

"Yes," Molly hissed back. Then she kissed Faye again, really not wanting the moment to shift or end, or to have to walk up the stairs to her bedroom on the second floor of the house. It would take a lot of her energy out of her. Faye would be doing all the work for certain.

Faye smirked. "Should we piss Amachon off then?"

Giggling, Molly grinned. "Yes. Come on."

Molly took out the IV from Faye's arm and settled it on the table next to the bed, so Amachon would know Molly had done it instead of Faye trying to escape his clutches. Without another hesitation, Faye stood up, cracked her neck, and then wrapped an arm around Molly's waist gently as they walked together out of the medical bay.

CHAPTER FIVE

BEN SAT in the middle of the medical bay three days after capturing the centivalk. It had taken him that long to get up the courage to even come down there and ask the questions that had been plaguing his mind ever since the failed creature capture and then the successful one even more so. What would the difference have been?

He couldn't stop. Joel had talked to him incessantly about it because his worry and anxiety had been so heightened that he needed to have an outlet and Joel was the perfect person for that. The room was cold like it always was, and he was sitting on the bed, waiting for Amachon to come in after Ben had requested him. He hoped that sitting on the bed would tell Amachon silently that he needed to be looked at instead of ignored and that he wasn't there just for chitchat.

He wrung his hands together, sweat slicking the skin as his nerves got the best of him. He had no idea how to make his request, but he knew something was wrong. He'd been off his medicine for months and there was no sign it was even out of system as far as he could tell. He wouldn't be able to shift if he still felt like he was confined by the chemical concoction Molly had made for him.

Amachon, thankfully, entered the medical bay and came straight over to him, concern written all over his large face. His eyes were soft as he stared down, and Ben tried to smile up at him but couldn't muster it.

"What's wrong?" Amachon said before grunting.

"I...I want to know what's wrong with me."

Amachon cocked his head to the side, his oversized hand from his giant of a body crowding into Ben's space, but it wasn't anything Ben wasn't used to. He'd been in the medical bay so many times he lost count, and Amachon was his best friend—almost. Had been a combination of a father figure and a friend. Faye was his best friend.

"What's wrong?" Amachon repeated his question from before.

Ben rolled his eyes and flung his hands up in the air. "I don't know. You're the medic. I don't know anything."

Amachon grunted loudly—his secondary way of speaking, or rather his primary if Ben thought about it. It was meant to silence Ben, to focus him, to narrow in on what it was that was bothering him. Ben suddenly wished he'd brought Joel because Joel would have been able to do all the speaking instead of Ben jumbling it up so bad no one knew what he was saying.

"I can't shift," Ben finally muttered.

Amachon narrowed his eyes and clapped Ben loudly on the shoulder. "You need practice."

"No...I guess...I don't feel any different. Shouldn't I feel different? I don't feel anything. I've been off my meds for months now. Shouldn't I feel something?" Ben refused to look at Amachon, wanting to have a giant black hole appear just under him and swallow him up before closing off to anyone and anything else. The conversation was utterly embarrassing.

Amachon slid onto the bed next to Ben and stared out the glass window into the medical area. Ben usually hated coming down there. Everyone did, for that matter. Joel called it Amachon's torture chamber. Ben agreed, but he wouldn't dare call it that out loud. As they sat in silence, Ben realized just how tight his chest felt. Reaching up, he rubbed his hand against his breastbone and tried to ease the tension.

"It takes time," Amachon whispered. "You need to use muscles you haven't used. Ever."

"So it's not going to happen in an instant?"

"Not at all." Amachon still didn't turn to look at him. "Why now?"

Ben shrugged, realizing he hadn't really explained it to anyone except Faye, Molly, and Joel. He barely wanted to think about it himself, but when they had moments like they did the other night, when he could have done something—anything—to make the situation better, to resolve it faster and sooner so no one got hurt, he felt he should.

They sat again in silence, Ben contemplating what to tell Amachon. Why did he want to be able to shift, really? It wasn't only because he wanted to be more useful. He was plenty useful doing all the technology for the house, with his inventions no matter how awry they went half the time. Molly always found a use for them. So why did he?

Shrugging again, Ben turned to Amachon. "I want to be more me."

"And who are you?"

"I'm Ben. I'm techie, and geeky, and funny."

Amachon tilted his large shoulder into Ben's, nearly knocking him onto his side. Ben rubbed his arm and stared up at Amachon, the giant's body towering over him.

"What was that for?"

"Feel better?"

"No."

"You sure?" Amachon grunted.

"I mean, I feel better, but I'm still not shifting."

"Time." Amachon pushed up from the bed and stood. He gave Ben one more glance before he shuffled his way out of the room.

Ben sat on the hospital bed for another ten minutes before he realized that was all the help he was going to get. He wasn't quite sure what he expected. They checked his blood weekly, so if there was anything up in that they would know already. But God, he didn't want to have to wait any longer to shift. Once the decision had been made, he just wanted to get it done and over with. He wanted to know how to control and contort his body.

He was twenty-seven-years-old. He should know how to do this by now. Everyone else in his family did, at least, he thought they did. The ones who were Tainted. But he didn't really know, did he? He hadn't seen his family since he was a little boy and had come to live with Molly, no one except his Aunt Deidre.

Climbing off the bed, Ben meandered out the door and instead of going down to his work area, he went up to Joel's room. Joel's room was always his sanctuary, his one place of calm in the entire house, and Joel would find him soon enough if he went there. He always did.

Sliding into the bedroom, Ben laid down on the bed and crossed his arms over his chest. He closed his eyes and drew in a deep breath, his nostrils filling with the scent of Joel—his cologne, his shampoo, his sweat.

It was almost near perfect. If only he knew how to morph his body into another creature.

Faye had spent the week annoying the crap out of Molly, as much as Molly would let her anyway. She checked on their centivalk friend, but mostly Faye had kept checking in on Molly, and every time Malek showed up to talk to Molly, Faye made sure she was there to break up the chitchat. She wanted his attention on her. She'd taken what Molly and she had discussed to heart, and she was going to figure out what he was up to.

She hadn't expected to ever see him again after they had relieved Molly of her curse, but she wouldn't lie if anyone asked because she had felt a tinge of a thrill when he'd shown up at the door all those months ago. Since then, he had kept his distance from her, which she found odd considering the shared history between vampires and witches.

Malek was the one who had shattered that glass for her. She had no idea of it until she'd convinced him to help Molly. Faye tapped her finger against her lips as she contemplated what to do next. Molly was good at manipulating, not only with her magic but with her wit. Faye was equally good at manipulating, albeit without magic.

Seduction was her preferred method. She would need to seduce him to get the right information, but Malek was also a witch, meaning he was good at manipulating with magic since that was all magic was. Faye pressed her back against the wall to the elevator as she waited for it to take her up to the main floor.

Making her way to Molly's office, she heard Malek's smooth voice and Molly's prim and proper one. Just from Molly's tone, Faye knew she was annoyed. Malek either knew that or he ignored it. Wiping her hands on her tattered jeans, Faye walked into the attic office at the top of the staircase without any warning.

Molly's office was huge and comfortable. Often the crew would hang out there, either in the middle the day and do their own work or chat with Molly if she was there. Faye smiled at Malek as he turned to face her with a sour look—it didn't suit his chiseled chin at all. Faye ignored it and stepped forward, swaying her hips more than necessary. Molly's eyes went wide before she covered her smirk behind the back of her hand.

"I've done my rounds," Faye announced for no other reason than to break the awkward silence and change the subject from whatever it was.

"Well, good." Molly's eyes were light with excitement.

Faye stopped walking just in front of Malek and pressed a hand to his forearm. Contact. That was always what men wanted. Molly wanted it fast and hard, usually, but men wanted to know she was interested instead of just being taken.

"Have you seen the centivalk in full daylight? He's beautiful."

"Beautiful is not the word I would use." Malek straightened his posture, that odd glare and sour look back on his face. "Molly and I were just discussing something—"

"That can easily wait for another time," Molly interrupted. Her next question she directed at Faye. "Have you spoken with Benjamin?"

"Not today."

"Please find the time. I think he needs to talk to his best friend."

"Right. I'll do that." Faye moved her hand from Malek's and leaned over the desk to focus in on Molly. Perhaps jealously would also add to his interest, though that hadn't swayed anything in the past few months since he'd been there. "I thought I would head into the city this weekend."

"Why?"

"Joel and I had fun last weekend, and I realized while I was with him that I haven't spent quite enough time with my friends from before I moved here. While I do like it here, Molly, I do have friends besides you."

Molly blanched. "I'm aware of that."

"Right, but last weekend reminded me how much I've neglected them, so I want to spend some time with them."

Narrowing her gaze, Faye knew Molly was about to tell her no, but she raised an eyebrow in a challenge. They both knew if Faye wanted to go then she was going to go. Nothing was going to stop her. Faye only hoped it wouldn't become an all-out argument. They'd been so good at avoiding a lot of that lately.

"All right, but I want some information if you're going out."

"I'll get it. Don't worry."

Molly's lips thinned. Faye straightened her back and turned on Malek then, wanting him to know she hadn't completely forgotten about him. She had to get him out of the office somehow, first so Molly would stop being annoyed with him, but secondly so she could have time with him without mother hen watching over.

"Want to take a walk? I have some questions Molly here refuses to answer."

"I...what?"

Faye refused to look at Molly, focusing everything she had on Malek. Once again, she touched a hand to his forearm.

"What kind of questions?" he asked, risking a glance to Molly.

"Oh, you know, Molly hasn't told me much of anything of our shared history, and all I know is what you and the others in the fold shared. I'd quite like to know more. She keeps everything too close." Faye gave him a brilliant yet sly smile.

Malek regarded her carefully before he eventually nodded and held out his arm for Faye to take. She clicked her tongue against her front teeth.

"Such a gentleman."

As they were walking away, Faye sent a look over her shoulder at Molly and winked. It surprised her to see the flare of jealously light Molly's eyes before she buried her face in whatever paperwork she had going on before Malek had interrupted her.

As soon as they were outside Molly's office, Faye spun on him and pressed him into the wall, her mouth against his hot and hungry. Malek grunted his surprise, but she pressed on as he started to give as much as he was getting. Faye finally pulled away with a smile on her lips.

"What was that for?" Malek questioned.

Faye shrugged. "I'm deeply curious, Malek, to find out what you taste like."

Trailing one sharp and elongated black nail down his neck from just under his chin to the collar of his polo shirt, Faye focused on the scent of his blood. While she wasn't a huge fan of feeding, she wanted to try it with him. Molly had told her once—as had Malek—that the older the witch, the stronger the blood. Faye wanted to know how strong he was, not to mention, what his personal flavor was. She found the witches she had tasted after meeting Molly, those who had more pure blood, each had their own unique and intoxicating flavor.

He smirked at her. "You can try, if you want, but I'm not sure you do."

"And why would you say that?"

"You and Molly..."

"Are not exclusive by any means."

"You have been since I've returned."

Faye grinned broadly. "I hadn't seen her in quite some time, and as much as I like to taste around, Molly's blood—" Faye drew in a deep breath as she remembered the salty-sweet flavor of her regular lover "—it's addicting. I imagine, however, yours might be just as enticing."

"It might." His voice was pulled tight, like he had to work hard to be able to speak at all. His hands were on Faye's hips, having not moved from when she'd pushed him against the wall.

Faye knew Molly could likely hear everything they said as they were only inches from the door, but she hoped Malek was unaware of that fact, or that he didn't care. "So?"

"We'll see."

"I'm surprised you haven't tried yet. You're the one who taught me of our interconnected paths, yet here you are, resisting the only vampire left in the world."

"Not the only," Malek muttered.

"What?"

"You're the only, you're right," he corrected. "It has been a long time since I have been with a vampire, especially one with as true a form as yours."

"See?" Faye grinned broadly. "You want it just as much as I do."

"Perhaps," he answered. "Right now I want to know what questions you had."

"Oh...well, not a whole lot of specific questions. But do tell me more about my history. I know I get as much energy as Molly does when we do things the right way. I know how my race was exterminated. But tell me, what is this matched thing Tess spoke about. I'm not sure I understand it."

"Molly hasn't told you?"

"She doesn't tell me anything." Faye sent a glare to the office door and then looped her arm into Malek's again. She wanted to walk with him and talk with him away from Molly's penetrating presence. It would be the only way she'd ever be able to seduce him outright.

Malek hummed as they took the first steps down the stairway and toward the second floor where the bedrooms for all of Molly's staff were. When they got to the main floor, Faye steered them outside and into the sunlight since it was such a beautiful day. She also knew they were less likely to be disturbed by anyone down there.

"So tell me, Malek, what does it mean to be matched?"

"It means everything." His lips thinned. "It means we are mated for life, like Reina and Corbin. It means we will have children."

"Kids? Really? Molly does not want kids."

"I'm aware." His tone turned from teaching and educationally minded to harsh with bottled up pain. Faye would have to watch that, especially since she'd used the excuse of trying to learn more about this one specific topic.

"Why did she leave the fold?"

"You'd have to ask her."

"I plan on it." Faye squeezed his hand and listened to him for the next hour as he told her more and more about the Tainted history she was so ill informed on. Perhaps her own father would have taught her about it someday if he knew she'd existed for her first seventy-two years of life. Instead, she'd grown up as an oddball in a human world, just trying to survive with an abusive and insane aunt and a cousin she thought of as a brother.

"Faye." Malek turned to her, cupping her cheek.

"Yes?" she inquired.

"Why do you want to taste me?"

"Curiosity. I'm always curious, and I'm always taking risks I probably shouldn't."

"Why would I be a risk?" He stared down into her eyes, and Faye shuddered.

"You're more than one risk, Malek. But I don't often listen to reason."

He stayed there without moving for at least a full minute before he bent his neck and brushed their lips together again. Faye listed her body into his, wanting him to know how much he affected her, even if he didn't. She could play the role she'd set herself up for. When he pulled away, he shook his head at her. "You're also a risk."

"I'm always a risk." Faye snorted. "I don't think anyone has ever told me I'm a safe bet."

"I'm thinking Molly believes differently."

Faye's lips quirked, and she shook her head. "Doubtful. I just stay here as long as I'm comfortable and have what I need. It's a place to stay with food and shelter and a really gorgeous regular fuck."

Malek's tongue dashed against his lips. "Well then, perhaps we can entertain you a bit more."

"I would love that."

CHAPTER SIX

SHE COULDN'T wait any longer. Faye's heart had been racing and her body jittery for the entire week. She'd tried to hold off on it as long as she could, but after a full week of waiting around and trying to get rid of the feeling, Faye knew the only way to truly push it to the side. She needed more of whatever that drug was.

She'd been through this before, the withdrawal. She used to take heroin all the time, but this drug was different. Whatever it was, she didn't have to take much of it for it to take her, which was beyond amazing. The heroin she'd had to take so much any normal person would have overdosed a dozen times over.

She waited until just after dinner, not wanting to make it seem like it was a huge deal. Faye picked up the van in the garage and told Molly she was going to do the supply run that night. There were no questions asked, which was exactly how she wanted it. Once she was in the driver's seat, her heart had already calmed knowing what she was about to do.

The drive to the train station didn't take long. She picked up the supplies she had promised she would so there would be even less questions asked in the morning. Then she drove around downtown, making circles back and forth until she stopped upon her good friend. There were a few stragglers here and there as the sun set, but Faye wasn't going to give up that easily.

Parking a few blocks away, she walked the rest of it to see her troll, climbing up onto his shoulder and her preferred place to sit.

She leaned in slightly and kissed his cheek, knowing that he would be aware of her presence even if he wouldn't transform just yet. Faye waited patiently until the cover of night when the crowds lessened. It took another hour for her troll to move, and even then, he didn't full transform or come alive.

"You are early," he whispered.

"Couldn't resist seeing you again. I realized last week just how long it had been."

He made a snort and disbelieving noise in the back of his throat. "Thank you for the taste."

"You're welcome. I also need to do that more often. I don't know how often you get those, but I know how much it helps."

"It does."

Faye sighed and put her head against the side of his face, breathing in his stony scent. She was still jittery, and while the sewers club was around the clock, she still wasn't sure she could get more of that drug or even what it was.

She rubbed her hands together, the chill in the air from the fall seeping into her bones. Molly would expect her back before midnight, and she'd have to manage that otherwise it would raise suspicions.

A person walked under the bridge below them but her troll friend didn't transform back into stone as she thought he might. Instead, he held completely still and waited as the man continued to walk with his shoulders hunched and his face to the ground as he didn't pay any attention.

As soon as he was out of sight, Faye turned to her troll. "Have you heard about a new drug on the streets?"

"What kind of drug?"

"I have no idea."

"Why do you want to know?"

Faye licked her lips. This was her chance. She could either hide under the guise of it being questions for the house or she could admit to him what she'd been thinking all week—she needed a damn fix. Faye put her hand to his cheek and closed her eyes, sighing.

"I took some the last time I was here. It was...exhilarating to say the least. Far different than any drug I've taken before. I would like some more."

Once again her troll friend clucked his tongue. "I've heard rumors."

"What kind?"

"Of a new drug, but no one I know has taken it."

He spoke so slowly sometimes and in a roundabout way that it frustrated Faye. She had to remember to be patient. She got the drug in the sewers from the bartender, so there would be no doubt she could try and get it there again, but she didn't want to become a regular either.

"What have you heard about it?" she finally asked.

The troll finally transformed the rest of his body that he could, which meant only down to the edge of his neck and his top of his shoulders. Faye had watched as he'd been able to transform more and more over the years. It was inch by tiny inch, but at least it was more. Perhaps he would get out of his prison eventually on his own.

"I have heard there is a new drug." He stopped talking. Faye kept waiting for him to go on, but he didn't.

"That's it?"

"Yes." He dragged out the last syllable of the word. "You find some and bring it to me."

Faye drew in a deep breath. Based on how Molly had said she'd reacted to it, she wasn't quite sure she wanted to give him any, he might truly break free from his prison then. Perhaps that was what he wanted. She patted his cheek. "I'll think about it. I got the first for free, no saying how much the second will cost."

"Your life."

"What?"

"Go, Faye. I will see you again."

Confused and curious, Faye jumped down from his shoulder. Waving goodbye to him from the sidewalk below, she hunched her shoulders and walked back to her van. She didn't want him to know where she was going to get it, and if she walked, he would no doubt know. Her troll friend was brilliantly smart as much as everyone thought he wasn't. He may be imprisoned for life or until Molly decided to release him, but that didn't mean he was stupid or unobservant.

Faye slid into the driver's seat of the van and drove the long way around her troll friend to get to the entrance to the sewers. As soon as she got to the sewer grate that she knew would take her directly to where she wanted to go, she slipped inside. The snake twins, Harsith and Gideon, were right there to greet her.

Many times Faye had allowed them to take her on the stairs down into the club, but tonight, she didn't want to. Between Molly and Malek she wanted to make sure she kept her focus. They came up to her, transforming from their snake forms into the more human-life forms, though they still both looked quite a bit like snakes with their gold eyes.

"Faye," Harsith whispered, nearly on a hiss.

"Harsith." She smiled at him. "I'm only here for a moment. I think I forgot something here last week."

He smiled at her like he knew, but surely he couldn't. Before Molly, Faye had come here to find a witch—a watered down one, but a witch nonetheless—to try and get some energy before she jumped recklessly off a building to try and find some answers about her father. Every lead she'd had for him stopped at Molly.

"Shall we let her pass, brother?" Harsith turned to Gideon, whom Faye had learned was the lesser forward of the two, though they both still had some balls on them.

"Yes, brother. She will pay her toll next time."

"Thank you!" Faye smiled at them and slipped between them on the thin stone stairwell. She didn't bother to look back as she walked into the club. The floor was covered in a fine moss, so her footsteps were softened as was the blaring music that would hurt her ears if she didn't force herself to ignore it and if she'd been in her vampiric form.

Faye didn't waste time. She went straight for the bar. Luckily, it was the same bartender that night as it had been the other night. Licking her lips, Faye leaned on the edge of the wood, knowing she might have to sweet talk her way into more of whatever she'd been given.

"What'll you have, love?"

Faye grinned. "Whatever that sweet stuff was you gave me last week."

The faerie, Aliya, looked a bit surprised but then she smiled. "I see you liked it."

"Loved it. Do you have more?"

"I may."

"Mind telling me what it's called?"

Aliya grinned as she reached into her bra and pulled out another small baggie with only two pills in it. Faye had been hoping for more, but two would have to do. Aliya leaned over the top of the counter, a smile on her lips and mystery in her eyes.

"Inanis. Kind of a boring name if you ask me."

Faye grunted. All these dealers coming up with new names for their drugs really needed to get more creative. Though this one might be accurate from everything Molly had told her. Faye didn't take the small bag from her immediately. Instead, she pressed her lips into a thin line.

"Did you like it?" Aliya asked.

"I did." Faye pressed her palm flat onto the top of the bar. "I don't suppose you're the one making it."

"I'm not. In fact, I've only gifted it twice. I know your taste for the wild."

Faye chuckled. "You could say that. Shall I pay you this time?"

Aliya shook her head in the slightest. "No, seeing you is enough."

Not quite sure where to go with that, Faye looked Aliya up and down. She would have done her at some point in her life, but she had a certain affinity for Molly now that she didn't before. She much preferred their regular fucking and understanding than she did trying to find random people—that and she didn't need sex to hide her energy feed any longer.

"I'll make sure to come here more often then."

"Molly keeps you busy."

"Yes." Faye's stomach churned at Aliya's fake pout. "But not too busy. I promise, especially if you have more of this."

"Be careful taking it, Faye."

"I'm always careful." Faye slipped the small bag into the palm of her hand and reveled at the feel of it against her skin.

Aliya laughed. "You're never careful."

"Well, can't fool you." Leaning in, Faye kissed Aliya's cheek. She wandered around the club for another ten minutes before slipping back up the stairs and out into the cold night air. She didn't have the time to waste taking it then and there as much as she wanted to. Molly would be expecting her home with the shipment of supplies any time soon, and she really needed to get them put away so she could disappear in the house where no one would find her before she could really take anything.

Molly sat at her desk, deep in the books she had scattered around about the centivalk. She wanted to know as much as she could about it, though she had zero desire to ask Malek. She wasn't even sure what he had told Benjamin was truth or not. She wouldn't put it past him to lie to anyone in the house to get her to pay attention to him, which she had been gladly avoiding since the day he had stepped foot into the house.

Sighing, Molly rubbed her temples. Perhaps Faye was right. They did need to tackle figuring out why he was actually there before too much longer passed. She heard him coming up the stairs before he got anywhere near the door. With a breath, Molly undid one button on her blouse to give him a bit better show. It was time to make some progress and to stop avoiding. She certainly wouldn't be as forthcoming as Faye had been, but she could manage just as well, if not better. Perhaps they could turn it into a game.

Molly made sure her nose was pressed into a book when he opened her office door and came into the room without so much as an invitation. She huffed a breath, still needing to keep up her air of annoyance before she'd allow him to sweet-talk her. Malek sat in one of the chairs on the opposite side of her desk, and when she did finally look up at him, he had a smirk on his lips.

"Not finding much, are you?"

"Nothing." Molly slammed the book shut even though she had found some interesting stories about centivalks in her archives. She wasn't about to share that with him.

"You could ask, you know."

"Ask what?" Leaning back into her chair, Molly made sure all her assets were best on display and she couldn't help the pleasure that soared through her chest when he glanced at her breasts before moving his gaze back up to her eyes. They had been matched at one point. They'd had sex, several dozen hundred times, in fact. But two centuries had passed since then, since she'd realized the folly and stupidity of the folds and how they'd eventually come to their own death. Leaving her fold had not been an easy decision, especially given the fact she'd needed Malek's permission to do it. She'd only managed to convince him of it by telling him she would one day return. It seemed he hadn't given up on that promise or come to collect her.

"What I know." He looked pleased as piss with himself.

Two centuries was a long time to go between seeing each other, but she was still able to read him easily enough. He was hiding something, something big, and she was pissed with herself for still not being able to figure out what it was. He wanted to be matched to her, yes, but that wasn't the only reason he had taken up residence in her house.

"And what do you know?"

He smirked. "Why would I share that wealth of knowledge with you, my love? You give me nothing in return."

Tension coiled in Molly's belly. She hated when people tried to manipulate her, but with this man in particular, it was far worse than anything. "What would you like?"

"What are you willing to give?"

Molly realized all too late they had both been speaking in questions since he'd pretty much entered the room. She had to put a stop to it.

Standing and coming around her desk, Molly slid into the chair opposite Malek and crossed her legs, making sure there was plenty of skin showing. For a moment she wondered if she was more like Faye than she had originally thought, but she shoved it to the side. "Then tell me, sweet Malek. What do you know of the centivalk?"

"I supposed your shifter boy has spoken to you already."

"He has."

Malek's lips thinned.

"There are no secrets in this house that I am not aware of."

Malek brushed a hand through his perfectly slicked hair before he stared her down. "I will give you information on the centivalk, Molly, but I do want something from you in return."

"And what is that? You've been here four months now and not once have you asked for something."

"I suppose you're right." He stared her up and down, intentionally this time. A shiver ran through Molly's body, and her nipples hardened against her will. "I want you to reconsider your stepping away from our match."

Molly's lips parted. She hadn't ever expected him to be so forward. He was nearly a hundred-fifty years older than her, but she had twice his power, not that he knew that. He had waited a century to be matched, and she had been it, only to walk away when she was a mere twenty years old.

"I will consider returning to the match in the future."

He narrowed his gaze at her. "I'll take that, I suppose."

"Malek," Molly stared, not quite sure if she wanted to ask her next question. "Is the match the only reason you're here?"

"What other reason would there be?"

And that was the question, wasn't it? She hadn't been able to put her finger on it, but his lack of answering pretty much told her there was at least one other reason Malek was there. She could only hope it wouldn't cause too much damage to her facility and network in the long-run or to the Tainted and creatures she housed. Molly had been running her own life for so long, she wasn't sure she could manage if he had any serious plans for her.

"Relax, Molly." He leaned forward and slid a hand onto her knee. "I'm not here to seduce you."

"But aren't you?"

He blushed, his cheeks lighting with fire as he pulled away as if her skin had burned him. "I suppose in some ways I am."

"Right." She eyed him carefully, dragging out the moment. "So tell me about the centivalk."

He grinned as he went on to explain all Benjamin had already told her and less than she had already discovered and read. It was any wonder that he would underestimate her abilities in research and her ability for knowledge. Two centuries was a long time, and she was no longer the young eager woman she had been when they'd first met. Perhaps it was time Malek got to learn who she really was and why she had walked away from the life she was supposed to live.

CHAPTER SEVEN

MOLLY HAD run through the house on one of her many rounds. She'd been up all night checking on the creatures and Tainted in her care. She often didn't sleep for days on end, part of the curse of living nearly forever. As much as she wanted to sleep sometimes to block out the world, she couldn't. Faye suffered from the same, it was part of what had drawn them together, she was sure of it—outside of the obvious, that there was no way to get around their attraction to each other since it was built into their bodies. She scoffed at the thought. It felt weird and odd to think of it like that.

In that way, Faye and Malek would be just as attracted to each other. However, Molly was fairly certain that if it were to come down to Faye choosing one over the other, Molly would win. Climbing the stairs back to her office, she turned to start inputting the data she had discovered on the centivalk into their network system. She'd meant to do it earlier that day, but Malek had distracted her along her ploy to try and figure out why he truly was there.

She was about to focus in on the work when there was a knock at her office door. The only one who ever dared knock was Amachon. Looking up, she smiled at him. He looked worn and weary. She forgot oftentimes just how old he was. They had met when he was a young doctor just trying to make his way in her fair part of the city nearly thirty years before, and they had worked together since. Eventually he had come to live with her at the house and became her own private doctor as she had sponsored more of his clinics that catered to Tainted.

"What can I do for you, old friend?"

He sat on the couch, which was odd for him. Normally he would stand in front of her to make his requests or tell her what was going on that she needed to know about. Molly checked the watch on her left wrist, noting it was well after midnight and far closer to dawn. He should have been asleep hours ago.

"What's wrong?"

His gaze shot up at her when she said that. Molly wasn't one to beat around the bush if she could avoid it, and with Amachon, she knew she didn't have to. His lips parted before they closed again. Molly shoved the papers in front of her farther onto the desk and stood up, walking to grab a snifter of whiskey from her cabinet in the far corner and bring it back for him.

He drank it quickly. "I've lost six patients this week."

"Six!" Alarm rang through her chest. "What on earth for?"

He grunted. "New drug on the streets. It's laced with something."

"With what?"

He shook his head. "Don't know."

Molly pressed her lips together as she leaned into the back of the couch with her shoulder, making sure to keep her body turned toward him. She didn't want him to think he didn't have her full support. Her heart raced. The last time they had lost this many people had been when the two of them had met, but then it hadn't been Tainted who were dying, it was humans. She'd put a stop to it, and they'd had thirty years of relative peace.

"Do you have any?"

Once again, he shook his head. "No."

"We need to get some. Test it."

"I know." Amachon rubbed his hands over his face after setting the drink down onto the table on the side of the couch. "I know, but not tonight."

She rubbed his arm carefully. Amachon usually wasn't one for physical touch, but Molly couldn't resist her own urges and feelings to give him what she thought he might need. In all the years she had known him, he largely kept to himself. He had no mates, no friends aside from who she brought into the house. He'd grown very fond of Benjamin and had taken him in under his wing, but he was far more a father figure than a friend.

Molly's mind spun a mile a minute. She had heard the rumors

but hadn't shared it with anyone. This was confirmation of what she already knew, and Molly realized, she should have gotten to work on the problem a lot faster. If six of his patients were dead this week, that would mean at least twice that many were dead in total, if not more.

"Amachon, I don't think we can wait until morning."

"I haven't the energy."

"Then you rest. I'll work." Molly went to stand up, but Amachon put a hand on her wrist and tugged her back down.

"No."

"What?"

"You also need rest."

Molly drew in a sharp breath. "I don't need rest like you do."

He shook his head at her. "You need it more."

With narrowed eyes, Molly found herself nodding before she shook her head as a reflex. "We can't wait on this. This drug is killing people, whether intentionally or not."

"Yes, and until we find someone who has some we can test, we have no answers."

Molly wanted to groan because he was right, and they both knew it, but she wanted answers then and there. Malek was one problem to have, but this was a much bigger and more pressing problem to resolve.

"All right. In the morning, we'll discuss it at the staff meeting."

"Good." Amachon pushed up from his seat and stepped toward the door, more like a stagger than a step, and Molly realized just how tired he must be for that to happen. She remained silent as he left her office, shutting the door behind him.

She had no idea how long she sat there before Faye opened the door and stepped inside. "You alone?"

"Yes?" Molly answered, echoing Faye's question.

"Good." Faye shut but didn't lock the door behind her.

Before Molly could say anything else, Faye pushed her back into the couch as she slid onto her lap to straddle her. Faye's mouth was on hers, a hand on Molly's throat, and fingers sliding down to Molly's blouse that she'd forgotten to button up from her visit with Malek.

Faye had the amazing ability to take her from zero to this within two seconds flat. She'd always been able to do that—which again, was either part of their biological connection from two very interdependent species or it was something else. Molly still couldn't quite tell, but she was pretty sure Faye had chosen not to think about it so she could move on with the fun bits of their relationship.

Faye sliced a long and sharp nail between the rest of the buttons on Molly's blouse, effectively opening it for her own pleasure. Faye's hand was on her breast in no time, pushing aside Molly's bra so she could fumble with her nipple, making circles on it before nipping at Molly's lower lip hard enough to draw a slight amount of blood.

"Touch me, Molly," Faye ordered.

Molly moved into action, having forgotten herself in her thoughts once again. She didn't work Faye up at all. Instead, she pulled apart the button on her jeans and shoved her hand down Faye's pants. They'd had quickies. They'd made love for hours. They'd done everything every which way they possibly could think of and more. Tonight was not for hours and drawing it out. Tonight was for a quick hard fuck to relieve the tension.

Shoving her fingers in hard, Molly smirked at Faye's grunt of approval. She worked her magic into the equation, wanting to feel the deep connection she knew it could provide and have Faye's own body restore her power even more than rest could ever accomplish. Molly set a rhythm she knew Faye would love, that would get her off in no time. Between two fingers inside her and her thumb at her clit, Molly moved her arm up and down as fast as she could.

Faye cried out her release, pressing her forehead into Molly's shoulder and closing her eyes. There was no bloodletting this time, no shared exchange of gifts. Faye gave entirely for Molly's benefit. Molly pressed kisses into Faye's neck, reveling the warmth and saltiness of her skin. Eventually Faye moved and scraped human teeth down Molly's neck and biting into her shoulder to mark her without breaking skin.

Keening, Molly shifted on the couch. Her own body betrayed how much she would love to have Faye between her legs, but it wouldn't be necessary. She could live without it so long as her magic was replenished. That would be enough of a give from Faye that night.

Faye's lips against her ears surprised her. Her words were so quiet Molly almost didn't catch them. "We have an audience. Would you like to continue or stop?"

Molly's heart rapped hard against her ribcage as she turned to look toward the door Faye had just come from. Sure enough, Malek stood with his shoulder pressed against the doorframe, watching everything. The choice was hers. It was just going to have to be one she made and quickly because Faye was not a patient person.

Lifting her chin as Faye nibbled across her neck to the other side, Molly kept her gaze locked on Malek, who stared back at her as if this was the most normal thing in the world. Anger surged in her chest, her magic pulling at her as it begged her to release the connection between her and Faye, but she didn't want to. She wanted it to mean something, not just for them but for Malek.

"Take my energy," Molly breathed out, fumbling her fingers against Faye's sides as she tried to find more skin.

"What?"

"You heard me. Fuck me, then take my energy."

"Molly, you know what too much will—"

"Do it, Faye." As commanding as Faye had been before, Molly pushed at Faye's hips until she slid to the floor. "Use your mouth."

It was perfect. Molly could watch Malek and see whatever he was doing while Faye would be utterly distracted with her task. Faye pushed Molly's skirt up with her help and then gripped Molly's head, pulling her down for a bruising kiss. When she backed away, Faye had a glint in her eyes.

"Playing at jealousy?" she whispered so only Molly would here. "Two can play at that, or rather three."

From that moment on, Molly knew everything Faye was doing was purely for show. Both of them could use it to their advantage in their manipulations of Malek. Molly was slick and wet, and unlike normal, Faye eased into it. Her tongue traced lines up and down, then circles before she slowly inserted one finger, pumping a few dozen times before adding a second.

Molly threw her head back against the couch as Faye tugged her hips down to have better access. Never once did Molly move her gaze from Malek, who stood cool as ice against the door frame leading into her office. She tensed as Faye brought her higher and higher, and she knew she wasn't going to last much longer.

Digging her fingers into Faye's shoulder-length blonde hair, she tugged hard. Faye pulled back with her mouth, replacing the motion her tongue had been doing with her finger until she dipped her head again and pressed her lips and mouth to the crease between Molly's thigh and hip. The pierce of her flesh was a surge of pleasure.

Molly gasped. Her back arched. Her fingers tightened impossibly in Faye's hair, but she wasn't going to let go. She wanted Malek to see and hear and feel everything she was. She was tempted to send him all she felt, but she didn't want to have the connection go both ways, which he would no doubt make it. Her power pulsed through her veins and her body as Faye urged more pleasure from her. She was in ecstasy.

Faye's rough tongue was such a contrast to the smooth burning feeling taking over her entire body. She convulsed as her orgasm ripped through her. Faye held her down as best as she could, but Molly couldn't help moving. Malek's tongue peeked out between his lips, wetting them, and Molly knew she had him.

As soon as Faye was done and moving away, Malek's cold voice shocked her. "The centivalk needs to feed."

"What?" Molly breathed heavily.

"If he doesn't eat, he'll die."

"Benjamin fed him."

"He didn't eat it. He needs something live."

She wanted to curse. "And what do you have in mind?"

"A creature or two. He needs enough until he'll hibernate."

Shifting to push her skirt back down her legs and button up her shirt, Molly brushed her fingers through her long locks and put it back in place. "Which one?"

"Your choice."

"Surely you have one in mind."

Faye stood up in front of her, zipping her pants up with a few small jumps and then flopping onto the couch next to her, their thighs grazing.

"I have several."

"Care to share with the class?"

"If you had a wyrm, I'd suggest that."

"Got rid of my last one, sorry." Molly's accent was thicker because she was beyond annoyed. It was as if nothing he had just witnessed made a dent of difference in his thick skull, and Faye trailing fingers over her bare arm and belly was not helping her distraction any. In fact, Faye hadn't said anything since she'd asked. Turning to Faye, Molly narrowed her gaze, trying to see how jittery Faye was because of the amount of blood she'd consumed that week.

"Then I have the perfect idea." Malek stepped into the room now that everything seemed calm. He grabbed Molly by the forearm on the opposite side of Faye and dragged her upward to stand.

Molly nearly protested but swallowed the retort quickly enough. Faye was up like a shot not two inches behind Molly. She was pretty sure this was the quietest she had seen Faye in ages. Confused by everything, Molly decided to deal with one problem at a time.

"I think I have the perfect beast. Faye, would you mind assisting?"

"Sure."

Molly wrenched her wrist from Malek's grip and led the way out of her office. The sun was already coming up over the horizon, and when she made it down to the secondary level, Benjamin was coming out of his door. His hair was skewed from sleep, his eyes puffy, and his pajamas a mix of wrinkles.

"Ben," Molly said by way of greeting as she passed him to make for the second stairway.

"Hey, I've been meaning to mention, Aunt Deidre is coming for a visit."

Molly's lips parted. "Now?"

"Soon."

"Do you think this is the proper time for a visit?"

He shrugged. "I know you don't like her, but she's the only family I've got."

"She's not—"

"She's staying here. She can have my room, and I'll crash somewhere else."

Molly's lips thinned at her dislike. "Fine. We'll discuss this later."

Without another step, she made her way to the main floor where the elevator was. Slipping inside with Malek and Faye following, she pressed the button for the habitat floor. "I believe the warthog-like creature I have will suffice."

"For today," Malek answered. "He'll need enough to get through a long hibernation."

"I'm aware. I've done my own research."

"Not enough."

Once again tamping down her own anger, Molly shifted her gaze to Faye. Faye's gaze flicked back and forth between Malek and Molly, eyes wide as she watched.

"Faye, are you all right?"

"Fine." Her voice broke on the word. Faye cleared her throat and tried again. "Fine. I'm fine."

"You're sure?"

"Yes."

"Okay. I'll need your help to move it."

"My brawn to your beauty?" Faye snarked with a glint in her eye.

There was the woman Molly had come to adore. Taking the chance to make her plan full, Molly stepped up to Faye as the elevator doors opened and pressed their mouths together in a heated embrace. When she backed away, she grinned. "Always."

CHAPTER EIGHT

FAYE SWUNG into Ben's workroom and pressed her hands to his shoulders. "What's happening, Benny-boy?"

"Don't call me that," he grumbled.

She smirked and pressed a kiss to his cheek loudly. "Molly said your aunt is coming. I didn't know you had an aunt."

He shrugged and continued to focus on his computer. "She doesn't like my aunt much."

"Why's that?"

"Have to keep everything hidden from her."

"You mean she doesn't know about Tainted?"

Ben shook his head and typed a bit on the computer, still not making eye contact with Faye. She couldn't quite get a read on him or what he was doing. If she narrowed her own gaze at the screen, she was pretty sure he wasn't actually doing anything, which for Ben was abnormal.

"Is something else bothering you?"

"No."

"All right then."

"It's my aunt."

"What about your aunt?"

Ben sighed and finally turned on his stool to face her. He squinted at her, but Faye ignored it largely, not wanting to point out what he was doing.

"I just...I don't know how much longer I'm going to be able to see her.”

“Is she old?”

“Well, I guess. She’s not really old, but you know our work.”

“I do.” Faye narrowed her gaze. “Did something happen?”

“You nearly killed Molly. If she hadn’t taken the brunt of whatever the hell you were doing, you could have killed all of us.” He stared directly at her, his words like ice daggers to her chest.

Faye sat on the stool opposite him, the one she would normally sit on when they would work a project together, but this time they weren’t working, they were talking, about very real things, which was something she sucked at. But she wanted to make this work, make this good. Sighing, Faye bit her lip and shook her head. “I didn’t know what I was doing.”

“I get that,” Ben muttered. “But it doesn’t mean it didn’t happen, and I was fucking useless to help.”

“Is this about whatever happened to me or whatever didn’t happen to you?”

He refused to look up at her. After a good amount of silence, Ben finally spoke, “I just think I should see my aunt before anything else happens.”

“What’s going to happen?”

“I don’t know, Faye, but that’s just the thing, isn’t it? We don’t know.”

“I’m not going to attack you. And you said you wanted to start learning your Tainted side months ago when I got back. If you still want to do that, you can.”

“To what end?”

“What do you mean?” Faye was utterly confused. She’d never thought they’d have deep conversations like this and it was trying her brain. She was someone who acted, not someone who discussed feelings.

Ben sighed and then rubbed both his temples. “If I start shifting, if that’s even an option at this point, then Molly will start putting me on more dangerous missions.”

“I’m pretty sure capturing a centivalk was a pretty dangerous mission.”

He glared. “You’re only proving my point.”

“What point?”

“That we don’t know when it’ll end, so I want to visit with my aunt now.” Tension rose in his voice, and his eyes were closed the entire time.

Faye put her hands up in a defensive motion then pressed

them back into her jean-clad thighs. "All right. So visit with your aunt."

"Please don't pull any stunts when she's here."

"Is she staying here?"

Ben nodded. He still didn't open his eyes.

"Are you okay?" Faye repeated, concerned there was something else going on that he wasn't telling her about.

"Yeah. I'm fine. Just a headache."

"Headache?"

His chin bobbed up and down twice before he settled. Faye reached forward and brushed fingers across his cheek.

"You're sure that's it?"

"There's an aura around you." His words slurred slightly, and his speech slowed down.

"An aura? I don't think anyone has ever told me I have an aura." She giggled but remained concerned, wanting to figure out just what was going on.

Ben didn't answer her. His shoulders slumped and then tensed. His jaw clenched tightly, not letting up. Faye kept her gaze on him the entire time. "Ben?"

He didn't answer. His body rocked forward and back a few times before he convulsed. His shoulders jerked; his legs flailed. He fell to the cold cement floor, his head cracking against it with a loud thud. Faye jumped up and back, panic welling in her chest. She shoved the stools aside as his feet tangled in his and knocked it over, but she was fast enough to keep it from hitting him.

Every muscle in his body was tense as the seizing fit captured him. Faye ran for the door and slapped her hand against the alarm, hoping someone would show up sooner rather than later because she had no idea what to do. Alarms echoed all around them, some loud that were nearer to where they were and some softer the farther away they were.

"Ben!" Faye knelt next to him, keeping his head from smacking into the leg on the metal work bench he used daily. "Ben!"

He didn't answer. His eyes rolled into the back of his head, drool moved out from between his lips. His hands clamped down on themselves so tightly she worried he'd break skin. Faye used her superior strength to keep him centered on the floor and not about to hit anything, but she still worried about the initial smack of his head against the cement.

She could hear footsteps against the ground outside, starting down at the elevator. It wouldn't take long before someone was there. Molly, she was sure of it, with her heels clacking rapidly as she ran. She was the only one.

Ben continued to convulse, whatever seizure had gripped him not letting up at all. Nothing about it seemed to be easing or getting better. The door slammed open. Faye looked up to see Molly standing before her, hair wild around her shoulders as she assessed the situation.

"How long?" Molly asked.

Faye shook her head. "I have no idea."

"Stay here. Keep him from hurting himself." Molly raced from the room again, but Faye had no idea where she was going.

She did as she was told and kept Ben as still as she could and away from anything that might injure him. Soon enough Molly was back. She took the long way around the workbench so she ended up on the other side of Ben. She pulled some type of liquid into a needle and pressed it into Ben's leg through his clothes, depressing the plunger.

"It'll take another minute."

"What'd you give him?"

"Something to end this, hopefully." Molly carded her fingers through his hair as Faye held him as still as she possibly could.

True to her word, it did take a minute or two before Ben's body began to calm down. The convulsions became less. His body relaxed. Faye pressed her hand to his shoulder lightly, wanting to know what the hell was going on. When she looked up at Molly, the question was on the tip of her tongue but it died there.

"Tell me what happened," Molly spoke as she checked Ben's vitals.

"We were just talking and he started doing this. He fell off the stool and hit his head pretty good."

"I'll have Amachon check that when he returns."

"He's coming back?"

"As soon as he can. He has some patients to deal with at the clinic."

Faye bit the inside of her lip. "What happened?"

"He told you he wanted to learn to shift, yes?"

"Yeah."

"He stopped his medication. He's been completely off it for months now but unable to shift—though I'm not sure how much he's actually tried—this is not uncommon in pubescents when they're coming into their shifting abilities. I expected this."

"You did?"

Molly nodded. "Yes. Now, help me get him to the medical bay."

Faye scooted her hands under Ben's body and lifted him almost effortlessly. It would have been far easier if she'd been in her vampiric form, but she didn't want to do that to him. They made their way to the medical bay slowly, and Faye put him onto a bed. Molly went to work. Faye wanted to stay, she really did, but the sight of Ben's limp form was almost too much.

"Does Joel know?"

"No."

"Where is he?"

"Out."

"Want me to find him?" Faye asked, wanting something to do other than just sit there.

"Yes, please. You can finish what he's doing?"

"Which is?"

"Call him, and he'll fill you in."

Faye spun out of the room and headed for her bedroom with the phone pressed to her ear. It wasn't a phone call she really wanted to make, but it was something she knew she was going to have to.

Molly was sequestered in her office. It had been a long day of work, and emergencies, but she worked still. She was exhausted. The rest of the house was quiet. She'd forced Joel to his own room after sitting with Ben for hours. Amachon had shown up, thankfully, to make sure Benjamin would recover.

Sighing, Molly stood up and got herself a drink of wine from her cabinet, selecting one of her favorite bottles to open. She needed it. The conversation she needed to have with Faye was not going to be a pleasant one, and she'd been avoiding it for as long as she could, but they needed more information.

She sat on her couch and was halfway through her glass of wine when Faye slipped into the office, locking the door behind her this time. Molly was curious if their evening was going to end like it had the other day, although she suspected it wouldn't. Faye'd had enough blood to last her months unless she was injured, and Molly had seen her struggle to keep control over her vampiric side. In fact, she was pretty sure Faye hadn't even known she was transforming when she lifted Ben's form from his work area and carried him down to the medical bay.

Faye sat next her, stealing her wine and chugging the rest of it.

"It sucks to be a vamp sometimes."

"If you want to get drunk, love, you're going to need something far stronger than wine."

Smirking, Faye shook her head. "I could probably drink all the alcohol in this room right now and not feel a lick of it."

Molly hummed, standing and refilling her glass so she could at least have more to drink. She needed to relax after a day like the one she'd had. Once again seated next to Faye, Molly rolled her shoulders. "Find anything with Malek?"

"No. Not yet. You?"

"Aside from his incessant need for me to rejoin the fold, which I was already aware of, no."

Faye settled her head on Molly's shoulder. "You still think there's more to it?"

"Yes. He's never been this insistent about the fold before."

"Perhaps they need you for something."

"Then he'd tell me that. Or Reina would."

"You've been in contact with Reina?"

Molly chuckled at Faye's wide eyes. She turned Faye's chin up to look down on her and brushed her thumb across Faye's lips. "Yes. Haven't you been?"

"Well, yeah, I just...did she tell you?"

"That you and she and Corbin had an exchange of energy? Yes. We keep no secrets in the fold."

"No wonder you don't fit in." Faye moved back to her previous position. "Is Ben okay?"

"I suspect he will be."

Faye didn't answer, not that Molly expected her to. They sat together in silence, Faye staring at something and Molly sipping at the wine she had refilled until it was nearly empty. She finished it off with a flourish and settled the glass on the table in front of them.

"We need to talk about the other night."

"O...kay. I didn't...I'm sorry about asking. I didn't think you'd mind, and I figured it might help."

"Are you speaking of the other night with Malek?"

"Isn't that what you're talking about?"

"No. But I didn't mind that. I think it may have worked to our advantage in several ways because I suspect, like Reina and Corbin, he knows this will be better with the three of us."

"Better?" Faye almost spat the word.

Molly narrowed her gaze. "They really didn't tell you

everything, did they?"

"I didn't ask."

"You wouldn't know what to ask." Molly sighed. "Witches in our fold are matched."

"So you've said."

"We're matched for life. With that comes the same ability you and I have, but with a vampire added in, it's intensified."

"Oh."

"Reina and Corbin got as much out of you as you did them."

"I guess that's good to know." Faye shifted uncomfortably. "What did you think we were talking about?"

Molly sighed and moved to look directly at Faye. She pulled one leg up onto the couch as she turned, her knee bent slightly and her ankle under her other knee. She wanted to have this conversation without making Faye feel as though she was being attacked.

"About the capture the other night."

Faye's nose scrunched. "I don't want to talk about that."

"You were high." Faye refused to look at Molly. "Please be honest with me. I don't want to have to go in search for information. I'm not looking to condemn you."

"You said no more drugs in this house."

"Well, you weren't in the house, to be fair." Molly quirked her lips up, hoping it would lighten the mood a bit and make Faye a little more amenable to talking. "What did you take?"

"Heroin."

"I've never seen you act like that on heroin."

Faye shrugged. "Maybe it was spiked with something."

"Did you get it from your regular dealer?" Molly knew it was an odd question to ask, but she wanted to know. Between what Amachon had told her and the rumors she had heard for months now, she needed more information.

"I did." Faye fiddled with the edge of her shirt.

Molly leaned forward and stilled Faye's fingers. "What did you take?"

"I bought heroin from him."

Narrowing her gaze, Molly ran a quick judgement. She'd agreed, at one point, never to manipulate Faye into telling her the truth again, but it was frustrating when she knew Faye was lying or at least avoiding the truth itself.

"What did you do with that heroin?"

Faye's lips thinned, and she rolled her eyes. "Fine. Joel and I went to visit the troll, and I gave him some. Joel was with me when I bought the heroin. I don't know why you haven't just asked him about it. He was with me the entire night. It's not like I could have done anything stupid without him knowing."

"All right." Molly reached forward and wrapped her fingers around Faye's wrist. "I believe you, though I wish you wouldn't visit him."

"He's in pain."

"As he should be." Her tone was far harsher than she had intended, Faye's surprised look told her as much.

"So you *are* the one who put him there."

"I am." Molly clenched her jaw.

"I always suspected, but he never outright said, and I never outright asked."

"I did." Molly really didn't want to have the conversation. "He deserves it. Enough said. I wish you wouldn't give him relief."

"He's in so much pain. And really, Molly, how long can you punish him?"

"You have no idea what he did to me."

Anger flared in Faye, her nostrils widening. "Whatever, Molly. You just continue to control the fate of the world in your fingertips and don't be asking the rest of us for advice or information."

Before Faye could stand, Molly grabbed her wrist again and held her in place. "Faye..."

"What?" Faye nearly yelled.

"You've transformed."

Faye looked down at her fingers then rolled her eyes, pulling her vampiric form back in so she reverted to her human side. "I've been doing that all day."

"I apologize about that. I shouldn't have asked—"

"It was worth it." The cocky grin Faye sent her smoothed a lot of Molly's ruffled feathers, but not all.

Lifting a hand to Faye's cheek, Molly pulled her in for a sweet and soft kiss. Faye tried to deepen it, but Molly resisted. "Not now."

"When?"

Molly chuckled. "When you tell me what drug you took."

Faye snorted. "Fat chance on that."

There was no resistance when Faye pushed into Molly again, their mouths moving against each other, Faye's body covering hers. Faye worked Molly up and then sat back, grinning like she had the world's biggest secret up her sleeve. Faye trailed a finger down Molly's rapidly rising and falling chest before she snorted and stood up, walking out of the room. Left frustrated for lack of information and sexually, Molly shook her head. She poured herself another glass of wine, grabbed the bottle, and made her way to her bedroom. She'd sleep on it before she attempted to get more information from Faye again.

Chapter Nine

MOLLY WAS down in the habitat area, looking in on the centivalk. He seemed fatter, for sure, although she wasn't happy about sacrificing some of her other inhabitants for it. The centivalk was a rare creature indeed, and she endeavored to keep it alive no matter the cost, even if she didn't like it.

They had kept feeding it, every day, a new creature that was alive and well. Molly had even sent Joel to go retrieve some, which was what he'd been out doing when Ben had fallen to his seizure. Faye had finished that up nicely enough. Molly stood with her arms crossed, watching as the centivalk captured his prey quickly.

He wrapped his two large pincer-like arms around it, the flipped on his side to wrap his entire body around the creature, effectively suffocating it while he drank the blood. Once the blood was drained, he would start in on the meat. By the next morning there would be absolutely nothing left.

A presence disturbed her. She knew he was coming before she could even see his face or hear his boots. *Malek.* The bman who had been the thorn in her side for the better part of her life. She'd been able to avoid him for the last two centuries for the most part, but his annoying presence in her house was a new trial she hadn't known she would have to face.

Taking the chance, Molly sent her magic toward him. If he slowly walked into it, closer with each second, then she might find a way to get into his mind without him noticing. It would be the only way she would be able to get information from him. She smiled when she finally heard his footsteps, and Molly stayed still, staring at the centivalk as it continued to eat.

"Molly." His voice was smooth as silk as always.

"Malek," she said back to him with the same sing-song tone. She wanted him to be comfortable while she worked her magic into his mind. Turning as he came right up to her, she smiled. "You were right."

"Of course I was."

Molly tried to hold in her quick remark she wanted to make. Malek was not always right. More often than not, she was the one who was right in their relationship, not that he would see that. "We never talked about the other night."

"What other night?"

Molly made eye contact with him, slightly demure just as he would like it. She could distract him with conversation. That would also be the best way to get information out of him. "When you interrupted us in my office."

"Oh, that night." Malek wiggled his eyebrows. "I wasn't invited in."

"You weren't." Molly put her hands down to her sides, wanting to appear as open to him as possible. She needed to be in order to get information.

Malek leaned in closer, his breath brushing against her cheek. "I don't recall being told to leave, either."

The smile lit her lips as much as she didn't want it to. He was always someone who could tear down the walls she tried to put up. "You weren't," she repeated. "Did you enjoy the little show Faye put on?"

"In more ways than you can possibly imagine."

But she could imagine, because as soon as he thought of them, the thoughts flashed through her mind. It wasn't a fantasy like she had expected. It was a memory. The two of them, centuries ago. Malek under her dress skirts as he did the exact same thing Faye had done, without the blood sucking.

She tried to control her breathing but couldn't help the gasp as the memory flooded her own mind, and she realized in her own distraction, she hadn't noticed Malek's power slip inside her. Warmth seeped through her and filled her. He was so much stronger than she was in the use of this spell. He was far more practiced at it, especially since Molly rarely used her magic anymore.

"Tell me, Molly..." he stepped impossibly closer "...why are you so resistant to the idea of rejoining the fold?"

"You know why."

"I really don't. It's been so long I've forgotten."

Molly's tongue dashed out against her lips, wetting them as her gaze flicked down to his mouth. She struggled to tear it away but finally looked up into his eyes. "I don't want to be matched."

"You didn't mind when you were younger."

"When I was naive and listened and did everything as my father told me. It's good thing he's dead now as I'm sure he's turning in his grave."

"And why is that, Molly? Because you've fallen in love with a woman or because you've left the fold."

"Both, actually." She raised a challenging eyebrow at him and didn't dare step away. As he worked further into her mind, she pushed back, putting up barriers and traps for him while also trying to work through his own thoughts. She mimicked his tone as she said, "Tell me, Malek, why are you here? And don't tell me it's because the fold sent you. They might have, but you are here for another reason entirely."

She was right. The thought was right there, but she wasn't able to break down the walls he had put into place. Malek's finger curled under her chin, lifting it up. He smiled at her. "Are you done playing your games yet, Molly?"

"What games would that be?"

"The ones where you attempt and I win."

"Hardly," she whispered. "I'm only just getting started. We're fairly evenly matched, you and me."

Molly stepped away from him then. She walked around to look at him over her shoulder with a seductive curl on her lips. Malek near fell over where he stood as he followed the line of her back down to the curve of her ass and hips. He was always weak to a woman's wiles, and Molly was sure to use that to her advantage.

He followed her, as she expected him to. "You think we're evenly matched. I taught you everything you know."

"Not quite everything." Her voice was husky. She kept working at that secret he held tightly in his mind, but thus far, she hadn't made a dent in trying to get in.

Malek grabbed her hand and jerked it, breaking her spell and his. "That was dangerous."

"No one has ever called me safe."

"You don't know what you're dealing with."

Molly stiffened but turned to face him full on. "Don't I? I have known you most of my life, Malek. I think I know you rather well by now, and I know you're not here just because the fold sent you."

"Reina and Corbin want you back."

"They understood why I left."

"Not anymore. We need all members."

"I'm not a member," she fired back, her jaw tight. "I gave that up ages ago, and you won't pull me in."

Malek's anger flared. She saw it in his eyes two seconds before he grabbed her other arm and spun her into the far wall. Her head collided with it, loudly, just before his mouth crushed hers. His arousal pressed into the side of her hip as his body covered hers. He held both of her wrists, pushing them against the wall up by her head so she couldn't move except to buck her hips, which she really didn't want to do.

The clapping surprised both of them, and Malek jerked back. Faye walked forward, her hands still clapping loudly as she gave applause. Molly moved her hands down to her sides, not slipping from the wall.

"I was wondering how long it would take you," Faye said, amusement dripping from every word.

"How long?" Malek questioned.

"Oh yes." Faye came up close to them. "See, I know your type, Malek. I've been around your type more than Molly here, and I understand how you work. You want her, and you'll do anything to get her. Your patience has worn thing, which is why you're here now, now that I brought you back into her life so unexpectedly."

Molly said nothing as she watched the pair of them.

"Molly needs to return to her proper place in the fold."

"She needs to do nothing other than what she wants and who she wants. I don't think she wants you." Faye put a hand against the center of his chest. "I, on the other hand, very much want, and I wouldn't mind being taken by the fold again either. That experience was quite...exhilarating."

Molly's heart raced. Faye had no idea what she was agreeing to. The fold would eat her alive literally if she were the only vampire for all of them. She would be so doped up on blood she wouldn't know which way was up and which way was down. Molly shifted to pull Faye back, but Faye stepped completely between her and Malek.

"Perhaps you'll join next time. Until then, Malek, I have something I need to discuss with Molly and you're not welcome for that conversation."

He seemed surprised, but he did step away. Bowing slightly

toward Molly, Malek walked the way he had come and disappeared around the corner. Molly didn't wait. "What's wrong?"

"Nothing. Joel's looking for you."

"That's it?"

"Yeah. I didn't like the way he was doing that."

Molly rolled her eyes. "I'm capable—"

"Of course you are. This was just easier, and I got to be the ass instead of you."

"It'll make it harder in the long run."

Faye shrugged. "I've always liked a challenge, quite like you were, and remember, I'm a walking risk."

Molly stopped at that, staring straight at Faye. "You're not wrong on that."

Joel sat in his office, writing up the report. He had no idea what had happened or how it had happened, but he knew Molly was going to want the report as soon as possible. He had tried to find her, get hold of her before getting back to his office, but it had been impossible. She'd all but disappeared, which worried him even more.

No one in the house had been hurt so far, but he knew it wouldn't take long before it reached them. Their house was large, with at least a hundred Tainted living in the underground floors, not to mention the creatures. Jesus, if the creatures got hold of what had happened, they'd be in shit so deep there would be no turning back.

He was just finishing his report when she stepped into his office. Joel breathed out a sigh of relief, forgetting the written report and focusing on the verbal one he was about to give. She raised an eyebrow at him as she stepped into his small office on the first underground floor.

"Shut the door," he beckoned.

"All right." Molly shut it behind her. "Why all the secrecy?"

"I don't want panic, and I assure you, there will likely be panic."

"Care to fill me in?"

Joel got up and sat on the small couch in his office. She sat next to him. "I'm not even sure where to begin. I was got a call about a patient early this morning, before anyone was up, that he was...I don't know...that something was wrong."

"Who called?"

"His wife. But I could hear him, and he was ranting like a

madman. I've never heard him say some of the things he was saying or even think about some of the things he was threatening."

Molly's eyes widened. "What happened, Joel?"

"He killed her. He tore out her throat, then he started eating her skin and body until I got there. Then he tried to attack me."

"You?"

Joel nodded. "I'm fine. I shocked him with the new toy Ben created, but then it was the oddest thing."

"What?"

"It didn't work. If anything, it did the opposite and only added to it."

"Joel, how did you escape?"

Joel skimmed his gaze over to Molly's, biting his lips from the inside. He didn't really want to tell her, but he knew he'd have to. There was no other way to get around it, and she was going to find out anyway. She was Molly. Eventually she knew everything. "I shot him."

"You killed him, you mean."

"He wasn't going to stop."

"I believe you." Molly brushed a hand through her hair and stared out the fake window in his wall, the one that pretended he was on the second floor of the house. "What happened?"

"Remember that feeling I got with Faye? That night we captured the centivalk?"

"Yeah."

"It was the same feeling from him. I couldn't get a read on his emotions at all. They were kind of all over the place—happy and angry at the exact same time. He had a thirst for blood and violence, that's for sure, but mentally, I'm not sure he understood it or wanted it. It's so weird."

"You think whatever she took, he took."

"I know it." Joel stared Molly straight in the eye. "I know whatever Faye took, Jason also did."

Molly pursed her lips. "I questioned Faye about it, and she insisted it was heroin."

Joel snorted. "She was not on heroin. We bought some that night, sure, but she gave it all to the troll."

"Yes, she told me that as well." Molly's jaw pulled tight, and her voice raised up in her distress.

The emotions coming off her in waves were anger and betrayal, but there was something lying underneath it all. Joel tried to pry through everything to get at it, to see what it was that always set her off about the troll because the feeling was there any time he came up in conversation. When she turned to face him, he knew what it was. Grief. Intense sadness and sorrow. It hit him hard. Joel's lips parted, and he reached out to cover Molly's hand with his, giving her a gentle squeeze, anything to try and ease that hurt.

"Wh-what is that?"

"What is what?" she asked, her voice terse.

"What you're feeling?"

"I'm feeling nothing." Molly stood up. "Has it reached the house?"

"My guess is it has. I've had reports of this happening a few times. I thought it was some type of virus, but witnessing it firsthand...Molly, whatever this drug is, it's powerful."

She nodded. "Amachon said as much as well."

"He's spoken to you?"

"Yes. He has had patients also succumb to this drug of choice and has witnessed perhaps not quite firsthand the aftermath of it."

"Has anyone survived it?"

Molly spun on him, surprise in her eyes and chest. "Faye."

"No one else?"

She shook her head. "Not that I'm aware of. Call Amachon."

"Right."

"We need to get on this. If this drug truly is killing as many as we suspect, then we need to deal with it now." Joel's heart was in his throat. He hadn't quite thought it was this bad, but Molly's alarm set him off. "Ben?"

"No, his seizure was not caused by this."

"Right." Joel let out a breath. "I suppose we're about to have a zero-tolerance policy in the house."

"We already had one," Molly responded.

Joel pursed his lips and stared her down. "With most Tainted, but not with all."

He knew he had her there. She couldn't deny that she'd looked the other way on Faye's drug use, although as far as he knew, Faye had been sober for close to a year at that point. He shouldn't have taken her to the sewers. That must have been where she got it.

"When you went out, was she ever alone?"

"A few times," Joel answered. "Never far, but I wasn't right next to her the entire time. She went and got us drinks or went to the bathroom. She could have gotten it at the club."

Molly nodded. "I suspect that is where she bought it. The question is from whom."

Joel nodded. "Yeah, and how much, because if Faye from that night could happen again, I don't know who can stop her, Molly. She's a vampire—she's one of the hardest Tainted to kill."

"Hard, yes, but not impossible."

"You wouldn't—"

"We may not have a choice if she chooses to imbibe again."

"Molly—"

Glaring, Molly turned toward the door and shook her head. She said nothing as she walked toward the door to his office. "Call Amachon. We all need to sit down and talk."

"Where are you going?"

Molly raised an eyebrow. "To find Faye."

CHAPTER TEN

THE SECOND time Faye had taken the small pills Aliya had given her, she knew she had to have more. The seconds of euphoria she felt from it was beyond anything she had ever felt before when it came to drugs, or really even life.

When she stepped into the sewer, she was surprised not to see the twins coming up the stairs toward her. They had been a mainstay since she'd visited the club since moving to the city and learning about it, but they were nowhere to be found.

"Interesting," Faye muttered as she stepped down the stone stairway to the floor of the club.

The bar was hopping, throngs of Tainted gyrating and drinking inside. For the middle of the afternoon, she was surprised to see so much activity. Faye recognized a couple of the regulars and Aliya, but that was it. The rest were strangers. She wished she had some heroin just to kick her off, but she hadn't thought that far ahead. All she'd known was that she wanted whatever Aliya had given her before.

Faye puttered around, dancing and drinking as she saw fit. Once again, Faye found herself wishing the alcohol would actually affect her without her having to drink an entire distillery to feel some of its effects. Just once she wished she was back to where she'd began, all those years ago before Molly, before she'd felt the true taste of pure blood.

Grinding her hips against the nearest Tainted, Faye lost herself in the sensation of hot bodies against her. Her head spun from the heat of the room, from the desire for the drug. It swam through her blood to the point it was nearly all she could think about. Molly was still in her head somewhere, she always was, but Faye focused on her need, her desire more than anything else.

The pulse of the music was loud, and she knew she couldn't linger. Molly would wonder where she had gone off to in the middle of the day without permission or without telling her.

When someone pressed up against her back, Faye leaned into them. She moved her ass around the person's front, waiting and wanting to know who they were until she had a moment to look. The music never stopped here. It kept going and going.

Finally, Faye moved around, and her eyes widened with Aliya's sweet face showed up as the one she'd been dancing with. Faye's lips parted with surprise for a moment before she grinned and tugged Aliya in for another round of dancing. The faerie's hands were small and nimble against Faye's body, enticing and then soothing. Faye had never been with a faerie before. She'd mostly stuck to humans since she hadn't really been accepted or involved in the Tainted world until Molly.

With Aliya's leg pressed firmly between hers, rubbing up and down, Faye understood perhaps why that was. Aliya was just as young as the rest of them, as the humans, as the ones Faye wasn't really interested in. They were good fun for dancing and going out, but no one had seen the world like she had—Molly and Malek excluded. And while Faye tended to ignore the fact she'd lived through the better part of seven decades, the more time she spent with Molly, the less she could.

Faye knew things. She had seen things, experienced things no one could fathom unless they'd also lived through it. As much as Molly admitted their attraction to each other was ordained or even manufactured because of their blood and species, Faye knew there was more to it than that. She wasn't attracted to Malek the same way she was Molly. She was curious about him, yes, enjoyed his odd little company and playing games with him, but there was something about Molly that always kept her coming back for more.

Her body was worked up into a nice hum of pleasure. Faye skimmed a hand down Aliya's side to her hip and then leaned in. "You've got some moves on you."

"Thought you might like to see them," Aliya answered. "But I supposed you're not here to dance with me."

Not one to give false hope but also one to constantly lie, Faye pulled Aliya in tight so their fronts were matched evenly. Aliya kept up the rhythm of her movements, and Faye realized a little too late how the changed angle was only that much better. Pulling Aliya's earlobe between her teeth and pulling, Faye let it go with a pop. "You're just an added bonus, a mighty talented one at that."

"I bet I taste pretty good. Faeries are known for being sweet."

Faye stiffened, her shoulders tightening, and her rhythm of dancing faltered. She pressed a kiss, finally, to Aliya's hot neck. "No offense, but no one tastes good except a witch, and that is not what I'm looking for tonight anyway."

"But you could."

"I won't," Faye responded firmly.

"I've heard it's pleasurable, and I'm always seeking more pleasure."

Faye cocked her head to the side as she stared at Aliya, wondering just where the conversation had gone off the rails. They had stopped dancing and stood in the middle of the moss-covered floor. "It can be pleasurable or it can be painful, but again, it's not what I'm seeking tonight."

"Right, you want this." Aliya pulled out another small baggie from her shirt just by her breast. When she pressed it into Faye's hand, she tugged Faye into her, hands firmly and confidently roaming over Faye's body this time. "I want payment this time. It's getting expensive for me."

Faye knew what Aliya was going to say, but she had to ask anyway. "And what kind of payment? Feeding is out of the question. I'll find the drugs elsewhere."

Aliya smirked. "Then if not that, something similar."

Without warning, Aliya pulled at Faye's hand until they were walking through the throngs of Tainted. Aliya led Faye to the side of the room where the tables were plenty. She leaned her shoulders against the wall and pulled her lower lip between her teeth. Faye raked her gaze up and down Aliya's body—at least if it were meant to be in public it would be quick and clothes would stay on.

"First this." Aliya took the baggie back from Faye and pressed one of the pills between her own lips, swallowing.

Faye had always taken two pills and wondered for a moment if she was only supposed to take one at a time. Aliya had never told her otherwise. The last time she'd taken them, she'd been smart, and locked herself in the catacombs at the house where no one would find her except perhaps Molly if she ventured that way. She had woken up as if from a trance a day later. It had been the best high yet. She'd dreamed, she'd been calm, calmer than ever. Aliya's hand against her cheek pulled her attention back.

"Where do you get this?"

Aliya shook her head. "Uh-uh, I want you to keep coming back here."

Faye gave her a small smirk. "I only ask because my body chemistry means I need a lot more than the normal Tainted."

"Oh?"

"Yeah, I don't want to run you dry and shortchange you money you're due."

Aliya shook her head. "I don't sell it. I give it away."

"You don't sell it?"

"Nope." Aliya's hand against Faye's breast was a sharp reminder of what she'd agreed to in order to get the drug. "Let's do this first, then I'll get you some more since you need it."

"And if you're not here?"

"You can find me."

"Aliya, I will gladly pay for it the same way I'm about to if I get it from you."

Aliya licked her lips, her gaze hardening. "After. First this."

"Right." Faye didn't hesitate again as she crashed their mouths together. Aliya moaned and wrapped her arms around Faye's neck and Faye lost all sense of what was happening. At some point, Aliya shoved two pills into her mouth, which Faye gladly swallowed. Faye made Aliya come several times against that wall. She was just urging her hand in and out once more when Aliya's demeanor completely changed, her body tensing but not from pleasure. Faye pulled back for a second to look her in the eye, but Aliya wasn't focused as her gaze darted around the room. Suddenly, there was a piercing pain at Faye's side, and when she looked down, blood spilled over her tight shirt and jeans.

Hissing, Faye spun around to see who had done it, but no one was there. The scene before her was shocking. Faye's heart ramped up. Aliya's hands pulled her back, wrapping around Faye's front so Faye covered most of Aliya's body, her ass once against pressed into the curve of Aliya's hips and belly. Teeth dug into Faye's neck, pain searing through all of her senses. Faye tried to move away, but Aliya was far stronger than she had been before.

The high from the pills she had taken worked into her head, and Faye had to blink three or four times to try and focus her eyes on what was happening in front of her. The throng of people still moved, but it was nothing she had wanted to see. Ever.

When Molly couldn't find Faye for the sixth hour that day, she took matters into her own hands. Her gut told her repeatedly something wasn't right, but she hadn't been able to get hold of Faye all day. No one had seen her, and she'd finally had Ben look up when Faye had left the property. No one had any idea where she'd gone, and Molly knew—she just knew—they were sliding back down the rabbit hole Faye had brought herself out of.

The only other time Faye had pulled stunts like this had been when she'd gone out to get heroin and bring it into the house or get high while she was gone. Molly had such hope they were done with all of that. As soon as she had a chance, Molly slipped into her Tesla. She needed to find Faye, and the one place she knew she'd gotten the drugs, whether Faye had said so or not, was the club.

It had been decades since Molly had stepped foot in there properly and it would probably be even longer. This was not a pleasure trip. Parking, she saw Faye's motorcycle and knew she was in the right place. Molly smoothed her hands down her tight green dress as she prepared to confront the snake-twins. They weren't her favorite breed of Tainted, but she had always appreciated their openness and honesty. They held nothing back sexually, unlike the way she had been raised.

Stepping into the sewers, Molly followed the familiar path she had treaded so very long ago. When she came to the wooden door, she wondered how she would get out of the twins advances that time. She hadn't managed the majority of her visits there. The door was, surprisingly, unlocked. Rubbing her lips together as the anxiety she had been feeling all day flared again, Molly pushed it open. The stairs beyond were completely empty.

Her heels clacked against the stone as she stepped down the stairway. As soon as she was on the main moss-covered floor, she knew something was wrong. The presence of people was lacking. Her senses were going wild. Molly opened the last door with a flick of her hand and magic to unlock it and gasped, a hand over her mouth as she stared at the blood bath in front of her.

Bodies were strewn about. Everywhere. The floor was covered with deceased Tainted. She bent down and pressed her hand into the moss. Pulling it back, it was covered in blood, so the moss was already doing its work at absorbing like it was trained to do. Molly's heart rapped hard against her chest as she stepped around, and over, and through torn up bodies. One after the other. No one was alive. No one was barely breathing. They were all dead.

She tried to see one familiar face but couldn't find it. If Faye had been there—who knew what type of damage she could have done. It was clear she wasn't the only one harming others. If Faye had been it, the damage to each body would have been worse, more violent. There would only be pieces of them left.

"Faye?" Molly asked, her voice ringing through the crowded room. "Faye, are you here?"

Molly walked through the entire main part of the club before she started on the back rooms. She had wondered at some point if Faye even knew they existed. More and more bodies were strewn about, but at least in the back area, they were far fewer. She really should call Joel and Benjamin, Amachon even, someone to come help her with this clean up. She had no doubt it was the same problem both Joel and Amachon had brought to her attention.

"Faye," Molly called again, her voice unsteady.

She heard the groan first. Turning sharply, Molly followed her instinct and pushed her way into a room at the very back of the club. As soon as she had the door open, the trail of blood was obnoxious. It looked as if someone had been dragged into the room, but her thoughts stopped, when she spied Faye on her back on the floor.

Racing to her, Molly squatted down and pressed her fingers to Faye's cheek. Her skin was still warm, but she wasn't breathing. Her eyes were open, but they didn't see anything. Molly cupped her cheek. "Faye, what happened?"

Faye didn't respond.

"Faye!"

With a jerk, Faye's body started breathing again. Molly shuddered as she tapped Faye's cheek again. "Faye, tell me what happened."

Faye said nothing, and her body was barely functioning. Molly pressed her fingers to Faye's wrist, catching her pulse as it stopped. Immediately, Molly tore at Faye's clothes to find the truth of the injury she'd no doubt endured with the amount of blood littering the floor. Molly knew she had to work quickly.

The slice in Faye's side was deep and no doubt the majority of the problem. There was a bite wound at her neck and shoulder, which also had a significant amount of blood pooling. Molly had never seen Faye so weak when she'd been so well fed before. She should have healed herself by then, a hundred times over.

Molly pressed her hand to Faye's side and was just about to start a healing spell when Faye jerked, her heart beating again and her lungs pulling air in and out of them. Molly paused for a moment, curious as to what was happening. It was as though Faye was dying over and over, like whatever had happened to her was preventing her from healing but that once in death her immortality kicked in to jumpstart her back to life.

"This won't do," Molly muttered.

The healing spell wove from her rapidly. She'd done it so many times over the years that she knew it by heart. Molly concentrated first on Faye's side, the wound tearing into her own body before disappearing into the ether. Then she started on Faye's neck. Those were the only two injuries she could see other than small scratches here and there.

Taking her time, Molly healed every single one of them. When she sat back on her heels, she carded her fingers through Faye's blood matted hair, wondering when her body would jumpstart her again. Sure enough, it only took a few seconds. This time, Faye continued to breath and her heart continued to beat. But she still didn't wake up.

Molly lifted the edge of her dress to pull out the small knife she kept pressed to her thigh. She slit her wrist. Opening Faye's lips with her free hand, Molly pressed her wrist to Faye's mouth. Faye sucked her blood down eagerly, waking as if from the dead. Soon enough her teeth joined in the feeding and Molly was as trapped against Faye as she could be, held by Faye's hand against the back of her head.

Waiting for Faye to sober up, Molly drew in deep breaths as Faye drank more, seeming unsatisfied. Like before, down at the pier, it was pain that seared through Molly's body, making it extremely difficult to concentrate and stay awake herself.

"Faye, you need to stop," Molly whispered, giving up her resisting and pressing her forehead into Faye's shoulder. "Stop."

Something must have clicked, because Faye did release her arm, but she still stayed silent on the floor. Both of them breathed heavily in the silence of the room. Molly wasn't sure how long she stayed there, pressed against Faye, but they were calm, so she took her time before trying to sit up. Faye had taken a lot of her energy, and Molly knew she was going to struggle to function.

"Are you sober?" Molly finally asked.

Faye shook her head. "Not totally, but close."

"Did the blood help?" Molly's head spun, and she knew she was going to have to work hard to focus and concentrate for the next chunk of the day while she tried to clean up the mess that was in the club.

"No." Faye's voice sounded rough and scratchy. "What happened?"

"The drug you took." Molly drew in a deep shuddering breath. "It...Faye, they're all dead."

"Who's dead?"

"Everyone who was here."

Faye tensed. "What?"

Molly nodded into Faye's shoulder, trying to hold back the tears. It had been years since she'd seen such a blood bath, but she couldn't help the memories surfacing. Molly formed a fist, slamming it down into Faye's chest. "What the hell were you thinking?"

"Molly..."

"No. Didn't you figure it from the first time what this drug made you capable of?"

Faye froze. "You don't...you don't think I did it, do you?"

Molly's jaw tightened, and she forced herself to sit up. "Who else has such a penchant for blood and the utter strength to kill so many so quickly?"

"I didn't—"

"You don't know that, Faye. You don't remember anything, do you? Absolutely nothing."

Faye's lips parted.

Molly closed her eyes and rubbed a hand through her hair. "Get up. You're going to help me clean this up."

"I'm...what?"

"You heard me." Molly pushed up as best as she could, but she had to grab onto a few chairs next to where Faye had dragged herself to stand upright. Faye had taken quite a bit from her, and the healing had cost her some, but she was still strong enough to do what needed done. It was only a momentary lapse from disuse.

Molly didn't wait as she walked out of the back room and into the hallway. She made it into the main area of the club and turned just in time to see Faye stumble out, her eyes widening in surprise. "I swear to you, I didn't do this."

"Yes, well, the moss will take care of it."

"What do you mean?"

Molly held her tongue in check as she stared at Faye. "You still have so much to learn. Bring all of the bodies in here please."

As soon as Faye had everyone in the main room, Molly called on her magic. Her eyes glowed as her power surged through her body. The spell was one she hadn't performed in ages, but it came to mind almost immediately. She knew what she had to do. No one else needed to witness this terror. It took her twenty minutes for the shadows to vanish the bodies and for her to stimulate the growth in the moss so it would work faster and absorb all the fluid that had been spilled. When she was done, Molly made sure to stand firm and glare at Faye.

"We're going home."

"That's it?"

"Yes."

"But this place—"

"Now." Molly walked out of the main part of the club and up the stairs. She needed rest, and she wasn't going to get it for quite some time. Sighing and still bloody from touching everything, including Faye and her own blood from healing Faye's wounds, Molly slid into the Tesla and headed for home. Faye would follow on her bike. They could handle the rest from the house.

CHAPTER ELEVEN

MOLLY STALKED through the house with a purpose. Just about everyone was still on edge after she'd discovered Faye at the club. Faye wasn't really speaking to her, and she had suspicions she was still high on something, though she wasn't sure it was whatever it had been before since she wasn't psychopathic and trying to kill or eat everyone.

Checking on each of the habits, especially the centivalk since he was their newest intake, she made her way toward the residential floor. She wanted to check in with Faye, again, and see if Faye would be willing to talk to her about what had happened. Molly had worked with the club for years, and this wasn't the first time something like this had happened. They would recover well enough. They were a sanctuary, a place where all Tainted could come together and be as free as possible.

She was just passing by the family room on the first floor when she paused before she reached the door. Malek's voice had that cool tone to it, the one he had when he was trying to seduce someone. Curious, Molly stood still, hoping she had been quiet enough when walking or Malek had been distracted enough that he hadn't noticed her. Casting a small spell, she hid her presence from him.

"I didn't realize Ben had any family."

Molly closed her eyes and pressed a fist to her chest. She'd forgotten Benjamin had told her his Aunt Deidre was coming for a visit. The timing could not have been worse, either. She understood his desire to be near family while he discovered himself, but that didn't make it any safer for Deidre to be in their house, not to mention, she was human. She had no idea about the Tainted world.

"I raised him when he was a little boy." Deidre's voice was calm but held a terse edge to it. Molly didn't know the woman well enough to be confident as to why she wasn't warming up to Malek.

She almost interjected, but she wanted to keep listening. Perhaps Malek would drop a hint as to what he wanted and why he was truly there. He certainly hadn't done that since he'd arrived at the house, but with Deidre, who knew. She was someone different, someone who had far less stakes in whatever was going to happen.

"Did you now? Well, I must say, you did a wonderful job. I only just met Ben a few months ago, but it's been a pleasure working with him."

Molly rolled her eyes. Deidre had been a part of Ben's life, but only when he was very young. As soon as he'd turned eight and shown some behavioral issues, she'd sent him off to what she thought was boarding school—year round. Molly had made sure to watch Ben closely since his mother had died, and when Deidre went in search of help, she was right there to step in.

"I suppose some of that credit goes to Molly," Deidre replied.

Surprised, Molly leaned in a little closer to hear better.

"Oh?"

"Ben moved here when he was eight to go to school. He hasn't left since, said he loved it here, and she gave him a job running the technology for the school."

"School?"

Cursing inwardly, Molly dropped the hiding spell and stepped closer to the door. She would have to break up the conversation if she didn't want Malek to slip up on what he didn't know. Someone should have warned him first, but no one had thought to do it. Stepping around the corner, Molly slid her clammy hands against the front of her suit jacket.

"Deidre, how good to see you again."

Deidre immediately shifted on the floral chair she sat in to stare into Molly's dark eyes. Molly gave her a brief smile before turning her glare on Malek. He must have seen or felt her annoyance because he raised his hands in the air like he was defending himself.

"Likewise, Molly."

"I didn't realize you were arriving today. Does Ben know you're here yet?" Molly realized a moment too late how odd her statement was, but she couldn't take it back. Pressing her lips into a thin line, she waited for an answer.

Deidre shook her head. "I haven't seen him yet. Joel picked me up at the airport."

"Right. I'll go get him, if you don't mind."

"I think Joel said he was doing that."

Molly's jaw tightened. She flicked her gaze from Deidre to Malek. Nodding her head toward the door at Malek, she hoped he'd get the hint that she wanted him to leave with her. He pushed up from the chair, thankfully. Molly turned back to Deidre. "I'll only be a minute, but I need to steal Malek here."

"All right."

As soon as they left the family area, Molly put a hand on Malek's wrist to stop him. She gave him a worried and serious look before walking toward the stairs, keeping him in tow behind her. She grabbed her cellphone and was just about to call Ben's number when an incoming call from Joel surprised her.

"What is it?" she asked, already sensing the urgency.

"It's Ben. He's having a seizure."

"Where are you?" Molly froze in the middle of the staircase, needing to know if she had to go up or down.

"His room."

"I'll be there in a minute." Spinning on Malek, she shook her head. "Go get Amachon. He's having a seizure."

Malek said nothing as he raced down the stairs. Molly moved up them. Her feet swiftly took her into Ben's room, and as soon as she opened the door, her heart broke. Ben was on the floor by the foot of the bed, his body jerking around like a fish out of water. She knelt next to him, holding his head carefully so it'd stop bumping into the corner of the dresser.

"How long?" Molly asked.

"I—I don't know. I came in and found him like this."

She drew in a deep breath. "Amachon's coming. Malek went to get him. I don't have anything on me."

"What do you need?"

"Paralytic."

"I've got it."

Joel raced from the bedroom and down the stairs. His feet pounded on the old wood. The one time Amachon wasn't at the house. She shook her head as she stared down at Ben. Amachon had been spending more and more time at the clinic with the outburst of drug overdoses. They'd have to figure out something, for

Ben and for the drug problem running rampant through the Tainted underbelly.

Ben had been seizing for at least four minutes by the time Joel returned, though Molly suspected it was far longer than that. He handed her a vial and a needle before he took over holding Ben's head away from the dresser. Molly filled the needle and plunged it into Ben's arm, depressing it. The liquid shot into his veins, but he didn't calm immediately. It was another two minutes before every muscle in his body stopped twitching.

Molly checked his pulse, his breathing, everything she could think of. Then she turned to look at Joel. "Put him on the bed, please."

"Shouldn't we take him downstairs?"

"Here will be fine."

Joel sighed and lifted Ben in his arms. Settling him on the bed, Molly sat on the edge of the mattress and gripped Ben's hand. She closed her eyes.

"What are you going to tell Deidre?"

Molly shook her head slowly as she stared down at the young boy she had practically raised. "I don't know yet. I'll figure something out."

"She doesn't know."

"Know what?"

"Anything."

"Well, she might learn something this visit."

Standing, Molly stepped toward the door after retrieving the medication and needle. "Stay with him, please. Let me know if his condition changes."

"I will."

With that Molly left the room, working out what lie she would be telling next.

The pills were easier to hide than baggies of heroin, that was for sure. Faye had taken to keeping them mostly on her person except any time Molly was in the room. She didn't trust Molly not to figure it out and take her stash. Faye had learned from the sewer club incident that she needed to cut the pills into a quarter instead of taking them all at once, as much as she wanted to. She could maintain the high and not want to suck everyone's blood at the same time. The high wasn't as good as if she'd take one or two pills, which she still did on occasion after locking herself in the catacombs, but it was enough to get her through the day.

After Aliya had died, she'd had to find another source for the little drugs, and this time, it cost her money. Faye's resources weren't as vast as Molly's but they did well enough in a pinch. Sliding a pill between her lips and thinking of her friend under the bridge, the one who had hooked her up with a new dealer, she swallowed the quarter of the pill. Stashing the small baggie behind a baseboard in her bedroom, she leaned against the wall and waited for the drug to hit her.

Sometimes it took too long, but she hated to let it wear off before she was slipping another pill between her lips and she hated the sensation of being sober after taking it. While high everything was perfect, warm, she felt as though she were in a bubble of happiness—something she had never experienced before.

Closing her eyes and leaning her head against the wall, Faye drew in a deep breath. She and Molly had talked weeks ago about banding together to find out why Malek was really at the house. Faye had done very little in the way of getting information from him. While she was curious, it was definitely more for Molly's benefit to find out than hers, and while she liked Molly, it didn't leave her motivated a whole lot.

It took some time, but the pill started to hit. First her head swam. Dizzy spell after dizzy spell worked through her mind, and she had to fling her eyelids open in order to focus her gaze to stop from feeling like she was going to fall over. Then the warmth came. This was her favorite part. She had been so cold, so left alone for years, and this felt like pure love to her. She'd never been loved like that. Snorting, Faye sneered. Probably would never be either.

Bending her knees up, Faye relaxed into the wall, her body pressed against the base of it like it was her lifeline, which she supposed it was. The urge to drink was still strong when she got high, but at least with only one quarter of the pill inside her, it was manageable. What wasn't manageable was her desire. She wanted Molly, though she supposed Molly was likely busy, and she suspected if Molly could figure out she was high, there would be no play time for the two of them. Instead, she would incur Molly's wrath.

Which would be a beautiful sight to see.

Molly was gorgeous when she was angry. The fire in her eyes, the sharp rise and fall of her chest, every muscle in her body tense and ready to go as soon as she commanded it. Molly was the perfect picture of control when she was pissed off about something.

As soon as Faye was sure the drug was in her system, she

pushed herself to stand, holding onto the wall to steady her wobbly knees. Straightening her spine, Faye stared at her door. She needed to do something for Molly before she could go find her. There would be no point in just seeking her out with nothing to offer.

Faye walked, although she felt as though she was gliding, to the door to her bedroom. *Malek.* She would start with him then work her way to Molly. If she had something to offer Molly perhaps Molly would be more inclined to what Faye wanted.

She spun around the corner of a hallway and ran right into the man she wanted to see. His blond hair was perfectly smoothed over the top of his head like he never had a bad hair day. Must be a witchy thing. Faye snickered. Molly was pretty much the same way except that one time they were in Beirut, that had been an adventure of Molly being flustered nearly the entire time. Faye had made it her mission to see her like that again at some point.

"Hey," Faye breathed the word out heavily. She pressed a hand right into Malek's chest, feeling his heart rap against his ribs in a steady thrum. She wasn't going to waste any more time if it could get her one step closer to something Molly wanted. "What are you up to?"

She sounded drunk. That wasn't a good start to this seduction. Faye needed to be able to think clearly, but the warmth was taking over all her senses, and she struggled to keep hold of herself. Fisting her fingers into his polo shirt he seemed to always wear, except a different color for each day of the week, which now that she thought about it, Monday's were always this weird pea-green color, so it must be a Monday. Not that she could tell because of the drug coursing through her veins.

"Are you high?" There was a note of disgust in each of his words.

Faye ignored it. "Why would you say that?"

"Because you're coming on to me like a woman in heat."

Sneering, Faye stepped away from him and glared. She realized Malek had grown up in a vastly different world and time than she had, but there was still something about him that made her feel squicky. She was also left near speechless, which was an odd sensation for her. Normally she had all kinds of quick quips to come back with, but something about Malek seemed to put her in her place.

He reached forward, cupping her cheek and tilting her head up so she had to stare into those cold eyes that were never quite readable. His thumb carded across her cheek, just under her eye.

Malek was quick. His arms were strong. He pulled Faye to him and spun her until her back was pressed against the wall and his front against hers. If she'd been sober, he never would have gotten the better of her. She was much stronger than he was even in her human state.

Malek moved in, his lips brushing against hers when he spoke. "I would very much like to know what it's like to kiss you, Faye, to fuck you."

The curse word was so strange coming from him, but it sent a shiver of pleasure through Faye's chest and down between her legs. Turning to seduction, which she knew she was good at, she bit her lip and lowered her lashes as she tilted her chin up to stare at him.

"But I want you sober for it. The power exchange is better that way."

"Power exchange?" Faye's voice was merely a whisper. Every time she had Malek like this, she usually learned something about herself in the process, something Molly most likely should have taught her.

His hand slid down to her neck, his thumb and forefinger pressing against her jugular and closing off her airway in the slightest. Faye remained utterly still. Malek ground his hips into her. "Has Molly not told you about that? Remember Reina and Corbin?"

"Hmmm, yes. I remember that. That's what you call it? Power exchange."

Malek nodded. Faye could play dumb if she needed, Malek seemed to like it. Being this close to him made the urge for his blood that much stronger, and she knew he would taste just as good as Molly. He had to. He was older, and he was purer blood than she was. His blood could last her even longer than Molly's.

His mouth was against hers again, his fingers tightened. "Sober up, and we'll talk about this again."

He was about to move away. Faye knew it. His hand left her neck, and he slid back, but she couldn't let him get off that easy. She had to take something, prove she was just as good at seduction as he was. Before he moved away too far, Faye gripped him behind his head and pulled him back to her, their mouths crashing together.

Arching her back, she jutted her breasts into his chest as her tongue pressed against his lips. Snaking her other hand around his back and up his spine, Faye held him to her. Malek's tongue plummeted her. Their breathing picked up as the tension and arousal grew. His hand was once again at her cheek, then her neck, pressing into her. His other hand groped her breast, harshly twisting her nipple through the fabric of her shirt and bra. He gave as good as he got. They would be an excellent match as soon as they got to that point.

Faye nipped his lip without breaking skin, wanting to give him a taste of what it would be like should they continue. Malek ripped backward, breathing heavily as he stared down at her. He nodded at her and stepped away to the middle of the hall.

"Next time, Faye, don't be high." He stalked away from her.

Whimpering, Faye wiped the back of her hand over her mouth to remove his saliva. Whether or not they fucked, she'd at least made progress into his inner circle. He wanted her. That was enough for her in that moment.

CHAPTER TWELVE

JOEL SAT heavily on the couch in his office, the weight of the past few weeks resting on his shoulders. Closing his eyes, he leaned his head back and let out a huge sigh of frustration. Deidre had stayed an extra week after Ben had confessed his seizure, though it was rather hard to hide it. Joel couldn't fault him. He'd want the extra support too if it was him.

While Joel was happy Ben was finally exploring his Tainted side, it worried him endlessly about what it could mean. He'd never seen anyone go to the extremes Ben did in suppressing his natural abilities. Medication, while it could do wonders, could also do a lot of harm, and Joel was pretty sure that Ben was discovering the fallout from it.

Rubbing his hands over his cheeks, Joel groaned. His worst fear was that Ben would have another seizure only the next time he wouldn't wake up, and Joel would be left without him. He never would have imagined when Molly had coerced him into working there nearly a decade ago that he would also have fallen in love in the process. They'd had a roundabout dating life, but through the thick and the thin, they'd stuck together.

Joel sat up straight when he heard his office door snick open. He pressed his palms to his thighs as he waited to see who it was. He'd been so engrossed in his own worry that he hadn't been paying attention to the emotions of those around him, and for the first time in a long time, he was surprised by who was at the door.

Ben pushed his way in, shutting and locking the door behind him. He gave Joel a wan smile before settling into the couch next to him, pressing his head against Joel's shoulder. Joel shifted and wrapped an arm around Ben's shoulders and tugged him in a little closer. Dropping a kiss onto Ben's head, Joel breathed in Ben's scent and closed his eyes. He wasn't sure if Ben knew, but this had been exactly what he'd needed.

"Aunt Deidre will be going home soon. She finally booked a flight."

Joel grunted. "Probably a good thing. At least Molly will be a little more relaxed if she's not in the house."

"Yeah."

Joel brought his hand up and threaded his fingers through Ben's messy mop of hair. "I worry about you."

"Why?"

"What going off this medication is doing to your body?"

"Molly and Amachon both say it should be out of my system already."

Joel pressed his lips together tightly before drawing in a deep breath. "Yeah, it should, but your body hadn't worked without it in a long time, so there are some adjustments to your own hormones and chemicals that it needs to figure out. I worry what damage is being caused by all this."

They fell into a long silence, Ben saying nothing, but his emotions were loud and clear. He went from concern, to anger, to frustration, and finally landed on determination. Ben turned his chin up, wrapped a hand around Joel's neck and brought their mouths together for a very long sweet and comforting kiss.

"Maybe. But couldn't you ask the same thing about taking the medication? What damage is being done by not allowing my body to be in its truest form?" With another quick peck to Joel's lips, Ben sighed. "I didn't come here to talk about this."

"Oh?"

Ben gave Joel a weak smile. "Molly."

"What about her?"

"She's up to something."

Joel smirked. "When is she not?"

"True."

"Do you know what it is?" Joel had an inkling of what it might be, but he wanted to see if Ben had come to the same conclusions he had. Then he would know they were on the right track.

Ben shook his head, and once again, they fell into a

comfortable silence. Joel had a patient coming within the hour, so they couldn't stay there much longer. Shifting in his seat, Joel reached over and pressed a hand firmly on Ben's thigh.

"When do you think you'll start trying to shift?"

Ben shrugged. "I have no idea. I haven't felt anything that might make me think I can at this point."

Joel raised an eyebrow. "What are you waiting for?"

Ben's lips parted and then closed. Shaking his head, his eyes wide, he said, "You know, I'm not really sure, I guess. I just thought I'd feel something."

"Like what?"

"I dunno."

"Have you talked to Faye about it?"

"Why would I talk to her?"

Joel narrowed his gaze. "She essentially shifts from one form to the other when she goes from being a human to a vampire and back. That, to me, is similar enough to what you're looking for that she might be able to answer the question."

"I hadn't really thought of it that way. I just asked her if it hurt, once, well, a long time ago I asked her that."

"What'd she say?"

"Yes."

Joel wondered if that was also part of the reason Ben was avoiding shifting, but he didn't want to comment on it. Bringing Ben closer with a firm hand to his cheek, Joel kissed him sweetly. "Ask her."

"I will."

"I've got a patient."

"And I've got work to do, no doubt Molly has something else she wants me to beef up security on."

Joel smirked. "You are the best at it."

"Some days," Ben trailed off as he stood up to leave. He turned last minute to stare down at Joel and shook his head. "I bet it's Malek."

"I know it's Malek. The question is what is Molly trying to get out of him."

Ben shrugged. "Your guess is as good as mine. You know she keeps that stuff pretty close to her until the rest of us to know. Besides, they have a history."

"They—what? They have a history? Wait...what does that mean?" Joel was standing before he even knew what he was doing. Ben's raised eyebrow of curiosity didn't sway Joel any.

"You mean…you don't know."

"Know what?"

"Crazy. I never know shit before you."

"Out with it, Benjamin."

Ben grinned and crossed his arms. "Molly and Malek have a history."

"So you said, and so I gathered from him being here, but what you said…it seemed more than just acquaintance."

"Do you know much about the ancient folds?"

Joel shook his head.

"Might want to research that."

"Why?"

"Very misogynistic if you ask me."

Joel narrowed his gaze. "There has to be more to it than that."

Chuckling, Ben stepped closer to Joel and ran a hand down his arm. "Oh, there is, but you get to do your own research on that. For now, just know that Malek and Molly were matched, she didn't want to be, he let her go, but I'm betting that he's back because he's tired of waiting."

"Waiting for what?"

"He wants the fold to continue."

"Stop being cryptic." Joel bit his lip when he realized his tone was edging on anger.

Ben snorted. "He wants bow-wow-chicka-wow-wow."

"Oh."

"He wants a baby."

"Yeah, I get it," Joel answered. "I still think there might be more to it than that."

"There probably is. You know immortals, they hide shit for days."

"Years."

Laughing, Ben nodded. "Yeah, you're right about that."

With one last peck to his lips, Ben left Joel's office. Joel turned toward his desk with a huff. He'd have to wait until after his patient left to dig into that one, but Ben had dropped probably the best hint into why Malek was there that he could hope for.

Molly stepped through the door to her office and stopped short. Faye sat on her couch, legs sprawled with a hand down her pants. Shutting the door immediately, Molly locked it from the inside—the only way the door would lock. She didn't dare take a step closer to Faye, whose dark eyes locked on her as the sun faded over the horizon. She wasn't sure what to say. For the first time in a long while, Molly was left speechless.

Faye, however, was not.

"Come over here." Her voice had that deep quality to it, the one that meant she wasn't in her human form, and Molly was sure that if she flicked the lights on to illuminate the room properly, she'd see Faye's long teeth and even longer nails, minus the ones on the hand currently down the front of her pants.

"I will not," Molly whispered, but her body wanted to move forward, to rest in Faye's embrace, to feel the excitement and heat and energy that only Faye could bring her.

"Molly." Faye dragged out her name.

Molly cocked her head to the side, and with a short breath, forced herself to move closer. Faye flicked her wrist toward the side lamp on the table next to the couch and it came to life. Sure enough, Faye sat in all her vampiric glory. She looked so much paler this way. Her skin had a silver glow to it, her eyes black as midnight, not just the irises but every part of it. When Faye turned her gaze on her, Molly shivered under the stare, her nipples standing to attention as the cold from the open parapet doors finally touched her skin.

"What's going on?" Molly slid onto the couch next to her. "This is wildly unlike you."

"I can't stop thinking about you."

Molly narrowed her gaze and gripped her fingers around Faye's wrist, feeling for her pulse. It was as rapid as if she was in the middle of a fight. Faye moved forward and pressed her nose to Molly's neck.

"I want to taste you."

"Yes, this is very much unlike you. I know you, Faye, and drinking my blood is not typically something you desire." Faye's teeth scraped against the hollow of Molly's neck, and Molly shuddered, thoughts and images rampaging through her mind as she almost gave in to Faye's sexual demands. This wasn't the blood-thirsty Faye from the docks, but this was a blood-thirsty Faye.

Faye's hand moved to the front of Molly's dress, cascading upward and over her breast. "I want you."

"I can see that." Molly tried to push Faye's hands down. "The question running through my mind is why."

"Because I love you."

Molly, startled, gripped Faye's wrist far tighter than she intended. "You do not."

"I do. I want to taste you."

Closing her eyes, Molly firmly moved Faye's hands from her body and pressed them into Faye's lap. "You don't. You're high. On what, I'm not entirely sure, but I suspect it's this."

The small baggie she held between her fingers was enough to get Faye's attention. Faye tried to grab at it, but Molly jerked it out of Faye's reach then settled it on the coffee table in front of the couch. She stared Faye down, wishing she could more often see her for this length of time in her vampiric form. In fact, this might be the longest Molly had ever sat with the vampire part of Faye, the longest she'd ever been allowed to gaze upon the beauty of force and nature that she was.

Cupping Faye's cheek, Molly held her gaze steady. She didn't have time to linger on wants or desires, she had to figure out what Faye was up to. "I see you cut the pills."

Faye nodded. "One is too much."

"You can control it better this way?"

Closing her eyes, Faye licked her lips. "The smell of your blood is alluring."

"Stay with me. Where did you get them?"

Faye eyes shot straight to Molly's face. "I won't tell you that. Then I'll never get more."

"Faye." Molly drew in a deep breath. "This drug is wreaking havoc all over my city. I need to take care of it."

"It's the best one I've ever had."

"Because you need so little?"

Faye's chin bobbed in her answer.

"Have you wondered how and why you need so little?"

At her parted lips, Molly knew she had her. At least Faye with only a quarter of the pill in her system was far easier to talk to than raging angry Faye with at least one or two pills in her.

"Do you remember the club?"

"Yes."

"Did you do it?"

Faye shook her head.

"Do you remember anything after you took the pill?"

At Faye's blank stare, Molly knew she had her. Faye took the drugs she was given and that was all she remembered until Molly showed up. She didn't need magic of manipulation to know that. Sighing, Molly brought their foreheads together and closed her eyes.

"How many times?"

"How many times what?"

Molly licked her lips. "How many times have you taken so much you've blacked out?"

Faye shook her head. "I don't remember."

"Fuck," Molly whispered and pulled back, grabbing at the small baggie again. "You do realize, Faye, that you are the only Tainted to survive taking this."

"I—I can't be."

"You are." Molly dropped the bag onto the wooden table to make her point. "You are the only one, and I'm betting it has to do with the fact you're immortal, which is a rare gift among our kind, but also because you have the gift of healing. I'm willing to bet that your blood thirst when you're high like this isn't because you want to rip my neck out but because your body is telling you that you need to heal."

Without warning, Faye transformed back to her human form. Slate-gray eyes stared up at Molly, wide with worry. Molly reached up and cupped her cheek again, brushing her thumb across Faye's lips.

"There you are."

"What did you mean I'm the only one to survive?"

"That's exactly what I meant."

Faye's lips parted in surprise, and Molly bent, pressing her lips to them for a brief moment of what she always seemed to take for granted, Faye's calm. Faye breathed out, her eyelids fluttered shut. "If you want me not to try for your blood, you better stay back."

"I will, just one more." With her fingers wrapped in the hair at the back of Faye's neck, Molly held their mouths together, swiping her tongue out along Faye's lips. She hesitated only for a moment when she ran into Faye's long vampiric teeth that must have come back out to play. She neatly avoided them as she tangled Faye's tongue with her own.

Faye jerked back. "Enough."

Molly smiled. "All right. Where did you get the drug?"

Faye's jaw tightened.

"Faye, please."

She shook her head. "I won't tell you."

"I need to know."

"No."

"You're not getting them at the club anymore, so where?"

"It's a stash that I had from there."

Molly narrowed her gaze and sat back, her spine rigid. Faye was lying. It didn't take her magic to see that, but what she couldn't figure out was why. "No more."

"Where have I heard that before?" Faye rolled her eyes and grumbled.

A light smile lit up Molly's lips. "Perhaps having a drug-addicted vampire in the house isn't such a good idea."

"You like it."

"I like you."

Faye's cheeks tinged with red, and Molly was pleased with herself.

"Have you seen Malek?" Molly changed the subject to give Faye the relief she needed.

"Yes."

"When?"

"The other day."

Molly grunted. "High or sober?"

Faye didn't answer, which told Molly as much as she needed to know. Blowing out a breath, Molly relaxed and took Faye's hand in hers. She'd thought they'd been making progress, but perhaps she had been too blind to what Faye could give her to truly look at what was happening in her house.

"We need to find out why he's here."

"I tried," Faye whined. "I did."

"You need to do it sober. Like me, he won't want you when you're high, and our blood seems to do nothing except feed an addiction much like the drug itself."

Pursing her lips, Faye raised her gaze without raising her chin, so her stare could be taken as either shameful or daring. "I'll stop."

"Please do." Molly raised Faye's head with a finger under her jaw. "Because I would very much like to see this again when you are sober."

Blushing furiously, Faye shoved up from the couch. "To Malek."

"Sober first."

"Fine." Faye heaved a sigh but zipped her jeans and walked out of Molly's office with an extra sway to her hips. Molly couldn't help but to follow every swing and then flush when Faye sent a knowing look over her shoulder before shutting the door behind her.

"Cheeky," Molly muttered.

CHAPTER THIRTEEN

MOLLY HAD given Faye two full days to sober up. She'd hoped Faye would, but she was far from surprised when Faye maintained her small high. How she'd gotten more drugs, or where she'd gotten them from, still remained a mystery, one she needed to rectify. If Faye wasn't going to give her that information, she was going to have to find it herself.

It was nearing dusk, and she finished up the paperwork she had on her desk. She'd run her plan by Joel, more like she told him what her plan was, and when she'd insisted on taking Malek with her, he'd hesitated. Molly knew Joel didn't trust Malek, which didn't surprise her any. People rarely trusted him because he wasn't very trustworthy. He had broken more than a dozen promises to her in the first few years they'd known each other, and one major promise by showing up at her house.

Since Faye was still flitting around high, she would have to take matters into her own hands to figure out why he was there. In some ways it felt as though she'd lost her partner in crime, but she knew even through Faye's haze, she was tactfully observant. She knew that for a fact, seeing as how Faye had been quite high the first few years they'd known each other and had managed to function properly just about every day she needed to.

Putting away her papers and closing down her computer after one more check through of the systems, she pushed away from her desk. *Malek.* She'd have to entice him to go with her. It shouldn't be too difficult, but she'd have to work a way to get information from him without divulging too much herself—that was the tricky part. He was her match in every way when it came to being cunning. Faye was her wild card, and she needed her in order to make everything work. They'd have to have another discussion.

Smoothing her hands down the front of her dress, Molly stepped from around her desk and toward the door to her office. The rest of the house would be doing exactly what they needed to be doing—checking on the creatures they housed, prepping for dinner, Amachon would still be at the clinics no doubt. His work had intensified lately in a way neither of them had ever expected.

Stepping from her office, she shut the door behind her and ran straight into Malek. Surprised, her lips parted before she caught herself. Cocking her head to the side, Molly eyed him carefully. "Did you need something?"

Her voice was huskier than she'd intended, but when he returned her look in full force, Molly decided it may have worked to her advantage.

"I was coming to make sure you were taking a break."

Raising a thin eyebrow, Molly smirked. "I doubt that was the only reason."

"It wasn't." He gave her a slight smile. "I wanted to see you."

"Well, good thing you did. I have a mission for us."

"Oh?" He threaded her arm through his as he turned to face the stairs.

Molly normally would have objected, but if she needed to get close to him to make any headway on obtaining information, she'd have to let him touch her and play that role. Taking her free hand, she wrapped it around his bicep and squeezed once before stepping forward toward the spiral staircase that would lead her down to the main floors of the house from her attic office.

"Yes, I need to know more about this drug."

"What drug?"

"Don't play ignorant, Malek. It's not your style."

"True. I assume the one the lovely Faye has been imbibing with."

"Yes, that one." She intentionally scraped her thumb nail against the skin on his arm just under the edge of his polo shirt. "I need more information about it, and my normal sources are proving fruitless."

"What are your normal sources?"

Molly stopped and turned, pressing her body into his side.

"That's for me to know."

"And me to find out?"

"You would think, wouldn't you? But no. I think I'll keep my sources to myself."

Malek's eye twitched, and she knew she'd irked him. Two hundred years ago, he would have come back at her roiling mad if she'd kept secrets from him, but two hundred years was a very long time, and just as she thought, he needed or wanted something from her as much as she wanted information from him. Malek getting angry would only hinder that progress for both of them.

"Would you come with me?"

"Come with you?"

"Yes." She grinned. "I would like the backup, and my normal crew is already busy tonight with other things. Would you like to get out of the house for a bit?"

"What do I get out of it?" He narrowed his gaze at her.

She chuckled and started down the steps again, coming to the second floor of the house where most of the bedrooms were for her main staff. "Oh, I don't know, time with your matched. Time out of this house and in the city."

She was outwardly flirting with him. It wasn't taking as much effort as she thought it would either. It may have been two centuries since she'd seen him face to face, but that spark was still there. As much as she may have wanted to deny it, she couldn't. They were matched, and that meant something.

"I'll go with you under one condition."

Molly knew what he was going to say before he even formulated the thought fully. Shaking her head, she eyed him carefully as they walked down the hall. "No, Malek."

"Yes."

"No. I broke away from the fold once. I won't go back."

"It's not even a functioning fold any longer."

That startled her. Every tidbit of information she'd garnered over the years had told her the opposite. They were more powerful and more in control of the world than they had ever been. With witches becoming a dying race, at least ones as pure as they were, that had meant there was free reign on open territories.

"Oh?" she asked, trying to get him to talk more. Perhaps he didn't know as much as she thought he did.

"We're fractured. I told you this would happen if you left, and you did it anyway."

"With your blessing, I'll have you remember that."

He paled. "It was for your happiness, nothing more. I couldn't keep you there against your will."

"And I thank you for that." They got to her bedroom, and she faced him, cupping his cheek. "Truly, I do."

Nodding, Malek bent his head so he was looking at the floor. "We need you."

"Malek, I don't think they need me."

"I need you." His confession hung in the air, building the tension already between them.

Once more, Molly reached up and cupped his cheek, drawing her finger across his skin just under his eye. "You don't need me."

"I do."

"Malek—"

"Please listen."

"All right, I'm listening." She stiffened her shoulders as a reflex, unable to control the slight move. "Share."

He rubbed his lips together and looked nervous. Not for the first time in her life did she wish she had Joel's ability to read people and feel their emotions. It would certainly come in handy in moments like this.

"The fold isn't right without you. We're weak. We're fractured, but more than that, I'm weak without you. You know what we could be together. We could be powerful."

"Reina and Corbin are powerful."

"Yes, but even they are aging, and it has been centuries since they've had a child."

Molly's lips parted and asked a question she already knew the answer to, but she didn't want him to know how kept she was on the fold. "How long has it been since a child has been born?"

Malek flushed. "Two centuries."

Letting out a snort, Molly clenched her jaw. "You will not blame this on me."

"It was our turn."

"I won't—"

"Just listen." Malek pleaded, his eyes boring straight into hers. "Because I need you, more than the fold does. You have always balanced me, you know that."

She wisely kept her mouth shut.

"I need that balance. Life has been long without it. I've kept tabs on you throughout the years, treasured the few times you have reached out to me, but I need more than that. I *want* more."

Molly wanted to tell him she didn't, wanted to staunchly stand firm in her decision all those years ago, but she couldn't. She needed him to open up to her. This was about more than just the fold. It had to be. No one had contacted her like this in nearly two centuries, not even when Pearl—she stopped that thought.

"Is there something wrong that the fold should feel the need to call me back after so long?"

He shook his head. "No, nothing like that."

"No war? No disease, no curse?"

"No."

"Then what is so urgent, Malek. Tell me, because I don't understand."

"*I* need you."

"You need no one."

"Maybe it's just that I want you. Isn't that enough?"

There was an edge to his tone Molly couldn't miss. She'd heard it there before. It wasn't just what the fold was made for, it was that she disagreed wholeheartedly with its purpose. "I will think about it. But right now, I have more pressing problems to deal with, especially if you say there is nothing wrong. Are you coming with me or not?"

He nodded his answer.

Molly turned around, leaning against her door with her hands over the knob as she faced him. "I'll be out in a minute."

She was halfway through undressing when the door to her room opened. Surprised, Molly turned to find Malek standing there with his hand on the knob. They both knew he was pushing his boundaries, but she needed information as much as he did, and she had agreed she would do this. Sending a flirtatious smile over her shoulder, Molly stripped the rest of her dress off before disappearing into her closet.

Coming back out, she made a show of pulling her leather pants on and a clean black shirt over her head. She flipped her hair up into a bun at the base of her neck, all the while staring him down. As soon as she was finished tying up her boots, she grabbed her jacket and moved to him.

"Ready?" he asked.

"Yes," she whispered, making her voice husky on purpose this time.

Malek pressed a hand to the small of her back as they left her room. Before she knew it, they were parking her Tesla at the corner nearby the club where she'd found Faye. What she really needed were Faye's contacts, but since Faye was being less than forthcoming with information, she'd have to rely on what she knew of Faye's contacts—which was probably far more than Faye dared to admit.

Molly walked confidently down the sidewalk toward the pier where she knew the man with the red head tended to hang out and sell. Even if he wasn't selling the drug, he would at least know if there was a new drug on the streets, maybe. He was Faye's dealer, and as far as Molly had ascertained, he was human and she couldn't figure out if he knew he was selling to Tainted or not.

Malek stayed close to her as they moved. It wasn't long before they came to a stop. Molly knelt down to the man who was far grungier than the last time she'd seen him. His head was tilted down, his life was in two rucksacks next to him. His shoes had no tread and his toes peeped out of one. His red cap lifted, and his eyes widened as he stared at her.

"I want some information."

"I got nothing for you."

Molly smirked. "I'm not the police. I won't arrest you. You're a dealer, I know that. You know my friend, she used to buy from you."

"I don't know anything." His teeth were mostly rotted from his mouth, and Molly had to hold her breath to squat close to him.

Drawing in a deep breath, Molly tried to soften her tone and worked her magic into his mind. He would at least be easy to manipulate. "Do you know about a new drug?"

He shook his head. Malek standing at her back made her more nervous than ever. Molly felt he was hiding something, but she couldn't quite see what it was yet. Working even more into his mind, she breathed magic into him.

"Have you lost customers lately?"

The man in the red cap nodded. "A few. Not unusual."

There she had him now. "And do you know about a new drug?"

He barely nodded.

"What is it?"

"I don't know anything."

"Do you sell it?"

"It's not for sale."

A shiver ran up Molly's spine. "What do you mean it's not for sale?"

"They give it away. They don't charge, but I tried it, and it didn't do anything."

Molly turned to glance at Malek, who shrugged at her as he

looked nervously around. "Someone's going to see us."

"Even if they do, you know how to deal with that." She shot back at him. Focusing once more on the man in the red cap, Molly pressed a hand to his leg to get his attention. "Who is giving it away?"

"Don't know. I got it from one of my regulars."

"Who might that be?"

"I don't share that information."

Molly clenched her jaw and worked even more into his mind. She'd eased up on her magic when he'd started talking, but clearly he had quite a few more barriers than she had anticipated, not to mention, he wasn't high like she had hoped. That would have helped her magic flow into him far more easily.

"You said it didn't do anything for you?"

"Nothing." He spat on the ground about a foot away from Molly's boots. "Tasted like shit, too."

Malek leaned down and pressed a hand to her shoulder. "We shouldn't linger."

"No one is coming," she whispered at him. "Stop worrying."

A slight rain fell over them, dampening everything at the edge of the pier. Drops clung to Molly's hair, and she knew it was going to get heavier as the hours wore on. She'd called on it, asked it to come.

"Who was it that gave it to you?"

"Ricky."

"Who is Ricky?"

"She's my ex."

Molly raised an eyebrow at that and twisted to see Malek. He was huddled under his jacket against the rain. "Where might I find Ricky?"

"Haven't seen her in a few weeks."

"Weeks?" Molly tightened her grasp on his leg, knowing the physical contact would help the connection. "Are you Ricky's only dealer?"

"Thought I was. Guess not."

"Where might she have gotten this drug?"

"Don't know."

"It's too much," Malek whispered. "He'll start resisting soon."

"You're not my trainer any longer. He can handle it."

"He can't."

"Shut up, Malek." The fire in her voice was strong, lightning crashing down in the city beyond them. Turning back to the man in the red cap, she pushed into his mind even more. "Where might Ricky have gone?"

It wasn't words that flashed through his mind so much as it was an image. Ricky in an apartment, raggedy with an old torn couch, one Molly recognized immediately. Pulling out of his mind, Molly stood up straight and turned into Malek's stiff form.

"Let's go," she ordered.

"Go where?"

"To an apartment."

They arrived at the high-rise shortly after. It was one she had been to years before when she'd first met Faye. It was any wonder. Faye wouldn't have just let the apartment go without giving it to someone she knew, and she'd given it to the man in the red cap, who had given it to Ricky. The walk up the stairs was long, and she was glad she was in boots this time.

She didn't hesitate as she formed a fist and pounded on the door. Sending out her magic, she felt for Ricky's presence inside the apartment, and sure enough, she was there, passed out on the old ratty couch.

"How did you know this place?" Malek asked.

"Long story," Molly muttered and pounded her fist for a second time. "Ricky, open the door."

It took five minutes before Ricky woke and cracked the door open. Molly stared her down, blonde hair a mess, eyes red and bulging. She must be human if she took the drug and survived. Molly didn't wait as she pushed her way inside.

"Hey!" Ricky shouted.

"Don't try me," Molly dared. "You have access to a drug. I want to know where you got it from."

"What drug?" Ricky's voice slurred.

Molly pushed her way into Ricky's mind, knowing she was using her magic more than she normally would, but she was tired of waiting for answers, and the pressure of Malek right behind her made her use it. "The new one. The one you've never had before. The one you shared with your ex."

"Oh." Ricky sneered. "That drug was shit. Did nothing."

"Good. Better than if it had worked. Now, where'd you get it?"

"Don't know."

"I'm tired of games tonight. Where did you get it?"

Ricky sighed. She headed for the small kitchen that was about as clean as when Faye had lived there, dishes and rotting food everywhere, mold up the wall behind the sink. It was a hell hole, and probably insanely cheap in the slum part of town. Ricky came back with a small black business card.

"Dunno. Gave me this, too."

Molly took it and flipped it over. Nothing was on it. It was a pure black card on both sides, no letters, no address, no number. "There's nothing here."

"I know." Ricky crossed her arms. "Never found the asshole again and since the pill didn't do shit, I wasn't really looking."

"Can I take this?"

"Have at."

"Thanks." Molly turned around and walked out, Malek following on a few steps behind her. She at least had some information. Whoever was handing out the drug didn't know human from Tainted, which at least narrowed what kind of Tainted it was, to an extent.

"What are you thinking?" Malek's voice shook her.

Molly sent him a glare before she slid behind the wheel of her Tesla. "I'm thinking this drug is specifically targeting Tainted."

"Agreed. But that's not uncommon."

"No, it's not. But for it to reach human hands? That *is* uncommon."

Just before she was about to shove the car into gear and step on the gas, Malek leaned over the center console and gripped her cheek. He pulled her in hard for a kiss, taking her by surprise. Molly gasped, her lips parting, and he swiped his tongue against her. Her eyelids fluttered shut, and she drew in a sharp breath. Malek's other hand came down, skimming over her breast to her waist and then back up to her breast, massaging gingerly while he nipped at her lower lip, just like he used to do.

Molly lost herself in the embrace. He'd always known how to kiss her, how to draw her attention away from whatever she was doing. That had been the curse of him. Giving as much as she got, Molly tangled their tongues together in a dance. Finally when she pulled back, she pressed their foreheads together, not daring to look him in the eye.

"What was that for?" she whispered.

"I want you to really think hard about it."

Molly hesitated before she answered, trying to make sure the lie would slide through undetected. "I will. I promise."

"That's all I can ask for."

"We can't let our race die."

"I said I'd think about it, Malek."

He pecked her lips again before resting in his own seat. "Then let's find us a dealer."

CHAPTER FOURTEEN

BEN WAS shoving the last of the needed equipment into the van when Molly pulled up in her Tesla, parking on the side of the house instead of the garage since it was full. Ben closed the van up and leaned against it as he waited for Molly to round the corner.

"What's going on?" her voice was firm and commanding.

"Creature capture," Ben answered, his voice full of excitement for the chase. Something felt different in him the last few days. There were tingles that ran throughout his entire body. At first, he'd tried to ignore them, but then they became so much part of his regular life that he couldn't, and he found himself not wanting to.

Molly didn't ask him another question, but the look on her face told him he better get to explaining soon. She stared him down with that on perfectly manicured eyebrow raised and aimed in his direction. Ben choked back a cough into his hand before he stood up straight.

"We got notification there's a skoll on the loose."

"You're kidding."

He shook his head. "Nope. So Joel and I were going to go get it. Weren't sure when you'd get back."

"Faye?" Molly asked.

Ben blanched. He'd gone to find Faye, and found her he had. She was throwing a fit in her room, tossing everything around it as she looked for something. He had no idea what, but Joel had told him to ignore her and leave her be.

Molly must have caught his look because she stepped in closer, a hand on his upper arm as she eyed him more carefully. "Is she all right?"

"She's upset," Joel's voice was strong as he came into the garage from the house the same time Malek joined them from the yard.

"What for?" Molly turned on Joel, and Ben let out a sigh of relief, glad he wasn't going to have to answer that question.

"Someone took her stash."

Molly gave the slightest snort, which told Ben she was the one who had found it. For a moment he was tossed back to two years ago when Molly had sent him on a manhunt throughout the entire facility—every single level and every single nook and cranny—to find the heroine Faye had stashed everywhere.

"Didn't realize she was using again so regularly," Ben muttered and turned toward the front of the van, getting behind the wheel.

The others continued to talk, but their voices were hushed. Ben pulled out his ever-present tablet and checked on the last known whereabouts of the skoll. There were more sightings and reports coming in as he went, paths of devastation left. He shuddered. He had a feeling he was going to be seeing and smelling a whole lot of blood that night. The sight he could nearly handle, but since he'd stopped his medication, the scent of things had become overwhelming. Every single person had their own scent, and it made his head spin as he walked around the building and ran into others. It'd been partly why he'd avoided everyone and stayed locked in his work area.

"Uh...Molly!" he called sharply and popped open the door, repeating himself so she could hear him.

Molly came over immediately. Ben handed her the tablet so she could see what he was seeing.

"We've got to get going."

"You're quite right." She turned to Malek and Joel. "Let's go."

They all piled into the van, and Ben pulled out of the house, drove along the winding driveway that would take them to the gate around the building. The gates opened automatically for them, and then they were off on a creature capture. They had yet to successfully bring home a skoll alive. The beasts were vicious.

It took ten minutes to get to the last sighting, and sure enough, as soon as they pulled up to the run-down building, they could see the trails of blood left in the skoll's wake. Ben parked while the others jumped out of the vehicle. Molly had slipped him a gun before she left and stashed her own in the back of her waistband.

He'd noticed she'd taken to avoiding weapons when Malek was around. He was curious about it but hadn't had the courage to ask yet.

The four of them walked around, Molly and Malek going off in one direction while he and Joel went the opposite. They didn't even need to speak to know what to do. They had all trained for this—well, except Malek, but Ben was pretty sure Malek wasn't going to let Molly wander away without him. In fact, he wasn't even sure why Malek was there or what the two of them had been doing before the skoll sighting had shown up.

Shaking the thought from his head, Ben focused on what was in front of him. He didn't want to get surprised by anything. Skolls were decently small, the size of a medium-sized dog, but they had very long necks, feet that were three times the size needed for their lithe forms, and claws that were deadly. Their silver color meant they blended in well at night, and they could move completely in silence, which made them doubly hard to track.

Ben kept his weapon in between his fingers, wanting to make sure he wasn't caught by surprise. Joel was doing the same. Together they walked around the building, checking the ins and outs of it and finding only more blood in its wake. There were dead small animals here and there, but nothing as big as would cause some of the blood trails. There had to be something else nearby that the skoll had killed.

Joel stopped short, and Ben stared at him. Joel nodded his head toward a door and went to it. Ben followed, his heart pounding. The scent of blood was overwhelming, but inside it, he smelled wet grass, which was flat out weird. The tingles that had become his constant companion over the past few weeks had ramped up and fluttered around his body like they were high on something or there was a dance party going on in his veins.

Putting a finger over his lips, Joel pointed to the bottom of the door where there was a hole in it. Small enough for a medium-sized dog to slide through. Joel pulled out his radio and clicked it three times. Ben hadn't even thought to do that. He was so distracted by the way his body was on fire. When he turned to look at Joel again as they waited for Molly's response, Joel's eyes got wide.

Ben mouthed the word "What?" without making any sound but he knew something was happening. Joel was suddenly a whole lot taller than him when they were normally right around the same height. A loud clatter echoed around the empty alleyway as his gun fell to the cement. Ben hunched down onto his hands and his knees, shaking out his head as the tingles fought their way into his mind, taking over everything.

When he stared back up at Joel once his body calmed, Joel was completely pale, and his lips were parted in shock. Ben opened his mouth to ask what was wrong, but no words would come out. Confused, Ben looked down at his hands against the cold and damp cement as the rain continued to fall on them and was shocked to find he didn't have hands anymore. He had paws. Large paws. Paws that were three times the size they needed to be for his body, and the thick pale claws were nested just inside the pads.

He looked back up at Joel and growled. He legit growled. Excited, Ben charged straight through the tiny hole in the door without a second look back. Every nerve ending in his body was alive. He ran until he couldn't run any longer, searching in each and every corner as he got used to how his body moved, how he needed to be running. He could see in the dark. He had to be doing that because there were no lights in the building, yet he could see everything like it was right in front of him, clear as day.

A call of voices came over his shoulder. Joel's voice first, then Molly's. They must have been whispering about him before they came in. This could be just the advantage they needed. Charging forward, Ben followed the scent of the skoll, the scent that was in the forefront of his mind. He would be the first to find the skoll, he would do this creature capture without them, and finally they would have the skoll alive like they'd always wanted.

Molly was shocked by Joel's description. If he was right, then Ben had taken a massive leap forward in his abilities. She hadn't expected this, especially that night of all times and places. Taking the lead, since Joel was at a loss for what to do, she held her hand over the door to unlock it with her magic then pushed it open, deafening the squeak with another small spell.

Malek took up position in the back, Joel between them. Everything in Molly's body was focused on finding Ben instead of finding the skoll. She'd love both, but Ben was her priority. If he wasn't fully aware of how he shifted, shifting back into his human form may take some trial and error. She'd seen it before, and it was not pleasant to watch. She could only hope Joel wouldn't have to witness it.

Holding her hands tightly to her side, Molly walked around the building, searching for any sign of a creature, whether it was Ben or the skoll. She found the trail of one of them quickly, and followed it after raising a hand to Joel and Malek, telling them what she'd found. They did everything in silence, which she was grateful for after the conversation she and Malek had had in her car before they'd returned to the house. She needed time to think. The pull to the fold was always strong, but she had to resist it. She'd done it for over two hundred years, so surely she could continue.

She stopped short when there was a rather large puddle of something on the ground her boot had landed in with her next step. Molly bent down, her knees bending as she reached out and touched her fingers to it. *Blood.* This time an entire pool of it. Shifting the debris against the stone wall, she moved it until she found the cold and very dead body of some Tainted she'd never seen before.

Molly clenched her jaw. They'd come back for him and figure out who he was to return him to his family if they could. If not, she still wouldn't leave him there. Sighing, Molly stood back up. There had been teeth marks and claw marks all across him, no doubt from the skoll in question that they were hunting.

She stepped away from the dead Tainted and went down another hallway. Her ears were tuned to anything odd or different that could be the skoll or Ben. Unfortunately, both would be deadly quiet. The growl surprised her. Turning sharply, Molly prepared for whatever may come at them. The growl grew louder.

She followed the direction of the noise, finding the skoll hiding under a pile of rubble in a den of sorts that it had obviously created. She squatted down, trying to seem less terrifying and less like the bad guy. She put her hand out, like she was talking to a scared little puppy, and waited to see if it would come out and check her out. The problem, based on Joel's description, was she had no idea if this was the skoll they were hunting or if this was Ben, and she did not want Ben to get hurt.

The creature growled louder, but Molly held firm. When its head reached beyond the cover of the den, Joel stepped sharply behind her, no doubt to protect her. She held her hand up in a fist, making sure he knew to be silent and not move. Then once again, she reached forward with her palm open and waited to see if the skoll would come forward.

She waited with bated breath. Molly held as still as possible, and sure enough, the skoll stepped out, one large paw at a time. Its neck craned around the corner of the den first, easily three times longer than it should have been to where it looked like an odd mix between a llama and a fox, but it was still beautiful. The long silver hair flowed down so when it ran it would look like running water in the moonlight.

Molly clenched her jaw and purposely loosened every muscle in her body. These creatures could sense fear and distrust, and she had to make them think they trusted her. She worked her magic, the tingles in her own body through her fingertips and sent a calming spell over everyone there. Malek was most resistant to it, but even he could see the cause for action and allowed the spell on himself.

With her hand held out still, Molly smiled as the skoll came forward and sniffed her fingers. "That's it," she whispered.

Malek jerked, his foot shuffling against the cement loudly. Molly inwardly cursed as the skoll she had coerced out ran back into hiding. When she turned to glare at Malek, she stopped short. There were dozens of skolls coming out from hiding, all with their heads down, growls coming from their lips.

"Fuck," Joel muttered.

Molly didn't hesitate, and neither did Malek. They were both thinking the same thing. She stood straight up, her magic weaving around Malek's like ribbons intertwining but not connecting as they cast the spells. Malek muttered the words while Molly stayed silent. She'd disliked saying the spells if she could help it. Malek's body and eyes glowed silver like the moon, and Molly knew her own body matched his with every breath. They stared for one second at each other before a powerful burst of magic flew from their bodies and pulsed outward into the sea of skolls before them.

It hit each and every one of them, knocking them onto their backs and sides. After the fourth pulse, Molly pulled back her magic as did Malek. Not one skoll moved. She shifted, her boots making a loud noise in the suddenly absolute silence of the large room they were in. There were dozens of skolls.

"We're going to need help," Molly stated. "Joel, call for extra hands, please."

He stood still, unmoving, his eyes riveted to one skoll in particular. "That's Ben."

Molly followed his gaze and tiptoed around the room until she found the one she thought Joel was pointing to. She could see why he thought it was Ben. Squatting down, Molly pressed a hand to the neck of the skoll, feeling for a pulse.

"He's fine, for now. We need to get him home."

"He—he shifted."

"I can see that," Molly muttered. "Isn't this what he wanted?"

"Yeah, but...I guess I didn't think I would see it."

She raised an eyebrow at Joel but turned to Ben when the pulse under her fingers sped up massively. She was about to call for help when Malek showed up right next to her. Ben's lifeless form in the shape of a skoll seized. His four legs flung out around him, body trying desperately to function as the pulses from the seizure ripped through him.

Molly wasn't surprised by what was happening. Ben had fully shifted on his first try of it, and his body had not been ready. "Joel, back to the van."

Malek scooped Ben up, cradling him like he would a child as he followed Joel. Molly glanced around the room as soon as she was alone and cast another spell, causing all of the skolls to sleep until she decided it was time for them to wake up. When she got to the van, she ripped through the small medical kit they kept with them. She'd insisted on putting some new medications in them since Ben had taking to seizures, and she was glad for it. She pulled out the paralytic and injected it into Ben's front leg. Soon enough, his body stilled.

She called for assistance, and as soon as a second and third van arrived, she sent Ben and Joel back to the house with a call in to Amachon already to join them and help with whatever Ben may need. She sighed. Her night of work was only just beginning.

Chapter Fifteen

Ben sat in the bed, covers over his legs with his tablet in front of him even though Amachon told him not to use it. He couldn't resist the temptation to skim through and see all they had captured from their creature hunt the night before. Amachon had released him in the morning once the seizure had stopped and he'd been sufficiently observed. He'd gladly gone back to his room to rest instead of hanging out in the medical bay.

Joel stepped into his room with a slight knock. His hair was still damp from the shower he'd taken, but he was dressed in his normal jeans, t-shirt and over shirt that was his standard uniform for work. Ben smiled at him and pressed the tablet into his lap, hoping Joel didn't say anything about him using it.

"How are you feeling?" Joel came over and sat on the bed with Ben, their thighs touching.

"Better. Groggy still, but not as bad as the last time."

"Interesting." Joel brushed his fingers against Ben's leg. "I think Molly said that might happen."

"She would know."

"She would." Joel nodded.

Ben watched curiously, sensing Joel had more that he wanted to say, but he couldn't figure out why Joel hesitated. Joel was normally always forthcoming in what he was thinking and feeling, one of the perks of being so in tune with emotions and what everyone else in the room was feeling.

Sitting up, Ben tugged Joel in and pressed their lips together in a quick kiss. "I hope I didn't scare you last night."

"You did, a bit. Not because you shifted but because you were seizing again. I worry about you."

"I can see that." Ben kissed him again. Joel pulled him back in and let their embrace linger and deepen. It wasn't meant as anything more than comfort. Joel's fingers slipped into Ben's hair, tugging before he sat back, his cheeks flushed.

"You're sure you're okay?"

"Yeah. I'm fine. I promise. I feel better than I have in a long time."

"Good. But how do you feel here." Joel put his hand to Ben's chest. "I mean, how are you doing, really?"

"I..." Ben stopped, trailing off. He wanted to be able to answer Joel honestly and fully. Thinking it over, he realized he hadn't evaluated how he was feeling about all the transitions in his life. Pursing his lips, tears sprang to his eyes and he shook his head as he fought them before giving in. "I miss her."

"Her?"

"Faye."

"She's right next door."

"She is," Ben started, "but she's not at the same time."

"I know what you mean." Joel squeezed Ben's thigh. "She's high again, so her behavior is erratic and self-indulgent."

"Yeah. She hasn't even checked in on me in a while. She said we were going to do this together, but we're not. She said she would be here for me, but she's not. She's nowhere. I haven't seen her in days, really. She's hiding out. I just...I miss her."

"I get it." Joel let out a sigh. "I'll talk to Molly about it too because it is starting to affect our work."

"It is. But more than that, Joel, I miss my friend."

"Then maybe you should talk to her. You will probably be able to pull her out of it easier than Molly."

"Really? Why would you say that?"

"Just trust me on this one. Please."

"I will, but I still want to know why you think that." Ben threaded their fingers together, playing his thumb over the top of Joel's hand.

"Because she trusts you in a way she doesn't trust Molly. Molly comes with complications. You come with simple friendship."

"Really?"

"I promise, Ben. It's that simple."

Ben flushed. He'd never thought his friendship with Faye would take quite that turn, but he felt the same way about her. He trusted her with his life, knew she would protect him and keep him safe if needed and support him through everything. Ben let out a shuddering breath. "I'll talk to her."

"Good. Until then, I want you to rest up. What you did last night was amazing, Ben. I don't want you to wear yourself out, but I do want you to do that again, especially if you want it."

"It was amazing." Bubbles burst in Ben's chest. "Seriously. I felt amazing. I have never felt so free, so in control of my body as I did in those moments."

"Good." Joel's eyes crinkled at the corners. "Then let's try to get more control over it."

"Yes."

Joel gave him one last kiss before leaving Ben's room. Ben leaned into the pillows behind him, waiting a moment before he picked up his tablet. He'd talk to Faye and see what had crawled up her butt lately, even if she didn't want it.

Malek had grabbed her hand when she'd walked by Faye's room and tugged her down the hall toward her room like he had a pretense of something serious. She could read through him two hundred years ago, and she could still do it then. He had nothing to tell her, but he wanted her alone. For what, she had a pretty good guess.

It had been three days since Ben had first shifted. Their world had calmed down, Faye was sober because Molly had taken the rest of her stash, and Malek had been waiting for an answer Molly was nowhere near ready to give him. They stopped outside her door, and before she could even ask him what he wanted, his mouth was on hers.

Moaning, Molly tilted her chin up, surprised by her physical reaction to him. His hand wrapped around the back of her neck and held her still as their tongues dueled for control. Molly knew she would win out. Malek was a gentleman, after all. He always had been. Sighing, she pressed a palm to his chest and pushed him away slightly, breaking the embrace.

"Have you thought about it?" He pressed kisses to her neck, behind her ear, and down the column of her throat.

Molly knew where he was headed. He knew every weak point on her body, every touch that would tackle her defenses. She had to find a way out of it because she wasn't ready to jump into bed with him, wasn't ready to make that commitment, or to tell him that she wasn't going back to the fold.

"I did," she whispered. It wasn't a lie. She had thought about it. She also knew that his tactic of talking about re-entering the fold was just that, a tactic. He wanted her distracted by that conversation. Licking her lips, she tangled her fingers in his hair, holding him to her body as he pressed her into the wall next to her bedroom.

They were only a few short steps away from a mattress, and she would love to take him, but her thoughts turned from him to Faye. Faye would always come first in her life, and Malek wouldn't understand that. He couldn't.

As if she'd been called, Faye stepped into the hallway, her eyes alight with mischief as she caught Malek pressed up against Molly. He didn't move, nor did he stop. Molly tightened her grip in his hair as she looked over his shoulder toward Faye, their gazes locking. For the first time in weeks, Faye's eyes looked bright and alive, clear. She was sober.

Breathing sigh of relief, Molly smiled as Malek licked lazy circles between her breasts. Faye only hesitated once before she stepped closer, her hand brushing up Malek's back until he stopped and stared between the two of them. Molly leaned against the wall, begging Faye to take over for just a minute.

Faye's voice was clear, commanding, and seductive all in one. "I think we should move this inside the bedroom."

"Are you joining?" Malek asked, his eyes locked on Faye's full lips.

"Yes," both Molly and Faye answered simultaneously.

Glad they had some effective silent communication, Molly took Faye's hand then Malek's after she opened the door to her room. He walked in first. Faye was the last to enter, and she locked the door, then held her hand over it. Molly heard the electricity humming as much as she felt it against her skin, making the hairs on her arms stand up straight. She and Faye had always meant to play with her electrical abilities during sex, but they'd never found the time. Perhaps next time. Tonight was for power and control and answers.

"Strip," Faye ordered, staring directly at Malek. "I want to know what we have to work with, and Molly, I do believe, has an advantage over me on that one."

Molly bit her tongue. That answered one question she'd been wondering. Faye had yet to seduce Malek. Malek did as he was told.

Faye turned into Molly, possessing her like she always did. Their mouths heated against each other, Faye's body aligning with hers. She was tempted to start the spell, the magic to exchange their gifts and empower both of them even more, but she did not want Malek to be involved with any of that. It would be far too close to being back in the fold.

Faye shoved Molly hard, and she fell onto the bed with a slight bounce. Faye crawled up on top of her, straddling her. She shoved a hand up Molly's shirt as soon as she found the edge and her lips to Molly's ear. It took Molly a second to realize Faye was whispering.

"This is what you want, right?"

"Yes," Molly hissed back. "But only you."

"You don't want him?"

Molly moaned as Faye twisted her nipple hard under her bra. This would be so much better than it had been in her office weeks before. She couldn't answer, and she knew Faye didn't expect one. Malek stood behind Faye. Molly caught sight of him out of the corner of her eye while Faye scraped dull nails down her belly.

"How much blood?" Faye asked to no one in particular.

Malek shook his head and held his hands out. Molly's lips parted as she tried to find an answer, but it was so hard to concentrate. She hadn't realized how much better Faye was at this than Malek, how much more practiced Faye was to her body, to every intonation of what she needed.

"None," Molly finally managed to say. "None."

"All right."

Faye's hands were at Molly's waist, and she pulled the zipper at the side of Molly's hip on her skirt, dragging it down slowly. Malek was behind Faye, his hands on her hips, in her pants, under her shirt until he shoved Faye's jeans to her ankles. Molly wondered if he would take Faye then, from behind without any warning at all.

His hand was between Faye's legs, his fingers disappearing in and out of her before Molly could even figure out how he moved so fast. Faye had her skirt off and on the floor, her blouse shoved up, over her breasts, and she lavished every inch of newly exposed skin. Molly allowed herself to become lost to the sensations, knowing she wouldn't be able to full focus on what Faye was doing for long. They were both there for a purpose.

Faye's mouth between her legs surprised her. The rocking sensation caused by Malek's thrusts into Faye and then Faye into her was far more tantalizing than she had expected. Faye thrusted two fingers into Molly, and Molly was lost. Every muscle in her body was on fire, tensing as pleasure coursed through her nerves, pulling together between her legs. Her voice broke the silence of the room as she fell over the edge with Faye being the one to push her. Without warning, Faye nipped at her inner thigh, teeth sharp and blood spilling. She didn't stay there long, the taste for Molly's blood far too strong, but as soon as Faye's tongue swiped over the entry wounds, they stopped up and Faye grunted her own release.

Molly's skin was hot and sticky. She sat up, pushing Faye off her as she stripped her shirt and bra. She knelt on the bed and raised an eyebrow at Faye who stood only half-naked in front of her. Faye mimicked her, stripping the rest of her clothes and following on to the bed. She stared directly into Molly's eyes as she ordered Malek to lay on his back on the bed. Once again Molly found her mouth occupied by Faye. When Faye finally pulled away, she was flushed and her chest rose and fell sharply with each passing second.

"Get behind me," Faye whispered.

Molly complied with the demand, letting Faye take complete control. It would serve Molly well because it would leave all her to focus on what they needed—access to Malek's mind while he was sufficiently distracted.

"Ready?"

Molly skimmed a hand down Faye's side from her breast to her hip. "Absolutely."

Faye turned and straddled Malek, slowly lowering her body until he was fully inside her. She rocked back and forth, urging her momentum to speed up. Molly straddled Malek's legs, her hips aligning with Faye's bottom as she pressed her front to Faye's back. Her hands snaked around Faye's body, and she began a torturous pattern against Faye's clit, knowing Faye always hated it slow, but the longer they had the better.

Malek dug his nails into Faye's thighs. Molly bit down into the cord along Faye's neck as she called on her magic. Faye worked Malek's body, keeping his mind focused on her while Molly slipped into his thoughts unnoticed. She wove herself around his mind, seeking information, memorizing what she could, and hiding when she needed to. She honestly couldn't have planned it better. It had been the perfect opportunity.

Faye groaned. Molly lifted a hand to cup her breast, squeezing the flesh in her fist and pinching Faye's nipple. Faye loved it rough— so did Molly, for that matter. And as soon as Molly had what they needed, she would send Faye over the edge on another orgasm.

She had it. Pushing a little further into Malek's mind, Molly followed the thread. She was so close to having what she wanted, but she couldn't get in. Swallowing, she bit down on Faye's shoulder hard. Faye's head knocked back into Molly, and Molly increased the pressure and sped up the pattern on Faye's clit.

Malek relaxed even more. Typical of almost every man Molly had been with in her long life. Rocking her hips right along with Faye's, Molly knew Faye was close. She wouldn't be able to hold back much longer. Malek groaned, his back arching as Faye pressed down into him.

It was just what Molly needed. Slipping behind the locked door, she caught a glimpse. But Faye crashed, her body clenching against her orgasm. Malek followed, spilling into her. Molly got her quick look before she backed out, not wanting to be discovered. Faye collapsed on Malek's chest. He rubbed hands over her back as Molly sat back on her haunches.

"Give me a minute," Faye muttered into Malek's skin. "I want you one more time, Molly."

"You can have me any time, Faye."

"Yeah, I know." Faye shot her a questioning look where Malek couldn't see.

Molly knew in an instant that her answer to one more round wasn't just an answer about sex. It was an answer to if it had worked. "Yes, then. One more."

"Good." Faye tapped Malek's chest with her palm. "You'll be a good boy and wait right here."

She pulled off him and flipped around faster than Molly had expected. Faye took her to the mattress, lying on top of her with a thigh pressed firmly between Molly's legs. She didn't wait this time. Molly didn't either. She wove the spell, strengthening her magic as Faye pierced her skin with small bite after small bite all over her chest and breasts as she rocked her hips. Pleasure shot through Molly like it always did when Faye did this.

Pressing her hands above her head, Molly gripped the footboard tightly and held on as Faye took her wherever they were going. She trusted Faye with everything she had. Chest to chest, body to body, Molly's second orgasm powered through her, Faye's final bite to her neck lasting as long as she needed and wanted. Molly carded her fingers gently through Faye's hair until she calmed and then brought their lips together in a gentle, loving kiss.

Malek cleared his throat, sitting up and staring at them. "I definitely would like to do this again."

Molly chuckled and rolled her eyes while Faye snorted and

dropped her forehead to Molly's shoulder. They both knew it was unlikely; however, they had gotten decently far in what they wanted. Perhaps one more round in a few weeks wouldn't be the end of the world. Shifting under Faye's weight, Molly moved to sit up.

"Well, you two can do whatever you would like. I have a house to run."

"Always working," Faye muttered as she sat cross-legged. "Take a night off already."

"It's the middle of the day," Molly retorted as she grabbed her clothes.

"So?"

Glancing from Faye to Malek, Molly knew if she stayed she would likely lose the battle. "It's the middle of the day. I will see you tonight, Faye, yes?"

"Yeah, yeah." Rolling her eyes, Faye plopped down onto the bed and rolled into Malek's side. "But don't get mad if I'm late."

Molly knew she wouldn't be.

Chapter Sixteen

Faye's body still hummed from fucking Malek and Molly. She slipped into Molly's office later that night, locking the door behind her and then electrically fusing the metal together in order to prevent anyone from coming in. It was her and Molly alone, and she was completely sober. It was the first time in a while since that had happened.

Sitting in the chair in front of Molly's desk, Faye crossed her legs and stared at her lover with a satisfied smirk on her lips. Molly was nose deep in something, she wasn't sure what, but she couldn't wait. She had plans for later that night, and she wanted to know what Molly had learned.

"Well?" Faye's voice was sharp as it rang through the quiet room.

"Two seconds," Molly muttered as she flipped another page and made a mark on it.

Faye sighed heavily and crossed her arms. Sinking into the chair, she stared out at the parapet. She had so many memories out there, but neither she nor Molly had spent much time there lately. She'd have to remedy that but after her outing.

"Molly, I've got shit to do."

"As do I." Molly's response was sharp and immediate. She still didn't look up at Faye.

Huffing, Faye rolled her eyes. If she didn't want to know what Molly had learned so badly, she would have walked out. Her friend wouldn't mind if she showed up early.

"There." Molly moved the papers to the side and folded her arms on top of the desk, shifting to stare directly at Faye. "You learn anything so far?"

"Not really," Faye muttered.

"I suppose we'll have to change that."

"Didn't you find something?"

Molly closed her eyes and rubbed the bridge of her nose. "Yes and no. Not as much as I had hoped, but enough to warrant exactly what we're doing."

"Quit being cryptic." Faye pouted. She'd gone without her drug for two days, and it was too much. She needed more to keep her even balance, and her friend's information called to her more than finding out whatever the fuck Malek was hiding.

"Earlier today was a perfect opportunity for me. Thank you for trusting me."

"I said we'd work together on this."

"Yes, and so far we have. I think it's going to take more time, however."

"I don't like him lurking around." What Faye really wanted to say was she didn't like him lurking around Molly, but she bit off the last word from her sentence and kept it to herself. If they were anything, they were not possessive over each other, but something about Malek made her on edge. He was fun to play with, but that was it.

"I don't either." Molly straightened her spine. "He continues to insist this is about the fold."

"I shouldn't have asked for their help."

"Faye, you did exactly what needed to be done. I was cursed. There was no other option to lift it. It needed their power and nothing else."

Faye wasn't quite sure what to say. She'd known from the start it had been the right decision, not only because the wicked witch was now back to the good witch, but Malek had taught Faye far more than she'd thought she needed to know about her own history and more. Changing subjects, Faye gritted her teeth. "So what'd you learn?"

"He's hiding something."

Faye dug her heel into the floor. "That's it?"

Molly's smile was saccharine. "Malek may be here in part because of the fold, but that isn't the only reason. I did catch glimpses of his conversations with the others and their desire for my return. That was not unexpected. They have always wanted me to be a part of the fold."

"And?"

"And I won't return. I'm satisfied with my life here, and I left for a reason."

"Just one?" Faye snorted.

"More than one." Molly amended.

They were getting nowhere fast, and she had a timeline to keep. "What else did you find out?"

"Malek knew about Caliban Troy before we told him."

Every muscle in Faye's body stiffened. She had never wanted to hear that name again. The man who had kidnapped, tortured, and raped her for over a month and then who she was sent back to in order to infiltrate could rot in the grave she'd put him in.

Molly must have sensed her unease, because she stood up and moved around the desk, kneeling in front of Faye's chair, effectively boxing her in. "I suspected this."

"How?"

"I don't know yet, but I suspected Malek was here for a purpose, you know that."

"Yes, but this?" Faye's eyes were wild, she knew it. Fear had latched onto her, and she struggled to get rid of it. "What does he know?"

"More than I could find out in that short of time. Faye."

At her name, Faye locked her gaze on Molly.

"Don't go back there. He's dead."

Jerking her chin in a nod, Faye drew in deep breaths like Amachon had taught her and tried to calm her racing nerves. Now more than ever she needed to meet with her friend.

"We'll have to try to get more information from him. Will you be able to help?"

"Of course." Her voice was rougher than she intended, but Faye didn't fix it.

Molly gripped Faye's fingers, pulling them into Faye's lap before she pressed kisses to the tops of Faye's hands. Faye was put off by the tenderness. They weren't known for being soft together. Their worlds revolved around each other, but they never were soft and loving.

"I should go," Faye whispered.

Molly raised her chin up and brought a hand up to Faye's cheek, cupping the side of her head. Faye turned into the touch, marveling in it as much as she resisted wanting to. There was always something about Molly she couldn't resist, and it wasn't until Malek had explained vampires and witches and their weird interconnected history that Faye understood why. She would always be attracted to Molly, and any witch for that matter, but the more powerful, the harder to resist. And she, being one of two vampires left, the only one who was born, she was a prize for any witch to behold. If only their attraction wasn't so manufactured.

"What are you thinking?" Molly's voice was gentle, probing, but Faye didn't feel the mental probes that she knew Molly would often use on others. They'd agreed long ago Molly would never manipulate her like that.

"That I have places to go and people to see."

Molly eyed her carefully. "Not quite true, but I'll let it pass this time. What we did today was very helpful. We may have to do that again."

Faye snorted. "It wasn't horrible."

"I'd prefer..." Molly trailed off and pulled her lower lip between her teeth, her cheeks flushing. "I would prefer if you took lead."

"You don't want to fuck him."

Molly nodded. "In essence, yes, if we can avoid that, I would prefer it."

"I can keep him occupied. It is in my talent wheel."

"That it is." Molly pulled Faye down for a kiss before standing. "Would you speak with Ben soon, please? I think he needs his best friend."

"Yeah, I'll get right on that." Faye pushed up from the chair and walked toward the door. She had to get out of there, had to get out of the house. Her skin crawled. It wasn't the first time she used her body to get what she wanted. In fact, that was exactly how her relationship with Molly started, but she had hoped to avoid it again. Malek was the first man she'd had sex with since Caliban, and the memories were almost too much.

Unlocking the door, Faye made her escape and found herself at the bottom of the spiral staircase. Her friend would know where she could go to get more of this new drug she'd discovered. He knew the oddest things. Grabbing her helmet and her motorcycle, Faye took off without looking back.

She waited at the base of the sculpture of the troll as his head broke from the stone. The grinding of rock against rock echoed under the bridge. His face morphed from being frozen in time to contorted with pain before he settled his gaze on her.

"My young friend."

She smirked. He was the only one allowed to call her that. Faye bit her lip as she climbed up his arm, the path familiar, and rested on his shoulder. She patted his cheek and rested her head against him. "Hello, my friend."

"You are visiting often now."

"I know." She wasn't quite sure what to say to him. She wanted information more than anything, knew he'd have it. For a troll who was stuck in one place, he had a wealth of gossip. His face was wrinkled. She'd noticed even with time he had more wrinkles gathering under his eyes and along his neck. She wondered if any of the patrons who visited him regularly would notice.

"Did you hear about the club?"

"I did." His voice was quiet, deep as it rumbled along with the rest of the sounds of the city at night. Each of his words was slowly spoken, each with care. She knew it took him a great amount of effort to speak, that each word hurt as he forced it beyond his lips. If she'd been thinking, she would have brought him some relief, but she'd been too selfish and thinking only of herself.

"Do you know anyone else who has this new drug?" She didn't want to wait around longer than necessary. She was already guilty about coming without offering him anything.

He turned to look at her, eyeing her carefully. "Why do you ask?"

"I'd like some."

"It is not safe."

"It's never safe. Drugs aren't made to be safe." Faye patted his cheek and bit her lip. "Do you know where I can get some?"

"There is something in it."

"I know." Faye sighed. "I know there is. Still, I want what I want."

He regarded her. "There is an underground city."

"There's what?"

He shot her a look, telling her to shut up. "Go to the club but take a left. Follow the path until it splits and take the one that leads you down."

"Who will I find there?"

"My brethren."

"And they'll have some of this drug?"

He groaned. "Yes. Next time, Faye, bring some relief."

"I will. I promise. I'm so sorry I forgot it this time."

He snorted, and dust billowed from his nose into the air in front of him. Faye kissed his cheek and climbed down the way she came up. By the time she was on the sidewalk again, he was already fully stone.

Faye followed his directions. She walked through the entrance to the club in the sewers, but instead of turning toward the door, she took a left. The moss still covered the ground and quieted her footsteps, at least for half a mile or so before it disappeared.

It seemed like she was walking for hours, but she knew it was barely even thirty minutes before she came to the split he had been talking about. Sure enough, one way led down and the other way stayed straight. With a deep breath, Faye turned and walked down the as she had been directed.

The halls became dark, and it was only because of her superior eyesight that she was able to see where she was going. Just for the hell of it, Faye held out her hand and send electricity shocking between all of her fingers, lighting up the way even more. She stopped when she realized there were paintings and drawings on the walls. Staring at them, she memorized as much of them as she could.

Faye eventually continued along the path, her boots making hardly any noise as she went. She came to a large opening. As she walked through it, Faye wished she could see everything, but it was even darker—pitch black. Focusing her hearing, she heard a rustling, a lot of rustling. There were definitely creatures surrounding her.

Before she knew what was happening, a flash of light nearly blinded her. Faye dropped her hand to the side, the electricity pulling back into her body. Glancing around, she saw the troll's brethren for the first time. Her spine stiffened, every muscle in her body tightening. She should not have come down there alone.

Faye pinpointed the one in charge as he stepped forward. He towered over her, and for the first time, Faye realized just how large her friend on the surface must be. "Your brethren sent me here."

The one in charge halted.

"He said I could come here, told me the way."

"For what purpose?" His voice was firm and deep just like her friend's.

Faye gulped. "He said you had something I was looking for, a drug."

"We have what you are looking for."

"M-may I have some?"

The troll nodded at something off to the side. Faye didn't dare turn to see what it was, but something plopped by her feet. She risked a glance down and was shocked to find a large bag of pills, enough to last her years if she kept it all to herself. Bending down, she snatched it up and held it close to her chest.

"Thank you."

"Share it."

The lights went out, the shuffling of feet against dirt and stone echoed until the room was silent. Faye let out a breath she didn't know she was holding and carefully walked back the way she had come. She'd have to do some research on that when she got back to the house and had a few spare moments. Not only was there an entire troll colony living underneath their city, but she had a sinking suspicion Molly knew about it, in detail.

Faye made it up to the first landing and ripped open the bag. She took two pills and swallowed them without pretense. Staring at the door to the club she had once frequented, Faye let out a sigh. She would miss that place, perhaps someday it would live again. Until then, she'd have to find a new place to party with Joel when they had a night off. Maybe they could even convince Ben to join them on the rare occasion.

Taking a risk, Faye popped a third pill between her lips and weighed her options as she held it there. She'd taken two pills before, and it had been the most glorious high she had ever experienced. She'd felt warm, fuzzy, peaceful for the first time in her long life. She wanted that peaceful experience again. It was everything she had craved with heroin and been unable to find.

Three pills might just put her there since she had grown her resistance to the drug itself through her low-dose usage of it. Swallowing the third white pill, Faye got onto her hands and her knees and found a place to stash the rest of the drugs. She'd want to come back for them later, when she was more with it, and when it would be worth it to her to take them with her. She'd have to find some new hiding places at the house, but that wasn't difficult. Molly could only have her eyes and ears in so many places at once, and Faye was resourceful if nothing else. She walked down the pathway she hadn't taken before as she waited for the drugs to kick in.

CHAPTER SEVENTEEN

MOLLY'S PHONE rang, waking her from a near dead sleep. Since she rarely slept, when she flipped onto her side to stare at her phone, she was surprised to see Malek's name flash across the screen. Rubbing her eyes, Molly pressed the phone to her ear and acted as if she'd been awake the entire time but not before glancing at her watch on the nightstand. Four-thirty in the morning. She was about to have to wake up anyway.

"This better be good." She didn't want to play games. Her mind was too slow to figure everything out and keep all the lies straight. Rubbing her temple, Molly waited for an answer, but she got none.

His breathing was somewhat heavy, but she couldn't hear anything beyond that. Narrowing her gaze, Molly shifted in her bed and sat up, continuing to listen rather than ask him what he wanted or why he was calling. Perhaps he hadn't meant to call her at all, and she was about to get a little piece of information she needed.

He grunted. "Molly."

"Yes," she answered, knowing finally he had meant to dial her number.

"It's Faye."

She turned immediately to the side of the bed next to her that was empty, not that she expected Faye to be in it. They hadn't seen each other in at least a day, and while Molly tended to keep close tabs on Faye especially when she was getting high regularly, she hadn't checked with Ben that day and had fallen into bed exhausted.

"Where is she?"

"We're downtown. East side."

"We? What were you doing with her?"

"I found her."

Molly swallowed and turned the lamp on her nightstand on. Her feet were over the edge of the mattress within seconds, and she was standing to get dressed, the phone still pressed to her ear as she waited for an answer. When she got none, she huffed. "Found her where?"

"In the sewer lines underneath the city."

Faltering in her step, Molly hesitated before she reached for a pair of black leather pants instead of a skirt suit she'd almost grabbed. "Where exactly are you?"

"Down by the piers. She looks like she was dragged here, or maybe crawled here. I can't quite tell."

Molly cradled the phone to her shoulder as she pulled the pants on and picked out a shirt. "And what were you doing there?"

"Molly, she needs medical attention. Something...something isn't right."

"What's wrong?"

"She's not responding at all. I can't get her to move. She's barely breathing and her breaths keep getting slower."

Cursing, Molly sped up getting dressed. "Text me a ping where you're at. I'll grab the van and get Amachon ready. But don't think this gets you out of explaining to me why you were down there."

Hanging up, Molly pulled her shirt over her head, grabbed her jacket, and called Amachon as she slid her feet into her boots. After alerting him to the situation, she moved through the halls and down to the garage. With the keys to the van in hand, Molly left the house and drove to Malek and Faye.

By the time she got there, her mind was a whir of possibilities. One thing she knew, Faye was likely high, but beyond that, Malek had given her very little details. Pulling up where her phone told her they were, she stopped. No one was in sight. The pier was empty, the warehouse next to it was closed up tight.

Stepping out of the van, Molly pocketed the keys and took her phone out. Before she could even call him, her phone was ringing again. Pressing it to her ear, that annoying flair of anger that seemed to lick at her any time she had to deal directly with Malek in any capacity came to life.

"Where are you?" she asked without pretense.

"Hold on. Turn around."

Spinning on her heel, Molly twisted to see Malek coming out of the shadows between two warehouses about two hundred feet from where she was. Hanging up, she pocketed her phone. She ducked her head and shoved her hands into her pockets as she walked toward him, but he didn't move to get closer to her. Beyond confused as to what was going on, Molly's anger ratcheted up a few notches as she made her way to him.

"I need to tell you that I have no idea what happened. I found her this way." His tone had an edge of worry in it.

Perhaps he knew if he'd done anything to Faye he would have to face Molly's wrath and he wouldn't survive. Clenching her jaw, she stopped short when Faye's body appeared in her view. She wasn't just lifeless, she was beaten and bruised. Molly knelt immediately by Faye's side, brushing her fingers over her cheek, a cheek that was split open and a nose clearly broken.

"What the hell happened to her?"

"I honestly have no idea. I found her like this."

"Found her where?" Accusation couldn't help but find its way into Molly's voice.

Malek shrugged and squatted down next to Molly. "I found her in the sewers like this. I told you that."

"You didn't tell me she was this close to death."

"She's a vampire."

Snorting, Molly rolled her eyes and carded her fingers over Faye's cheek. "Why haven't you given her any blood yet?"

"I did. The blood on her lips is mine. It didn't work."

Turning to him sharply, Molly kept her mouth shut. If his blood wasn't working, then Faye was definitely high on the same drug she'd been taking. There was no way to sober her up except to wait, but just because their blood didn't work didn't mean their magic was fruitless.

"Did you attempt to heal her?"

"Yes," he whispered and pressed a hand to the small of Molly's back. "Twice and neither time did I make any progress. I was only able to heal a few small cuts, but you are far more talented at healing than I am. Don't think I didn't know you helped me when she ripped out your side."

Molly chose not to answer him. She'd hoped he hadn't noticed, but she'd known she wouldn't have been able to hide it from him at the same time. Melding magic together like that had a completely different feel to it than using one's own magic.

"We need to get her home. Perhaps Amachon can do something."

"I didn't find any drugs on her."

Cocking her head to the side, Molly thinned her lips. "Did you expect to?"

"I think she's taken more than she's ever taken."

"Most likely. Any idea where she got it?"

"Not a clue."

Molly's heart sunk. Malek had lied. If there was one thing she had learned all those years ago, it was how to determine when he was lying, which he had done to her fairly often in those first few years, claiming she wasn't ready to understand the ins and outs of the fold. Little had he known, her father had shared far more than he had.

"Let's get her home." Molly's voice was barely above a whisper as she bent and pressed her lips to Faye's in a gentle kiss. "Amachon is waiting."

"You'll have to..." Malek waved his hand at Faye. "I'm not sure I've the energy."

Molly clenched her jaw again, trying to figure out why Malek had depleted a lot of his resources or if this was a ploy for him to determine just how powerful she was without him. He'd had a taste of her magic the last time they were on the pier together, perhaps he wanted to know the true source of it, but that was something she'd never share with him.

Standing, Molly stared down at him and Faye before waving her hand. Faye's body moved in the exact position it had been upward from the ground until she was floating. Molly's power surged through her chest and into her fingers, and she had to work hard to control it and keep it at bay. She always struggled with that when her emotions were heavy, one of the things Malek had chided her over throughout the years of training she'd endured.

Without a word, Molly directed Faye's lifeless body to the back of the van. Malek opened the doors with a grunt. Molly lifted Faye's body a little higher and slid her into the van, lowering her down gently. She crawled in and checked on her again. No doubt she'd at least be able to heal some of the wounds Faye had endured from whatever she'd been through, but she had no desire to do that in front of Malek and let him in on how powerful she had become in the intervening years since she'd seen him last.

Molly kissed Faye's forehead and then crawled up to the

driver's seat. Malek shut the back doors and before he could even get in the passenger side, Molly stepped on the gas and took off. He found his own way to the docks, he could find his own way home.

Driving rapidly, Molly pulled into the garage. Faye was home. She was in good hands. That was all that mattered for now. Crawling into the back without alerting Amachon she was home yet—he'd figure that out shortly—she kneeled over Faye's body in the small, confined space.

"What have you been doing, Faye?"

Faye didn't answer, nor did she move. Her breathing was so shallow, Molly worried she would stop at any moment. Pressing a hand to the center of Faye's chest, Molly closed her eyes. Power pulled through her, growing as it compounded on top of her. With a sharp breath, she worked her way into Faye's body, feeling all her injuries. Malek hadn't been wrong, and neither had Molly—Faye was near death.

Molly focused on the physical injuries she could heal, but every time she would mend a rib, it would break again. Every time she was magically sew a cut together, it would stay only for a moment before ripping open again. After her fourth attempt, Molly gave up.

Malek ripped open the back of the van, his eyes narrowing as they focused in on Molly. "What are you doing?"

"Nothing that is working."

"Let's get her to Amachon."

He reached forward, cupping her cheek. Molly turned into the soft touch, the exhaustion hitting her fast, but it wasn't physical exhaustion. Closing her eyes, she let out a sigh. She'd already been through this fiasco with Faye once, and while she loved her, she wasn't sure she wanted to sober her up again without Faye wanting to work on that herself.

Malek moved his thumb, and Molly opened her eyes. "Amachon's coming."

"How do you know?"

The door to the garage opened, and Amachon rolled a stretcher in. As he reached the back of the van, he grunted at Molly, who moved out of the way. The giant reached in, pulled Faye by her ankles until he could reach her torso. Then he lifted her onto the stretcher and pushed her out of the room. Molly and Malek shared a glance before she scrambled to follow.

Ben sat cross-legged on his bed as the sun crested over the edge of town. Joel was passed out in the bed next to him. Ben smiled at the sight of his lover. They'd barely been apart since the incident with the skolls. Joel hadn't wanted to leave him except when necessary, not that Ben could blame him.

They'd been together for the better part of six years, and for the first time ever, Ben quite enjoyed having Joel nearby almost constantly. Lying down next to Joel, Ben ran his hand over his belly, waking him slowly. Joel rubbed his eyes, blinking wearily.

"What's wrong?" Joel's voice was full of sleep.

"I want to show you something."

"What?"

"Sit up." Ben kissed Joel's cheek then moved back into the position he had been in for near an hour while he watched his lover sleep. Maybe it was time they make more of a commitment to each other. He'd feared when Molly had backed away from their relationship that he wouldn't be able to be what Joel needed, but all those fears had proven false in the intervening years.

Joel pulled up to lean against the headboard, rubbing the sleep out of his eyes before he reached for his glasses. As soon as Ben knew he had Joel's full attention, he closed his eyes. The tingles Faye had told him about were there, though on second thought, he wasn't sure he'd describe them as tingles. It felt more like a rushing surge of water, like a flash flood.

Smiling when the flood hit him, Ben drew in a sharp breath. With the power came pain, just like it had the first time. Heat scoured through each limb of his body until the entirety of his body burned as if he was on fire. Every nerve, every inch of skin was alight. Grimacing, Ben focused on the creature—the wings, the feathers, the beak.

Joel gasped, and Ben couldn't help the small grin that lit up his face. Drawing in a deep breath as the pain receded, he glanced up at Joel, cocking his head to the side. He didn't have to look to know he'd transformed, he'd shifted from his human state into that of a creature, a new creature. Joel jerked back before he sat up and leaned forward slightly.

"Ben...when did you...how did you?"

Ben squawked, since that was all he could do in that form. He pranced around the top of the mattress like he was on a runway, showing off. Joel chuckled and held out his hand. Ben stepped closer, and when Joel's fingers touched him, it was ice to the fire still burning through him. He stayed in that form a little longer before he got up the courage to change back. This time, like the last, he was prepared for the pain that was about to take over him. He'd never been one to want to experience pain in any kind. He always avoided it if he could, but this was his life now. He was a shifter, and he needed to be able to withstand the pain.

As soon as he was back in his human form, naked and lying on the bed next to Joel, Ben let out a sigh and pressed his forehead into Joel's shoulder. "What do you think?"

"I think you're getting the hang of this pretty fast."

Ben grunted. "It hurts so much to shift."

"I imagine. It hurts Faye just as much."

"Really?"

Joel nodded, and for some reason, knowing Faye felt the same level of pain made his own a little more bearable.

"She never says anything."

"She's been shifting for seventy plus years, Ben. I'm sure she barely even thinks of it now."

Ben nodded. "I guess."

Joel kissed his temple. "You going to tell Molly?"

"Eventually. For now, let's keep this between us. I don't want to have to shift unless I know I can."

"All right."

Joel grinned. He gripped Ben's cheeks and pulled him in for a deep kiss, turning so he laid half on top of Ben, covering his body and skimming a hand down Ben's side. Ben groaned under the touches. Yes, they did need to have at least one more talk, and maybe they wouldn't have separate rooms anymore. Giving as good as he got, Ben lost himself in Joel's body.

CHAPTER EIGHTEEN

EVERYTHING AMACHON had tried failed. He'd eventually left Faye, hooked up to just about every machine he had in the medical area, Molly swore, just to keep her alive. She hadn't left. Malek had been in and out several times, but no one else had joined her. She wasn't sure if they even knew. Molly rubbed her hand over Faye's, working her healing magic into Faye's body to try again and see if she could make some progress. Nothing. As soon as the cut was healed, it would come right back, and Molly couldn't keep going through that pain herself without the progress of Faye actually healing.

Molly closed her eyes and listened to the house. Everything was calm around her. Malek was nearby, but she expected nothing less. Faye was the only vampire alive as far as he knew, he would want to make sure she survived if only for his own personal gain. Molly focused on Faye, trying to get a feel for her. She broke her rule and pushed into Faye's mind, but she found nothing there. Faye was a blank slate, which was worrying. Even those in sleep or in induced sleep from injuries should be thinking something. Their minds didn't just stop.

Standing, Molly walked to the glass door to the medical area. She shut it behind her as she stepped out into the hallway, finding Malek standing there with his arms crossed over his chest. "I have an idea."

"We need to cleanse her blood." Molly mimicked his move and

crossed her arms.

"Yes. How did you..."

"I'm not unaware of what goes on in my house, Malek, as much as you may think. She has been increasing the amount of the drug. I have no idea how much she has taken this time, but no magic has seemed to work on her when she's intoxicated."

He gave a sharp nod. "It's dangerous."

"Are you frightened?" Molly's lip parted slightly as she taunted him, but it wasn't a full tease. She wanted to know just how far he would go to save Faye. It would tell her a lot in the long run. Molly stepped in closer to him, getting into his space. Her hands on his arms, she stared up into his blue eyes. She wanted to work her magic into him, see what he was thinking, but if they truly were going to cleanse Faye, she would need all the magic she had left. He had no idea how much she'd used, but there was no doubt both of them would be near depleted by the end.

"No." Malek bent his head, his face impossibly close to hers. He cupped her cheek again and shifted in even closer. "I'm not frightened. Are you?"

"Hardly. I've done this before."

He gave a small quirk of his lips, the wrinkles near his eyes new with his added age, and she hadn't noticed them before. As much as he was the same man she had left over two hundred years before, he was so vastly different. Malek bent down and pressed a kiss to the corner of her lips. Giving in because as much as she wanted the comfort, she also needed to keep up the pretense she and Faye had started, Molly turned into the kiss and deepened it.

When Molly moved away, she gripped his hand, twining their fingers, and gave him a sweet smile. He did always like his women strong but subordinate, which posed the question as to why he was so interested in Faye because she was anything but submissive.

"Ready?" she asked.

"Let's do this."

They walked together into the medical area. Malek stood on one side of Faye's prone form while Molly stood on the other. Each of them gripped one of Faye's hands. Molly reached over Faye's body and held her fingers for Malek to take. The smile he gave her sent a shiver down her spine. Turning to focus on Faye, Molly drew in a sharp breath.

Malek's magic already worked into her body. Molly added her magic into Malek's, but held back a good chunk of it. She absolutely did not want him to know how powerful she was, and if she had to divert her focus to keep that from him, she would.

Closing her eyes, Molly focused on Faye's body instead of on Malek. Faye was who they needed to help, and this was Molly's last chance of hope for a magical cure. Outside of this, she was going to have to start researching medical ways to bring people around after they'd consumed the drug.

Once again concentrating on Faye, Molly closed in on her injuries. She felt Malek working right alongside her, his presence stuck to her as she moved. Surprisingly, he wasn't leading and didn't seem to be taking that control like he normally would.

Finding broken bones and bruised organs, a punctured lung and liver, Molly cringed. They would have to work quickly. She sent out her magic in ribbons to wrap around the liver first, squeezing and holding secure. Next she focused on Faye's lungs and regulating her breathing. Pulling back to herself, Molly saw Faye's vitals normalize in the slightest which gave her hope.

Pushing back into Faye, she knew Malek was right there with her. Molly went into each cell she could find, using her magic and Malek's magic to cleanse the individual cells she could find. She knew whoever walked by the medical area was going to see them and wonder what they were doing, but they would hopefully be left alone.

She was halfway through Faye's body when weariness took over. Drawing a steady breath, Molly pushed on. She had to complete the ritual and while Malek was there to help, his magic wasn't doing as much as she had hoped. Risking it, Molly added more of her magic into their pool and worked faster.

Another hour and Faye's liver healed. Molly released the spell she had done to bind it and refocused that magic on Faye's blood. Thirty minutes more and Faye's lungs healed. Molly wanted to clear out the rest of the drug from Faye's body, but Malek's mind nudged hers and she pulled back. If Faye's body was back to healing itself, then they were at least close enough that her innate healing abilities would kick in.

Breaking the spell, Molly stared directly into Malek's eyes. He blinked at her, his lips parting as if he was going to say something, but he remained silent. His cheeks paled, the color draining from them, and he gripped the edge of the bed.

"Malek?" Molly leaned forward to grip his hand, but he dropped, his body crumbling to the ground. "Malek!"

Racing around the bed, Molly knelt next to him. She reached for his wrist and checked his pulse before she tapped his cheek to try and get him to come back around. Cursing, Molly stood up and ran straight for the wall where the alarm was. She hit it and went back to Malek.

"Malek, wake up." Tapping his cheek again, Molly drew in a deep breath. He'd only told her about Faye's injuries, not that she'd asked about his, but surely he wasn't injured as well.

Not knowing what to do while she waited for Amachon, Molly began the healing spell again. This time she focused on Malek, learning the ins and outs of his body as he drew in deep ragged breaths. She went through every limb before pulling away. She pushed her hair out of her face and relaxed. He wasn't hurt. He was expended.

Amachon rushed in, his breathing heavy. Molly put a hand on his arm to still him. "He's fine. Exhausted. Put him in a bed, will you?"

Grunting, Amachon lifted Malek and settled him in a bed in a completely different room than Faye. Molly pulled herself up, her own exhaustion finally filtering into her senses. She settled on the bed next to Faye and reached for her hand. Already Faye's skin was warmer than it had been. The scratches were gone from her knuckles, the bruising vanishing from her face as Molly watched.

Amachon came back in, a large hand on Molly's shoulder. "What did you do?"

"We rebooted her, so to say." Molly didn't take her eyes away from Faye. She'd seen her heal on her own so many times and each time it was a wonder. "Get me a scalpel, please."

Amachon listened. Taking it, Molly nicked her wrist and pressed it to Faye's mouth. Drops of her blood slid between Faye's lips, but Faye remained still. With bated breath, Molly waited. It took her to the count of thirty-six before Faye's chest surged upward, her hands flying to Molly's arm as she held Molly against her mouth as lapped at the energy Molly so willingly gave.

When Faye finally eased up, Molly ripped her hand from Faye's mouth and leaned down, pressing their lips together in a heated kiss. Faye's fangs were still long, scratching at Molly's tongue and lips. Closing her eyes, the iron tang on her own tastebuds, Molly lost herself in Faye. They had to stop this. Faye had been close to death too many times in the last four years. While she may have been willing to take the risk, Molly wasn't sure she could handle the fallout any longer.

Faye chuckled as she pushed Molly away. "I know what you're thinking, and stop it. I'm alive."

Molly punched Faye lightly in the shoulder. "Barely."

"But alive."

"Not for lack of trying." Molly turned serious, raising an eyebrow at Faye. "I need rest. You leave this bed before Amachon releases you, and I'll kill you myself."

"Yes, ma'am." Faye gave a half-ass salute.

Standing, Molly made sure her feet were steady before she walked away. She needed space, and she needed sleep. She would get no work done for the next few days. Crashing onto her mattress, Molly fell asleep, happy in the thought Faye was still alive.

Molly woke with a start. The door to her room shut quietly, too quietly for it to be anyone but her old friend. Rubbing her eyes, she turned on her side to see the giant shuffle toward her. She shifted to allow him space to sit next to her and tried to keep her eyes open, but the bleariness was next to impossible to get rid of.

"How long has it been?" she asked.

He reached up and put the back of his hand against her forehead. "Three days."

"Three—damn it. I have work to get done."

"Tomorrow," he muttered with a grunt on the end, handing her a magical tea he always seemed to give her when she'd exerted herself. "You need rest."

"I need to work."

His glare chided her back into silence. She could get up to work after he left and he would be none the wiser for some time. Molly wetted her lips and moved to sit up and lean against her headboard.

"How are the patients?"

"Faye."

She chuckled at just his tone of voice, which told her everything she needed to know. "Did you release her yet?"

"No." He grunted. "You needed rest."

"Faye would let me rest."

Amachon shook his head. "No. She needs to speak with you."

Molly nodded. "I'll see her soon, then. And Malek?"

Withdrawing into himself, Amachon stilled. Molly reached out and curled her fingers around his wrist and gave him a gentle squeeze. They stayed silent, Amachon not answering Molly's question and Molly waiting for him to actually answer.

"He's not woken."

"What? I used far more magic than he did."

"And you are stronger." He eyed her carefully.

Molly drew in a breath. "You said you would never speak of it."

"Only to you."

Pursing her lips, she stared at the ceiling, settling into the bed. "He is powerful enough that he should have woken by now."

"Something is wrong."

Molly rubbed her temple, a headache settling in, and she knew she'd have to sleep again to make it vanish completely. "I'll check on him."

"Not now."

"No, my friend, not now." She expected him to leave. Normally he would have, but Amachon stayed right where he was, unmoving. When another few minutes had passed, Molly touched his arm again. "What is it?"

"This drug is killing my patients."

"I know."

He shook his head. "No, it's increasing."

"Increasing?" Her voice rose in surprise. "How many?"

"Too many."

"Statistics, Amachon."

He grunted a few times at her in frustration before settling down again. "I lose at least six a night."

"Six!" Shock rang through her chest and out into her limbs. She hadn't realized the number had gotten so high. "Where are they getting the drug?"

"By the time they get to me, Molly, they aren't talking."

Sighing, Molly rubbed her temple again. "How are they finding you?"

"Someone brings them."

"Different someone, I assume."

"Friends, family, partners. It doesn't matter. Someone brings them to me for medical care, but as soon as they take it, they're as good as dead."

"Do they get angry like Faye?" She hadn't realized the question had been the first one she wanted to ask, but as soon as it was past her lips, she couldn't take it back. She needed to know, without a doubt, if Faye had killed all those people in the club or if it had been a cacophony of murder.

"Yes, but by the time they find me, they're comatose."

"Interesting, do you have a timeline at all for when it happens?"

"Depends on the Tainted."

Molly longed for her table or even pen and paper to write this down, but her eyes were still bleary and she wasn't sure she'd be able to even if she wanted. "Tell me more. What else have you observed?"

"Now is not the time, Molly."

"Now is the only time."

He grunted at her in anger, but she remained still and kept as much of her gaze focused on him as she could to wait him out. When he was done trying to intimidate her into lying down again, he finally answered.

"No one survives if they're around after the drug is taken."

"Is it only swallowed in pill form?"

"So far."

Molly nodded and closed her eyes, listening to her old friend speak.

"From what I can tell, after the violence has worn off, if they are still alive, they go into a comatose state until they're bodies seize uncontrollably until the heart stops."

"Any other damage?"

"To the brain." Amachon tapped his head. "But I've been hesitant to autopsy."

"Because you don't want to be infected with whatever they may have."

He nodded at her.

Sighing again, Molly nodded. "We'll do an autopsy here. Under close supervision. My tests on the drugs I took from Faye have proven fruitless. Get me what you can, and I'll start research as soon as I'm rested."

She said the last bit for his benefit since she wasn't even going to attempt to get out of bed quite yet unless she had to. He stood up without a word, leaving her alone. Just as he reached the door, Molly called to him.

"We'll figure this out, my friend. I promise."

"Hopefully before we're all dead."

"Faye will live through it, I'm sure."

"Not if she keeps going."

Molly had no response for that. Without a doubt, Amachon was right. Molly just didn't want to admit it.

CHAPTER NINETEEN

FAYE GLANCED around the medical area and slipped from the stretcher she'd been confined to for the better part of three days. Her bare feet hit the cold floor, sending a shiver straight up her spine. Molly had yet to be down to see her, but that wasn't a surprise. Faye had seen her pale cheeks, her heavy-lidded eyes, and the struggle she'd had just to stay there and talk for the few minutes she did.

Padding barefoot, Faye left the small room she'd been confined to and walked into the next one over. Malek lay on another bed, his hair a mess, his clothes stripped. He was hooked up to machines like Faye had been when she woke up. Amachon must have been worried. He never hooked Molly up to those things when she overexerted herself.

Faye slipped onto the edge of the bed. Three days was a long time. The last time she'd seen him like this it had lasted a little over a full day before he recovered. His skin was ashen, like he was truly sick instead of just having exhausted his magical powers. Drawing in a deep breath, Faye debated what to do. She'd been told to leave him alone, but she was awful at listening to rules, they knew that.

Taking his hand, Faye trailed her thumb across the back of his in a circular pattern. She'd felt attraction to him from the moment they'd met, much like with Molly but also so very different. With Malek, while there was physical sexual attraction, that was it. Molly held something else over her. Malek had told her about the odd interdependency between vampires and witches, something Molly had failed to share with her. Faye was certain that was why she felt anything for Malek at all. They were built to make sure the other survived. They needed each other.

"Malek," her voice was soft, a whisper nearly. "Malek, you need to wake up."

"I am awake," he muttered. "I don't want to open my eyes."

"Headache?"

He nodded very slowly, his chin moving up and down, but he curled his fingers around her hand and squeezed.

"Molly gets those when she's depleted her magic as well."

Snorting, Malek squeezed her hand again before shifting on the bed. "Where is she?"

"Resting in her room according to Amachon."

"And I'm relegated to the medical area." The disdain in his tone was strong.

Faye chuckled at it. "She wasn't as bad off as you to begin with, but this is also her house. We follow all the wise witch's orders quite well here."

"Do you?" Malek popped one eye open and reached up, brushing his fingers across Faye's cheek in a loving touch. "You don't seem as someone who follows orders well."

"Didn't say I did it well. Everyone else, however, does."

Malek groaned as he shifted on the bed, turning so he was on his side and facing her. "Turn the lights off, would you?"

"Sure." Faye stood up, hit the light switch, and came back to right where she had been. She took his hand once more between both of hers and stared down at it.

"Why do you stay here, Faye?"

Faye cocked her head at him. "What do you mean?"

"You don't fit in. Vampires aren't built for fitting in, being with others, other than witches, that is. Why not come back to the fold with me? We could use you. You could use us. We have lots we could teach you about your own history."

Faye sighed. "I haven't heard very kind things about your fold."

"Oh?"

"Well, not really. I haven't heard much of anything about it, actually." Faye bit her lip, staring down at his wide eyes. Now that it was dark, he stared right at her. "Why do you want me and her to go back with you so badly?"

"You're the only living vampire."

Faye raised an eyebrow at that. She was not the only living

vampire, although she didn't know how much Malek knew. Her father was a point of contention in her life, and she'd rather not think about him if she could. However, his statement still raised some questions. "Are you saying that because I'm the only born vampire?"

"There is quite a difference." His voice was soft when he spoke. "Your abilities and power to start with."

"And what else?"

"Your abilities to rejuvenate."

"You or the fold?"

He chuckled lightly. "Both."

"See? I knew there was something else there, that this wasn't just because you liked me or I fucked you."

Malek's lips quirked into a smile. "That was most pleasant."

"Sure." Faye's cheeks heated. It hadn't been bad sex, though she'd much preferred sex with Molly when they would initiate the magical bond between them, something Molly had been adamant about not doing with Malek, which didn't surprise Faye in the least. Even what she'd done with Reina and Corbin that had been a one-off had been better sex than what she, Malek, and Molly had managed, but she wasn't about to tell him that. "I'd help you out now, but I'm not sure you'd be able to handle it in your current state."

"You're probably right," he muttered. "How is Molly fairing?"

"Haven't seen her, so I imagine about as good as you."

"She hasn't visited?"

"Not at all." Faye drew in a deep breath. Once again she found herself rubbing up and down his arm. "Malek, why are you here? Really."

"Some things have changed in the fold since you arrived on my doorstep."

Faye pressed her lips tightly together, not sure what she could have changed except asking for their help in healing Molly from a curse that was determined to make her batshit crazy for the rest of her life. She'd really gone off the deep end, and it had taken them far too long to figure out what was wrong before they'd found a way to break the curse.

"What changed?"

"First the realization of the others that vampires are not as dead as they once thought."

Faye hummed. "I might not be dead, or undead, but my race certainly is."

"You could always grow it back if you wanted. That's the beauty of vampires, they can repopulate rapidly."

"Not really my style." Faye sneered at the thought, repulsed. The conversation was taking a very similar turn to one she'd had with Caliban Troy, the asshole who'd kidnapped her to try and revive the dead race of vampires using Faye as his personal baby making machine.

"I thought as much." Malek's eyes closed again, and he drew in a sharp breath.

Faye bent down close to him and kissed his cheek. "You should rest."

"In a minute I will. They want me to bring you and Molly back into the fold. We need you as much as you need us."

"I've lived seventy some-odd years without you. I think I'm good."

Malek gave a wry smile. "Yes, but you have no idea what we can offer."

"Sex. I know that."

"Yes, sex." He blinked slowly. "But also so much more."

"I'll think about it."

"That's all I can ask."

"You have neatly avoided my question, however. Why are you here, Malek? I know it is more than just bringing us back to the fold."

"That's all, I swear. They sent me here to convince you to come home."

The word "home" sent a shiver down Faye's spine, and not in a good way. Letting the conversation drop, Faye kissed his lips and cupped his cheek. "Rest, Malek. There will be time to talk later."

"Faye?"

"Yeah." She stood up, staying nearby.

"Don't take that drug again."

Snorting, Faye laughed as she walked away from his bed with an extra sway to her hips as she went. No one told her what to do, and that drug was the only relief she got from her demons in the past few years. It was a wonderful respite to have despite what the others thought. Settling back onto her own bed, Faye stood up immediately.

She'd listened enough. It was time to do something else and get out of the medical area. She was healed, and there was no reason for her to be stuck there. Walking out the door, she slipped into the halls and headed straight for her room.

Faye wanted fresh clothes before she left her room and headed straight for Molly's. Amachon didn't know, but Faye could be very helpful for Molly in her recovery. She jumped in the shower and cleaned up. Stepping out of the bathroom, Faye was completely naked, her hair wrapped up in a towel on top of her head. She stopped short. Ben stared back at her from her bed with wide eyes before he flung his hands up over his face.

"Oh my God! I did not need to see that."

"You liked it, don't deny it." Faye smirked and walked closer to him. "I know you did."

"Faye..." Ben whined, still covering his face with his hands and not even taking a peek.

Chuckling, Faye headed for her closet and grabbed a clean outfit. She took her time getting dressed, wanting to make Ben pay the toll for coming into her room unexpectedly. When she was finally dressed, she sat next to him on the bed and moved his hands.

"You're a dork."

He scrunched his nose at her. "Feeling better?"

"Loads. What's up?" Faye didn't want to make Molly wait any longer when she could very easily help her power rejuvenate.

Ben sighed and covered his face again. "Joel told me to come see you."

"O...kay? What about?"

"I've managed to shift twice now."

"Really? That's awesome." Faye clapped him on the shoulder and stood up like the conversation was over. She wished she'd been there to see him shift, but with the current state of her life, it was probably better she wasn't.

"It is for the most part." He scratched the back of his head. "I just...I don't know how to ask this, but you're the only other Tainted in this house who actually shifts form even though you're not a shifter like me, but I thought you might have a clue what to do because I'm not sure what to do—"

"Benjamin." Faye shook her head and put her hands on her hips, staring him down. "Out with it."

He looked at her like a little kid who was completely lost. His voice was so quiet and demure, she worried she had misheard him.

"Does it always hurt?"

"Oh." Faye drew in a deep breath, looked at the ceiling to try and figure out what the hell to say, and sat on the edge of the mattress next to him again. "Yeah, it does."

"Great." Ben paled.

She reached over and grabbed his fingers, squeezing them in a comforting gesture. "Look, I've been shifting into my vampiric form since I was a kid. It hurts. It's always hurt. I remember the first time truly that I did it intentionally, not just to feed on some energy but to actually shift on purpose. Oh my fucking God, Ben, that hurt. I nearly passed out from the pain."

"Really?" A light of hope echoed in his eyes.

"Yeah, really. It hurt. It took me months to even want to try to shift on purpose again. The difference, I think anyway, was that I wasn't in a rush to feed and having more issues with being hungry than with shifting. Anyway, when I was twelve or so, I couldn't take it any longer. My aunt had these pain pills she used to take and I snuck into her bathroom one night and downed the entire bottle."

"No shit!"

Faye nodded and stretched her back as she shifted to stare at the floor instead of him. Faye clenched her jaw. "My aunt was so pissed."

"I'd be pissed too if I found you'd taken a whole bottle."

Snorting, Faye rolled her eyes. "She wasn't mad because I got high. She was mad that I took *her* drugs to get high. She wanted them."

"Your aunt did drugs?"

"Yeah. Runs in the family, I guess. Anyway, I took pain pills for a long time to make it easier to go back and forth between the two. Eventually, I guess, I just got used to the pain, and it wasn't as big of a deal to take them before I became a vampire."

Ben wrapped an arm around her shoulders. "So that's why you started taking drugs?"

"Yup. Not why I continued. That's a whole different story."

"Tell me, then. I'm not sure you've ever shared that with me."

"It's not that good of a story."

"I want to know."

Groaning, Faye brushed her hand through her damp hair. "Fine. We have to feed as vampires, right? I hate it. It's disgusting. And I didn't know any vampires or Tainted who would willingly do it like Molly. Human blood is stronger than animal blood, and sometimes, depending on what shit I'd gotten myself into, I'd need human blood or even Tainted if I could find some, but that was harder. I hated doing it."

"You still do, I think."

"Yeah, mostly, unless it's with Molly."

Ben gave her a wan smile.

"I was at this party one night. My ex had invited me to it. Everyone was drinking, which sucked because alcohol barely makes a dent in me unless I have a lot of it. They were getting high, smoking joints, dropping acid, whatever floated their boat. I've tried it all, Ben. Heroin, however, is its own master."

"How so?"

"God, it makes you feel so good. It gets you all warm and tingly and hot and bothered." Her eyes lit up. "It's amazing."

"Why'd you need it to feed?"

"Taking energy can be pleasurable if it's done the right way, and if I'm going to take energy from someone, I'm going to do it where they at least get something out of it. I don't want to be the asshole who only gets something she needs."

"Now that sounds like you." Ben gave her a cocky half-grin.

Faye laughed. "Heroin would get me in the mood to get there for whoever I was taking energy from. That's why I started taking it."

"Ah. I don't think I'm going to take drugs."

"No. Probably not. Though, if you want, I know which ones should work well." She winked at him. "You'll get used to the pain. I promise. It sucks for a while, but it does get easier to deal with, and you'll find the better positions to stand in to shift more quickly."

"I...hadn't thought of that."

"Time, Ben. Time. Now, get out. I have things to do and people to see."

"Molly?"

"Yes, and if you interrupt us, I'll kill you myself."

Ben put both his hands up as he stood and walked backward toward the door. "I promise you I will not intrude again."

"Good. And knock next time."

"I did. You didn't answer."

"Maybe because I was in the shower!" Faye laughed as he blushed furiously. "And don't think I know you didn't look."

"I did not look!" Ben's voice rose in pitch. "I swear."

"Uh huh, sure." Faye shut the door behind him, spun around in a circle to make sure she had everything she needed, and left the room herself. She was on a mission to find Molly and give back the way Molly had given days before.

CHAPTER TWENTY

MOLLY SET her tablet down when the door to her bedroom snicked open. She rested her head into the headboard and smiled as Joel gave her stern look before shutting the door behind him. Even in her respite, she wouldn't deny him. Amachon and Joel typically kept everyone away when she needed to rest.

"You're not supposed to be working."

Her eyes crinkled as her smile broadened. "It was just a little work."

"Molly, you need to rest and get better. You can't do that if you keep working."

"Yes, sir." She gave him a half-salute like Faye had given her before she'd left the medical area. Amachon had given her fair warning Faye had escaped the medical bay, and Molly was slightly surprised Faye hadn't joined her yet. "What can I do for you?"

Joel moved to join her on the bed, much as Amachon had, only Joel was far more comfortable in her space. He ran a hand up and down her thigh through the covers and let out a long sigh. Molly kept her mouth closed, sensing Joel needed to come around to whatever he wanted to tell her on his own.

She settled the tablet on the opposite side and folded her hands together, waiting as patiently as she could. When minutes went by and he said nothing, she covered his hand with hers and squeezed to get his attention.

"What is it?" her voice was tender and soft, almost motherly as she tried to coax whatever was bothering him out.

"It's Faye."

Molly's stomach clenched. She had a flashback to four years prior when Joel held her up in her office one evening to talk to her about Faye, only then they'd thought her name was Caroline because of all the lies she'd told, but once again Molly felt Joel was about to explain all Faye was doing that she shouldn't.

"What did Faye do?"

"Well, it's not so much Faye as it is what she represents."

Molly squinted her eyes at him. "You'll have to help me here, Joel. I still have a migraine, and I don't have the ability to read between the lines. Plain words, if you will."

"I'm sorry. I should leave. This can wait."

Molly leaned forward and reached for him, holding him in place. "This is bothering you. Tell me what it is."

Joel drew in a deep breath and let it out slowly. He rubbed a hand over his eyes and then behind his head. "The drug, whatever drug she's been taking, it's becoming wider spread. My patient load has drastically increased, but it's all stories about someone who has taken it and gone insane before dying."

"Amachon tells the same stories."

Joel nodded. "I've talked with him already."

"Have you found any information about who might be dealing it?"

"That's just it. They don't charge for it ever."

Molly snorted. "Figures. This drug only affects Tainted."

"Really?"

"Malek and I, the other night, went to speak with Faye's old dealer—"

"Current dealer."

Molly's lips parted in surprise. "What do you mean current dealer?"

Joel narrowed one eye at her. "She still buys heroin, all the time."

"She doesn't take it." Molly's heart raced at the thought Faye might be still taking drugs and she had no idea it was happening. But that didn't make any sense at all. Faye, while good at hiding her intoxication, wasn't perfect at it. This new drug proved that.

"She buys it for the troll."

"Oh." Molly pressed her lips hard together and refused to look at Joel. She'd visited the troll several times over the years when she needed information or suspected him of something, but she had no desire to visit him ever again. Faye, however, seemed to be best friends with him, even before she'd crash landed in Molly's maple tree four years before.

"You didn't know?"

"I knew she visited with him."

"She gives it to him to ease his pain. That prison he's in is a torture device."

Molly clenched her jaw, pressing her tongue to the roof of her mouth. She wasn't going to say anything. Joel did not need to know, and if he hadn't figured it out already like Faye had, she wasn't going to be the one to break the news.

"I can't imagine anything he did to deserve to be put in that thing. You know I asked Faye once why he was there and she said she had no idea."

"That doesn't surprise me," Molly muttered. "Would you mind warming my tea? Amachon brought it up when he visited earlier."

Joel stood up and took her cup from her nightstand and walked toward the dresser where the tea tray was. "I figured Faye of all people would know. They're like best of friends."

Molly glanced at her tablet, hoping for something to change the topic to. "You were talking about the fallout from the drugs."

"Right, I was." He came back with a fresh cup of tea and handed it over. He took up his vacated spot on the edge of her mattress.

Wrapping her hands around the cup, Molly let the warmth seep into her skin. "What did you find out about a dealer?"

"Nothing. They just give it away."

"Who is they?"

Joel shrugged. "No idea. I think normally the dealer also ends up dead in the entire exchange of everything."

"We need to find out not only who is dealing this to the second level dealers, but we need to find out who is making this drug." Molly took a sip of the hot tea, thankful for its warmth. She refused to look up at Joel again. If she did, she worried he'd be able to see what she was hiding. It was hard enough to keep things from him.

"What's got you so anxious?"

Cursing inwardly, Molly set her cup on the nightstand and crossed her arms. "I'm not anxious, Joel. I'm simply tired."

"No, this is anxiety, which is very rare for you."

Molly held the silence. She didn't want to answer him, didn't feel she needed to. It was none of his business. She tried to relax her muscles, focus on what they were originally discussing, take her mind off what she was hiding. That was the best way to keep him on his toes and away from what she wanted to keep hidden.

Joel was about to speak when he froze. His jaw dropped and then closed. His chest rose and fell rapidly. Molly panicked. She was had. She knew it. Joel stood up from the bed, his arms at his sides and his hands in fists.

"You didn't."

"I did nothing wrong."

"*You.* You are the one who put him there."

Growling, Molly tried to get up, but a wave of dizziness forced her to stay put. "I did nothing wrong, Joel. The punishment was justified."

"What the hell can justify a torture prison for three decades, Molly? Tell me that? Did he commit genocide?"

"Not yet," she muttered.

"Did he start a war?"

"Attempt may be a better phrase." Molly closed her eyes and pinched the bridge of her nose. "It was justified, Joel. Leave it at that."

"No! You don't do this. You are fair and even-keeled. You might push ethical boundaries, but you don't do this. This wasn't because he did anything except piss you off. This was pure revenge."

"He killed her!" Molly's voice reverberated in the room, booming through his panicked accusations. "That was enough for me."

Joel stared at her, wide-eyed, like he'd never seen her before. Panic hit Molly. Her grasp on him slipped. Everything he had seen of her in the last few years, this was the final straw that could break everything they had built up together.

"Who did he kill?"

"I don't want to talk about it." Molly clammed up. She couldn't force herself to say her name, to even think it in this situation was to taint her memory.

"Who, Molly?"

Shaking her head, she glared. "It doesn't matter. It was justified."

"For killing one person he has been tortured for thirty years? Not justified, and you know it. That's what makes this so much worse. You know he doesn't deserve it."

"Get out." Molly's voice was low, a dark edge in it.

"What?" Joel sounded shocked.

"Get out, Joel."

She knew she shocked him. There was no getting around it, but she had to get away from the conversation. She had to step back, collect her thoughts, figure out what she was going to tell him. He had been a child when she'd put the troll in his prison, and honestly, it was none of his business.

"Now."

At her final word, Joel spun on his toes and stalked to the door, slamming it shut behind him. Molly released a breath she'd held pent up and closed her eyes. That had been near a disaster, and she'd almost lost everything she had built up with him. She still might. A tear slipped from the corner of her eye, and she brushed it away angrily. She would not cry anymore because of the pain he had caused. She'd done what she'd needed to do all those years ago, and she hadn't regretted it once.

Molly moved to sit on the edge of the bed, gripping the fabric of the sheets tightly between her fingers. As much as she tried to hold it back, the tears were going to come. They were going to spill over her cheeks, and there was nothing she could do about it. Her breathing quickened. Her eyes stung. Reaching for her tea, she flung it across the room with a scream, listening as it shattered against the wall. Every precious ounce of control Molly had been so careful to build up over the years vanished in an instant. It always did when Pearl was involved.

When the door opened, Molly's magic unleashed from her fingers. She flung her hand out, slamming it and whoever it was against the wall, invisible fingers tightening around her victim's neck. She didn't dare open her eyes. She knew it wasn't Joel. He wouldn't come back so soon.

When she heard the sharp gasp for breath, Molly glanced up. Faye's slate-gray eyes stared stoically at her. Releasing her magic, Faye dropped to the ground, coughing and sputtering as she tried to regain her breath. Finally kneeling on the floor, Faye made eye contact with Molly.

"If I knew you wanted that, all you had to do was prepare me a little."

Without another word, Faye surged forward. Her superior speed meant she was in front of Molly before she could even think about speaking. Faye knocked her back onto the bed with a hand wrapped around Molly's neck and lips pressed hard to Molly's mouth.

This. This was exactly what she needed.

Molly surged up, shoving Faye onto her back. Straddling Faye, Molly continued the bruising kiss, adding in nips that threatened to break skin. Roughly she grabbed Faye's breast and gave a hard squeeze that she knew would hurt. Faye gasped again, this time a mix of pleasure and pain.

"You better make this good," Molly ordered.

"Wanting to forget something?"

"Shut your mouth."

"Shut it, or use it?" Faye bucked her hips, knocking Molly to the floor with a thud.

The air rushed from Molly's lungs, and Faye was on top of her as she caught her bearings. Faye's nails were long as she ripped through the fabric of Molly's clothes, tearing them off. With her breasts bared, Faye's long teeth sunk into the flesh. Molly's back arched as a moan escaped her throat. She dug her fingers into Faye's damp hair, holding Faye's head to her body.

Her magic came unbidden as it flashed from her into Faye. The connection made, she let it simmer in the background as she coaxed Faye away from her body. "Don't stop there."

Faye grunted, her long black nails scraping down Molly's side and leaving bloody welts in their wake. "Need to take your mind off something, Molly?"

Molly swallowed, trying to hold back the scream of pleasure building. She did not want to let Faye in on what she and Joel had been discussing. No good would come of that. She'd known Faye had been aware that she was the cause of the troll's imprisonment, but they'd never discussed it further.

Breathing heavily, Molly licked her lips and reached down to smear the blood Faye had so graciously not lapped up against her skin and against Faye's cheek. Every second they stayed connected, her power grew that much faster. Faye knew it. It was why she'd shown up, and Molly had been expecting her as soon as Amachon had told her she'd escaped.

"What is it, Molly?"

Not answering, Molly pushed Faye off her and leaned up. "I'm not here to talk."

"What if I am?" Faye eyed her suspiciously.

"You've never been a talker."

"Is that your polite way of tell me to shut it and shove it?"

Molly didn't have time to answer as two of Faye's fingers pushed inside her. Molly's body clenched against the intrusion, but she relaxed after a moment, and shifted to give Faye better and easier access. "Make it good."

"Don't I always?" Faye's arm moved rapidly and forcefully.

Molly wrapped her arms around Faye's shoulders, digging her nails into her scalp and dragging them against the tender flesh. Rocking her hips to each of Faye's thrusts, Molly closed her eyes. Faye's nails and teeth dug into her wherever they could reach, little pinpricks of pain and pleasure all mixed in together. Each of her senses was overwhelmed as Faye held her in place, forcing her body to react exactly how she wanted it.

When she crested over her orgasm, Molly moaned, her lips against Faye's ear. Reaching between her legs, she ripped Faye's hand from her body, heaving breaths as she tried to center on what they were doing and what needed to happen next.

"Faye..." her voice broke.

"Don't worry about it. It's not the point."

"But I want to."

"Not right now. Wanna tell me what got you in such a tizzy?"

Grunting, Molly pressed her forehead into Faye's shoulder and closed her eyes to shake her head. "No, not really."

"I saw Joel leaving. He looked pretty upset."

"He is."

"What about?"

Molly kissed Faye's shoulder, then the hot skin at her neck. Maybe she could still distract her if she tried hard enough. She had the energy now that Faye had given her what she truly needed. Nipping at Faye's skin, Molly pressed her hips into Faye's body. "Did you help Malek yet?"

"No."

The vehemence in Faye's voice surprised her. Molly pulled away, staring down into those slate-gray eyes she had come to love over again. "Are you going to?"

Faye scrunched her nose. "No."

"Faye, you should help him. You know you can."

"Can we not talk about me fucking a man while my fingers are still sticky from you?"

Molly bent her neck and pressed their mouths together, tangling their tongues. She pushed Faye to the ground, covering her body, ready to give Faye as much as she had received if not more. Faye pushed at her shoulder and tilted Molly's body to the side.

"I said that was enough."

Masking the pout she wanted to give, Molly turned onto her back and stared at the ceiling. If Faye was done, they were done for the night. Her skin cooled from Faye's heated touches, her nipples hardening as a reaction. Faye pushed up on her elbow, tracing one thin long black nail against her skin, which sent shivers through all of her nerves and goosebumps along her skin.

"Malek—"

"Not now, Molly. What did you say to Joel?"

"Nothing."

"Fine, what does Joel think you said?"

Sighing, Molly closed her eyes. "He made a connection I'm surprised he hasn't made prior."

"Connection to what?"

Molly stared Faye straight in the eye. "The troll under the bridge is there because I put him in the prison."

"I know. Want to tell me why?"

"No." Molly pushed to sit up and then stand. Stalking to her closet, she grabbed a robe and slid it over her shoulders. If Faye wasn't going to let her reciprocate, then she was done with the conversation.

"I have ways to find out."

"Then use them." Molly glared. Two of them attacking her on this in one night was nearly too much. She wouldn't be able to hold her tongue much longer, especially with the migraine still lingering. Though that should be vanishing soon enough thanks to Faye.

Faye stood and followed Molly, still perfectly dressed in her tight jeans and low-cut black tank. Molly longed to touch, to distract, to strengthen the bond they still shared. She was loath to give it up and break it until she had to.

"I don't want to bite Malek."

"Then don't." Molly threw her hand up. "It's your choice, but it would be a nice thanks for what he did for you."

"He didn't do much if I recall."

Molly stilled. "You recall? Do you remember? Because he's the one who found you."

"I'm aware, and aside from bringing me back here, he didn't do much. I don't know what you think he did or didn't do, Molly, but the magical effort to cleanse my blood was far more you than him. Think about it."

"I already know."

"Then why would you suggest it."

"Because that is the purpose of using sex to get answers, is it not? He did something for you, you must do something for him. Create that trust and that bond." Molly stepped in closer to Faye, taking her hand gently. "You can do this."

"I don't want to."

"Since when as that ever stopped you."

"Fair."

Molly carded her fingers against Faye's cheek before cupping the side of her face and pull her in for a kiss. "I'll tell you someday. I promise, but please, not today."

"I'll hold you to that." Faye kissed her hard. "Guess I'm being sent on my way."

Laughing, Molly pinched Faye's ass and gave her a tap. "On your way then."

"I could bring him up here."

"You could, but I think this is something you need to do. Malek trusts me. He's trying to earn mine. He needs to know you trust him."

"I get it, Molly. Go fuck the other witch and leave this one alone for a bit."

"You always have such a way with words."

Faye raised an eyebrow at her before leaving the room and Molly alone. Sitting at her desk, Molly pulled open the drawer in the center, lifted the papers on top and slid out the picture. She smiled down at it, good memories finally flooding into her mind. It was all worth it, and she still maintained, it was justified.

CHAPTER TWENTY-ONE

AFTER FAYE had left her room, Molly couldn't settle. Her bare feet padded across the floor as she paced back and forth, caught between her rage for her conversation with Joel and Faye, her desire to keep everything hidden, and guilt. For the first time in three decades, Molly felt a tinge of guilt tickling at the back of her heart.

Perhaps Joel had been right. Thirty years ago she had overreacted and done something she perhaps shouldn't have and Lamek had suffered the consequences since. Cursing, she pulled off her robe and slipped into her favorite green dress. Joel had no idea what he was talking about and regret was not something Molly allowed herself.

The four-inch heels Molly put on were perfect for what she needed, a distraction. With Faye's help, she was feeling much better than hours before. Futzing with her hair and putting on a new layer of makeup, Molly stepped out of her bedroom for the first time in days. The halls felt so familiar yet so different.

Everything crumbled around her. Molly pressed her hand to the wall of the house, the house she had built from the ground up so many years before. Tears stung at her eyes. It was as though the house was living around her, that she could do nothing but feel the pulse beat beneath her fingers.

The house had been with her through thick and thin, through so much. Molly smiled and stepped away. She took the elevator down to the third floor and stepped out to find Amachon staring at her. The tears once again came unbidden, only this time she couldn't hide them. And she didn't need to.

Wrapping her arms around Amachon's middle without warning, she burred her face in his chest. Amachon hesitated to put his arms around her, but eventually he hugged her back, dragging his large hand up and down her back. She melted into him.

"What is this about?" he asked slowly after a few minutes.

Molly shook her head into his chest, then drew in a deep breath. "Joel brought something up."

"What?"

Sighing, Molly pulled back and wiped her eyes. "Pearl."

Amachon grunted and stepped away. "You haven't spoken of your sister since she died."

Whimpering, Molly shook her head. "I haven't had cause to think of her."

"You think of her."

She couldn't fault him. Molly remembered her sister, and since Malek's reappearance, she thought of Pearl quite often. Brushing her fingers through her hair, she stepped farther away from him. "It's nothing."

"It's not nothing."

"Is Malek awake?"

He grunted an affirmation.

"I think I'll speak with him." She went to move away, but Amachon put a hand on her arm to stop her. She stared down at it before turning her chin up at him to stare into those golden eyes.

"It's okay to miss her."

"I do." She gave him a wan smile. "I do miss her."

"Tell Faye. She'll understand."

Molly gave him a disbelieving look before she walked away and into the medical area. Malek was sitting up on the bed, staring at her over a book as she came in. She curled her lips up to try and seem as if she was in control. It was the first time she felt completely out of control since the curse. As soon as she stood next to Malek, he reached for her hand and took her fingers in his.

"You seem to be faring better than me."

"Faye helped a little."

"Oh." His lips pressed together.

"I assume she hasn't been back down here."

He shook his head.

"I told her to come."

Malek sighed. "As much as I appreciate the sentiment, Molly, I don't like the idea of Faye doing that."

"And why is that?" She regarded him carefully. "That's the purpose of the bond."

"I understand." He set the book on the edge of the bed. "But I don't like the idea of sex solely for the purpose of the bond. I never have."

"I don't think it would be just for that." Molly didn't dare look him in the eye. Faye's relationship with him, nor hers for that matter, was solely about gaining more power. "She likes you, Malek."

He narrowed his eye. "She likes what I can give her, which is information you withhold."

Molly tsked. "Perhaps, but I think it's more than that. I've known her for years, and Faye doesn't act like this with everyone."

"It's nothing more than the bond."

"It is more than that." Molly slipped onto the edge of the bed and took his hand in hers. "There is a connection between the two of you."

"There is still a connection between us."

Molly tensed. She wasn't quite sure what to say. She still needed to give off the air she was interested in him that she was thinking about his offer to return to the fold, but it was getting harder to keep up that facade, especially when Faye was so much better at it than she was. Then she realized she didn't have to lie. Nearly three hundred years of history meant they would always have a connection of some sort, and there was no use denying it.

Bending down, she kissed his lips tenderly. "You're right. There is."

He pulled her in for a deep, slow kiss. Everything in Molly's body calmed as his tongue danced with hers. Malek carded fingers through her hair and held her tight to him. She pressed into him even more, her chest brushing against his. When she finally pulled back, she sighed. "I'll see if Faye will come visit you."

"Don't. She can do whatever she wants. It's you who I want."

Parting her lips in surprise, Molly shook her head. She wanted to tell him he wouldn't get her without Faye, but the words wouldn't come. Instead, she brushed her thumb across his lips. "Then perhaps we can all join together later."

"I would like that. I wanted to talk to you about something."

"Oh?"

"I've been thinking about how we healed Faye, and perhaps the cure for this drug isn't medical but magical."

"I had the same thought, somewhere between the hours of sleep and rest. I even started working on it."

Malek's face lit up a blush creeping into his cheeks. "I should have known you would have thought of it already."

"I will need your help to test the theory."

"I don't know how much help I'll be in that matter."

"Yes, your magic."

He nodded. Molly didn't press, unsure how to ask the question. There was no logical reason other than the fold restricting Malek's magic as to why he didn't have access to everything. She wasn't sure she wanted to know what he had done to deserve that punishment.

"It's because of you," he whispered.

"Because of me?" Molly's brow drew together in confusion.

"It was the risk I took in convincing the others to help." He cupped her cheek, drawing her attention back to him. "It was a risk that was worth it."

"I'm not going back."

"I know," he whispered. "I never thought you would, but I needed to try."

"Then why are you here, Malek? It's not because you want me back, particularly if you understand why I won't go back."

"Because of Pearl."

Molly couldn't get away from her sister no matter how much she tried. "It's not only because of Pearl."

"I know, but she was the deciding factor in that moment."

"How would you feel to be told your blood wasn't pure enough to be part of the fold or to be looked down upon because of your heritage?"

"She was your half-sister, Molly. Nothing more."

"My older sister. She was my older sister, regardless of who her mother was, she was a witch and a very talented witch at that."

"Yes, she was very skilled. I suppose you taught her."

Molly chuckled. "No, our father did."

Reaching up, she took his hand from her face and held it between her fingers. Perhaps Malek would be the perfect person to talk to about Pearl. He'd at least known her unlike anyone else in the house. Amachon had met her briefly, but it was only days into their acquaintanceship when Pearl was killed.

"I taught her some," she admitted.

"I know you did. I allowed it, remember? I also pushed the boundaries of the fold then as well."

"I'm aware." Molly blinked slowly. "She was very powerful."

"I was sorry to hear of her passing."

"How did you?"

"How did I what?"

"How did you hear of it? Neither of us was connected to the fold at that point. We were here, nowhere near you or the others. Our parents were all dead. How did you hear she'd died?"

Malek's jaw tightened. "This is not the first time I've come looking for you."

"Oh?"

"When you moved here."

"Pearl was alive then."

"Yes. But she was getting older. It was only a matter of time. Her blood wasn't as pure as ours, and that means she aged far more quickly."

"She still had years left," Molly whispered, ignoring that fact even thirty years after Pearl's death.

"She did. Want to tell me how she died?"

"She was killed while on a mission." When Malek didn't press, Molly stared at the ceiling and closed her eyes to prevent the tears from falling again. "We were solving a case, and there was an accident. That's all."

"I think it was more than that."

"I couldn't save her."

"Her life was well-lived, Molly. I wish she'd been able to learn with you formally. It would have helped her control her magic well."

Molly didn't answer him. She stayed seated for another minute before standing and brushing her palms down the front of her dress. "I should check in, seeing as how I've been under the weather for a few days. Let me know when you're feeling more able to discuss a magical cure to our little problem."

"I will."

"And I'll send Faye down."

"Don't bother. She'll come here if she wants to."

Molly was about to walk out the door when she stopped. "You've changed, Malek. And it's not for the worse."

Without another word, she left the medical area. She made her rounds, checking on everything she had missed in the last few days. By the time she was done, her anger was back. She let it settle deep into the pit of her stomach. It was better than grief, so she held onto it as best as she could.

Joel found Faye in his office when he walked in, which surprised him. Shutting the door, he sat next to her on the single couch and patted her knee. "Good to see you up and running again."

She snorted. "Don't you ever feel like that conversation gets old?"

"Every time we have it." He closed his eyes and leaned his head back. "Are you going to tell me about this drug yet?"

"Why would I do that?"

"Because you're getting high again and you know exactly how this conversation is going to go."

Joel focused on Faye's emotions. For the first time in a while, they were clear instead of conflicted. Every time she'd been high recently, he'd known it. The two overwhelming emotions floating through here were pure pleasure and pure rage, complete opposites that never truly existed together for long except when Faye was high, no matter how little of the drug she took.

"Did Ben talk to you?"

Joel opened his eyes at that, turning his head on the couch to face her. "What do you think he said?"

She narrowed her gaze and shook her head, a smile tugging at the corner of her lips. "Uh, nope. I'm not falling for that."

"No, Ben did not speak to me."

"He came to tell me about shifting and pain."

"And you told him it was why you started getting high."

"He did talk to you!"

Joel snorted. "No, but it's an obvious conclusion for someone who is a trained psychologist. You tend to forget that, don't you?"

"How can I forget?" Faye crossed her arms over and pouted. "You're always reminding everyone."

"Am not."

"Sure, you're not."

Joel smacked her knee lightly. "What do you need?"

"I thought I could be of some help to you, actually."

"Are you going to tell me where you've been getting the drugs?"

Faye pursed her lips and gave him a sideways glance. Her mood went from teasing to serious, and he could tell she was weighing her options and the outcomes. While he found her lack of filter on emotion annoying at times, he did admire how quickly her mind worked and how well she made decisions.

"I got them at the sewers that first night."

"I thought as much, but that doesn't tell me who gave them to you."

"Aliya." Faye blushed.

"The bartender?"

Shrugging, Faye turned to face him. The lick of embarrassment that had flashed through her body vanished as she focused on confidence. He also admired her ability to do that.

"She just gave it to you?"

"Said the first one was free."

"Because she thought it'd be the only one. Where did Aliya get it?"

"Don't know. I didn't ask. It was a new drug, and I thought I'd give it a try."

"Try you did." Joel sighed. "And almost ripped Molly in half in the process."

"She's fine."

"Because Malek was there."

"No, because she's Molly, and she would have figured something out."

"Do you not remember what you did to her?"

Faye raised an eyebrow in his direction before shaking her head slowly. "I don't remember anything from when I'm high on this drug. It's one of the benefits."

"You're the only one who has ever survived taking it, and I'm pretty sure that's because of your unusual body chemistry and the fact you're essentially immortal."

"I can die."

"It's not easy to kill you."

"True." Faye gave him a cocky grin. "You on the other hand would be very easy to kill."

"Yes. So are the majority of my patients." Joel paused. "You said the first time. Where else have you gotten the drugs?"

"Here and there. No one ever seems to deal it out more than once. Aliya did, though, but I only got it from her twice."

"Twice?"

"The second time we took some together while we...uh...while I fucked her against a wall."

"At the club."

"On the dance floor."

"Shit, Faye." Joel covered his eyes. "I did not need that image in my head. Does Molly know?"

"Yeah. She's the one who found me sobering up, and she's the one who took care of the mess."

"The mess?"

"Everyone was dead." Faye paled. "I was in the back storage room. Molly cleaned up, and we left."

"Jesus."

"She didn't tell you?"

"Not a word." Joel scratched at the stubble of hair on his chin. "Does she know you and Aliya...?"

"I don't know. Doesn't really matter." Faye's defenses skyrocketed, and she built another wall Joel would have to tear down.

"It doesn't... You're committed to Molly."

"Absolutely not. I am committed to no one, and Molly is very aware of that just as she is not committed to me in any way."

"I'm confused."

"Then be confused. It's none of your business." Faye pouted. "I did ask my troll friend if he knew where I could get more."

Joel's ears perked up at that. It would add into what he'd already discovered about the drug itself. "Did he know where?"

"He told me I should stay away from it."

"Oh really?"

"Yeah, obviously I didn't listen to him."

"Clearly." Joel clenched his jaw, eyeing her carefully. "And why not?"

"I like how it makes me feel."

"And forget."

"That too." Faye winked at him. "I've got to run."

"Run where?"

"I think Malek needs a hand." Faye made an obscene gesture, which forced Joel to flush. She laughed at his reaction before waltzing out the door to his office.

Shaking his head at her, Joel moved to his desk. He had a bit more research to do before he brought his new discovery to Molly.

Chapter Twenty-Two

MOLLY LEFT the house under the dark of the night when no one was around. Faye was still awake, but the rest were in their own rooms, sleeping and resting as they should be. She pulled out of the driveway in her Tesla.

A light rain fell from the sky, no doubt from the change in her mood. Molly had to focus on the anger before she went on this particular mission, before she took the step to confront him. It had been two days since she and Joel had their argument, and they had barely spoken since. They'd neatly avoided one another.

Every muscle in her body was laden with tension as she drove away from the house. No one knew where she was going, and that was probably a good thing. After speaking again with Faye about her drug usage and getting nowhere, Molly knew she had to find answers sooner rather than later. They couldn't wait until the entire Tainted race was killed before they were able to figure out who was making the drug and distributing it.

Overwhelmed by the number of problems compounding on top of each other, Molly took a risk she normally wouldn't, at least not without backup and someone knowing where she was going, but the sensitivity of the topic prevented her from asking for any help.

The drive was quick. Molly parked a block away, knowing he wouldn't know she was there. She sat in the driver's seat of her car, running through conversation after conversation in her mind. She had to find a way to break the ice. She'd only gone to visit him a few times over the years and every time had to do with Faye and her drug problem. She knew the two of them were close, that Faye got information from him in exchange for something, she wasn't sure. Joel had mentioned Faye brought him drugs to ease his pain, but that couldn't be all he got out of it.

Molly could exchange the lessening of his sentence for information, perhaps ease the pain levels. Though, she'd prefer not to. She would never release him. She hadn't lied to Joel when she said his punishment was justified. She truly believed it and that there was no reason to let him loose on their city again. His kind of Tainted needed to be controlled, and if she could have imprisoned every troll out there, she would have.

Getting out of the vehicle, Molly stepped slowly toward the bridge. Her heels clicked against the asphalt as she moved. The rain caught in her hair and covered the jacket she'd thrown on before sneaking away from the house. She made it to the bridge, but still had not a clue how she was going to start the conversation or even convince him to halfway wake up and speak with her. She doubted he wanted to see her as much as she wanted to be there.

Standing at the base of the troll's prison, Molly stared up at him. He was aging even in his prison that was meant to keep him alive forever. The lines around his eyes and mouth had elongated. His skin pulled away from his bones even more. He looked skinnier. She may have to modify the prison so he wouldn't escape if he was able to get loose.

He didn't move. Molly knew he was aware of her presence. He should be able to feel everyone walking in the vicinity, know who they were. Part of that was his abilities as a troll. The race was made to keep guard, so their skills in observation were strong. She'd put him there after all, and she had no doubt that he had memorized how she felt in the air.

Snapping her magic to attention, Molly jerked her hand in his direction. A bolt of electricity moved from the underground wire in the base of the bridge into him. He didn't move. Molly's lips quirked as she did it repeatedly. Waking him up this way was far more pleasant than she had anticipated. Pouring her anger from the last few days into gaining his attention, Molly flicked him with electricity until she grew bored with that.

She moved in with heat. That had worked the last time she'd had to do this, if she remembered correctly. Making sure no one was in the area, Molly closed her eyes and drew her magic into her chest. Calling on the elements, she walked herself through fire. Then she sent it out to him. Starting at his toes that were cemented under the ground, she moved the heat into him. She increased it.

It took a full minute before his head rustled, the grinding of stone against stone as he moved and woke from his slumber. Smirking, Molly kept the heat up until he was fully bared to her as much as he could be. Just his head and neck moved. He groaned and snorted, dust coming out of his nose.

"Stop." His voice boomed through the underside of the bridge.

Molly kept it going. His order wasn't going to stop her one way or another. It felt so good to let loose on someone after keeping everything pulled inside her for days.

"Stop!" he shouted.

Pulling back, Molly kept the heat as a very real threat in case he dared to defy her or ignore her. "I need answers."

"I have nothing for you." His voice was slow still, but there was a sense of urgency to his words. She had no doubt that the pain was very present in his body that he couldn't move away from it.

"Answers or your fate will be no different."

"I did not intend to kill her."

Molly's lips parted, but she barreled right through that confession. He had said it all to her before, but she didn't care to listen. He had killed her, and that was all she cared to know. She'd witnessed every second of it. "Are you dealing the drugs?"

He laughed. His voice boomed through the underside of the bridge, this time sending shivers down her spine and into her toes. Molly increased the heat, not wanting to deal with his antics that night. She wanted answers then she wanted to get out of there. "Where are they coming from?"

"I have nothing to give you."

"I want answers!" Her voice rose in rage.

"I know nothing."

"Horse shit." Molly stepped closer, still staring up at him and having to crane her neck to look into his pitch-black eyes. "You may be stuck here by my hand, but you're fully aware of what is going on. Tell me what you know."

He didn't respond. Cranking up the level on the heat, Molly added in a few sparks of electricity to make her point.

"They're killing Tainted."

"I know."

Finally, she was getting somewhere. "Tell me who is doing it."

"I do not know."

Looking up into his eyes, she knew he was telling her the truth. She let up on the electricity but kept the heat as a constant reminder of all she could and would do to him. "Tell me."

"I know nothing."

"Tell me!" Molly yelled, her voice burst from her in a lash of anger. Her chest rose and fell in sharp gasps as she tried to control herself while at the same time wanting to let it all go. This was why she didn't ever tread down to the bridge to see him.

"Faye came here to get drugs. Where did you send her?"

"Nowhere."

"Don't lie to me!" She raised the heat and intensified the electricity. "Where did you send her?"

"I do not know anything. What am I going to learn from here? I am in prison."

His words stung. Molly let out a breath. He was right. What could he do from his position? He had access to some things, he had information for sure, but there was no way he was the one manufacturing the drug or even handing it out to other dealers.

Frustrated, Molly increased the heat in one last time to try and get an answer, but she had little hope she would. Molly swung her hand out behind her, ending the spell before she got into her vehicle. Slamming the door, she pressed her forehead to the steering wheel and let out a sigh. She needed to get a hold of herself. She couldn't slip back into what she had been a year before when she was cursed. With no more answers than when she'd come, Molly headed home.

Faye slipped into Ben's room after knocking and making sure he was alone. After her last encounter with Joel, she would be fine with not seeing him again for a little bit. She wasn't as mad at him as Molly was, but she didn't want to see him either. Ben sat at his computer, the sun setting over the horizon behind him through the window.

Bouncing on his bed, she backed up on it until she could sit comfortably. "Let's do this."

"Do what?" He spun around to face her, eyes wide and confused.

"Shift."

"What?"

"Let's train you to shift without pain. I've been thinking about it, and I'm the perfect person to teach you how to do it."

"You literally just told me it's always going to hurt."

Scoffing, Faye rolled her eyes and landed flat on her back on the messy bed. "I did, but that doesn't mean you can't learn to make it easier. So let's do that."

"Let's not." Ben focused on his computer, typing away.

Faye gave him a minute before she sat up and moved over to him at the computer. She spun him around in his chair so he had to face her and leaned over so that her face was right in his. "You need to learn."

"I will, but not with you."

"Why?" Faye stood up straight and crossed her arms offended. "You don't trust me or something?"

"I don't want it to hurt."

"Ben, it's going to hurt whether you do it with me or not, but let me teach you this. Come on. I'm the one who's going to know the most, you know that."

Ben gave her a hard stare. "What do I get out of it?"

"Uh...a lesson from yours truly."

Rolling his eyes, Ben glared. "No."

"Come on, Benny-boy."

"I've told you not to call me that."

"Get up." Faye grabbed his hand and pulled him to stand. "What did you change into?"

"Skoll."

"Okay, do you want to change into something else? Like...a fish?"

"Won't I die from not being able to breathe?" Ben paled.

"Doubt it. You can breathe out of water, so your shifted form should be able to as well."

"Can I breathe underwater?"

"We'll have to find out. Maybe not today though unless we're jumping in with the sharks in the river."

"There's sharks in the river?"

Laughing, Faye put her hands on her hips. "You have no idea what is in this city, do you?"

Ben's lips parted, but he closed them sharply with no retort. She'd called him on something he didn't want to admit. Bypassing that conversation for another day, Faye grabbed his hand.

"Something easy then. If you shifted into a skoll, then let's try a dog or a cat."

"Okay." Ben let out a breath. "Okay."

"I want you to think about it. Whichever one you want. Think about the shape of the body. Think about the feel of the fur. The lines of muscles. The breath in your lungs."

Ben didn't say anything, but he closed his eyes. Faye walked around him, giving him space he needed. She knew this was a huge ask, but if he was willing to give it a shot, then she was willing to teach what she knew.

"When you're ready, feel for your powers, pull it in to you, focus on it, and then turn it to the wild."

Keeping quiet, Faye stayed back. He would need the room. She pressed her lips together, and when she sensed he was about to shift, she gave him one more piece of advice. "Loosen up every muscle in your body, Ben. You don't want to be tense."

He shook out his arms and his legs, his knees trembling. It wouldn't be perfect, but she had faith he would succeed. They stood there in silence for another two minutes before he popped his eyes open and stared directly at her. Faye held her breath, waiting to see what would happen.

Before her eyes, Ben shifted down to the ground, his back arching up, hair sprouting along his spine and his skin as his clothes ripped to make room for the new him. When his hands touched the floor, they didn't have fingers but paws. He looked up at her, his eyes reflecting surprise at her in his gaze.

Faye grinned. She got down onto her knees and held her hand out for him. Ben walked toward her, his gait unnatural. They could work on that later, and she knew he'd get more used to it as he moved and became more comfortable with his body. Ben's head moved against her hand, his back arching as she scratched it and under his chin. He made the cutest little cat there was.

He waltzed around the room, prancing from one side to the next. As he came back to her, he jumped up on the bed, stretched his back, and hopped down to meet up with her again. Faye patted his head.

"Whenever you're ready, Ben, you can come back into your human form. I'll get you some clothes."

He didn't shift back right away. Faye waited patiently, enjoying watching him explore his shifter side. As he got closer to her, she realized his scent had changed to reflect that of a feline. Interested and curious, she drew in a deeper breath to try and catch more of his exact smell. There was still a faint hint of him underneath it all, and that earthy smell that had come to the forefront of his blood since he'd stopped his medication. He was still Ben, no matter what form he took.

Ben got up on his keyboard, stomped around the keys as they

clicked under the weight of his paws. Faye giggled. He meowed and walked back to her. He brushed his head against her arm and walked to the center of the room where he had originally shifted. Faye knew without him saying anything that he was going to shift back to his human form.

Getting up onto her feet, she grabbed a pair of jeans. As soon as he was back to him, she tossed them at him. Ben groaned when he moved his arms and his legs. "It hurts."

"That will go away the more you get used to it. It's like starting to work out when you haven't in forever. It takes your muscles time to get used to it."

"I get that, but it still hurts."

"Take a hot shower."

Ben gave her a sharp look.

"What? It helps. I'd suggest a bath, but I don't think that's quite your style."

"Yeah. That was good though."

"You're definitely getting the hang of this. You should try something other than a mammal next time. I'm curious just what all you can shift into."

"I think it's limitless."

"Maybe." Faye sat on the edge of the bed as Ben went back to his chair. "You'll also likely have to work on doing that much more quickly. Can't be taking your time when we're in a true emergency."

"Faye—"

"Practice, Ben. It just takes practice. Don't give up on it yet."

"I wasn't giving up on it." A slight whine was in the edge of his tone.

"Maybe not, but you weren't practicing either. We'll set up some more times to practice."

"Great."

Chuckling, Faye clapped him on the shoulder. "If you'll excuse me, I need to go wrangle Malek, per Molly's request."

"Oh? What did he do now?"

Faye heaved a sigh. "Exist."

CHAPTER TWENTY-THREE

FAYE SKIPPED seeing Malek and went straight for her motorcycle. With the machine between her legs, she pulled out of the garage while Molly pulled in. Cursing her luck, Faye tried to escape, but Molly was fast and grabbed her wrist to keep her still.

"Where are you going?"

"Out." Faye was thankful for the helmet hiding every facial reaction she had.

"There is no reason for you to be out tonight."

"Other than I want to be. I did my chores, Mom." Rolling her eyes, Faye shifted to a more relaxed stance. "I can go have some fun."

"You're going to get more drugs."

Faye didn't want to respond, though she doubted she could hide it much more. Molly was anything but stupid. Her shoulders tensed, and she pulled her helmet off to give her more time to find an answer.

"This is the first time I've been sober in weeks, Molly. What makes you think I'm going to go get more drugs?"

Molly's dark brown eyes narrowed in her direction, eyeing her up and down. Faye shuddered. She loved having that gaze on her, and she wanted to feel it again over and over. No matter what she did, it was as though she was addicted to everything Molly. Molly was her drug of choice, but she was also one she couldn't freely have whenever she wanted.

"I want you to talk to your friend."

Groaning, Faye settled her helmet on the bars of her bike. "That is stupid. He doesn't know anything."

"He knows something. Joel agrees. More Tainted have been coming to us where these drugs are concerned."

"He wouldn't talk to you, would he?"

Molly's tongue dashed against her lips before her jaw clenched. Faye inwardly smirked, knowing she had caught Molly right where she didn't want to be caught. "No."

"And did you torture him like last time as well?"

Molly drew in a sharp breath. "He wouldn't answer my questions."

"What the hell? He's a troll that you've put in a prison of constant torture and then you up and go add more pain to that and expect him to answer you? That's not how to get information."

"Lofty coming from the likes of you."

Faye gritted her teeth.

"You know I may use my skills to my benefit, but rarely do I cross the ethical boundary into torture."

Molly gave her a hard stare.

"What crawled up your butt these last few days? Seriously. Everyone has avoided you."

Brushing a hand through her hair, Molly stared from the Tesla to the door to the garage that would lead her inside. Faye had a feeling she was looking to run, which was also very unlike Molly. Normally she would confront this head on. Faye cocked her head to the side, wanting and waiting for an answer. Since when had she become the patient one?

"I don't have time for this." Molly turned to leave, but Faye gripped her arm this time.

Something compelled her to try and get an answer. Whatever it was, clearly it was a weight she hadn't expected to bear. "No, you do."

Molly's lips thinned. "I don't."

"Then make it." Faye held Molly's gaze. "I'll tell you this is reminiscent of your curse, and the boys are pretty scared of you right now. I had the advantage to not being here for that."

"You wouldn't understand."

Faye snorted. "Well, with that attitude, I certainly won't. Grow up, Molly."

Plopping the helmet back on her head, Faye roared the engine to life on her bike. She pressed down on the clutch and was about to release the gas when Molly's hand on hers stopped her again. Easing up so the engine made less noise, Faye focused on Molly.

"I had a sister, and he killed her."

"So you torture him daily for the rest of his life?"

Molly's eyes widened. "It was an unjustified killing."

Faye got into Molly's face. "Since she was your sister, I'm going to also assume she was a witch—"

"She was a half-witch."

Surprised, Faye pointed a finger at her. "We're going to come back to that because you have not shared that one with me. Either way, she had some sort of magical power since she is your sister, which means she was able to protect herself, and knowing you as I do, I strongly suspect you and she were in the middle of something you probably could have avoided if you'd just stuck to yourselves. So was it really unjustified? And is torturing the Tainted who killed her for thirty years a justified reaction?"

When Molly said nothing in response, Faye shook her head and revved her engine. In second, she sped out of the garage. Her first stop was to see her friend under the bridge. He transformed only his head as soon as she arrived. Faye had no idea why Molly had allowed only his head to be free from the prison on occasion, but she was glad for it.

Climbing up on his hand and then his arm, Faye made her way up to him. She patted his cheek and pressed her forehead to his rough leathery skin. "How bad was it?"

"What do you speak of?"

"Don't try to hide it from me. I talked to Molly, and I know what she did. How bad was it?"

He didn't answer, which meant it was awful. Faye ran her fingers over his skin and closed her eyes. On a deep breath, she had made a decision.

"I'll go get you something."

"I do not need it."

"Stop being the tough guy. Take what I can offer, please."

He remained silent. Faye was about to climb down when she stopped to give him one last look. He was already shifting back into his stone facade that was his protection. Faye got onto her bike and sped off toward the docks. She should have gone there first. She'd known Molly had done something to him, and she should have gone to get him something to ease the pain before even thinking about seeing him.

The man in the red cap was in a new spot. He probably had to move for fear of getting caught by someone. He was a few blocks away from where she'd last found him. Faye pulled her helmet off and shook her hair out before straightening her back and stalking toward him.

As soon as he saw her, he grinned, his rotted teeth making an appearance. She was so glad she'd never have to deal with that. One distinct advantage to being a vampire she had learned to love from the start.

"Hello, my friend," she started.

"Ryan. Come once again for what I can offer?"

"Yeah, but not as much this time. It's for a friend."

"It's always for a friend now. When do I get to serve you again?"

Faye pressed her lips together. "Probably not for some time. Would you mind? My friend is in a lot of pain."

He held out the bag, and Faye slipped him some money. She pocketed the drugs and popped her helmet back over her head. She would be happy to never see him again, but he had always been good to her. She would have to stop seeing him at some point because he'd figure out she wasn't aging and she'd have to find a new dealer if she were to continue to visit her friend under the bridge, but until that time came, she was going to use him.

As soon as she was back at the troll, she injected the drug into his neck. He sighed as it worked through his system. Unlike her, he took very little drugs to ease his pain and find a high. Something about the makeup of their bodies. She'd read about it in one of Molly's books ages ago when she'd been curious enough to go searching and, well, bored enough.

She could tell when the drugs hit him fully. The tension in his face eased up and he seemed far more relaxed. Faye sat on his shoulder and waited for him to be able to talk with her.

"Thank you, my friend."

"Any time." She patted his cheek again. "Any time. And I'm sorry about what she did."

"Her anger is justified."

"Why does everyone keep saying that when it's not? Ugh, I don't want to talk about Molly. She's got her own demons to slay, and I'm not about to help her with them. She'll figure out she's wrong at some point."

"So upstanding."

"Not always." Faye's eyes scrunched. "I've always been hot or cold when it comes to ethics and morals, you know that."

"Not always."

She chuckled. "You're right. I used to follow all the lines. I thought it made me more human."

"You are Tainted."

"I am." The acceptance settled into Faye's chest. She had tried to play at being human for so long she'd forgotten to even think about her Tainted nature, which had been exactly what she wanted, but it hadn't landed her in a good place at all. At least now she mostly accepted both sides of herself.

"I was wondering if you knew where I could get more of that new drug."

"I told you to stay away from it." Anger laced each of his words, and it was the fastest she had ever heard him speak. "It is not good for you."

Faye furrowed her brow. "I've only taken what I can handle."

"You have taken it? And survived?"

"Yes."

They lapsed into a silence. Faye brushed her fingers together as she thought about all he was saying. Her question was twofold. She wanted more drugs, especially since she'd lost the last bunch, or at least, couldn't remember where she'd stupidly hidden them in the throes of taking far too much, but she also didn't want Molly to come back and question him. If she could get the answers Molly was looking for, then it would be better for everyone.

"The same as before," he answered.

"I met some of your people down there, but I suppose you already thought that might happen. I had to use your name to stay out of trouble."

He chuckled. "They do not like Molly."

"I don't suppose they would."

"They like you."

"Have you spoken with them?"

He gave a slight nod.

Faye drew in a breath. She hadn't realized how he must have missed them. From what she'd read, trolls were a closed community. They needed every one of them to survive. Faye put her palm flat against him. "Are they making the drug?"

"No."

"Then why are they giving it out if they're Tainted. I mean, this drug kills us, you've said so yourself."

"They are not."

Faye drew in a sharp breath. "Then why did you send me to get it from them?"

"They collect it."

"To keep it from others. Why didn't I think about that before." Closing her eyes, Faye let out a sigh. She should have known he would be trying to help instead of trying to incite. There was nothing in it for him if all Tainted were gone. If Molly died, then he'd never get out of this prison, though perhaps someone from the fold might be able to undo the spell, without Molly out of the way, she likely wouldn't let them.

"Thank you, my friend."

He turned to her. "Be careful, friend. This drug is dangerous."

"I know." She leaned in, kissed his cheek tenderly, and pushed back so she could walk down his shoulder and then his arm to her bike. She gave him one last wave and mounted. She had at least one more stop that night before she headed back to the odd little whitewashed house.

The sewers were the same. She wasn't quite sure why she expected them to be different, but they had been quiet for weeks instead of with the loud booming of music that normally would play there. Maybe that was what she looked for.

Instead of following the path down the club, she moved along the path she had taken the last time she was there. The trolls were the obvious answer to get more information, whether Molly had wanted to admit that or not, though she suspected Molly wouldn't be able to get answers from them. She had burned that bridge and continued to keep the flame lit.

The soft moss ground gave way to dirt, and Faye continued to move. She used the electricity in her fingers to light the way. Stopping short, she narrowed her gaze at the corner of a rock. Curious, she bent down and moved it, then dug with her sharp nails into the hardened soil. It took her a few minutes before she felt the smooth confines of the baggie. Grinning, Faye pulled out the bag of pills she had hidden.

"Well, lookie here."

She shoved them into her leather jacket and zipped the jacket closed to keep them in place. Facing down the trolls again was not necessarily something she wanted to do, but she had to see them and know if her friend was hinting at something else.

She was just about to step into the wide, pitch-black room when she stopped short. Perking her ears up, Faye listened carefully. Rapid breathing echoed all around her. Her heart ramped up its pace. She wanted to step back, but answers loomed. Staying completely still, Faye waited to see what was going to happen next. If she moved, they might attack. If she didn't, they still might attack.

The breathing became heavier. For someone with superior eyes, it pissed her off to no end that she could see nothing in the dark. Waiting with bated breath, Faye listened to see if she could figure out where they were. More than one surrounded her, but her back seemed to still be free, though she wasn't sure how long that would be.

Molly had known where she'd gone, but she'd done a good job of pissing Molly off before she left too, so it could be a while before anyone came looking for her. She had to calm down, think of a plan to get out of there, and go from there. Swallowing down the bile and fear working its way around her belly, Faye shifted her foot back.

The breathing turned into a growl.

"Fuck," she muttered.

Faye spun around, flinging her hand out with electricity from her fingers into any direction she thought they might be. She couldn't even see what they hell they were, but they were not trolls. She hit nothing. Not bothering to create another electrical field, Faye booked it the way she had come in. One of them caught up to her, grabbing her ankle and dragging her down so she landed hard on her face.

It pulled at her pants, shaking her leg as its head whipped side to side. The tingles in Faye's chest worked overtime, and she let loose. Her nails elongated, and her fangs descended. Flipping over, Faye kicked hard, knocking the creature back, the creature she still didn't have a good view of. Crying out, Faye winced as more fangs sunk into her arms and into her shoulder.

"Fuck this," she muttered, her voice low as she pushed to get them off her.

Kicking and screaming out, she managed to sink her nails into the side of one of them. Hot wet fluid poured over her hand as she ripped out whatever she could grab at. She must have done some good damage if not killed the creature because she flung something wet and sticky away from her.

Reaching for the next one, Faye did the same. She ripped her way through them until they gave up and ran out toward the exit into the street. Faye lay still, catching her breath. Reaching up, she checked her store of drugs and found them safe and tucked inside her jacket. As much as she wanted to continue down to the trolls for a chat, she knew she wouldn't be able to do that with the rampage of beasts running wild on the surface. She still had no idea what they were.

Faye pushed herself up to sit and recalled her vampiric form. Ben would be able to shift as fast as her eventually. The thought of him made her smile as she turned onto her knees and used the wall of the sewer to help her stand up. Creating the electric field, Faye held her hand around the ground to try and see what it was that had attacked her.

Blood littered the now damp soil but no creatures. Cursing again, she took a step toward the club. She had to warn Molly at least, get someone out there to do damage control because that was all it could be with a pack of something running loose. Faye reached for her phone but had no service that far underground. Groaning, Faye stumbled her way toward the entrance to the sewers. She stopped short when she saw the black fur, the hind legs, the barely rising and falling chest.

"So I did get you." Smirking at herself, Faye knelt down just as the beasts last breath shuddered through its body.

When it didn't transform into a human form, she was confused for a moment. Running her fingers over its head, she sighed. She still had no idea what creature it was. It looked like a wolf, but its tail was long and covered in scales while the rest of its body had black fur all over it. Whatever it was, it was ugly. Snapping a picture of it on her phone, Faye stood up straight and booked it for the surface. She had to call Molly, as much as she didn't want to.

CHAPTER TWENTY-FOUR

MALEK HAD spent over a week in the medical bay before Amachon finally released him. Faye walked through the halls with a purpose in her steps, her high on a low level since she'd gone back to cutting the pills into quarters before taking them. Malek stopped her with a hand on her arm, and Faye spun into him, smiling in his direction as she hoped it came off as seductive. She was pretty sure that was still what she was supposed to do with him, but she and Molly hadn't talked about it recently.

His lips worked up into a saccharine smile. It set Faye on edge. She cocked her head to the side as she eyed him to figure out what he was up to. Malek had never been this sweet with her. His demeanor was normally far more standoffish, but she supposed that could have changed since she'd fucked him into oblivion, though she'd done that more to save Molly from the task.

"Yes?" she asked, still trying to get some sort of answer from him.

"How are you?"

"I'm fine." Faye raised an eyebrow as she judged him. "And you? You're the one who has taken far longer to recover."

"I'm well, thank you." He gripped her upper arm. "I see the cleanse was a folly."

"Oh?"

"You've been taking more drugs."

"Not as much." Faye winked at him and leaned against the wall in the corridor. She wanted to see how far she could take this. She did have to gain his trust, make him think she liked him, which was almost a feat in and of itself. It wasn't that she disliked him. He was useful for information, but that was about it. She was pretty sure all he saw in her was vampire, which was such a stark contrast to Molly.

As she anticipated, Malek moved against her, his body pressing into hers. He kissed the corner of her lips. "Let's go out."

"Out where?"

"Let's get out of this house."

"Malek," Faye put a hand on his chest, "You'll have to tell me why we're leaving not just that we're leaving."

He kissed her neck. Dutifully, Faye turned her chin up and gave him more access.

"Is it for a date?"

"I thought we might be able to find some information for Molly. She's been in such a sour mood lately, I thought perhaps some information on this project of hers might brighten her mood."

"So this is for Molly?" Faye ran her fingers down his side until she reached his hip. She wasn't sure what he was thinking, but sneaking out of the house without Molly knowing would most likely not please Molly at all. In fact, his plan was likely to do the complete opposite, and Faye had just gotten back into Molly's good graces after her argument and the subsequent creature attack.

"Be honest with me, Faye, when do you do something that isn't for Molly?"

Faye could think of plenty of times she ignored what Molly would want and went her own way, including the time she'd literally left the house for months to find her own recovery. The time she'd gotten sober for herself not because Molly had told her to. She wasn't about to tell him that. "You're right, I do everything for her."

"Then let's do this."

"This as in what?"

"You have contacts."

"When do I not?"

"You're in tune enough with Molly's contacts that I would imagine you'd be able to do your own investigation. She's too consumed by research right now, trying to find a cure."

Faye rubbed her lips together and turned to face him, her chin pointing down. She remembered something about Molly saying Malek liked his women submissive. She could play that role. She'd done it on more than one occasion, and when she was born, it was almost natural for women to play that role.

"What research is she doing?"

"Finding a cure."

"Cure for a drug someone can chose to take or not?" Faye walked her fingers up his chest. Maybe she could get him into bed and then the crazy notion of leaving the house would be out of his head.

"For the drug, yes. She wants a counter to it."

"I thought Amachon had tried everything."

"Amachon isn't a witch."

Pouting, Faye turned her chin up to look him in the eye. "You're saying she's looking for a magical cure?"

"Yes." Malek pressed an arm above her head and leaned over her.

"Then why aren't you helping her?"

Malek narrowed his eyes at her. "You know Molly, she works better alone."

"Like you do, I suppose."

"And yourself."

Faye couldn't help the chuckle that left her lips. "You're right about that."

"So tell me, Faye, will you try to solve the mystery with me?"

"You ask so nicely, as though I have a choice. I bet I need to go with you so you don't run into trouble."

"I don't have the contacts here you do. Unlike last year when you came to be for help, this time I'm coming to you."

Sighing, Faye knocked her head back into the wall. Her eyes picked up Ben shuffling down the hall, his shoes brushing against the cement as he walked, never even. She would know that gait anywhere. Raising her tone so he would hear, Faye answered, "I guess we could go to the sewers, Malek. I do have a few contacts I haven't resorted to using yet."

"See? I knew you'd be useful."

Faye let out a small noise in the back of her throat. Somehow, she thought Malek meant more than just in this situation. Ben's footsteps stopped. Faye held her breath and kissed Malek swiftly. "Let's go."

Ben's heart raced. Something was wrong with what was happening in that hallway, and he had a gut feeling about it. Taking a chance, Ben held his breath as he loosened every one of his muscles like Faye had taught him. He focused on a spider, small but stealthy. Its eight long legs that would carry him almost anywhere he wanted to go.

As soon as he started shifting, the pain scorched through his body. He bit his tongue until he tasted blood and kept from crying out. He stopped paying full attention to what they were saying as his muscles changed, his bones broke and mended.

As soon as he was an arachnid, Ben let out a breath, the immediately the pain receded although it still lingered in other ways. He crawled up the wall to try and get a better look at Faye and Malek, but they were already heading his way. Faye's eyes darted from side to side and down the hall as they moved, Malek's hand at her back as he guided her. It made Ben's stomach twist.

Faye turned the corner where Ben had been standing and froze, stopping suddenly. Ben panicked for her. Malek gave her a curious look. Faye, in true Faye style, rolled her eyes and shoved him against the wall with her mouth pressed to his. She ran her hands up and down his sides. Her breathing quickened.

Ben's mind spun. He did not want to be witness to any of what was going on. He cringed at just the thought of it. Faye's hand slapped down above Malek's head, only inches from where Ben clung to the wall. Her gaze turned from Malek to Ben, and once more Ben panicked. Inching forward, he stepped onto her pale skin and skittered from her fingers to the top of her hand to the backside of her arm.

His tiny body moved along until he got to her hair where he burrowed his way under the locks at the back of her head. Malek's hand skimmed through the base of Faye's neck and a little into her hair, and Ben moved upward even more. Faye's voice was soft when she whispered to Malek, "I suppose we should save this for another time perhaps."

"Yes. Molly will only be distracted for so long."

Bile worked its way into Ben's stomach. Whatever the two of them were doing, Molly was not to be involved, which worried him. He knew Faye's and Molly's relationship was anything but conventional, and something he really didn't want to know the details of if he thought about it. He saw enough of it by accident, exactly like this, though perhaps this time Faye had done it on purpose for his benefit.

Faye leaned into Malek's side, and his hand was around her waist. Ben relaxed as his hand was far away from where Ben clung to Faye in hiding. It was going to be quite the journey to see what the two of them were up to. They walked to the garage, and Faye handed Malek a helmet for her motorcycle and then popped her own on. Ben had to squeeze against her skull in order to fit into it without getting smooshed.

It took him another few seconds before he was brave enough to walk around to the side and stare out the front of her helmet. They got on the bike, Malek behind Faye as she drove. Her hands twisted on the bars, and the roaring came to life under her. They then were off. Ben barely noticed the movement as he held on to Faye's hair to keep himself steady. He still had no idea where they were going, but he was along for whatever trouble they were going to find themselves in.

Molly's back ached. She'd been holed up in her lab for days with very little breaks. Amachon had checked on her, and informed her he was releasing Malek. Faye had even been in once or twice but that was it. Molly closed her eyes and pinched the bridge of her nose.

Her lab was usually a place of sanctuary for her from the rest of the house, but this time it was so vastly different. Instead of using science to solve the problem, she was using magic, magic she wasn't even sure how to make work without her. Groaning under the pressure and confusion, she straightened her back and rubbed along the small of her back to try and ease the ache that had taken up residence there.

The spell to cleanse was simple enough, but she had to find a way to keep that spell alive without her being present, otherwise she'd be taking over damage control instead of Amachon, and there was no way she could manage that and still focus on solving the greater issue of who was creating the drug and who was distributing it.

Molly walked around the lab, pacing back and forth. Her magic was barely spent. It was far easier to do a cleansing on a blood sample than on a whole body. That was the other issue. With the amount of magic it had taken to cleanse Faye's blood, she wasn't sure she could pour that amount of energy into more than one Tainted at a time without a week of recovery after each incident. Malek had proved unhelpful in that arena, and while she was powerful, her magic was not unlimited.

Needing a break, Molly stepped out of her lab. It felt as though it had been weeks since she'd been outside those four walls. Sighing, she glided down the hallway in her four-inch heels she insisted on wearing and toward the elevator. She took it down, checking on the creatures she'd captured and making sure their habitats were up to date. The centivalk had calmed, and she was pretty sure he was going to start hibernation in the next month, although he'd need to feed a few more times before then.

The skolls were a different story. Their habitat took up the majority of one of the lower floors. They'd designed it to look like the tundra with rocks and trees for them to hide in. They were largely nocturnal, so at night, if they all listened carefully, they could hear them rustling around, howling and chattering at each other. Faye had complained of it on more than one occasion. Molly had put in a work order with Ben to get more soundproofing, but he was thoroughly distracted by advancing his shifting abilities, something Molly was proud of but at the same time she couldn't have him neglecting his duties.

Taking a turn, she went up a few floors until she knew she was close to Benjamin's work areas. Molly walked down the hall with confidence in her step. She was going to have a quick chat with him, remind him of the rest of his work duties, and then she'd be on her way again to work out the problem in her own lab.

When she got to his work area, she was surprised to find it empty. It only confirmed the fact he was neglecting his duties. Rubbing her temple, Molly went back to the elevator and took it up to the next floor. From there she stepped into Joel's office with a scowl on her face, quickly replaced when she saw him sitting with Amachon.

Cocking her head to the side, Molly gave both of them a hard stare and waited for them to speak. It wasn't improper for them to be speaking together, but she had a feeling the conversation was about the very problem she'd been trying to solve. When Joel nodded his head toward the chair sitting opposite the two of them, she knew she had been right.

"We were just discussing this drug," Joel explained.

"Oh?" Molly asked, trying to glean what she could from their already halfway over conversation.

"Faye said she wasn't able to find any information from her contacts downtown. The dealer is never the same, and no one seems to know where the drug comes from since the dealers imbibe and the result in the same fate as everyone else."

Sighing, Molly stiffened her spine. "Except for Faye."

"Her blood," Amachon grunted out. "She is unexpected."

"In quite a few ways."

"She's been taking them again, so she went out and got more drugs."

"Has she?" Molly's eyes widened momentarily. She should have been more in tune with Faye's drug habits, but it was honestly exhausting to keep track of them, and she had bigger issues to try and solve. Placing her hands together in her lap, Molly stared at Joel. "I hadn't noticed."

"You've been locked away in your lab. I'm not surprised."

"Where did she get them?"

Joel shook his head. "Not a clue."

"Have you asked?"

"Which resulted in very evasive tactics which Faye is known for."

"Yes, she does seem to be able to outsmart an answer when she doesn't want to give one." Molly couldn't help the smile that lit up her lips. It was one of the things that attracted her to Faye in the first place. "Speaking of, have you seen Faye or Malek? I wanted to pick Malek's brain over a problem I'm having."

Joel shook his head. "No, not for hours."

Pressing her lips together, Molly stared at him. "Feel her anywhere in the house?"

Concentrating, Joel slowly shook his head. "Actually, no."

"Wonderful." Molly sighed. "Malek?"

"Not him either."

"Perfect." Standing in a huff, Molly walked toward the door. "I'll figure it out on my own then."

"Molly...stay a minute." Joel nodded to Amachon, who left in a scurry. Joel moved to Molly, grabbed her hand and dragged her to the couch with him. "What's going on?"

"Nothing that shouldn't be happening."

"I've noticed the two of them. Their emotions, heightened. I know what happened the other night."

Molly's lips thinned and pulled tight. "It's planned."

"Is it?" Joel gripped her chin to turn it up so he could look in her eyes. "Because what I'm feeling from you something I have never felt before."

"Jealousy," she whispered the word, barely wanting to admit it to herself.

"Yeah."

Molly bided her time before answering, but she knew she'd never get away without giving him some sort of answer, and even beyond that, she knew she'd feel better if she could say it out loud. "There is a reason I never shared with Faye about the fold, about Malek. I won't tell you that reason, but this was one of my fears."

"I'll tell you, Molly, from my experience, although it is slightly breaking ethical lines, I don't think Faye will mind, what she feels for you is vastly different than what she feels for Malek, not just in what she feels but in intensity."

Molly gave a sharp nod. "I need to get back to work."

"Take a break every now and then, please."

"What do you think I'm doing now?" Molly stood after patting his thigh and walked out of the office. That had been enough of a break for her, though she was doubly curious what Faye and Malek were up to that couldn't involve her.

CHAPTER TWENTY-FIVE

FAYE DROVE right to her old friend then passed him by. She didn't want Malek to know who he was or what he was doing under that bridge, though perhaps Malek would be able to release him from the prison Molly had put him in. She still was unsettled by the fact Molly had done it in a moment of grief and rage yet after thirty years still maintained he deserved it.

Parking downtown, Faye stared at the entrance to the sewers. If Malek wanted to find answers, Faye could only think of one group of Tainted who would have some, and the week before when she'd tried to speak with them, she'd been cornered and attacked by stupid dog creatures with creepy ass tails.

She dismounted her bike after Malek got off and pulled his helmet off. He looked so odd with the sleek black helmet on his head and his pristine khaki pants and polo shirt that she was glad when he handed it over to her. Faye settled them onto the bike and put her hands on her hips. Ben was still with her, she hoped, if not he'd have to hitch his own ride back to the house and explain what he'd done to leave it to Molly, but she wasn't about to save him the embarrassment of finding a way home naked, that was his stupid bloody choice.

"What are we doing here?" Malek's voice as full of curiosity.

"This is where my contacts are, though I have to warn you, the last time I tried to go see them I somehow incited a pack of rampant...something. What did Molly call them?" Faye ran her fingers through her hair, tugging to try and find the right name for the creatures. "Trachen, or something like that."

"Trankyn."

"Sure, that." Faye dropped her hands to her sides. "I found a wild pack of them, and they attacked me, and I attacked them. Whatever, it wasn't pretty."

"I heard whispers of that in the house but hadn't thought anything of it until now. They are quite a rare breed to find."

"So is everything we've been finding lately." Faye turned toward the sewer entrance in the back alley between two tall buildings. She'd walked that way so many times she couldn't count, but that didn't mean anything since the blood bath made it easier.

Malek bypassed her comment and stepped closer to the building. "Is it this way?"

"Yes." Faye let out a sigh and walked in front of him. "My contacts are a bit shy about others, so you know. They may not show face if you're with me."

"I'm not letting you go alone."

"Aww, what a cheesy and stupid sentiment." Faye snorted as she bent down and popped the top on the manhole cover. It'd taken her three times of visiting the club to finally ask where the real entrance was instead of squeezing through the way she had gone before. It was much easier to get there this way.

Sliding it off, Faye rolled her eyes at him as she stayed in a squatting position. "I'm a vampire, idiot. I can defend myself. Also, my contacts really don't like witches."

Without another word, she dropped down the manhole, her feet landing on soft mossy ground. She stood still, her eyes adjusting rapidly to the lack of light. None of the soft lights had been on since the massacre in the club. She wondered if the club would ever recover and open back up. She'd heard rumors of similar things happening there but had never witnessed it. Though the trick with the floor and been an interesting insight, and something Molly had clearly already known.

"Ben," Faye whispered as she stared up to see if Malek was coming down. "If you're still with me, prepare for a ride. This is going to get rough."

Malek's feet landed next to hers. "Did you say something?"

"You're hearing things, old man."

Malek's lips quirked up. "I am not old."

"Uh, yeah, you are. Ancient practically." Faye turned to look down the long line of the sewer that would lead her toward the club's entrance. They'd have to go that way before they split off to head in the other direction.

Malek gripped her hand and threw her into the side of the sewer. Her breath left her lungs sharply, but she caught herself before he was pressed against her front again. "It's far easier to do this here without prying eyes."

Faye immediately thought of Ben, if only Malek knew they very likely still had prying eyes, but it also wasn't the purpose of them being there. Faye pressed their mouths together, already working through a plan to put a stop to what he wanted to happen before it got anywhere near that. She drew in a sharp breath when Malek bit her lip hard enough to draw her own blood.

Shoving him back, Faye shook her head at him. Molly may like blood play, but they never spilled her own, and she did it solely for Molly not because she wanted it. Faye reversed their positions and ran her hands up and down his sides before sneaking her fingers under his shirt to caress his skin.

"I really don't think this is the time or the place," she said against his neck as she sunk her dull human teeth into him. She couldn't put her finger on why she resisted biting him as a vampire. He hadn't tried to make the magical bond with her either, and she had no idea why since it would benefit him as much as it would her.

Her high was wearing off, which had also not been in her plans, but Faye had forgotten to bring any more of the drug with her so she'd just have to deal with it. Perhaps the trolls would have more for her and she could slip some without Malek or Ben noticing. Having him along could certainly hinder her ability to get high.

Faye stepped away from Malek with a smirk on her lips. "I thought we were here to see my contacts."

"And we are." Malek heaved a breath.

Faye walked toward the club, following the very familiar path. She glanced behind her at Malek occasionally, sending him heated looks. There was definitely a pull to him like there was with Molly, but it was nowhere near as strong. The connection was interesting, and only proved to her that whatever was between her and Molly was far more than the stupid biological bond that had been created between vampires and witches.

As she wandered toward the door to the club, she felt something crawling along the skin of her collar bone. She was about to reach up and swipe it away when she stopped and held out her hand. A small spider crawled onto her fingers and stood still as she stared down at it. She knew without a doubt Ben sat in her hand. She took another step and put her hand back toward her shoulder until Ben got off it and settled wherever the hell he'd been hiding. It was good to know she'd at least have some kind of backup and he was getting good practice in for his shifting abilities.

"Have you ever been to this club?" she asked Malek.

"Once or twice, I'm surprised it's still functioning."

"It's not right now. It's this way." She turned sharply away from the door to the club and down the secondary path she had never noticed until her friend had pointed it out. The moss still covered the ground, and she wondered if it was the same moss that covered the floor in the club itself. If she bled, would it absorb the fluid like it had everything that night? Had it absorbed the Trankyn she had killed or had Molly disposed of it?

Shaking the thought from her mind, Faye followed the path as it grew darker and darker. She didn't dare use her electrical power since she didn't know where Ben was on her body, and she worried she might accidentally electrocute him if he were to step on her skin while she held the electricity in place. Turning to Malek, she raised an eyebrow at him.

"I can see fine, but if you need some light, you might want to get on that."

"I can see."

"All right." Faye turned back to lead the way. She was pretty sure he couldn't but had no idea why he was so resistant to lighting the way for them with a flame or something. It would make sense for him to do it because he was already tripping up and stumbling and the room they were about to go in was pitch black to the point she couldn't even see.

As soon as she stepped in, Faye knew something was wrong. The entire feel was different. Instead of the easy tension it had been the first time, this time felt far more like the last she'd been there. The call against her head made her ears ring. Malek grunted. Faye urged her body to create electricity so she could see who and what was coming at her.

Whether it was because of the ringing in her ears or whoever was out there being utterly silent, she couldn't hear a thing and figure out where anyone was. Her heart raced. The tingles worked though her body and begged for release, but she had nowhere to aim it at. Pushing to her feet, Faye elongated her nails, hissing and cracking her neck to make a show of her power and abilities.

Malek whimpered. He must have gotten hit by whatever it was

too. Air rushed by her head, and Faye dodged out the way, faster than Malek would have been able to. As whatever had been thrown tumbled against the wall behind her, she realized it was a large rock. No wonder her ears rang.

"We're here to talk!" Faye shouted, her voice low because of her Tainted form, an octave below what it normally was. Malek still whimpered next to her before he grunted and started shouting.

Giving in, Faye shot electricity through her palm. The blue light reached far across the room they stood in but not as far as the end of it. It did give her a good view of a huddled rock-looking creature dragging Malek by his ankle. Faye heaved a breath and ran for him, but she was knocked back by another rock that hit her square in the chest.

She fell against the ground. Her fingers touched dirt, which surprised her. Faye jumped up again, trying to go after Malek. Charging forward, she was shoved back again. Electricity against the dark showed her a large looming face inches from hers. Gasping in shock, Faye scrambled backward.

"Do not move," it whispered.

Faye froze. The noise from Malek's body vanished, his screaming disappearing. She had no idea why he wasn't doing anything. He was still weak no doubt, but he should be able to do something to protect himself. As soon as there was silence, a loud clapping of rock against rock echoed and fire flashed to life in four corners of the room.

She was surrounded by trolls. They towered over her, her friend's size nothing in comparison to these beasts. Drawing her tingles back into her chest, Faye relaxed into her human form. Her ears still rang, and she shook her head to try and get her hearing back to normal but couldn't. Reaching up, her fingers covered in a fine layer of dust she touched the side of her head and found blood dripping down her face. That would heal up soon enough, but they must have hit her harder than expected.

"What do you think you're doing? We're here to talk, nothing more."

The one that knelt before her raised his deep-set eyes as he glanced over her. "He is a witch."

"So?" Faye scoffed and pushed herself to stand. "I'm a vampire, what difference does that make?"

"Lamek."

Faye clenched her fists. "I don't know what you're talking about. He is my friend. What have you done with him?"

"He is a witch."

"So what? You're going to kill him because he is a witch?"

"Lamek."

"Stop saying that!" Faye screeched.

"Lamek is your friend."

Faye was about to rage again when she halted. Every muscle in her body tensed. "You want him to let Lamek go?"

"He is a witch."

"He's not the witch who put Lamek there, and unless he knows what spell she used, he won't be able to do much, trust me. He's not going to be that useful to you."

The troll in front of her cocked his head back and forth, staring at her like he was trying to figure her out. "Vampires and witches are the same."

"We most definitely are not, but if you're going to kill him, I want to see him first."

The troll's leathery lips were wetted with a tongue. Faye cringed at the scent of his breath and waited to see what they would say. This had been unexpected. If she'd known they were going to kidnap Malek, she would not have taken him down there.

"Let him go."

"No."

"Then take me to him. I can make him do whatever you want him to."

Once again she was regarded carefully.

"It's that or you talk to me about these drugs."

"We try to find them."

"I know that. Who is making them?"

"Lamek first."

Growling, Faye's frustration grew. "Answers first."

"No." A large hand came up over top of her and flung down.

Faye found herself encapsulated in a giant fist. She pushed as best as she could to try and pry open his fingers but didn't make a dent. Shifting into her vampiric form, she tried again to no avail. Scratching and clawing at his skin didn't seem to make a difference either since she barely managed to cut his thick leathery skin.

She was dumped unceremoniously onto the ground, hitting her head against a stone before a large metal frame was latched around her. Looking up and around, Faye had no clue where she was. It wasn't pitch black, but she was definitely in a cage of some sort. She touched the bars and tried to bend them, but her strength proved futile. Looking around, she saw Malek pressed against the far end, blood coming from the side of his head like it had hers.

"Fuck." Racing to him, she knelt down and pressed a hand to his cheek. "Wakey, wakey!"

Malek groaned in pain.

"Malek. Wake the fuck up already."

His eyes blinked. "We've got to get out of here."

"Couldn't agree more."

"You're bleeding."

"I can heal myself in a minute." He coughed. "Just need to catch my bearings."

Faye nodded and stood up. She walked around their cage, which was larger than she had originally anticipated. She hoped Ben was still with her, but she hadn't seen him since they'd first gone into the sewers. He could be their only hope to get out of there.

"What do they want?"

Malek surprised her coming up right behind her. She sighed. "Molly put one of their buddies in a prison, not sure if you knew that, and they want you to get him out."

"I can't."

"I know that." Faye turned to look through the bars on their cage again. "I mean, I'm sure you could with more information, but Molly is tricky, and I wouldn't put it past her to put some surprises in there for anyone who did try to get him out."

Malek grabbed her arm. "No, I can't. I don't have the magic to do it."

"You're a witch, and you're older than Molly, so you're more powerful. Why wouldn't you be able to?"

"Long story, but trust me on this one."

"Sure, okay. Whatever." Faye went back to trying to find a way out of where they were. "First things first, we've got to get the fuck out of here."

He snorted. "Agreed."

Chapter Twenty-Six

Molly couldn't get Faye out of her mind, and every time she sat to concentrate on a counteragent to the drug, she would go right back to thinking about Faye. They had been gone for hours at the very least. Surely they wouldn't have gotten themselves into trouble. Staring from her computer to her notes on her tablet in front of her, Molly gave up, knowing that trouble followed Faye no matter where she went.

Walking to Benjamin's work area, she stopped short when he still wasn't there. Curious, she moved to his computer and booted it up. She checked to see who had left the house through the gate at least and found no one except Faye and Malek leaving.

Sighing, Molly gripped her phone and called Joel.

"What's up, boss?"

"Have you seen Benjamin? I need him for something."

"Nope. I think he's working."

"Working where?"

"His computer?" Joel sounded suddenly suspicious.

"I'm in his work area, and he is not." Molly glanced at the door. "I came here earlier and he wasn't here then either."

"I'll be right down."

Molly slipped into Ben's chair and clicked through his computer. She pulled up the cameras in that room specifically to figure out when he'd been in there last. The computer was still rewinding the footage when Joel joined her.

"He said he was going to work in here before he started on that soundproofing problem with the skoll habitat."

"He still hasn't worked on that. Faye has reminded me endlessly."

Joel smirked. "Have you called him?"

Molly's lips parted, and she shook her head. "I haven't."

With his phone to his ear, Joel stood back while Molly continued to go through the video footage. Finding Benjamin was not normally an issue. He was always around when she needed him, and he was never far from his tablet or his computer, both of which were on his desk. Curious she picked up the tablet to look at what he'd been working on last. Sure enough, it was plans for the soundproofing that pulled up first.

"No answer." Joel slipped his phone into his pocket. "You try."

Molly called, but she already had a feeling there wasn't going to be an answer. As soon as it went to his voicemail, she set the phone down and shook her head at Joel. "Do you feel him nearby?"

"No."

Cursing under her breath, Molly went through what footage she could find until he popped up on the screen. It was over seven hours ago. She followed him as he worked a few minutes in the room she and Joel stood in and then left to walk down the hall. It took some trial and error for her to follow him down to the habitat wing.

Her heart thundered when she caught sight of Faye and Malek on the cameras. Joel pressed a hand to her shoulder and gave her a slight squeeze. Molly wasn't sure she wanted to see whatever they were doing, but she couldn't rip her gaze away. Something still didn't sit right about Malek being there. It wasn't because of the fold. It wasn't because he wanted her to rejoin. Something else niggled at the back of her mind.

Malek pressed Faye up against the wall. Ben stopped short before he stepped behind a door and they couldn't see him anymore. Molly paused the video and tried to find another camera that aimed in that direction, but there was nothing. She went through camera after camera and never found him again.

Eventually, giving up, she checked on the footage of Faye and Malek, watched as they walked together toward the elevator and then followed them to the garage where they left. "I'm going to check the videos again. It's as though he just vanished."

"You don't have some weird secret room in there, do you?"

Molly pressed her lips together tightly. She knew it was a

running joke that she had hidden rooms and hallways all over the house, and while it was mostly true, she wasn't about to share that with anyone who didn't need to know. Faye had discovered some of them in her late-night explorations of the house when everyone else was sleeping and Molly was still in the middle of work. Faye had been most interested in the underground tunnels that led to different buildings in the nearby areas, new and different ways to escape Molly's clutches, as Faye had so bluntly put it. Though, she'd never used them to run away. Faye always walked right out the front door with all the confidence Molly wouldn't chase after her.

"We should go check to be sure he's not still there."

Standing, Molly gripped her phone tightly in the palm of her hand. Her magic was strong and ready for whatever may lay ahead. Maybe Ben was stuck in one of the rooms. As they walked, Joel kept pace with her.

"Where do you think Malek and Faye went off to?"

"I'm willing to bet they went to seek out some of Faye's contacts."

"Without telling you?"

"Hmmm, yes. Malek is trying to prove his worthiness."

"So he took Faye?"

"He doesn't have the connections she does, and he's trying to get her help as well."

"For what?"

Molly didn't answer him as she pushed open the door to the room she'd seen Ben walk into. There was nothing in it except some storage items shoved into the back corner of it. Joel stepped out, but something caught Molly's attention out of the corner of her eye. She paused for a moment as she focused on it. Joel popped his head back in.

"Find something?"

"Clothes."

"What?"

"Ben's clothes. He shifted."

"He did what?" Joel's eyes were wide as he pushed Molly to the side and grabbed the neatly folded clothes in the corner of the room. He pressed them to his chest. "Oh my God."

"He'll be fine, especially if he is where I think he is."

"And where's that?"

"With Faye." Molly stalked out of the room, her heels clacking against the cement floor as she swiftly moved toward the elevator.

"Where are you going?"

"To find Faye!"

Joel muttered, "Well, that's a comment you say about every day."

She shot a glare over her shoulder as she pushed the button for the elevator. "You can join if you'd like, or you can stay here and take over. Your choice."

"I'll come."

"Good." Molly stepped into the elevator. "I'll meet you in the garage in ten minutes."

"How do you even know where we're going?"

"Because I know Faye."

"You're the only one."

"Joel, watch your tone. Faye has been an asset to this team for years, you can't deny that."

"I like her better when she's sober."

Molly wanted to voice her agreement, but she kept her mouth shut. It wouldn't do good to share that with him. They all knew it anyway. As the elevator doors opened on the main floor of the house, Molly walked ahead of him and into her room. She had to find Faye, again, but she would. This time she only hoped it wouldn't be as dangerous as the last.

Faye heaved her shoulder into the metal to try to make it budge. She did it so hard, she popped her shoulder out of the socket. Wincing and crying out from the sudden pain, she dropped to the dirt ground and shook her head at Malek. "It's useless."

"Let me help you." He gripped her arm and popped it back into place.

Faye scrunched her nose and let out a sigh. She shouldn't have gotten high so much. It had been weeks since she'd drank from Molly, but between that, the Trankyn attack, and the drugs, her body was wearing out far faster than she intended. Maybe there was a long-term effect to the drugs she hadn't anticipated.

"What are you thinking?" Malek's voice was strong as he spoke as if he hadn't been injured at all, but Faye could see the paleness in his skin and the slowness to his steps.

"We have to get out of here. They're going to go berserk when they figure out you can't do what they want you to."

"Do you know what spell Molly used on Lamek?"

Faye shook her head. "We've never really talked about it."

"What?"

Faye snorted. "Why the hell does that even surprise you? She's a closed book. You know that. I knew she was the one who put him there, but I never asked and she never shared why until just the other day and even then she wasn't very forthcoming about it."

Standing, she walked around the cage to try and find a weak point in it. They hadn't been bothered since Faye had been thrown in there with Malek. They would only have so much energy for so long, and while the others had likely noticed their absence, being found was a different story. Faye wasn't even sure where they were.

"She needs to share with you."

"No shit." Gripping the bars, Faye shook them, but they were welded together so tightly they didn't even rattle.

She nearly sneezed when she felt something crawling on her face again. Resisting the urge to smack it away, Faye nodded toward Malek. "I need to piss. Stay over here."

"I've seen all there is to see of you, Faye."

She glared. "Stay here."

Faye stalked to the far side of the cage over by some large boulders that had been imprisoned with them. She hid behind one of them and held out her hand. Ben crawled down her arm and over to her palm. He again didn't move. Faye had no idea how the hell she was supposed to communicate with a spider, so she just stared at Ben to see what he would do.

Ben spun web and glided from her hand to the dirt floor. She watched as he walked toward the edge of the cage and vanished. Still not sure what the hell he was doing, Faye stared and waited. She only had so much more time before Malek would be wondering what she was up to because she definitely wasn't taking a piss.

She turned to glance at Malek to make sure he wasn't coming closer, and when she turned back around she nearly jumped out of her shoes. Ben stood before her, fully human and fully naked. She kept her gaze up toward his eyes and grinned at him, still not speaking in case Malek heard. He held a finger to his lips to indicate she had been right in not saying anything.

Faye hugged him around the middle before Ben drew in the dirt a crude picture of something breaking and a foot. Ben's body melted in front of her to a small creature no taller than her knee. He moved close to the metal barrier and glanced at her. Faye squared her shoulders as he coughed and a splat of liquid moved from his mouth onto the metal. Faye coughed to cover it up.

"You okay over there?" Malek asked.

"Yeah, just lost my breath for a second."

Ben shifted again, this time vanishing completely from her

sight. Faye tuned her ears into the metal, and it didn't take long before she heard what was happening. His arachnid form crawled up her leg and back onto her shoulder. Normally she would hate to have a spider on her, but since this was her best friend, she let it go for now.

Stepping from around the rock, Faye kept her ears attuned to the metal as it melted away. Ben had been brilliant. "I think I found a way out. There's a weakness in the metal over here."

"Really?" Hope littered Malek's voice.

"Yup. I think I can pry it open."

"Try it. Maybe I can help."

They went back over to the part of the cage Ben had spat on. Faye gripped two bars above where the saliva had come out. She just needed to make the opening wide enough for them to slip through without touching any of the saliva itself. That wouldn't hurt her, but it would do actual damage to Malek.

With a deep breath, Faye pushed against the bars. They didn't budge. She hadn't waited long enough. Faye moved her boot against them and kicked hard, her shoe slipping on the wet metal until she fell into the salvia. The acid burned her skin, eating away at it. Hissing, Faye jerked back and tried to wipe it off her arm and shoulder but got it all over her hand at the same time.

Malek moved in and gripped her hard to keep her still. He stared at the injuries and shook his head. "What is that?"

"I don't know." Which was true. She hadn't known whatever the hell creature Ben had shifted into, but whatever it was, it fucking hurt, and she wasn't healing. Malek reached down into the dirt and threw it onto the wounds.

Faye cried out as her pain doubled, but the continuous spread of the acid did stop as soon as the dirt hit. Tears brimmed in her eyes as she leaned against the boulder she'd hid behind before. Calming her racing heart, Faye waited until she could see through the pain again. Malek leaned right in front of her.

"You need to feed."

"No." Faye sniffed hard. "I'm fine."

"Faye, this drug you've been taking—"

"I said I'm fine, Malek." And she meant it. If she could avoid drinking from him, she would. Faye pushed herself up, sure that she could try it again. If anything, she'd rather take the hit of the acid than Malek. She was much better at healing. Water-like liquid poured from her injuries, wetting the dirt he had put into her wounds.

Faye kicked out and managed to break the metal this time, shattering it until he could safely fit through. She helped him get out first and avoid touching the acid still left on the metal. Faye, however, wasn't so lucky when she slipped through the bars, her leg hitting it again. Hissing, she rolled onto her side and then her back to get away from it. Malek didn't hesitate as he threw the dirt in it again.

Faye gripped his arm and stood up, running. Malek followed behind her as best as he could, but she knew he must still be weak from that head injury. He was far too slow with following her even though she was in her human form.

Keeping her eyes pierced for some place to hide, Faye moved forward without looking back. As soon as they noticed they were gone, they were going to be pissed as fuck, and she did not want to be on the receiving end of that. Faye found a cave and aimed for that. She paid barely any attention to their surroundings as she pushed forward. The more she moved, the harder it became.

Her body ached. The wounds on her arm, shoulder, and leg opened back up. Cursing her own stupidity, Faye dodged into the cave and shoved Malek against the wall, her body covering his as a troll stepped right by them. He held his breath, Faye put her forehead to the cold stone in cold air to her lungs. It felt so good. Maybe she had even accidentally inhaled the damn acid. She was going to have to ask Ben what the hell kind of creature that was because she wanted to murder each and every one of them and suck them dry.

Not that she would, but the thought at least calmed her racing heart. As soon as she could tell the troll was out of the way, Faye stepped back from Malek and shook her head. "We have to hide. I have no clue where the hell we are."

"We're under the city."

"Well, I'm not that stupid." She glanced toward the entrance. "This way."

A roar startled her. Faye jerked with a start and stared to where they had come. Their escape had been discovered. Gripping Malek's hand, Faye took off running. They moved through the dark cave until she had to use her electrical powers to light the way. Malek stumbled so many times she lost count. Her muscles burned so badly she wasn't sure she'd make it to the surface again. Finding a little alcove, Faye shoved Malek in and rested next to him, drawing in as deep breaths as she could. They were going to have to hide out there for a bit until she had enough energy to keep going.

CHAPTER TWENTY-SEVEN

FAYE HADN'T heard from anything that sounded like trolls in at least the thirty minutes they'd been hiding in the tiny alcove. She wondered if they were even small enough to get into the caves, but she really didn't want to find out, or know how they would. Surely they had a way to the surface even if they didn't use it all that often.

She knocked her head back into the stone wall and drew in a deep breath. She'd much rather be down there with Molly, though she was pretty sure if it had been Molly, that they all would have been dead. Molly was preferable for the trolls than Malek, but he'd been powerful enough to for them to know he was worth something.

"Do you know much about trolls?" Faye asked as she tried to will her body to heal. It still wasn't.

Malek turned to look at her. "Some. They're not common in Europe like they are here."

"I don't think they're all that common here."

"Well, now they're not common at all."

Faye glared at him. "Speak, my friend. You obviously know more than I do."

Malek gripped her arm to look at it. "Your injury is not healing."

"It's fine."

"You know how to solve this problem."

"It's not a problem yet. Stop changing the topic. Tell me about the trolls. My friend, Lamek, is a troll, but he's never shared much."

Nodding, Malek released her hand. "Trolls are isolationists."

"Like agoraphobic but trolls not humans?"

"Yes." Malek gripped her hand again. "They don't leave. It's a community thing. They do live longer than humans, but not like us."

"Witches, you mean."

"Correct. Or vampires. A troll may live to be a hundred easily but as soon as they age over that their health drastically declines."

"I wonder how old Lamek is."

"I would anticipate it was fairly young when Molly imprisoned him."

"So she's just going to keep him there the rest of his life?"

Malek shook his head. "I don't know Molly's intensions with him. I didn't even know she had imprisoned him."

"She did it because he killed her sister."

Malek paled.

Faye cocked her head at him and then narrowed her gaze. "You knew her sister, didn't you?"

"Yes. I knew Pearl."

"Pearl? Her name was Pearl?"

Malek gave the slightest nod. "They were only a few years apart in age, which is very rare for witches."

Faye wanted to correct him the way Molly had, but she held her tongue, keeping that information to herself, not to mention, she knew Ben was lingering around somewhere, and she wasn't sure how much Molly had shared with him. "Because you guys are control freaks."

Snorting, Malek nodded. "You could say that."

"No, I know it. It's ingrained in Molly's blood. Trust me. She can't let go of anything."

"I believe that is why she likes you so well." Malek reached up and cupped Faye's cheek. "She can't control you as much as she wants to."

"Pretty sure it's my ass she likes." Faye held a finger up to her lips to quiet him. Malek understood and remained silent. Faye stared out at the entrance to the little alcove they had found because she thought she heard something off in the distance.

Sure enough, she could hear something burrowing its way through the tunnel they had traveled down. Faye swallowed as panic worked its way into her chest. There was no way out of the alcove they had found themselves in. She was going to have to fight whatever it was, and she was pretty darn sure it wasn't a troll.

Faye pushed to her knees and waited for it to come. Malek stayed quiet, leaning against the wall. She glanced back at him. If this went how she figured it would, she might have to take his energy like he'd offered, though she wouldn't have any time to make the bond or make it pleasurable for him like she preferred.

Whipping her head toward the entrance, Faye braced her body. The pawing, the growling, the heavy breathing. It was all reminiscent of what she'd heard the last time she'd come to make contact with the trolls. Faye tensed her muscles, preparing for when they'd shift around and smell them. She had no doubt they were following the blood trail.

She bounced on her toes as her energy kicked up to full gear. She changed into her vampiric form at the last minute and hissed as she pushed her way out into the main part of the tunnel, taking one of the trankyns with her. Its head lodged against the wall, bursting with blood that made her nose scrunch from it. Malek would be a much better option than whatever the hell these things were, though if it was down to live or die, she'd drink from it.

Three more came at her. Two took her arms while the third landed its paws right on her chest. Faye groaned as she landed hard on the ground, the air pushed from her lungs. She dug her long black nails into the neck of one of them, ripping as much of it with her as she tore her hand away. It cried before its breath was gone.

Faye focused in on the next one, the one gnawing at her already acid-eaten arm. She briefly wondered if Ben had jumped off her or if he was still planted somewhere as she fought off the next creature. She flung it hard, her feet kicking out until it landed with its brethren dead against the wall. She was far more prepared this time than she had been the last, which was to her advantage. And she could see better, though her eyes kept blearing over when she least expected it.

Crying out as heat and liquid surged around her neck, Faye curled in on herself. Everything was difficult. It was hard to breathe, hard to think, hard to move her limbs. She must have blood pouring from her somewhere. Having to refocus her brain and her eyes, Faye looked up just in time to see the trankyn pounce at her. She lifted her arm to block him but failed. Drawing in short sharp breaths, Faye did the only thing she could think of. She plunged her hand in the direction she knew it was in. Her fingers collided with something soft, something that burst and streamed liquid down her hand and arm to her chest.

Claws dug into her chest as it tried to get away, but she couldn't bring herself to pull out. Faye wrapped her arm around its body and pulled it in tighter to her, digging her deadly fingers in farther to whatever bit of flesh she'd managed to get hold of. When it finally collapsed on top of her, she wasn't sure she had the energy to get it off. She laid there, completely silent and still until Malek came over and pushed the thing off her chest.

Faye gasped. Malek dragged her back toward the alcove, but they only made it to the entrance when he shook his head at her. "You're out of options."

"Shit balls." She expected him to offer a wrist.

Instead Malek kissed her hard as his hands skimmed up to her cheeks. Holding her head as his tongue swept around hers, small nicks here and there appearing on his flesh, she tasted him. Every witch had a unique flavor, at least of all the ones she'd taken energy from, but Malek did not taste good.

He moved from her mouth down to her chin and her neck. She still didn't feel the bond begin, which she assumed he would start since he'd need magic as much as she would need energy. Confused but not willing to give up what he was offering so freely, Faye plunged her teeth into the side of his neck as she gripped the back of his head to hold him still.

The rotten flavor hit the back of her tongue, and she wanted to withdraw from him. Instead, she swirled her tongue in circles, soothing the bite and easing the blood flow. She took as much as she thought she could stand and he could lose before moving away. Without warning, Malek kissed her, this time not as furiously and with far more tenderness.

When he slowed until he pulled away, he closed his eyes. "Molly doesn't know what she has."

Faye was about to ask him what he meant when she jerked with a start as Ben stared at them over Malek's shoulder, his hands on his hips and a glare on his face.

Ben had seen everything. From Faye saving Malek, to her idiotic attempt to fight her way out of the cave. He decided he couldn't hide any longer. They had to talk to form a plan to get out of there. He was the only one who could travel around without being suspected since no one knew he was even there. Shifting in the dark corner of the cave, Ben watched as Faye took energy from Malek, as they kissed, as they connected.

When they finally stopped, he wasn't sure what to say. He'd

listened to Faye defend Molly's attraction to her, listened as Faye insisted Molly and she were together, but then this? He didn't understand it in the least. This was different than what he and Joel had done with Molly years before, and as soon as Faye had shown up, that had all stopped.

Faye stared directly at him, her chest rising and falling as Malek continued to kneel over her. Her voice was the first to ring through the quiet of the alcove. "We have help."

"What?" Malek asked as he sat back on his haunches and turned around to face Ben. "Should have known. You're what got us out of the cage?"

"The one and only." Ben glared at him. He hadn't liked Malek much from the start, but this whole weird relationship thing he was doing with Faye was pushing it toward the edge of downright hatred. "You can thank me later when I get us out of here."

Faye smiled. "Glad to see you embrace your shifter nature."

Ben didn't say anything to her. He still wasn't fully comfortable being naked, but there was no other option at that point. He walked into the cave and back. Squatting down, he gripped Faye's arm and dragged her up until they were covered in shadows.

"What's the plan, Benny-boy?"

"I told you not to call me that."

"This is your day, Ben. Tell us where we're going."

"I'll have to explore a little."

"Then do that. I'm going to take a minute more because of this acid shit you decided to use. What the hell was that thing, anyway?"

"Cropeck."

"Seriously? I'll have to look that up in the database when we get out of here."

"If we get out of here."

"Then find us a way out, Ben." Faye sighed and held up her arm to watch as it healed.

Ben wanted to make sure she was in as good a shape as she could be before he walked away from her and left her with Malek and no one as backup. He didn't trust Malek, and he was surprised Faye did.

"I'm going to check out the rest of the cave and see where it goes."

"You do that. I'll stand guard here."

Ben walked away from them and around the corner. So long as no one else or nothing else was coming after them, he was going to stay in his human form. The shifting so much was exhausting him more than he and anticipated.

Ben's bare feet on the dirt was an odd feeling. He was so used to wearing shoes that he struggled to get used to it. A fine layer of dirt covered the hard stone floor, so it was cold but soft at the same time. Focusing on what he could find, Ben wandered around the cave, not too far off that he would get lost. He wished he'd had his tablet with him because he'd be able to map the cave better.

When he got back to the alcove, Faye looked to be in far better condition than when he'd left them. Malek still didn't look all that great though. Ben sat on the ground, trying to hide half his body. Faye tugged off her jacket and threw it at him. Thankful, Ben covered his hips with it.

"I think our best bet is to go farther into the cave."

"Any idea where we are?" Faye asked.

Ben shook his head. "Not one clue. Without my tablet, it's hard to tell. It all looks the same to me, and while I may be Tainted, my eyesight is not as good in this form as yours is."

"Right." She turned to Malek. "You up for walking?"

"I'll have to be."

Ben rubbed a hand along the back of his neck. "I don't think the trolls can fit down the cave, but that doesn't mean they don't have more creatures to send in after us."

"They're pissed," Faye commented.

"How can you tell?"

She pointed to her ear. "I can hear them. They're moving around more than I have ever seen them."

"You've seen them before."

Faye locked eyes with him, and she gave a slight nod of affirmation.

"When?"

"Only once before. My friend sent me down here."

"For what?"

Faye pursed her lips. She glanced from Ben to Malek and then back to Ben. "For Inanis."

"For what?"

"This drug everyone is going on about."

Ben wrinkled his nose. "They're making them? Wait, it has a name?"

"No! And yes, it has a name." Faye held her hand up to stop him from continuing. "They are not making them. They're actually collecting them from dealers, or they're sending people to do it? I don't know. But they're trying to get it off the streets and out of the hands of Tainted."

"Interesting," Malek whispered. "They don't come to the surface, so they're definitely sending someone else out."

"They don't come to the surface?" Ben asked.

"Never." Malek stared at Ben. "That's why the punishment for Lamek is so humiliating. He's forced to the surface for onlookers to stare at and admire him. It's literally degradation every second he's stuck there."

"Wonderful." Faye rolled her eyes.

Ben ignored her. "You didn't finish telling Faye about the trolls."

"Some other time."

Ben couldn't fault Malek. They needed to get out, not get a history lesson, though he was now curious how much Molly had kept from him in the long term of things. She'd help him hide his Tainted side for decades but at what cost. Had she not let him fully into her world because he didn't want to be?

"Ben, focus."

"Yeah. Let's get going before they realize Faye went all vamp on the trankyn."

"Shut it. It was the only way out."

"I know." Faye helped Malek up.

Ben wrapped the jacket as best as he could around his hips and continued to walk. If he had more energy and felt safer, he would shift back into something to hitch a ride with Faye just so he wouldn't have to be butt-ass naked around them. Though, neither Faye nor Malek had commented on it. He led the way as Faye kept her arm wrapped around Malek's waist while they walked.

Chapter Twenty-Eight

FAYE GRABBED Ben by the shoulder and held him still as she listened.

"What is it?"

"I hear cars."

Ben grew a broad smile. Faye pointed up. She had no idea how far below the surface they were, but they had to be decently close for her to hear them. Faye walked a little faster as the sounds grew louder.

Ben helped Malek while Faye moved ahead of them. Something else was coming up behind them in the tunnel, and she did not want to find out what it was. Faye shifted into her vampiric form and ran as fast as she could until the rock under her foot changed to be harder and more solid. Slowing down, she saw the door out in front of her.

Faye pushed it open, finding a tried-and-true sewer line. The bottom was covered in at least six to twelve inches of sewage, which she turned her nose up at, but there was a door, which meant they could shut out whatever was coming.

Racing back, Faye stopped and pressed her hands to her knees. "We've got to move. Ben, you're going to have to either shift into the spider or something that can run fast."

"What? Why?"

"Something is coming."

"What about Malek?" Ben pointed his thumb in Malek's

direction.

"I'm going to have to carry him."

"You will not," Malek argued.

"Try me. I dare you." Faye glared at him. Ben shook his head. "Come on, Ben. I know it hurts, but you've got to. I can't carry both of you at the same time like this and we've got to move. They're not that far behind us."

"What is it?"

"I have no idea, and I don't want to find out, but it slithers. It doesn't run."

Ben shuddered before he tensed.

"Loosen your muscles, Benjamin. Don't tense."

"It hurts."

"It'll hurt more like that." Faye pointed at him and transformed into her vampiric form. Malek glared at her before looking at Ben whose body morphed in front of them to the skoll he'd first shifted into. Faye smiled and held her hand out for Malek. "Now. There isn't time."

"How do you know something is coming?"

"I can hear it, smartass. Would you like to wait and find out if I'm pulling your leg?"

"No."

"Good." Faye didn't give him a second chance to back out. She gripped his arm and wrapped his body around her shoulders. Her knees bent under his weight, and he definitely slowed her down, but she was still able to move faster than her human form with him on top of her.

Ben beat her to the door, but he hadn't shifted to open it. Faye set Malek down and opened the door. Ben whimpered at her, but she sent him a serious look right back. He took the hint and hopped through, the splash loud when he landed. Malek climbed through next, and Faye went through last.

She glanced through the door before shutting it behind her. She could only hope whatever the hell was following them didn't have hands. They walked together this time, Faye back in her human form but Ben still shifted into a skoll. Malek hobbled, struggling to slog through the twelve inches of sewage at their feet.

Faye tried to hold her breath, but it was impossible. She was going to burn her skin off when she got to the house, literally. It would be the only way to get the scent off her, and she could take the pain. With Molly's blood, she'd even be able to heal right away unlike with Malek's. Thinking about his blood caused the bile to rise in her throat again, and she had to swallow it down. His blood had done the trick in a pinch, but there was something off about it. She'd have to ask Molly.

It didn't take them too long to find a ladder and a manhole. Faye went first because she was the only one with thumbs and not a bruised ego. As soon as she breathed in the fresh air, she felt so much better. She stayed up there, helping Malek out and then Ben after he shifted back to his human form. Faye handed over the jacket as they leaned against the brick building wherever the hell they were.

Faye covered the manhole again and walked toward the road from the alley they'd found themselves in. She glanced around, looking up and down the street to try and figure out where they were. Grabbing her phone, she called the only person she could think of who wouldn't ask questions first.

"Molly."

"Where are you?" There was a sense of urgency in Molly's tone, a hint of fear, but also a touch of anger, which was what Faye had hoped to avoid.

"Um...downtown."

"Where downtown?"

Faye scrunched her nose. "The other side of downtown, in my old neighborhood. Bring the van would you? Malek is—I don't know, weak. Ben is fine though, but naked if you can bring some clothes."

"Benjamin is with you?"

"Ben?" Joel's voice was loud through the line.

"Yeah. Were you looking for him?"

"We'll be there in thirty minutes."

Hanging up, Faye wandered back down the alley. She looked at both of the men she was with and shrugged. "Molly said she'll be here in thirty."

"You called her?" Ben's eyes widened.

"Who else was I supposed to call?"

"Joel."

"He's with her." Faye rolled her eyes. "Besides, I'm not going to walk back to the house with you naked and Malek here barely able to stand on his own."

She saw Malek's lips part to object, but she cut him off by holding a hand up to stop him.

"Molly was going to find out anyway. This way, we can go into the conversation expecting the interrogation."

"Interrogation?" Malek questioned.

"Oh yeah. She's not going to let this go," Ben added in as he shifted the jacket on his hips.

"So what's our story?" Faye asked.

Malek shook his head and turned to Ben. "How did you follow us?"

"I uh...caught you talking in the hallway and shifted into a spider and hitched a ride on Faye."

She tried to hold back her smirk, knowing Ben had done that the entire time, but she let him. It was a good experience for him and good practice. Though, she could have done without being nearly killed herself or being imprisoned.

"You can tell her that," Faye pushed. "She'll get mad at me for letting you come with us."

"I'm not going to dump her anger all on you."

Faye lifted one shoulder in a half-shrug. "Might as well. I can use that to my advantage."

Ben narrowed his gaze at her before he flushed. "I don't want to know that."

"You knew it already." She laughed. "But first I think we all need to hose ourselves off."

"Did you tell her that?"

"Uh, no. I was worried she'd make us walk home if she knew that."

"She wouldn't—" Malek started.

Faye interrupted. "Oh, she would. She's done it before."

"You've been in the sewers before."

"Many, many times." Faye winked at him. Stretching her back, she walked out toward the road again. It hadn't been that long since she'd hung up the phone, but she had a feeling Joel and Molly were already in a vehicle when she'd called, something about the closeness of Joel to be able to hear Faye and the sounds in the background.

Sure enough, just as she had anticipated, the van turned around the corner up ahead. Faye stepped back toward the alley as soon as she knew they'd seen her. Joel was driving, and he pulled up at the curb. Molly was out of the vehicle in two seconds, anger written all over her beautiful face.

"What were you thinking?" She stopped short of walking right into Faye.

Faye grinned. "Oh, is there something wrong?"

"The sewers? Again?"

Faye laughed. "Got the clothes?"

Joel came around with a pair of sweats from the back of the van, which meant they hadn't gone home and they had been driving around somewhere when she'd called. Faye grabbed them and stalked to the dark recesses of the alley. Tossing them at Ben, she helped Malek to stand and wrapped an arm around his waist as he wrapped one around her shoulder.

They moved together toward the van. Molly crossed her arms over her chest as she glared at the two of them. Faye raised an eyebrow in her direction, daring her to make one more comment about what they were doing out there, but Faye was not going to answer when everyone else was around.

She helped Malek into the back, and he closed his eyes as he leaned against the wall of the van. She patted his knee in comfort before shutting one half of the back doors. Ben jumped in after, the sweats super loose on his hips to the point that he had to hold them up with a hand, but they were at least better than her jacket, which he handed to her.

Faye snorted. She was going to burn every article of clothing she wore including her boots because there was no way she was wearing them again after that experience. She shut the door behind Ben and was about to turn to walk toward the side door when Molly stopped her with a hand on her arm.

"We're going to talk about this," Molly's clipped British tone was clear.

"I've no doubt of that." Faye raised a defiant eyebrow at her.

"You can't leave like this without telling me where you're going."

"Nothing was supposed to happen."

"Nothing is ever supposed to happen, Faye. This is why we communicate."

"Look who's talking about communication."

Molly's lips parted in surprise. "I don't want to argue right now."

"Then why are we still talking."

Molly paused before she spoke. Stepping in closer, she cupped Faye's cheek and brought their mouths together in a tender and brief kiss. "I'm glad you're all right."

"I'm perfect. But I want to talk to you about Malek."

"Did you find something out?"

"Maybe. Later, when there aren't so many ears."

Molly nodded sharply and kissed Faye again before she stepped away to get into the passenger seat. The aroma of the three of them in the closed confines of the van was nearly too much. Joel rolled down every window possible but it still reeked to high heavens. As soon as they pulled into the garage, all the doors were opened and Faye shot out of it as fast as she could.

Molly helped Malek to stand and sat him in a wheelchair Faye had brought over. She knelt before him and drew in a sharp breath. "What else is broken?"

"Broken?" Faye's voice echoed. "He didn't break anything. He got hit in the head with a rock."

Molly's eyes widened as she turned to look over her shoulder at Faye. "His ankle is quite obviously broken."

Faye bent at her waist and looked at it. Sure enough, Molly was right. Whenever he had done that, she had no idea, but she wasn't about to ask either. Malek would tell Molly whatever he wanted to. Faye was about to wheel him out of the room when Molly stopped her with a glance.

Molly placed her bare hands on Malek's disgusting pants and sock and shoe. Faye gagged. Molly shot her a glare, her eyes already turning golden as her magic worked through her body and into him. She drew in a sharp breath and shifted. Faye knew the break lanced through Molly's ankle before healing itself completely.

Her body glowed for longer as she no doubt made sure Malek had no other injuries. When Molly moved away from him, she stared up at Malek and then shifted her glance to Faye. "It's far harder to heal yourself than another."

Faye couldn't figure out why there was an explanation being given, especially considering Malek obviously did not have the magical ability Molly did, for whatever reason. Shifting in her stance, Faye scrunched her nose.

"Does this mean he can shower on his own now?"

"I don't see why not." Molly pushed herself to stand and held out a hand for Malek. "He is well and healed."

Malek pressed his hand into Molly's and stood up. His cheeks were still pale, but he was at least moving better than he had been before. Faye rolled her eyes as he stared down at Molly, definitely looking down her shirt. Faye had done that on so many occasions there was no way to count them all.

"Good, because I feel disgusting." Faye let go of the handles on the wheelchair that they weren't going to use and stalked out of the garage, leaving the two of them on their own. She beelined it for her room and the bathroom.

Stripping out of her clothes, she dropped them into a plastic bag and tied it shut tight before hopping in the shower, turning the water on as hot as it would go. It might burn, but she hadn't lied when she'd thought about burning her skin off so it would regrow. She scrubbed and scrubbed her entire body to try and get rid of the stench.

The water at her feet was so murky to begin with she could barely stand to look at it. By the time she'd been in there thirty minutes and was running out of soap, the water was at least clear. Dunking her head under the spray, Faye cleaned out the dust and the dirt she'd accumulated between the cage and the cave, tunnel, alcove, whatever they had managed to find themselves in.

She checked her arm and her leg, finding the skin completely healed. Her stomach still churned at the lingering flavor of Malek's blood. It was so odd. She'd never been so turned off by blood before. Well, the thought of it, yes, but not the actual blood she'd consumed. She always found that enticing.

The door opened, and Faye popped her head out of the curtain to find Molly raising an eyebrow at her, arms crossed, and her dark curly hair in tumbles around her shoulders. "When you're done—"

"Yes, we'll talk."

"I'll be outside."

Faye moved back into the shower. Somewhere in the back of her mind, she had hoped Molly would wait for that conversation, but that last hope had been dashed. Distracted by Molly's presence, Faye finished her shower, wrapped a towel around her middle, glared, and turned her nose up at her ruined clothes and left the bathroom.

CHAPTER TWENTY-NINE

MOLLY SAT on the edge of Faye's bed as she listened to the water turning off in the ensuite bathroom. She'd thought about starting with the others, but Faye's comment outside the van had pulled her in this direction.

When Faye came out, wrapped only in a towel, her skin pink and moist since she hadn't bothered to dry herself, her hair dripping onto the floor, Molly's heart clenched. She gripped her hands tightly together in her lap and dragged her gaze up and down Faye's body.

"Like what you see?" Faye's voice was strong, edgy, toward a tone of anger.

Molly was breathless. "Always."

Faye's hardness softened, and she stepped toward Molly, plopping down on the bed next to her. "I want to burn those clothes."

Smiling, Molly held open her palm, found a flame in it and then closed her fist. "Done."

"I wanted to do it." Faye pouted.

She shrugged. "They reeked, Faye. Trust me, this was the faster and better way."

"I trust you."

"Do you?" Molly turned her chin up at Faye, her hair dragging over her shoulder. "I wasn't sure after tonight."

"Look, you wanted me to get close to him, so I did. You

wanted me to find out information, I did. That's what I'm doing, nothing more. I really didn't think anything bad was going to happen, especially since the last time it had all gone to shit, but apparently they had more of those little fuckers hidden around there."

"Trankyns?"

"Yeah. Though, it started with the trolls."

Molly drew in a sharp breath. "You met with the trolls."

"Yes." Faye's slate-gray eyes stared straight into her soul. Molly wanted to get out of the conversation without explaining everything, but she also felt she owed Faye the truth.

Molly cupped Faye's cheek. "I'm glad you're all right. Truly."

"I'm fine. Had to drink from Malek. That was gross."

"Gross?"

"He tasted like rotten, moldy cheese."

"What?" Molly's eyes widened as her mind spun.

"Yeah. Most disgusting thing I've ever taken energy from, and I've got say, I've had a lot of nasty things, including already dead things, but this took the cake by far."

"He didn't taste good."

"Yeah. Why? What's that mean?"

Molly's eyes locked of Faye's. "It means he didn't lie."

"What do you mean?"

"They bound his magic. They put a block on him."

"For what? What could he have possibly done to deserve that?"

Molly shook her head. "I have no idea, but it must have been pretty serious. They don't take this kind of betrayal lightly."

"Betrayal? Molly, you're light-years ahead of me here. What's going on?"

"I haven't explained much about the fold to you. That's my own fault."

"You didn't want me to know."

Molly bypassed that comment and moved on. "The fold has immeasurable power if we're all together. As you witnessed last year."

"Yeah. That was…something else, though I was mostly focused on you not killing me at the time."

With a smile playing on her face, Molly brushed a thumb across Faye's full lips. "One of the punishments for betrayal, well, the only punishment, is to have your powers bound. He'll still have access to certain magic."

"Magic like what? Healing?"

"Yes. Because it's benign. He can't harm anyone with it."

"That makes sense."

"What?"

"Well he had quite the cut to his head since we both got smacked in the face with a giant stone."

"Faye." Molly's voice broke, and she moved her hand up to the side of Faye's head, trying to look for an injury she intuitively knew wasn't there. "You should have told me."

"I'm fine. Why aren't your powers bound?"

"Why would they be?"

"You left the fold."

Molly swallowed. "I did, but I had permission."

"You asked for permission?"

Her head bobbed from side to side as she thought about how to answer that question. "I more insisted on permission."

"That makes more sense." Faye grinned.

"We'll have to find out what Malek did to deserve this."

"Was it deserved?"

"No doubt." Molly stared Faye directly in the eye. "The fold does not make these decisions lightly."

"How would he go about fixing it?"

"Depends on what they told him. It could be anything. I've only ever seen this happen one other time in my lifetime, Faye. I mean it when this is a rare punishment for betrayal."

A drop of water moved from Faye's hair over her shoulder and down her chest until it vanished into the cotton of the towel still wrapped around her middle. Molly reached a finger, the edge of it brushing along the damp trail the droplet made until she skimmed Faye's neck. Faye moaned, her head carding to the side.

"Why did you go down there?"

"Thought I could find some answers."

"Trolls never tell the entire truth."

"Well, I might know that if you told me there were trolls who lived underneath the city."

"They don't like outsiders."

"Figured that out pretty quick." Faye smirked, her lips curling up. "But I think they like me, actually."

"Because of your friend."

"Yes."

A stillness came over the conversation. Molly traced the damp trail of another water droplet. She brought the water to her lips, dashing her tongue out to taste it. When she glanced up, Faye's eyes were locked on her mouth.

"Will you tell me about Pearl someday?"

Molly froze, but the sincerity and curiosity in Faye's tone told her it wasn't an attack or a prying for information. She genuinely wanted to know. "Why?"

"You said she was a half-witch."

"She was my half-sister."

Faye's gaze was still locked on Molly's mouth. "That explains something else Malek said."

"He told you about Pearl?"

"He told me her name, that she was only a few years older or younger than you."

"She was older. My big sister." Once more Molly's finger traced the trails of water as she distracted herself. "My father had a human mistress and got her pregnant. When Pearl was born, her mother died during childbirth, which was not uncommon in those days, so he took her home to raise her."

Molly blinked slowly, tears forming in her eyes, but she let them. This was the most she had spoken about Pearl in decades, and it felt so good to talk about her.

"We grew up together, but the fold wouldn't train her because she was seen as impure."

"Well, she was by their standards, which are fucking high if you ask me."

"Yes." Molly's lips curled up slightly. "I left the fold partially because of her and their hatred of who she was because of her blood and partially because I vehemently disagreed with their way of life. I had to do it under their rules, however, otherwise I would have ended up like Malek."

"Bound."

"Yes. I convinced Malek to release me from my obligation to him, and then he and I went against the fold to release my obligation to them."

Faye's lips parted. "He fought for you?"

Molly pressed her palm to Faye's cheek and turned her so they stared into each other's eyes. "He did. He put my interests over and above his. He could not be matched with someone else, and he knew that."

"He gave up everything for you."

"Not everything. Only matching."

"And you."

"Perhaps." Molly scraped her nail against Faye's lower lip. "I don't really want to talk about Malek."

"I can see that." Faye smirked. "Was there something else you wanted to talk about?"

"Talk?"

"No."

"You want to do something else then?" Faye pressed the tip of her tongue against Molly's nail.

"God yes."

Molly pushed at Faye's shoulder so she laid back on the bed. Crawling over her, she slipped her hand against the cotton of the towel and back up, cupping her breast and squeezing. Their mouths connected, heatedly dueling with each other as they each fought for control.

Her hair fell over her shoulders as she held herself above Faye, running her free hand up and down. Faye's skin was still hot from the water, still damp. Molly would have loved to have joined her, but she understood the need for Faye to feel clean. Faye moaned when Molly pulled open the towel and pinched her nipple hard between her thumb and forefinger, twisting until she knew there was enough pain to cause Faye to arch her back. And that was exactly what she did.

Initiating the bond was almost second nature for her at that point. Molly called her magic, surrounding them each with it, letting it flow through her body as well as Faye's. It found every recess imaginable. Each time she scraped the edge of her nail against Faye's nipple the same pleasure shot through her own body.

Breaking the kiss, Molly nibbled her way down Faye's neck to her chest. She covered Faye's breast with her mouth, sucking hard and twirling her tongue in the same way her fingers had just been moving. Faye gripped the back of her head, fingers tangled in her long locks as she tugged sharply before pushing Molly's face back into her.

Molly grinned before moving to Faye's other breast and doing the same. Faye's hips bucked up, catching Molly off-guard. Faye twisted until she was planted firmly underneath Faye's wet chest. Grinning up into the eyes of her lover, Molly moved her knee up to press it hard against Faye's core.

Faye let out a noise from the back of her throat as her forehead dropped to Molly's shoulder when Molly did it again and again, creating a fast rhythm. Faye suddenly pushed up and away from her, cocking her head to the side.

"You've got way too many clothes on."

"So take them off." Molly pulled her lower lip between her teeth, smiling up at Faye.

"Slowly or my way?"

"Your choice."

"This isn't your favorite dress, is it?"

"Hardly."

"Good."

One long nail on the tip of Faye's finger cut sharply and perfectly into the material against Molly's chest. Molly gasped as the sharp edge of her nail scraped along her sensitive skin but didn't cut her. Her own nipples hardened in response as heat pooled between her legs. That was what she loved about this, the threat of danger but so deeply controlled. It was perfect.

Faye ripped apart her dress, pushing the pieces to the side before she glided her hand downward, coming straight into contact with Molly's body. Faye snorted and moved her fingers through the hair between Molly's thighs.

"Commando, again? Anticipating something?"

"Hoping. They're in my pocket." Molly's chest rose sharply.

"You're incorrigible."

"Like I said. Hopeful."

As Faye moved her mouth downward, Molly lifted up to pull the dress from her arms and tossed it over the side of the bed. Just as Faye was about to go down on her, she shoved her body backward. She wanted Faye to go first this time. It hadn't been that way in long enough, and after Faye's day, she deserved it. Molly sent Faye a wicked grin.

"Up on your knees."

"This is about to get interesting."

"Isn't it always?"

Faye complied, and Molly spun on her butt until she was facing the opposite direction she had been. She pushed her body down until her head was planted firmly between Faye's legs, and when she looked up, she was greeted with the most beautiful sight she'd ever seen.

Wrapping her arms around Faye's hips, Molly lowered her down until her tongue could reach. She swirled her tongue in circles before flattening it out and moving her head side to side. Faye gripped the sheets on the bed as she fell forward, her hips jerking as pleasure coursed through her, the echoing pleasure moving right through Molly.

Faye sighed. Molly pulled her down tighter and focused

everything she had on bringing Faye to her first orgasm of the night. She definitely intended to do this until dawn if she could manage to keep Faye occupied that long. She jerked with a start when Faye's fingers touched her, slid inside her, moved slowly in and out, her thumb pressing hard against Molly's own clit.

She sent the pulse of pleasure through their bond, opening the connection between them even more. She wanted Faye to bite her, but she could truly wait for that to happen until they were far more satisfied and the pleasure wouldn't be as sharp but more like a nice warm bath. Faye's body collapsed on top of her as her hips rocked in time with the orgasm pulsing through her. Her fingers continued their pattern on Molly's body, bring Molly even closer to the edge.

What put her over, like it did most times they had sex, was the sweet sensation of Faye's teeth digging into her skin. The taste of her own blood echoed in her throat as Faye drank her, the sweetness, the spice, the familiarity of it all. Faye sucked, and Molly held still under her. They would not be done just then that was for sure. Molly would have her all night.

CHAPTER THIRTY

FAYE HAD spent the week doing all her normal duties and meeting with Molly to discuss a more detailed plan of how to get information from Malek. They shared everything they knew about him recently, though Faye wouldn't lie, she was still quite curious as to who Malek was back when Molly had met him—and their relationship.

Turning into the game room, Faye went to find Joel and Ben to have a fun easy night and was surprised to find Malek in there instead. She eyed him carefully, curious as to why he was there since the game room was not his normal hang out. No one else was in the room. Faye waltzed around the large cushiony couch and sank down next to him.

"What's up, bright eyes?"

"Bright eyes?" He raised a thin blond eyebrow at here.

Faye shrugged. "Bored out of your wits yet?"

"I find I have less to do than expected."

Chuckling, Faye clapped his thigh. "We can change that. I have a list of shit Molly has given me to do. You can join me, though I'm done for today. It'll have to wait until tomorrow. I was looking for Joel and Ben, have you seen them?"

"No."

"Oh." Faye turned to stare at the television that was off and noticed the book in Malek's lap. Picking it up, she read over the cover and tossed it back at him. "Interesting read?"

"Not in the least."

"Molly has a whole store of books in this house if you wanted to read something else."

"Interest doesn't mean it isn't knowledgeable."

"Whatever." Faye sighed, not seeming like she was making any progress with him. She and Molly had agreed she needed to continue her seduction. For some reason, Malek had found a liking to her and was interested in pursing both her and Molly, though Faye had an inkling it was just so he could get to Molly in the long run.

"It's important to know history." Malek reached along the back of the couch, his arm behind Faye's shoulders.

She shuddered as he leaned in closer. "You think so, but I'm not sold on that."

"If we don't know history, it might repeat itself."

"To be fair, you're kind of living history, and I will be too eventually. Kind of already am, but not as much as you are."

"In the scheme of things, Faye, I am quite young."

She wrinkled her nose. "No, I'm young. You're getting close to four hundred years old. That is anything but young."

His laugh echoed through the room, and he shook his head at her. "Reina and Corbin are far older than that."

"And who's next in the fold? Age-wise. You have to be up there, right?"

"Molly was not the last to join our fold. Tess was, but she is one of the younger ones. We stopped adding to it during the war."

"And what war was that?" Faye glanced at the door, thinking she saw Ben coming in, but no one was there.

"World War Two."

Pressing her lips tightly together, Faye turned slowly to him. "That's the war that eradicated vampires."

"Yes, all but you, apparently."

"Well, me and my father."

Malek's lips quirked up to one side. Faye shivered, sensing they weren't alone in the room, but she couldn't see anyone else there. She focused on Malek, curious as to why the news that her father was still alive didn't surprise him.

"You survived because no one knew you existed." He brushed his fingers over her cheek.

Faye turned into the touch, trying to convey she was interested in him no matter what. "True. I'm young in comparison, which I think was my point in the beginning. Why are you reading about old wars?"

Malek shook his head. "No reason except to expand my knowledge. Did you know there was a war amongst the trolls?"

"Nope. I don't read often."

"You should. It's quite useful."

"So is asking questions," Faye muttered. "What was the war about?"

Malek drew in a deep breath and let it out slowly. "The war took place here. It was about rising to the surface or remaining underground."

"Isolation or inclusion. Seems to be what most wars are about."

"You're not wrong on that."

"And clearly the isolationists won."

"But not without great cost."

"How many trolls are left?"

"A handful." Malek brushed his fingers across her lips.

Faye wanted to bat his hand away because it was annoying, but she let him continue, once again trying to play the role she and Molly had ordained for her. "Just the ones underground here?"

He nodded.

"They can't make troll babies?"

"No. They've become sterile. They will die out in the next generation."

"How sad." Faye immediately thought of Lamek. He'd never shared any of that with her, though she'd never asked him either. They had an odd friendship, one that followed only one line of thought—drugs, sex, and fulfilling immediate needs.

Malek shifted on the couch and brought Faye's mouth to his for a quick kiss. "I can see your mind turning. What are you thinking?"

"It's sad he'll never be with his friends and family again, and I hate that he's stuck on display for the world to see."

"Ah, yes. You could convince Molly to release him."

"You've met Molly, right?"

Malek chuckled. "I think of all Tainted in this world, you would be the one who could convince her of such a duty."

"Duty?"

"He does not deserve to be imprisoned for a crime unworthy of such a punishment."

Faye clenched her jaw. In order to get Molly to let Lamek out of his prison, she'd have to first get Molly to think about Pearl. She'd started that process, but not in the way Molly needed to in order to release Lamek. If there was one thing Faye had learned about Molly in the past four years is that was if Molly made a decision, she rarely changed her mind, which was why the whole re-entering the fold seemed utterly futile to her.

"I don't think he deserves it, but I also wasn't there when it happened, and unless you talk to Molly and figure out what happened, I highly doubt you're going to be able to convince her to let him go."

"He doesn't deserve a prison for life for killing one person, who was not so innocent."

"What do you mean not innocent?"

"Do you think Molly is innocent?"

"No," Faye said confidently. "Absolutely not."

"Why would you assume Pearl was?"

"I didn't." Faye stared at him. She could see why his power specialty was mental manipulation. He was as good at it as Molly or Faye combined because no way had Faye said Pearl or Molly were innocent in the entire situation. If anything, she thought the complete opposite. But Malek had her for a quick second wondering if she had said that. She stared him down, waiting for a response. He didn't need magic to read her mind. "I think Molly did it for revenge. You never want to get on her bad side."

"That's true."

"So, how did you get on her bad side, Malek?"

He sucked in a breath. She was pretty sure he hadn't thought the conversation would take that turn. Faye waited patiently for an answer, wanting to at least start down that path. Not only would it give her information potentially as to why he was there but it would give her more insight into Molly and Malek before he'd shown up at the house.

"Who said I was on her bad side?"

Faye smirked. "I suppose no one did, and since you're still alive and not in pain, you can't have done something too horrible, but she did ignore you for the better part of two hundred years and pretend you didn't exist, so you did something."

"It's more what I represent for her."

"The fold."

"Yes, along with the confines of what the fold represents. She knew the fold before it was in modern times. She doesn't understand how it has changed."

"You mean sexism?"

"Some, yes. She is a powerful witch, and we knew that even

when she was young. It took a lot of training for Molly to learn to control her magic."

"I imagine it would for anyone."

He nodded. "But more so with her."

Faye remained quiet, hoping he would continue. She felt a crawling along her skin at her leg, and when she glanced down, she saw a spider staring at her. Rolling her eyes, Faye brushed Ben off her and focused on Malek.

"Why did she need more training?"

"Control. She is not as controlled as you may think she is."

Faye couldn't quite argue with him on that one. She might have control over her magic, but beyond that, Faye wasn't so convinced Molly was as unlike herself as Molly claimed. Faye leaned in to Malek.

"Why do you think you have more control than her?"

"I trained her."

"Doesn't mean you do. Students often surpass their mentors."

His eyes danced with joy at Faye. "You're quite like your father."

"Oh? Did you know him?"

"Yes. Though I can't say knowing him was pleasurable."

Faye laughed. "Yeah, I hear that a lot. Don't worry. Next time I see him, he'll be dead."

Kissing Malek hard on the lips, Faye pushed to her feet. "I'm off to get some work done. You keep busy with your damn book."

"Please consider talking to Molly about Lamek."

"Why do you want him released so much?"

"I can only imagine what the fold might do to her if they discover what she's been up to."

Faye drew in a sharp breath and let it out on a whistle. Then, unexpectedly, she bent down over him, her hands on the back of the couch as she got into his face. "Some might take that as a threat, Malek, since you are still part of the fold and she is not. However, I will give you the benefit of the doubt with that statement." Tracing a path down his chest, Faye followed her fingers with her eyes before locking her gaze on his. "But somehow I'm pretty sure the fold is absolutely aware of what Molly has been up to these last two hundred years, and I'm pretty sure she damn well knows it."

Wrinkling her nose, Faye straightened her back and turned toward the door. She didn't dare look back at him as she tossed over her shoulder, "See you tomorrow, Malek."

As soon as she was out of the room, Faye let out a breath and shook her head. Everything with him was odd. Hot and cold, freezing and burning. She couldn't quite get a handle on what was happening, but she did know he hadn't tried to magically manipulate her since he'd gotten to the house. Maybe he couldn't if it was true that the fold had bound his magic. She still wanted to know why though.

Ben stood behind the hallway and waited as Faye walked toward him. He'd listened in on a lot of the conversation with Malek before racing out of the room when he realized Faye was getting ready to leave. Shifting into a snake, he slithered as fast as he could to the end of the hall and then shifted into his human form and waited for her to show up.

As soon as she stepped to where he could reach, Ben grabbed her arm and shoved her against the wall with a hand over her mouth. Faye gave him an odd look, staring at him while he held on. Ben grinned at her and jerked his hand back when he felt her tongue against his palm.

"That is disgusting."

"So is pressing up against me naked. Dude, disgusting." Ben tried to cover himself, but Faye rolled her eyes. "Like I haven't seen it before, or seen naked men before. You're going to have to get used to that."

"Shh, I don't want him to know I was listening."

"He's clueless."

"You're sure?"

"Yeah. However, you need to be more subtle. I saw you walking by and then felt you come into the room."

"Felt me?"

"Yeah." Faye rolled her eyes. "You're not super sneaky. What'd you think of Malek's request?"

"I think it'd be worth it to talk to her about the troll, and I think he's right. You're the only one who could potentially convince her."

"Great." Faye slapped his back. "Go get some clothes, Benny-boy. I want to have some fun tonight."

"Molly gave me work to do."

"You're shitting me. We were supposed to get drunk."

"Well, I was supposed to get drunk. You don't get drunk easy."

"True." Faye pouted. "Did she give Joel something to do, too?"

Ben nodded.

"Fuck this." Faye's fists clenched. "She's messing with all my fun."

"Part of being the boss." Ben looked Faye up and down. "I'm sure you can find something to do, or someone."

"What's that supposed to mean?"

"What's going on with you and Malek? I've seen you two together."

"Nothing." Faye sighed. "Ignore it. It won't last. He won't be here long."

"What do you mean?"

"Nothing. Don't you have work to do?"

Ben shrugged. "I guess."

"Then get to. I don't want a pissed Molly on the rampage and I doubt you do either. Then we'll never have a get-drunk night again."

"Truth." Ben smirked and moved his stance. He shifted into the snake again and slithered his way around Faye's leg and up to her hip.

She gripped him around his head and dropped him on the floor with a loud slap. "No need to get too close, Benny-boy. Do your thing. I'll see you later."

She walked off in one direction, leaving Ben on the floor coiled up. He wished he could speak to her when he was shifted, but at least he could still hear her. Uncoiling, he stretched out his muscles and slithered along the floor to the next room over. He was supposed to be checking on the habitats and working on tracing the drugs origins with the list of ingredients Molly had given him to check out, but the urge to shift was far too strong, and he hadn't managed to stay at his computer for more than a few hours that day. He loved the freedom he was finding in shifting from one creature to the next.

Ben moved through the lower floors of the house. He got to the stairwell and shifted into an ant to walk under the door before moving back into the snake to climb the railing to take him up to the main floor of the house. He wanted to see Molly and listen in on whatever she was up to. That would be interesting for sure.

Twice more he had to shift from the snake to the ant to get into her office in the attic. The door to her office had been shut, but until he was inside, he didn't know if it was locked. Ben went from his ant form into a small little beetle that could move far more rapidly than the ant.

Molly sat at her desk, her hair falling over one shoulder as she was bent over some papers. Ben climbed up the backside of the desk and stopped right behind the computer. He could see her, and if he moved slowly enough, he hoped she wouldn't be able to see him. His muscles ached from shifting so much, but Faye had been right, the pain wasn't as bad as that first time, and the desire to shift kept pushing him to do it more.

Molly flipped a sheet of paper and rubbed her temple as she squinted. Ben inched forward, trying to read what she was working on. It was simple financials for the house, something he was very glad he never had to deal with. Backing up, Ben decided he'd have to either show face to her to gloat about his improving shifting abilities or he'd have to sneak back out and pretend he was never in there.

Ben climbed off the desk and was just about to shift back into the ant to sneak out of the room when something in his body felt off and funny. He tried shaking his head to get rid of the feeling, but he couldn't. It was as if he was floating. His brain wouldn't work right, and every time he tried to focus, he'd wander off on a cloud. Drawing in a deep breath, Ben shook his head again.

Something wasn't right.

CHAPTER THIRTY-ONE

MOLLY JUMPED, her hands flying to the top of her desk as she pushed herself up to stare over it. Ben's naked form flopped around on the center of her floor just by the coffee table. She grabbed her radio and flew around her desk as fast as she could. Shoving the table to the side and out of the way so Ben wouldn't hurt himself anymore, she depressed the button on her radio.

"Joel, get the emergency medical kit and bring it to my office, now. Call Amachon and have him return."

She tossed the radio to the side as she held Ben's head to try and keep him from bumping it into anything and causing even more damage. She wished she could heal whatever it was that was making this happen, but she couldn't. Healing was not her mastery skill. They would need Tess for that, and not for the first time, she was tempted to call her and beg for help. She hated seeing Ben like this.

Brushing her fingers over his cheek as his head jerked, she counted the seconds and the minutes as his seizure continued. His legs flung around him, his arms thumping against the floor as the seizure wracked through his body. Fear sprung in Molly's chest as she worried about what this would do to him, how much it would hurt him in the long run if these seizures didn't stop. She'd read as much as she could find on shifting, but none of it included latent shifting abilities or suppressing them since it had never been done before. Not for the first time, Molly regretted making the medication.

Faye got to her office first, sliding on her knees to the other side of Ben's uncontrolled form. Faye blocked him from injury on that side, and they shared a look over his body. Faye's lips parted, her eyes wide. "What happened?"

"No idea," Molly answered. "I was working. Then he was here, seizing."

"Did he talk to you first? Tell you something?"

Molly shook her head. "No, he wasn't here and then he was."

"He was shifting, a lot." Faye stared down at Ben's face.

Molly could easily see the love Faye held for him. As much as she teased him, he was like her little brother in many ways, and Faye would never want to see harm come to him. It was part of why she always sent the two of them on missions together, to protect Ben. Faye would never let anything happen to him if she could help it.

"Shifting how much?"

"Spider, then snake, then human, then snake."

"He was not a snake when he entered this room. He was much smaller."

"Then that's at least one more shift. Did you call Amachon?"

"Joel. I haven't heard beyond that."

Faye's hand cupped Ben's cheek. "It's slowing."

"It is." Molly closed her eyes, thankful the seizure was ending. Joel would be too late, but at least he wouldn't have to see Ben seize again. It was as much a toll on him as it was on her and Faye. Molly drew in a sharp breath, bolstering herself for Joel to burst into the room because she knew he was nearby, his pounding feet against the stairs gave him away.

Molly's heart broke as Joel skidded into the room. He flung the medical kit in Molly's direction as he took Ben's head into his lap. His chest rose and fell heavily as he'd no doubt run the entire way. "What happened?"

"Best guess is he was shifting too much too quickly for now." Molly carded her fingers across Ben's still cheek.

"You said this would stop."

Molly nodded. "It will. It takes time as his body gets used to everything going on."

"He shouldn't still be doing this. He was making so much progress."

"He still is." Molly shared a glance with Faye. They had to get Ben down to the medical area, and Faye was the best bet since she was strong enough to lift and carry him down the stairs without

Amachon there. "Amachon?"

"I...didn't get him called."

"I'll do it," Faye piped up as she moved away from them with her phone in her hand.

Molly stared down at Ben, remembering when he'd first come to live with her. It hadn't been that hard to convince Deidre to let him stay there. She'd lied, of course, as she did a lot of the time, but it was for Ben's own interest. He'd shifted once, and Molly wasn't even sure he remembered doing it all those years ago, but it had scared him so much she'd agreed to find a way to help him stop temporarily. Well, temporary became more permanent. It was so hard to remember twenty years to her was not the same as twenty years to someone with a normal life span.

She brushed fingers through his messy hair he'd never been able to tame. He'd fallen hard for Joel when she'd hired him, and as much as she'd tried to stay out of it, Ben had convinced her to help him out. Everything had tumbled from there. When she looked up, Joel was staring right at her.

"What?" Her brow drew together sharply.

"Why are you sad?"

"No reason." Molly turned to Faye. "Is he coming?"

"In an hour when he has a break in patients. He said since Ben's not seizing any more that he'd be all right if you take care of him."

"All right." Molly pushed onto her knees. "Would you bring him to his room?"

"Not the medical bay?"

"I think he'll be fine and far more comfortable in his own room. Take all the electronics though. I don't want him working."

"I'll do that," Joel spoke up.

Faye bent down next to Ben and slid her arms under his shoulders and his legs. Molly watched her as she stood up, groaning under Ben's weight even though Molly knew it was next to nothing for her to lift him, only awkward at positioning. Joel followed them to the door and stopped as Faye started down the stairs.

He turned back to Molly. "Tell me."

"Another day, Joel."

He came forward into the room as Molly cleaned up what had been left on the floor and stood herself. He helped her move the coffee table back into place and set everything in order before he gripped her hand and tugged her so she had to face him.

"Tell me." His voice broke, as if he was begging her to let him in a little.

Tears flashed in her eyes again, but she held them back. Stepping closer to Joel, she pressed a hand to his cheek and shook her head at him. "I met you the first time when you were five. Do you remember?"

"No."

She gave him a sweet smile. "I'm not surprised. I met Ben the first time shortly after he was born. I held him, protected him."

"Really? He's never told me that."

"I'm not sure he knows. Deidre might never have told him, and I haven't."

"Why not?"

Molly stepped away, taking her time and sitting on the couch, crossing her legs as she stared up at him. "Go to him. You don't want him waking up with Faye as his company, do you?"

She could tell he was hesitating, but with a little more encouragement, he stepped out of the door and down the stairs. Once again alone in her office, Molly stared out the window to her parapet. She'd been mournful since she'd opened up to Faye about Pearl. It was beginning to affect every aspect of her thoughts, which was not something that should be happening.

Taking the time for herself, for once, Molly settled into the couch with a glass of whiskey. She could take a few hours to think about those she had lost over the last century, and those in her house she would lose because she would outlive all of them.

Joel sat in his office after having taken the day off to sit with Ben while he recovered, but he had to play catch up. He was filing paperwork when Faye popped her head through the door, a grin on face as she eyed him up and down.

"How's Ben?"

"Still recovering," Joel muttered before focusing on his work. He didn't pay her any attention. Faye was not someone who would stick around if there was something she wanted, and she also wasn't one to beat around the bush if she thought she needed something. When she did actually need something, she could avoid with the best of them.

The door clicking shut surprised him. Joel looked up to find Faye standing. "Ben said something about making the room quiet?"

"Uh...yes? I can do that, but why?"

"Ears."

"Faye, not to sound obtuse, but what is this about?"

"Malek."

Joel clenched his jaw. He'd known for months Faye and Molly were up to something with Malek, but he hadn't been able to quite figure out what. Suddenly intrigued, Joel held up a finger as he pulled over his tablet. He logged into the system in a roundabout way Ben had showed him and input the code. Narrowing his gaze at the device, he hoped it worked.

"I'm not Ben, but I think it worked. You'd know better than me." He handed the tablet to her.

Faye took it, skimmed through it, hit a few buttons and handed it back. "There. I added a backdoor so even if people suspect, it'll confuse them to find out."

"That makes no sense to me."

"Doesn't have to. Just know I upgraded Ben's system."

"Just like that? In like three swipes of your finger?"

"Yup." Faye smirked. "Now, Malek."

"Yes, tell me all about Malek."

Faye plopped into the chair on the opposite side of his desk and slapped her palms onto her knees. "Well, he's obviously here for some reason and we haven't figured out what that is, and it's frustrating the fuck out of me."

Joel glanced from her to the door. "Is that it?"

"Pretty much. You know anything?"

"No."

"Weren't you also working on this?"

"Sort of." Joel leaned into his chair, relaxing. "You needed me to turn everything off for this?"

"I don't trust him."

"That's probably wise."

"What do his emotions tell you?"

"He's very hard to read."

"Like me?"

Joel shook his head. "No, not like you. Your emotions are easy to read, figuring out what they mean to you is hard. For Malek, he's very even-keeled. Much more like Molly."

Faye scoffed. "Why does that not surprise me?"

"What have you learned so far?" He could tell Faye was hesitating. He knew just about everything Molly did in the house that she wanted him to know, but since Ben had taken on shifting full-force and the drug had been introduced into their city, he'd been far more distracted and not as much of a listening ear to Molly as he normally was. Perhaps that had been what the day before had been about. He needed to set some time aside to sit with her.

Faye said something, and he realized too late, he hadn't heard her.

"I'm sorry, what?"

"Malek wants me to convince Molly to release Lamek."

Joel furrowed his brow. "Who?"

"The troll."

"Oh! Oh...well, that's interesting. Did he say why?"

Faye crossed her arms. "Other than he thinks it was wrong and when the fold finds out she'll be in trouble, no."

"Do you agree with that assessment?"

"Yes, but I think there's more to it."

Joel drew in a deep breath. "Did you know Molly was the one who put him there?"

"Yes. Didn't you?"

"No."

"Oh. I knew before I even met Molly, but he and I were friends far longer than that."

"His name is Lamek?"

"Apparently." Faye cocked her head at him. "Are you still mad at her for it?"

"A little."

"She thinks she had a good reason for it."

"I understand that."

"You disagree?"

"Yes."

Faye chuckled. "Least I'm not the only one."

"I agree with Malek. If anyone was going to convince her to release him, it would be you."

"Why does everyone keep saying that?" Faye pouted as she stared at the floor. "Still, why does he want Lamek released? Because I don't think it has anything to do with the fold."

"Good question."

"Malek is good at manipulating. Like, you thought Molly was good? Nope. He's better."

"Actually, I thought you were fairly good at it, better than Molly." Faye gave him a funny look, so he continued. "Molly is easy to read when she's hiding something, not what she is hiding but that she is. You're so all over the place it keeps everyone on their toes."

"Thanks. I think."

Joel chuckled. "What do you want to do about it?"

"I don't know, but I do know that I want to keep him out of whatever business I can manage."

"Is that why you're here?"

"Yup." Faye pointed at him. "You're smart."

"Why are you here, Faye?"

"We have to figure out who is behind this drug."

"Oh? Is it not your preferred drug of choice anymore?"

"Do I look high to you?"

Joel paused to really look her over. She'd come in like she normally would have. Her eyes seemed clear. Her emotions—well, that was always another story, but they did seem to at least be steady. Shaking his head, he answered her. "Not in this moment, but that doesn't rule out any other time."

"I'm not."

"Good for you. Have you gone back to sobering up or is this temporary?"

She shrugged, and he had his answer. She'd sobered up enough to get something from him, but an addict was an addict, and Joel was pretty sure that as long as he was alive, he'd be wondering if Faye was slipping herself some drug somewhere. The least he could ask for was that she was honest about it, which she seemed to be for now.

"Why do you want to find the dealer so bad?"

"I think the dealer will lead us to who is making it."

"Your troll friends didn't give you any hints?"

"I don't think they have any clue about it. They're just trying to keep it off the street."

"Why? I mean, they don't come to the surface ever, what would they care?"

Faye froze. "You know, I hadn't thought about that."

Joel stiffened his shoulders as he leaned forward on the desk. "Okay, so let's lay out what we know already. There is a new drug. It only affects Tainted, and it is deadly. Not just to those who take it, but to those around anyone who has taken it."

"Yup. And they're giving it away for free, so to me that says they want the deadly affect."

"Agreed." Joel held his breath. "Who would want that?"

"Someone who is really ticked off about Tainted folk."

"Human?"

"That'd be my guess. Someone who knows about us. Someone who has a beef with us."

"The drug is just here though, only in this city."

"So far." Faye stared at him. "Who's to say it won't go elsewhere?"

Joel's heart thumped hard. Faye was right. They needed to figure out who was behind everything sooner than he'd thought. "Has Molly said anything about anyone?"

"No, but I haven't asked her."

"You...what have you two been talking about?"

"Malek."

"So who's been working on finding the dealer?"

Faye blew air into her cheeks and shook her head. "No one?"

"You're joking. What has she been doing?"

"Malek."

Joel ran his hands over his face. "What the hell, Faye?"

"Don't ask me. But I'm tired of watching people die, aren't you?"

"Yeah, that's what I told her weeks ago. That's what Amachon's been telling her for weeks. What has she been working on?"

"Some type of magical cure that Malek told her to work on and figuring out why Malek is here to begin with, not to mention avoiding her own issues."

"Where do we begin?"

"First we have to find the dealers. Molly has Ben looking up some of the drug's supplies—well, had, until the other day. I have no idea how far he got into that, but I'll look and see."

"I've spoken with my patients but since none of them actually got the drug or were with their friends and family when they got it and took it, they haven't been very helpful in that arena."

Faye rolled her eyes. "That's brilliant. Hand out the drug to kill everyone and no one can trace it back to you."

"Right? Where did you get it?"

"The club. I told you that. But they're all dead. I got the rest from the trolls. A whole big bag of it."

"Faye."

"What?" She grinned at him. "No, I'm not giving it to you."

"Do you really need it?"

"Probably not, but I want it. I gave some to Molly so she could run experiments on it, but she's so focused on this magical cure I think she stopped trying to find out where everything is coming from."

Joel sighed. "Okay. Dealer. Where do we start?"

"Downtown."

"Isn't that where everything starts?"

"Yup." Faye giggled. "We're going out tonight."

"Tonight?"

"Joel." Faye's tone turned to chiding. "Since when have you seen dealers out in the middle of the day where they can get caught?"

"You're right. Tonight."

"And no Molly. She doesn't need to know a thing."

"You're sure?"

"Yes. I don't want Malek to find out, and she's just one more person who might tell him."

"You don't trust her that much?"

"Where it concerns Malek? Not at all." Faye gripped the tablet, hit a few buttons and slid it across the desk to Joel. "See you at ten."

"I'll bring the coffee."

Laughing, Faye waved her hand at him as she walked out of his office. Joel closed his eyes, he really needed to dig deeper into what Molly had been doing and just exactly who might be making the drug. Pulling up Molly's files on his computer, he got to work.

CHAPTER THIRTY-TWO

UNDER THE cover of dark, Faye walked her motorcycle out of the garage and waited for Joel to show up. He slipped onto the back without a word as they were near the gate. She started the engine, and they were off. For the first time ever, Faye wondered if this was what her friendship with Joel could be if she allowed it. She'd always been so focused on Ben and Molly and avoiding Joel since his abilities still gave her the heebie-jeebies most of the time.

He was wrapped around her back, holding on tight to her middle. Faye felt his fear, which was odd. He was the one who was supposed to know what she was feeling, not the other way around. They rode in silence until Faye reached downtown near Lamek. She parked her bike and pulled off her helmet, hanging it on the handlebar.

"You scared or something?" she teased.

"With you? Pretty much always."

"What's that supposed to mean?" Faye wrinkled her nose.

"You're a bit reckless."

"I may be immortal, but you're not, and I know that. I drove slow."

Joel snorted. "Maybe for you that was slow, but not for the rest of us mere mortals."

Faye punched him lightly on the arm. "Did you happen to figure out where we're starting?"

Joel got off the bike and stretched his back. It was nightfall, and raining, which gave off this eerie glow of lights from the asphalt. Faye was used to hiding in the shadows, but since she'd met Molly, she'd slowly been going on more during the day. Still the two of them preferred the night. Joel was a day-walker.

Faye stayed rooted on the bike. She had a list of places they could start, but they were all her contacts. He might have access to information she didn't. Though she probably should have hacked into Molly's system and done a little more research before they left. She'd been far too busy making up for Ben's lack of work and covering her steps so it looked like he'd done it.

She hoped Molly didn't figure it out. Ben was in enough shit with her as was.

"What are you thinking?" Joel grabbed Faye's wrist.

"Nothing."

He narrowed his gaze at her suspiciously.

Faye lifted and dropped one shoulder in a half-shrug. "I'm thinking about Ben."

"He's fine."

"Yeah, but Molly's mad at him."

"Not mad." Joel shook his head and let go of her wrist.

Faye disagreed with Joel's assessment, but she wasn't sure she wanted to tell him that. Swinging her leg over the bike, Faye propped it so it would stand on its own. They only had so much time before Molly would expect them at work in the morning, and if Faye wasn't careful, Molly might be looking for her in the middle of the night as had been her habit lately.

"Where are we starting?" Faye repeated her question from earlier and tried to refocus their mission.

"What dealers do you know?"

"A few. What dealers do you know?" She eyed him.

Joel rolled his eyes. "Now is not the time for a power play of information."

"I already talked to Lamek, and he doesn't know anything."

"Really?" Joel cocked his head at her. "That's kind of odd. He normally has a lot of information about what's going on out here."

"You're right. But I asked. So did Molly." She said the last bit on a mutter.

"Molly?"

"Tortured him."

Joel drew in a sharp breath. "She's out of control."

"Not quite my assessment, but I do think she overstepped her boundaries. Anyway, where are we starting? Because standing here is getting old real quick."

"I don't have near the contacts you do in the drug industry."

"Most of my contacts are humans."

"Don't you think they would have some awareness of what was going on?"

"Maybe. Fine then." Faye stalked off down the steep sidewalk and toward the waterfront.

She'd taken him to the man in the red hat and hopefully be able to find someone who had some information on what was going on, but if the drug only affected Tainted, she doubted they would know anything. They walked in silence until they reached near the entrance to the club. The thrum of music, the beating base surprised her.

She grabbed Joel by the arm to halt his forward movement. "Do you hear that?"

"Hear what?"

"The music."

"What music?"

Faye glared at him. "I can't tell if you're shitting me or if you can't actually hear it."

"Look, vamp, not all of us have excellent, beyond perfect hearing."

Rolling her eyes, Faye pointed toward the entrance to the club in the sewers that had started the entire adventure. "There's music coming from the club."

"You're kidding."

"I'm not." Faye pressed her lips together and popped them out. "We're trying there."

"You sure?"

"Trust me." She grinned at him.

Joel hesitated before he shifted his direction to follow Faye. They walked together until they got to the second interior door, where Faye had originally met the snake twins. She held her breath as she walked through and waited to see if they would show back up. Something about the feel of the club had changed but it was also the same. It confused her.

She stopped him with a hand. "What do you feel?"

"What?"

"For once, just answer the question without asking another question," Faye pleaded. "What do feel?"

Blowing out a breath, Joel closed his eyes in concentration. Faye waited as patiently as she could, but she worried it wouldn't be fast enough. Someone, or rather, something was coming up the stairs and they had heavy footsteps.

"Joel?"

"Nothing abnormal. I feel a lot of Tainted down there. Joy. Sex. Frustration. Anger."

"Can you tell if they're high?"

"What?"

"Joel," she snapped.

He shook his head. "No, they feel normal."

"Good."

"Why?"

Faye held a finger to her lips and spun around to face the giant who was as big as Amachon but far grouchier. He filled the passageway they needed to take to get down to the club itself. "Who are you?"

He didn't grunt like Amachon, and he definitely didn't have the calming disposition Amachon did either. Faye lifted her chin up to stare him in the eye. "Patrons."

"Who sent you?"

"He did." She figured it worked the first time she'd ever gone down there, perhaps it would work the second.

"He who?" The giant was absolutely demanding. She missed the previous bouncers already.

Faye didn't dare shift a glance to Joel and only hoped he was holding as firm as she did. "The troll."

"He's not welcome here."

"Well, he's not here. He sent me."

"What for?"

"Look. We're here to party. Heard the club's back to business. Want to join in. Who the hell are you to tell us otherwise?"

His yellow eyes widened before he bent down over her, trying to intimidate. Faye held her ground, but she felt Joel shift and take a step back. "I'm the new bouncer."

"Then bounce. We're paying patrons."

He snorted and turned his body so he was squished against the wall. Faye and Joel had to walk single file past him, and they still ended up squeezing in between him and the railing. As soon as they got to the bottom of the stairs, Joel spun Faye so her back was against the stone wall.

"I can't believe you did that."

"Did what?" She grinned. "Argued back? Don't you know much about giants?"

Joel shook his head.

"You need to read up and learn up."

"I've only met Amachon."

"Well, Amachon is the most pleasant giant I have ever run into."

"And when have you met others?"

Faye scrunched her nose. "Remember that mission Molly sent Ben and I on a few years ago to Ireland?" At Joel's nod, Faye continued. "That's when I met the giants. Ben didn't, but I did."

"They're from Ireland?"

"Um, not quite, but they like the climate there so they kind of took over it when they could. Come on." Faye pushed open the last door and they walked into the club, her arm wrapped in his.

Everything was exactly as the last time they had been there together. Faye remembered what it looked like in the in-between, blood spattered everywhere, dead bodies lying around. Glancing around the room, she had a fleeting hope of seeing Aliya again, but the faerie was nowhere to be found.

Faye moved through the room like she owned it, Joel sticking close to her. She grabbed a drink at the bar and faced the rest of the crowd as they danced on the moss-covered floor, moss that Faye now knew was there for quite the purpose. Faye eyed customer after customer, watching for anyone dealing out her newest drug of choice.

Joel leaned into her ear, his lips far too close if they weren't in such a loud environment. "See anyone you know?"

"Nope. I gave Molly the rest of the drugs before we left." She took a casual sip. "You were right. So was Ben, for that matter."

"I...what?"

She smirked at him. "I need to stop running."

"When did I say that?"

"Frequently." Laughing, Faye grabbed him, and they moved out onto the dance floor. She pressed her butt into his hips and rocked her body to the beat. Joel moved with her, a little stiffly, but she kept up the ruse they were there for fun and not for work.

She saw the deal go down in the corner of the room. Spinning around, Faye gripped Joel by the shoulders and lowered her body on his thigh. Coming back up, she confirmed who the dealer was. A small little man who looked more tweaked than she did. She was surprised they would come back to the club so soon.

"You ready?" she whispered into Joel's ear.

"See something?"

"Yup."

"Any time you are." He pulled out his phone, sent Molly a text, and glanced up at her. "I'll follow you. This is your crazy plan."

"It always is." Giggling, Faye moved away from him and toward the dealer.

As she got closer, she recognized the man for what he was, nothing more than a watered-down witch. His scent was nowhere near intoxicating, but it held that same quality Malek's and Molly's did. Faye sidled up next to him.

"You going to share some of those goods? I'll pay whatever you're asking."

"You don't even know what it is."

"I've heard rumors of how good it is. Trust me. I want to try some. I'm always looking for the newest thing out there."

The man glanced up into her eyes before holding out a small baggie with only two pills in it. "Sure. Next time it'll cost you."

"So sweet." She almost popped one between her lips, but instead, Faye pocketed the drugs and grabbed the man hard on his upper arm. She pulled him back toward the storage room she had become so acquainted with.

Joel was only a few steps behind her when the entire club went dark. Faye's eyes adjusted rapidly. The man she held quivered in fear. She shushed him as others screamed. Her ears perked up as she tried to listen to what was happening. There were no orders shouted, but the screams started.

Faye reached for Joel, but he was gone. Looking where he'd just been standing, Faye balked. He was nowhere. "Joel!"

The man she held snickered and gripped her neck, digging his fingers into her throat. Rolling her eyes, Faye gripped his wrist and snapped it in two. He fell back against the wall as she searched once more.

"Joel!" The screaming in the other room picked up in volume but it was no longer screams of fear but screams of rage. It was happening again, only this time she was completely sober. Or...she wasn't. The flicker of the drug she'd wanted bit in her belly. "What the hell?"

She spun around to the man huddled against the wall.

"Did you put it in the drinks?"

He sneered at her. "*I* didn't."

"Fuck this." Faye snapped his neck and barreled through the room with her eyes wide. "Joel! Where are you? Joel!"

When she got no answer, Faye panicked. Molly would kill her.

Joel had texted her, so there was no time to try and find him before Molly would show up.

"Joel!"

The second bloodbath of the club's history that year began. Faye ducked in and around people, swinging her fist when she needed to get through. The wounds she sustained healed, but she still couldn't find him. Faye spun in circles, lost as she searched and searched.

"Joel!"

"Faye!"

She spun in his direction, catching a glimpse of his curly head as he was dragged through a door. "Shit."

Molly had Malek next to her in the Tesla as she drove. He'd convinced her to go out there, but she still wasn't sure she wanted to. As she drove through the streets and parked under the bridge, she sighed and turned to him.

"You sure you're up for this?" he asked.

"No." Molly pressed her lips tightly together. "But you have convinced me."

"Have I? I sense I haven't."

Molly smiled and turned toward the troll. She stared him down as he remained stoically frozen in place. "You know me too well. Why don't you release him? Then I won't have to be the one to do it."

"Why are you so opposed to it? Molly—" Malek turned to face her fully "—you have to see how unfair this has been to him."

"You weren't there."

"I know I wasn't, but killing one person does not deserve a lifetime of punishment."

Molly bolstered herself. She had been making the argument since the last time Faye had brought it up. She knew the conversation would come to haunt her, but she hadn't expected it to be Malek who brought her there. "He may not for that, but he had other crimes."

"What did he do?"

"It doesn't matter. If you want to release him, I won't stop you."

Malek turned to look at the troll. The car remained silent for minutes as Molly waited for him to say it. She knew why he wasn't lifting the spell, but she still didn't know the cause, and this was one of her last hopes for finding out why or at least giving in the opportunity to tell her without her using magical means to get the result.

"I can't," he whispered.

"Because your magic has been bound."

"How did you know?"

Molly gave him a sweet smile and rested her head against the seat of the car. "Malek, I have known you a very long time. I'm surprised I didn't pick up on it sooner, but I have repressed my own abilities for decades. I'm sorry to admit, I wasn't paying attention."

Malek gripped her hand tightly in his. "I haven't been bound that long."

"I figured it out when we cleansed Faye. I had to use far more magic than you did yet you grew far weaker than me."

"You had help recovering."

A flush tinged Molly's cheeks. He wasn't wrong. She did have help, but that still didn't mean she was wrong either. "Either way, you were not up to your full abilities."

"You're right."

"What did you do to deserve your magical binding?"

Malek drew in a deep breath and let it out slowly. "You know the fold. Any little thing against them and they take it as an affront."

"Sometimes." Molly squeezed his fingers back. "What was it this time?"

He shook his head. "I'd rather not say."

"I can't help you if you don't tell me."

"They made me a deal."

Molly glanced out at the troll before staring into Malek's cold blue eyes. "Bring me back and receive your magic in return?"

He nodded.

Snorting, Molly nodded her chin. "They never took kindly to my leaving."

"They didn't. You could return, but only if you want to. I don't want to force you into anything for my sake."

"Maybe one day you will release him. Until then, he will remain in his prison." Molly stared out at the troll. Her phone buzzed, but she ignored it. "Tell me how the fold has changed."

"They haven't. At least, not much. We're smaller."

"Reina?"

"She misses you dearly."

"I miss her, too." Molly's eyes crinkled at the corners. If anyone was a mentor for her magic outside of Malek, it had been Reina.

The two of them had spent hours together as she'd refined her skills. Though when Reina had found out Molly was in turn teaching Pearl, the upset afterward was beyond anything she had expected.

"What if I help you find who is making this drug, will you release him then?"

"Why are you so eager for me to release him?"

Malek didn't answer right away. He stared across the street at the statue under the bridge. He spoke toward the window, not turning to face her. "I know what it's like to live in a lifetime prison. You got out, Molly. I stayed in for your sake."

She mulled over the comment. There may very well be some truth to what he'd said, but she still knew he held back. The fold had to want her back for a reason. It wasn't to be matched to him. They had all the time in the universe for that. Something else was happening, something he hadn't even begun to share.

"I will consider that."

"Then let's find us a drug lord."

Molly smiled at his grin before reaching for her phone. She read the text from Joel and her eyes lit up. "Seems like we may have a lead."

"Oh?"

Handing the phone over to him, Molly put the car into gear and drove toward the club.

CHAPTER THIRTY-THREE

AS SOON as Ben realized everyone was out of the house, he snuck down to his work area and booted up the computer. He sat on his stool, and he glanced over his shoulder to make sure no one was just showing back up. After sleeping on and off for the day and a half since his seizure, he couldn't stand to be in bed any longer.

Joel had given him the heads up they were leaving, but when Molly had walked by with Malek and talked about taking him out of the house, Ben couldn't let the opportunity pass up. The computer screen came to life, and he input his passwords to get into the systems. Triple-checking to make sure Molly, Faye, and Joel were truly out of the house, Ben let out a sigh of relief. The list of chemicals Molly had left him at least a week ago still sat next to his workstation.

He should have been working on that instead of skittering around the house like a shifter on steroids. He started searching through each and every one of them and was surprised when results popped up within seconds of entering the data. Narrowing his gaze, Ben leaned forward to look up and down the reports.

"Faye." He smiled and shook his head.

The electronic signature she made sure to leave on everything was plain and clear, though he'd be the only other one in the house to know to even look for it. Chuckling, Ben read the reports to get caught up on how far she'd gotten, which hadn't been that far at all. It had seemed she'd done enough to keep him in Molly's good graces but no more.

"Figures."

Typing away at the keyboard, Ben started new searches up. He needed to find some answers for Molly, and for Joel. He'd seen the way everything had been weighing on him lately, and he'd been a crap boyfriend in hardly paying attention. Ben had been so wrapped up in his own shifting abilities that he forgot other people had problems too.

He pulled his feet up onto the middle rung of his stool, leaning over to stare at the computer screen as he made progress on a job he should have already done. He combined some of the chemicals, worked to try and figure out where they could be made and what type of environment would be needed. Molly would have been helpful for those questions, but since he wasn't supposed to be working on it and she was up to something with Malek, he ignored the easy way out as best he could.

The grunting over his shoulder scared the shit out of him. Ben jerked with a start and spun around to find Amachon glaring at him.

"What?" Ben said innocently. "I felt bad. Not bad sick, bad as in guilty."

Amachon grunted again. "Find anything?"

"Found Faye came in here and did some work, which is astounding." Ben rolled his eyes. "She didn't do much but enough."

"Find anything new?"

Ben shook his head slowly. "Not yet. Where did Molly go?"

"Lamek."

"Who's Lamek?"

Amachon's large hand clasped over Ben's shoulder. "Troll."

"Oh. He has a name?"

"Apparently." Amachon pointed at the computer screen. "What's that?"

Ben shifted to look at the screen, his eyes widening. "That, my friend, is a lead."

He clicked through several screens, following the search as every muscle in his body tensed with anticipation. Amachon stayed close by as he shifted through the raw data. Chemicals, locations, people. Ben got to one more screen and drew in a sharp breath.

"Did Molly suspect anyone?" Ben asked.

"Trolls."

"She may be right, still."

"She does not suspect them anymore."

"Really?" Ben turned with eyes wide. "She may want to reconsider that."

"Why?"

Pointing at the computer screen, Ben nearly bounced out of his chair with excitement. "This right here."

"Says what? I don't read computer."

"So this is two of the chemicals she gave me on this list that would make up the basics of the drug. Not the part that makes you crazy, apparently. But combining them together, you get this sort of weird chemical thing. I don't know what it's called."

"Compound."

"Right, chemical compound. That has been purchased recently and sent here."

"To where?"

Ben flushed. "Trolls."

"They live underground and are xenophobic."

Turning with a sharp glare, Ben shook his head. "They're not xenophobic. They're isolationist, which is why this does make sense. They don't like other Tainted or humans, so it stands to make sense they would want to get rid of them."

"Humans, not Tainted. They only don't like witches because of Molly."

Ben snorted. "That's fair."

Grunting in Ben's direction, Amachon got Ben's attention. "Why trolls? You haven't answered that."

"A few years ago, when Faye told me about her troll friend, whatever his name was, I got curious about trolls and started to put searches out for them. I wanted to know how many more of them we had in the city, well, under the city. Which surprisingly they live in a city of their own, did you know that? It's like a whole city under this city, like we're built right on top of it."

Amachon squeezed Ben's shoulder tight.

"All right, back on topic. They have drop points for supplies they get from the surface. They're not as isolationist as they make it out to be, but since the troll has been on the surface, they've started to emerge from underground a little more. One of the drop points is where this chemical was sent."

"Where is it?"

"With the troll on the surface."

Amachon grunted. "Call Molly."

"Why?"

"She's there now."

"Oh, yeah, right." Ben grabbed for his phone and fumbled with it for a few seconds before he managed to get it open to Molly's name. He dialed her and put the phone to his ear but turned to Amachon while he waited for Molly to answer. "I have no idea who's running the stuff though."

"She'll find out."

"You sure? I doubt the trolls are actually coming to the surface, and the one stuck here isn't going anywhere. So who do they trust to run things to them?" As soon as he asked the question, he knew he had an answer, at least a partial answer. *Faye.* They would trust her because Lamek trusted her. But she hadn't mentioned anything about trolls.

When Molly didn't answer, he hung up and dialed again. He shook his head at Amachon when he sent her a questioning look.

"I'll keep trying."

"Good." Amachon clapped Ben on the shoulder and shifted out of the room silently.

Ben stared after him as Molly's phone once again went to voicemail. He tried Joel, and then Faye, and then Molly again, but the result was the same. No one was answering. Pouting at being left behind on a mission again, Ben continued his research, trying Molly's phone at every opportunity he got.

Faye pushed her way through the throng of drugged up people and to the door. Slipping behind it, she locked it tight and let out a sigh of relief when she turned to find it empty. The drug was hitting her system, though it wasn't near as effective as it had once been, meaning she was building up resistance to it and she hadn't had that much to drink. She'd never finished hers, and Joel hadn't even bothered to get one.

The room she found herself in was a storage room, one she hadn't been in before. Lights flickered above her, but her superior eyes adjusted rapidly. She was alone, but she swore she had seen Joel go through that door, or rather be half-dragged through it. Fumbling around, Faye moved aside boxes and crates of supplies, trying to find an exit other than the door she hadn't looked away from as soon as she'd seen it shut.

Her heart raced with fear. She couldn't lose him. Ben would kill her. Or try to. Molly would actually kill her. Faye flung aside one more crate and froze. A door in the floor, wooden, like it had been there for centuries. She bent down to the small circular hole in it and dipped her finger inside. Pulling the wooden square up, she dropped it to the side. It was pitch black below, and as much as she wanted to send a shoot of electricity down to see how far down it went, she didn't want to tell them she was there, whoever *they* were.

Faye put her boot through and found the first rung on the ladder. Joel was probably shoved down it, so it couldn't be that far down. Drawing in a deep breath, Faye lowered herself down. As soon as her head was below the surface of the floor above, silence reverberated as if she was in a bubble. The noises from the club were completely gone, and the only thing she knew of that could cause that was magic.

Faye kept climbing down, her heart racing and her feet steady on the rungs of the ladder. It was farther than she'd originally thought, but when her boots touched solid ground, she turned around, her eyes adjusting to the dark. She was alone in a long hallway, one she suspected mimicked the sewer lines above her from their length and depth.

She hadn't had time to research it, but she suspected the trolls had built their own city mimicked on the one above, one that was a mirror image on a grander scale to accommodate their large size. This would be a sewer line, although it wouldn't have actual use because trolls weren't human or disgusting.

Faye stepped down the long stone hall. She kept her lips closed as she waited to see if she could hear or see anything to indicate where Joel might have been taken. She'd spent more time below the surface of the city than she'd ever wanted to. Following the line of hall, Faye stopped when she came to a door. It was metal, curved like it had been made specifically for that space, or stolen from a similar space.

With no other sight of a door, Faye gritted her teeth as she twisted the large circular handle in the center of the door and creaked it open. It was anything but silent, and if they were watching and waiting for her, no doubt would she just have given away her position.

Stepping through, Faye found herself in the heart of what she could only call a troll city. The buildings were huge. She hadn't realized how far underground she was, but the stonework was magnificent. Faye scrunched her nose as she tried to follow Joel's scent, but everything was so clean and pure that it was washed away the moment she stepped through.

She and Malek must have only been on the outskirts of the city or even nowhere near it when they'd been down there. She stared in awe at the world before her she'd never expected to see. Trolls moved easily and confidently as she stayed put and tried to figure out where the hell she was supposed to go next.

Hiding behind a building, Faye pressed up against the white marble base and looked from side to side. She was just about to step forward after making a decision when she had to press back against the wall as a troll walked by. Crouching, Faye tried to hide, but there was nothing except the wall to conceal her.

The troll stopped short in its walk, then bent down, sniffing her. The long face eyed her carefully. Faye straightened her spine as she stood up, putting her hands on her hips. If she was going to have to face the trolls, she would do it without looking back. After all, Lamek was her friend, maybe that would get her a bit farther than she'd originally thought.

The giant troll wrinkled its nose at her, its nose that was at least twice her size. "You are old blood."

"I am." Faye swallowed, the conversation very reminiscent of the first one she'd had with Lamek all those years ago when she was looking for a witch before she met Molly officially. Faye stood her ground, curious as to where this was going and how far it would take her.

"Come with me." The troll lowered its large hand out.

Faye climbed on, sitting cross-legged. She hoped she was making the right decision and wasn't giving herself up for death. The troll straightened, its hand remaining perfectly even to carry Faye.

"I am Titsui."

"I'm Faye."

"Lamek's friend."

"Yeah." Faye gave a small smile. At least they were still calling her friend. "Have you seen my friend? Joel?"

Titsui nodded. "I shall take you to him."

"Oh good." The question gnawing at her from the inside out was ready to burst forth. Faye tried to channel Molly and not ask, but she couldn't resist. "Did you take him?"

"No. We saved him."

"I thought you didn't like other Tainted."

"Humans. Tainted we like."

"But not witches?"

"No."

Faye nodded. Titsui walked slowly, but for every step she took, she encompassed at least ten times the distance Faye could manage in her human form with that time. She was brought to the center of the city and from Titsui's height, she was afforded a beautiful view of the architecture and buildings around her.

Titsui stopped and settled Faye on the ground. She pointed at a building and opened the door for Faye. Together they walked inside. As soon as Faye saw the light, which she hadn't been able to figure out where it was coming from, and the corner of the room, she ran. Joel stood up with a start, his eyes wide as he stared at her.

"Thank God you're here!" Joel stated as she reached him.

"You're okay?"

"Yeah. I don't know what happened."

Faye drew in a sharp breath and turned to Titsui who followed them in. "Can you tell us what happened?"

Titsui nodded and moved to sit cross legged in the center of the large floor. Faye grabbed Joel's hand, and they walked forward together. Faye climbed up Titsui's leg to sit on her lap, making Joel come with her. The trolls had never been anything but kind to her, and Titsui seemed to be following in that line.

"Your friend was taken."

"I know that." Faye smiled. "Who took him? Why did they take him? How did you even know about it?"

Titsui held up a large palm to stop Faye. "Lamek has told us about you and your questions."

Flushing, Faye turned her chin up. "Then you know I have a lot of them and I don't leave without answers."

"Yes. Your friend was taken because of the witch."

"Because he works for her?" Faye shot Joel a look, hoping he'd stay quiet.

Titsui nodded. "This drug, it kills."

"I know. We've seen it."

"We are trying to stop it. It takes time and is difficult when we do not dwell on the surface."

Faye clenched her jaw. She knew from Lamek that interrupting with another question would only slow down the process, but she wanted answers already. Joel sent her calming waves of emotion, which she silently thanked him for. She had a feeling Titsui was far higher in rank, whatever rank the trolls had, than Lamek or even the last few trolls she'd run into. Titsui's language was clearer and more precise, though she still spoke slowly.

"We use Tainted to collect the drug and bring it here."

"Then what do you do with it?" Joel asked.

Titsui turned to him. "We gave it to Faye."

So they did know her name. Faye looked into Titsui's eyes with surprise. "That was all of it you had?"

Titsui nodded. Faye knew there had to be more. The bag, while it was large bag of drugs, was not a whole lot. To manufacture something in that small of a batch wouldn't make sense if the idea was to get rid of Tainted in the city. Joel must have had the same line of thought because they shared a glance.

"Thank you," Faye said. "We've been trying to figure out who's making the drug, not just distributing it, although that would be helpful, too."

"We do not know who makes it. They employ a gang to distribute it."

"A Tainted gang?" Faye stared with disbelief, but Joel's hand on her arm caught her attention.

"There are a few in town."

"Are you serious?"

He nodded. "But they aren't the ones with the drugs. They were the first places we checked."

Faye turned to Titsui. "Who are you getting the drugs from?"

"Anyone we can."

"The club. Did you get them from Aliya?"

Titsui nodded. Faye's chest rose and fell sharply. Turning to Joel, she stared him right in the eye. "Aliya was the one with the drugs first, and she didn't take them for weeks, not until I went back to get more from her, and even then, she only took it because I gave it to her. Why wouldn't she take it when she got it? If she's into drugs..."

"You think the faeries are behind this?"

"Maybe not making it but definitely distributing it."

Titsui make a noise in the back of her throat. "We do not want more Tainted to die."

"Why would faeries want Tainted to die? I mean...we're all part of the same group, right?" Faye looked from Titsui to Joel, hoping someone had an answer. Both of them shook their heads at her. "All right. How do we find the faeries?"

"Your witch will know."

The hate in Titsui's tone did not go unnoticed. Faye cocked her head to the side. Since she didn't know when she'd be back down there, she wanted answers. "Why do you hate witches so much?"

"Your witch, I will not say her name, tortures Lamek."

"I know." Faye shook her head. "I hate it."

"Me too," Joel piped up. "We're working on getting her to

release him, but we don't have the magic to do it."

"She will not."

"Do you know why she did it?" Joel asked. When Faye shot him a glare, he shrugged. "What? I can't get it out of her."

"He killed her sister," Faye muttered.

"There's more to it than that. Molly wouldn't imprison someone for life because they killed her sister."

Titsui blew a huge breath on them, silencing them. "Before I was elected official, my predecessor wanted to rise to the surface. He took actions to accomplish this."

"Actions, like what actions?" Joel leaned forward, catching every word Titsui said, and Faye would be remiss if she didn't hear everything too.

"War on humans. He wanted them gone from this part of the city, making room enough for us to rise."

"Shit. There was a war," Joel muttered.

Faye raised an eyebrow at him. "Told you."

"How did her sister die?"

"Accident. Lamek is young. He was angry and a believer. He wanted to surface."

"So how did she die?"

Titsui shook her head. "I was not there. I cannot tell you. But it ended the war."

Faye shot Joel a look. "All right. Um…are we free to leave? I think we need to go find these faeries and figure out what the hell is going on."

At Titsui's nod, Faye shifted and climbed down her leg. Joel followed her. Faye put her hands on her hips and stared around the building. "We're really free to go, just like that? Last time you put me in a cage."

"You were with a witch. Do not bring him back here."

"Got it." Faye bowed down to Titsui, not quite sure what she was doing or why she was doing it, but she felt as though some type of revere was deserved. "Thank you."

"Goodbye, Lamek's friend."

Faye gripped Joel's hand, and they walked back the way she had come. As soon as they were through the door into the tunnel, she gripped his shoulder. "You're fine, right?"

"Yeah. They snatched me about two seconds after I came down this thing."

"How did they even know?"

"I have a feeling they know a whole lot more than they get

credit for. Trolls deal in information, not goods."

Faye snorted. "Did your research, did you?"

"Some." He flushed "We going to find these faeries?"

"Yup."

CHAPTER THIRTY-FOUR

MOLLY PARKED the Tesla near the club, slamming the door as she got out. Her chest heaved as she raced toward, not paying attention to Malek and whether he was coming or not. She pushed her way inside, her heels making it difficult to run, and she wished she had changed before leaving the house, but she hadn't known this was going to happen.

The giant standing guard gave her an odd look until he recognized her, and then he stepped back without protest. Molly pursed her lips in his direction before clicking her way down the stone staircase to the last door into the club. Malek's footsteps echoed behind her as he followed.

With the last door pushed open, Molly froze. It was just as she feared. She pulled her magic from the center of her belly and flung it outward at everyone in the room, freezing them in place. Twisting to look at Malek as the spell worked, she shook her head at him.

"I'm going to need your help."

"You know I can't."

"We can't let them die!"

"Put them to sleep and bind them. We'll do it one at a time as we have magic to spare if we can't find another cure. But I'm of no use to you."

She sent a stream of her magic into every Tainted there, ushering them into sleep. Awake and live bodies fell on dead bodies, crashing onto the moss-covered floor below. Molly worked her magic again, binding them to sleep until she herself woke them.

When all was said and done, Molly sighed and turned to Malek, a grin on her face. "This might work."

"We shall see." His own smile echoed hers.

"Do you see Joel or Faye? He said they were here." Molly walked around the bodies on the floor, searching through them for a sign of her staff and her love. Malek walked in a different direction. When she glanced up to check with him, he shook his head at her. Molly went to the back storerooms and found no one there.

Coming out into the main room, Malek handed Molly her phone. She glanced at it and noted all the missed calls from Ben. She raised the device to her ear. "Benjamin?"

"I think it's the trolls."

"Distributing or making?"

"Both."

"All right. Would you get Amachon and bring a few vans down to the club. I need you to take these individuals back to the house under supervision. I'll deal with them when I have a minute."

"Umm...okay? Can I get more information than that?"

"No. But they won't be a problem."

"Whatever you say, boss."

Molly pressed the phone into the pocket of her suit jacket and bent down to take a closer look at one of the injuries on a man lying on the floor. Amachon would have to look at him otherwise the injury might end his life before she could cleanse his blood, though she'd make the most injured her first priority if she had to.

"What are you thinking?"

Molly stared up at Malek. "That this was planned. Again. This is the second time this club has seen such a fate."

"Oh?"

"Faye was here the first time as well."

"She has bad luck."

Smirking, Molly turned toward one of the storerooms when she thought she heard a bang and grunting. Holding her hand up to Malek to tell him to be quiet, she walked toward the room and pulled a gun from the back of her waistband. Malek raised an eyebrow at her, and she shrugged.

"It's easier than magic sometimes."

"I suppose I should take to carrying one of those around if I'm going to continue working with you."

"We work together now?"

"Seems like it."

Molly would have scoffed, but voices echoed through the closed door. She cocked her head at Malek before focusing on the room behind the door. Flinging the door open, she held her gun out in front of her to protect the both of them when she stopped short. Faye sat on the floor, her legs dangling down in something, and she pulled backward, falling as Joel popped up and fell on top of her. Joel gave her a funny look and laughed before cringing and whining.

"What happened?" Molly asked, shoving her gun into her waistband as she moved next to Joel.

"Princess here got injured, like he does on any damn mission," Faye snorted.

Molly shot Faye a serious look, but Faye raised an eyebrow right back at her in a challenge. "What happened?"

"He fell down. Twice."

Joel winced. "It hurt."

"I had to carry him the rest of the way and drag him up the damn ladder."

"Where were you?"

"Talking to trolls." Faye pulled all the way out of the trap door and saw Malek over her shoulder. She sent him a sizzling glance Molly did not miss and stood up to walked over him, gripping his arm to stand close. "Much better this way than through the sewers."

"Hmm, you smell better, too."

"Aww, you see that, Molly? He must like me. I don't know why you keep telling me Malek doesn't like me."

Molly closed her eyes and didn't look at Faye, knowing the jibing was just that and nothing more. They still had to get information from Malek, and Faye knew how to do it her way best. "Where does it hurt?"

"Everywhere," Joel moaned.

"Joel."

"What?"

"Where specifically does it hurt?"

He narrowed his gaze. "Everywhere."

"He fell about ten feet, Molly. He's not lying."

Molly cast a glance over her shoulder to see Faye hanging off Malek. Keeping her mouth shut, she turned to Joel. "Do you want me to heal it now or later?"

"When later?"

"Faye and I have a mission we need to go on."

"Do we?" Faye asked.

"Do it when you have energy, Molly, or Amachon can fix me up. I don't want you to run out of magic."

"We don't run out of magic, just energy." Molly stood up and twisted to face Malek. "You will take him home and help with Ben and Amachon."

"If that's what you want."

"It is. Faye?" Molly beckoned Faye with one glance and crook of her finger. "You're with me."

"Where are we going?"

"To finish this."

Molly gripped Faye's hand and took her out of the room. Faye gasped as they walked through the main room with all the bodies and squeezed Molly's fingers tight. "There's so much blood."

"Ignore it. Mine's better."

"Damn straight. You put them to sleep?"

"For now, so they'd stop killing each other."

"Not a bad idea. What are you going to do when they wake up?"

Molly shot a look to Faye. "No idea."

They walked up the stairs, past the brooding giant at the door, and out of it. Instead of walking toward the exit, Molly took a path that should be decently familiar to Faye at that point. Faye turned and stopped her, shoving her against the wall until their lips crashed together. Molly moaned, gripped Faye's hair, and kissed with everything she had.

When Faye pulled away, she grinned broadly. "Where are we going?"

"Ben called and said he traced the purchases to the trolls."

Faye kissed Molly again. "I love Ben, and he does good work, but Joel and I were just down with the trolls. Long story I may or may not tell you. They aren't the ones doing this, and if you walk down there, Molly, they will kill you."

"I can protect myself."

"I don't think you understand how much they want to kill you."

"Fine." Molly put both her hands in the air. "If it isn't the trolls, who is it?"

"Aliya."

Molly pulled a face at Faye. "Who?"

"Oh, that's right, you don't come to the club with normal people and leave me to fend for myself when I get here, Ms. I'm-too-good-for-those-things."

"Faye."

"What?"

"Who is Aliya?"

"The bartender. Decent fuck, too."

Molly's cheeks flushed, and her chest constricted. She had no idea how to respond, and she hated when Faye said things that knocked her flat on her ass. Clenching her jaw, Molly stood as still as possible and waited for Faye to continue, hoping she wasn't waiting for some kind of specific reaction.

"She's a faerie, Molly. Relax."

Molly held her tongue.

"She's the one who gave me the drugs the first time. And the second time. But she also didn't take them until I gave them to her."

"You're speaking gibberish."

Faye grinned and pulled Molly back in for a kiss, pressing her hard against the wall of the cavern, their breasts pushing into each other. Every nerve in Molly's body felt as though it had fire in it. Molly slipped a hand up Faye's back to try and stop her, but she was so lost, she could only hold on for the ride. Faye's lips moved from her mouth to her chin to her ear.

"Don't worry. I'll always come back to you."

"You better," Molly whispered, relief flooding through her. "Who is Aliya?"

"She's a faerie, and I'm pretty sure the faeries are the ones making this drug."

"Why?"

"Haven't figured that one out because it would pretty much kill business at the club, but considering they own and operate it, and it's back up to running weeks after the first massacre, I'm really betting they're it."

Molly's tongue dashed against her lips, Faye's taste dancing in her mouth. "So we go to the faeries."

"Yup."

"Do you know where to find them?" Molly trailed a finger down Faye's cheek. "Or do I still know more than you?"

"Smart ass."

"Where's your bike?"

"Outside. Are you going dressed like that?"

"Don't start with me, Faye."

"It's hot. I'm just saying it's not very practical."

"I was not anticipating Joel's SOS."

Faye snorted. "Kid can't handle blood."

"And you live on it. Is that too much of a surprise?" Molly pushed Faye away from her and started toward the entrance. They slipped out the door and down the street toward Faye's motorcycle, catching sight of Ben driving a van.

Faye waved before she pulled the helmet over her head and handed the other one to Molly. "Don't want to smash your pretty face."

Molly carefully slipped a leg over the back of the bike and wrapped her arms around Faye's middle. "Just remember how much of a distraction I can be."

"I'd like to see you try. Where are we headed?"

"Lion's Park."

Faye pulled up at the park and helped Molly off the bike as she teetered on her four-inch heels. Biting back the retort, Faye turned toward the play equipment and back to Molly.

"The faeries live in a park?"

"In it is a precise way of saying that."

"What does that mean?"

Molly winked at Faye as she walked around her and into the grass, her heels sinking in as she went.

"No, seriously, what does that mean?"

"You really need to finish your training for the job, Faye. It's been four years since you started working for me. You should know these things."

"Do you know how much information you jam packed into that stupid training class? For someone who had no involvement with Tainted life until you, you have to give me a break."

Molly spun to face Faye, humming as she looked her over. "And here I thought you were smarter than that."

"Than what?"

"Procrastination."

Faye growled. "You overestimate my ability for the mundane."

"Hardly, Faye. You enjoy classes. You have received numerous degrees from universities. Why would I think my specifically designed course would be any different?"

Thoroughly chastised, Faye put her hands on her hips and stared around the park. "Well? Where are they?"

"Close your eyes."

"What?"

"Close your eyes. I don't want you getting sick all over my shoes."

"Molly. This is stupid."

"Fine. Have it your way." Molly stepped under a large maple tree and smirked. "Coming?"

Faye moved in close to Molly, who held her tightly around her waist. Molly raised her fist above her head and touched the tree with her palm, pushing in. All the air in Faye's lungs was sucked out of her. She squeezed tight to Molly, holding on for dear life as they did whatever the hell they did. Faye groaned as they stopped moving, the tense pressure that had felt as though it was trying to burst her relieving, finally.

"What the hell was that?"

"I told you to close your eyes."

"Like that would have helped."

"Don't get sick on my shoes."

Faye shook her head. "I'm not going to get sick. Just trying to breathe normally."

Molly turned sharply and held up a hand to silence Faye. Faye complied and watched as Molly glanced around. The mood turned from teasing to tense in an instant. Faye's stomach clenched as she held her breath and looked around. They were somewhere, she wasn't sure, but it didn't look like a park at all. It looked like a city. They were on a street, lamps lit to ward off the dark, but the street was completely empty.

"Where is everyone?" Molly whispered.

"Hell if I know. I didn't even know this place existed."

Molly stepped forward, her heels clacking against the stone street as she went. Faye moved much more silently, wondering if they would even find the dealer. They walked along the empty street until Molly stopped sharply, Faye bumping into her from behind.

Bouncing back, Faye stared down the street and froze. She moved around Molly, stepping in front of her as she cocked her head to the side. The woman down the way definitely looked familiar—her pixie like features, her hair, the slight smirk on her lips. But it couldn't be her.

"Aliya," Faye whispered. As much as she wanted to run forward and see if it really was her, Faye hesitated. She needed to know what was going on, why Aliya stood in front of her, why she was alive and not dead.

Molly stood next to her. "We do this together."

"Yeah," Faye answered. "Together."

They waited as Aliya came toward them, and the closer she got the clearer it was to Faye it truly was her. While Faye tensed every muscle in her body, Molly stayed calm and relaxed. Faye envied her ability to do that. They stood shoulder to shoulder as Aliya got closer.

"I was wondering how long it would take the famous Molly to grace us with her presence."

"Who is us?" Faye snarked. "I just see you."

Aliya raked her gaze over Faye. "You are so good until you talk. Then you...I don't know...disappoint."

"All right," Faye answered. She had no clue what that was supposed to mean, but she could tell Aliya meant it as an insult, not that it bothered her any.

Molly moved slightly ahead of Faye and took charge. "Where is everyone?"

"They have abandoned this place."

"Why?"

Tingles worked into Faye's chest, and she tried to hold them at bay as long as she could. She needed to wait until the prime moment to shift, if she needed to, and she really wanted to know how the hell Aliya was alive. She'd seen her die, been the one to kill her, hadn't she?

"They weren't welcome here anymore. Only my allies are welcome, and you, Molly, are not an ally."

Faye's heart raced. Molly barely moved an inch, but Faye caught her jaw clenching out of the corner of her eye. She prepared for whatever may happen next. Faye tensed as others joined Aliya, surrounding them. Faye was at a disadvantage, not knowing where exactly they were or how to get out of there. Molly had all that knowledge, and suddenly, Faye regretted not listening and learning more about the Tainted world. She'd taken it all for advantage. They also hadn't told anyone where they were going.

"I don't like this," Faye muttered.

"Shush," Molly answered before calling out to Aliya. "Where's King Jakob?"

"Dead."

"How?"

"I killed him."

Molly's jaw clenched again, her hands forming into fists. Faye knew instinctively her magic swirled under the surface, waiting for Molly to release it. They could do this together. Sure they were outnumbered by a bunch of murderous faeries, but they'd found themselves in worse pickles before. Though they at least had somewhat of a plan before going in those times.

Bouncing in her boots, Faye was ready to shift and to take them down. Molly didn't turn toward her. Glancing around, Faye counted how many they were outnumbered by. It was a lot—easily by thirty. It was going to be a bloodbath of a different nature. Swallowing, Faye bounced even more in her boots, letting the tingles roam freely in her chest. All she had to do was wait for the cue from Molly.

Aliya walked even closer until she stood ten feet from where they were. "I am the Queen."

"And why are you manufacturing this drug?"

"Isn't it obvious?"

"Not quite." That trite tone of Molly's set Faye on edge. Molly was close to bursting. "Explain it to those inferior to you."

A blush rushed to Aliya's cheeks, and Faye knew what Molly was doing. Placating and pleasing the one who held the most power in the room. "Your kind disgusts me."

"My kind?" Molly hissed out a breath. Faye reached forward to hold her back.

"Witches. Vampires. Immortals. You take this world for advantage, for your own benefits."

"But you're killing those who aren't immortal," Faye shot back. "What about them?"

"They support you."

"So for their support they lose their lives? And why so violently? Why not poison the water?"

Aliya faltered. Faye cocked her head to the side curious. It was as if Aliya hadn't thought of that, which made zero sense for someone who was a faerie and had the actual ability to do that. Pursing her lips, Faye went to speak, but Molly beat her to the punch.

"Suppose that was a bit much to ask from a child."

"I am a queen!" Aliya stomped her foot down. Tree roots grew up from the ground, snaking around Molly's ankles and up her legs. Molly ignored it.

Faye pulled the tingles from her chest, her nails elongating, her teeth descending. Cracking her neck, she hissed as she prepared to take down whoever got to them first. She would protect Molly while Molly did whatever she was going to do.

The others descended on them. Faye spun around, taking down the first one with a slice to her neck. She spun around to take down the next. Ducking down, Faye moved as swiftly as she could. She kicked, sliced, worked her way through the crowd of faeries as she went. Catching sight of Molly, Faye's breath left her. Her entire body glowed like someone took a light and shoved it inside her.

Faltering, Faye lost her footing and fell flat on her face. Twisting onto her back, she cried out when roots wrapped around her arms and her legs, holding her down. Cursing, Faye bent her wrist and sliced through some of them to get her hand loose. She jerked her legs up and down, but it was nearly impossible to move as more roots wrapped around her and kept her down.

A burst of light flung from Molly's body. Faye shut her eyes tight against it, unable to cover her eyes in anyway. The faeries nearby her were knocked to the ground, and when she turned to see them, she noticed the roots were gone, withering away like someone had dumped poison on them. Pushing up from the ground, Faye ran to Molly, grabbed the gun out of the back of her waistband and aimed it at the faeries coming toward her. She had to defend them.

Molly was still wrapped up tight in tree roots, unable to move. Faye sliced her way through them, but they kept piling on, faster than she was able to break through. The hit to her side surprised her. Turning to look down, a tree root was shoved between her ribs, or rather, into them as she no doubt had a few broken ones with the size of the root.

"Oh fuck," Faye muttered.

Molly couldn't even turn her head to look, but her eyes slid toward her.

"I'm fine." Flinging her hand down, Faye sliced the root off and pulled out the part that was stuck in her. Blood poured from her side before healing up. Faye drew in a deep breath as she moved to avoid being struck again. "Molly, end this."

Once again a bright burst of light flung from Molly's body, knocking Faye on her ass as it went through her. She drew in a sharp breath as her ribs popped back into place. When she glanced up, Molly was free from the roots, and Aliya lay on the stone street, her neck at an awkward angle. Everyone else stood still around them as they stared at Aliya's dead form.

This time Faye knew she was dead. Turning on her side, Faye pushed herself up and stumbled over to Molly. Her chest rose and fell rapidly as she caught her breath. None of the other faeries moved.

"They'll want to deal with her body properly," Molly whispered. "But I need to make sure she's dead."

"How do they do that?"

Molly gave Faye a serious look. "There's rituals before her body will become one with the earth."

"Makes sense."

Faye watched as Molly stepped forward and bent down in front of Aliya's broken form. She pressed fingers to her neck and sat back on her feet. Faye moved next to her to help her stand, their hands staying folded together as Molly turned to face the rest of the remaining faeries.

"You have a choice to make. Carry on Aliya's charge or follow the other faeries who have left. The choice is yours, but know which one you need to make if you want a different fate."

The others bowed down to Molly, getting on one knee. When all the faeries knelt as if Molly were their queen, Molly turned to Faye.

"We should go."

"Right. How exactly do we get out of her."

Letting out a small chuckle, Molly gripped Faye's fingers. "Close your eyes."

Faye listened this time, but the experience was just as bad as the first time. When she opened her eyes, she was pressed against Molly but back in Lion's Park. Faye let out a breath. "We can never go there again, please."

"Unfortunately, I imagine we'll be spending quite some time with the faeries while they rebuild."

"Joy." Faye whined. "You really think this was all just Aliya's crazy plot?"

Molly stared at Faye. "No. I've known the faeries for a long time, and they are not known for violence. The way she was acting...something else is at play here."

"Okay, what?"

"No idea. For now, I think we've stopped the main problem. Let's work on the rest tomorrow."

Faye straightened her shoulders. "Sounds like a plan. What now?"

"Home." Molly cupped her cheek and kissed her lips gently. "Now we go home."

CHAPTER THIRTY-FIVE

BEN WAS at the door when they returned. Faye heaved a breath as she shoved her helmet onto the handlebars. Molly handed over hers and ran her hand along Faye's shoulder and down her arm. She loved touching Faye like that and had taken to doing it often as the months had passed.

"You two will never believe what I found."

Faye scoffed, but Molly was genuinely curious. She put up a hand to stop him from rambling. "Before you go on, did you retrieve all the individuals from the club?"

"Yes."

"Clean everything up?"

"Yes."

"Amachon?"

"Dealing with them." Ben bounced as he held his tablet close to his chest. "Can I tell you yet?"

"Go ahead."

Faye shot Molly a look of annoyance, but Molly focused on Benjamin. He clearly had something the wanted to share, and she wasn't about to ignore him. Faye sat on her bike while Molly stood next to her and waited for Ben to go on.

"Okay, so while you were gone, I found something."

"You found something in that short period of a time?" Faye sneered.

Ben shot her a glare. "Not all of us are lazy."

"Ouch." She smiled at him through her false hurt.

"Enough," Molly interjected. "What did you discover?"

"A manifest." Ben handed his tablet over. "I don't know why I didn't find it before."

"Because you weren't looking," Faye muttered.

Molly's lips parted, but she couldn't find the words she wanted, so she ignored Faye and focused on the screen in front of her. Ben wasn't lying. The document was full of hate for Tainted, particularly those who were immortal, which meant pure witches and vampires. She skimmed through it, flipping page after page of hate for the control they exerted. Anyone who had hundreds of years of experience would have control over their gifts.

Handing it to Faye, she turned to Ben. "When was it written?"

"Within the last couple years."

"Why is there so much hatred of vampires then? Faye and Marcellus are the only vampires living."

"I've only read it through once and haven't done any searches on keywords to match it up with potential previous documents, but I'd think it's pretty obvious. Vampires are the epitome of immortals."

"Yeah, except we were all but exterminated." Faye wrinkled her nose, handing the tablet back to Ben. "So much for immortal."

"She's not wrong." Molly crossed her arms. "I don't know about this. It seems too convenient."

"Yeah," Faye agreed.

"What?" Ben's eyes widened. "It's not. I spent hours searching for this."

"And it just happened to show up after Faye and I learned who was dealing and making this drug? Call me skeptical, but I don't trust it."

Faye pressed her lips together. "Not to mention I still don't get why. Why would another Tainted attack all other Tainted? It makes no sense to me."

"Purity is one reason, but I have never known a faerie to be racist toward other Tainted. Ever, and I have known my fair share of them."

"You would," Faye accused.

Ben's gaze bounced from one to the other before he sighed. "All right, so bypassing that statement, no one else could have made the drug."

"Even if they did make it," Molly stated, "that doesn't explain why. And then there's the issue of Aliya."

"What issue?" Ben asked.

Molly looked around the garage. She really didn't want to be having the conversation out in the open. Her office was a much better place, where she could control the environment and where she knew there would be no prying ears listening in.

"Where's Malek?"

"With Joel. Why?"

Molly waved her hand and closed the garage door as she stalked through the door. Ben and Faye followed her, Ben quickly and Faye dragging her feet. Molly didn't stop until she was in her office, and as soon as the three of them were inside, she locked the door.

"Aliya, I believe, was under the influence of a greater force."

"Why do you say that?" Faye asked.

"Did she act normal to you?"

"No, but that whole situation was messed up."

"Benjamin, what else have you found?"

"Just this so far."

"Keep looking. I want to know who came up with the formula for that drug. All right?"

"Got it, boss." Ben skittered away, leaving Faye and Molly alone.

Faye pursed her lips and stared at Molly with a raised eyebrow.

"What?" Molly asked.

"Are you going to share with the class what you're thinking or do I have to guess?"

"The door."

Faye waved her hand and the door slammed shut and the lock moved into place. Molly sat on the edge of the couch, brushing her hands under her butt as she moved. Faye remained standing, lording over her.

"Watching Aliya tonight was eerily similar to watching a turned vampire from a born vampire, one who is under the influence of its master."

"I have not turned anyone." Faye paled.

Molly shook her head and waved her hands, trying to calm Faye down. "No, I don't think that. Sit down, please."

Faye plopped down on the couch.

"I realize you haven't seen that as you weren't alive the last time it happened, but the amount of power and influence someone had over her was very strong. There is magic that can do that, but it is blood magic and there are not many witches who know how to use it."

"Are there any other methods of control like that?"

Molly drew in a deep breath. "Some telepaths can. Certain Elementals, though that gift is very rare."

Faye gnawed on her lip. "So what are you thinking?"

"I'm thinking we have only scratched the surface."

Faye nodded. "I agree. But I'm not entirely sure where to go from here in terms of searching for another answer."

"Ben will find something."

"You're placing a lot of trust in a man who has barely stepped foot in his work area in weeks."

Molly frowned. "I agree, but he will come around. It's natural for him to be overwhelmed and distracted right now."

"Maybe."

"I'm serious. Give him some room to grow. He certainly gave it to you."

Faye folded her arms in a pout, leaning into the couch. Molly tried to hide the quirk of her lips, but she couldn't. Turning into Faye, she cupped her cheek before trailing a hand downward over Faye's breast and arms to her belly and hip.

"I think we should celebrate."

"Celebrate what? You just said it was all a bunch of bullshit anyway."

"But we did take down the dealer and main manufacturer of the drug. Let's celebrate that win for today, yes?"

"By celebrate...do you mean...?"

"What else would I mean, Faye? I used plenty of magic tonight. I should think after your blood loss a reciprocation of gifts would be welcome."

"Is that all it is?" Faye's slate-gray eyes were wide.

"Hardly." Molly raised her hand up and dragged her thumb across Faye's lower lip. "You know that by now, whether you'll admit it or not."

They held the silence, Molly staring deep into those beautiful eyes she couldn't get out of her mind. Finally, with a light smile, Molly pushed Faye down onto the couch, covering her body. The bond was there in an instant. Molly barely had to work for it. Faye's cheeks flushed as she was overwhelmed with Molly's emotions, but she wasn't going to hold back any longer. Faye needed to know everything.

Faye was completely naked, her body warm, or rather hot, as she pried her eyes open to find the sun staring back at her. It had been ages since she'd slept through dawn. She turned to get off the bed, but a hand pressed to her chest, curling around her as hot breath rushed against her back.

"Don't move."

Faye chuckled. "Molly, it's past dawn."

"The house will survive."

Faye settled down where she had been, taking Molly's hand in hers and folding their fingers together. Molly definitely wasn't going back to sleep, but she could appreciate Molly's desire to stay put in the warmth of the bed after a busy few days.

"You know someone will come find you sooner rather than later."

"Please don't let it be Malek," Molly whispered.

Faye licked her lips and turned over. She brushed fingers over Molly's lips, staring into those dark brown, nearly black eyes. Curling her Molly's long tresses around her fingers, Faye sighed. "What is it you have against him?"

Molly muttered. "Drop it."

"Why are you so afraid to have sex with him?" Molly tensed, and almost instantly, Faye regretted asking the question. "I'm sorry."

"No, no, it's a valid question." Sighing, Molly shifted onto her back and flung an arm over her head. "We were matched at one point, Faye. That means something to the fold, and to me, as much as I don't want it to. I worry if I give in to that again, I'll never find my way back to you."

"That's ridiculous. I'm good for a fuck, but that's about it."

Molly's lips parted in surprise. Faye tried to get out of the bed, but Molly pulled her back. "Wait."

"No. If you're matched to him, go be with him if you want. If not, be with him and have some fun while you're at it. Sex doesn't mean you have a lifetime commitment."

"It will to him."

Faye sighed and relaxed. "And you don't want it to? You can't control what he thinks or feels."

"No, but I can avoid encouraging him."

"True."

They lapsed into silence. Molly moved into Faye, wrapping around her side and brushing her fingers over the injury Faye had sustained the night before. It was completely healed. Only Molly would know that something had been there to begin with.

Molly kissed a line along Faye's neck to her collarbone, tweaking her nipple as she moved her hand across Faye's body. "Besides, I'd much rather have you."

"Why don't you release him?"

"Malek?"

"No, Lamek, but yes, also Malek. Can you release him?"

"I could, but it's more complicated than that."

"What do you mean?"

Molly twirled her tongue against the column of Faye's neck. "I would lose the protection of the fold."

"I'm sorry, how is that any different than how you already live?"

"It means when I get cursed again, they won't help."

"They barely helped this last time." Faye pouted. "So really, why wouldn't you release him?"

"I don't think he'd accept."

"That's his problem."

"He has to accept for it to be final."

"Who makes up these dumb rules?"

Molly laughed as she pressed her hand between Faye's legs, causing Faye to gasp. "The rules have been in place for eons."

"Well, they're stupid," Faye whispered on a groan.

"I agree. That's why I left."

Faye moaned as Molly's fingers pressed into her. Her back arched as Molly made the magical bond. Faye much preferred sex with Molly to include the bond, but they'd done that pretty much all night, and she wanted to talk about Lamek.

"Molly?"

"Hmmm?" Molly nipped into the skin just at the underside of Faye's breast.

Faye squirmed as pleasure coursed through her body. "What about Lamek?"

"What about him?" Molly's fingers pumped harder into Faye, just like she liked it.

Raising her legs up, Faye gripped Molly's wrist and changed the angle to be exactly what she wanted and needed. She pulled out her nails, digging them into the skin around Molly's wrist. "Release him."

Molly's rhythm didn't hesitate, but she did bite down a little harder into the soft flesh at Faye's stomach. Faye jumped and tossed her head back against the pillow.

"Release him, Molly. He doesn't deserve to be stuck there."

"All right. Now come."

Faye's body shuddered as her orgasm ripped through her. As soon as she was calm enough, she pulled her hand away from Molly's wrist and licked up the blood that spilled onto her fingers. Molly laid next to her again, making slow designs into Faye's chest and abdomen.

"You really mean that?" Faye asked, scared about what answer she might receive.

"Yes. I will release him."

"Thank you."

Molly sighed. "But perhaps we can use this to our advantage."

"What do you mean?"

"I want to know why Malek is truly here, don't you?"

"Yes."

"Let's use this to confront him. I'm tired of waiting around for other methods to work."

Faye tapped Molly's temple. "What are you thinking?"

"Let's ask him to reverse the spell. We know he can't. I've talked to him about it already, but this time, I'll press him for information, or you will. You should."

"I should? Why?" Faye licked her suddenly dry lips.

"Because while you are pushing him, I'll weave a spell. Either way, we'll get what we want, whether you pull it from him or I do."

"Are you sure?"

"Yes." Molly flopped onto her back. "I want an answer."

"And you always get what you want. Everyone knows that."

Molly erupted in laughter. At Faye's confused look, she answered, "Hardly. It's amusing you think that."

"Experience," Faye muttered. "Pretty sure everyone else would agree with me."

Molly stilled. "It's not true."

"Seems like it to us."

"Maybe I should share more often, then."

"Whatever. Your choice." Faye rolled her eyes and pushed out of the bed. "Time's up, buttercup. It's morning, and there's work to do."

Molly narrowed her gaze in Faye's direction. "Why are you wanting to get work done? Usually you're the one who wants to stay in bed and I'm the one vying to get back into the game."

"Maybe you're rubbing off on me."

"Doubtful." Molly stayed right where she was, her hair strewn over the pillow, the blankets wrapped half-around her. "Truly, Faye, what is it?"

Faye shrugged and walked into Molly's bathroom, shutting the door. If Molly wasn't going to join her, then she would do whatever she wanted. She didn't need Molly to tell her where to go or what to do any more than she needed to lay in bed all day. When she walked back out of the bathroom, Molly was still in bed. Faye growled as she grabbed her clothes, dressed, and walked out to begin her round of chores.

CHAPTER THIRTY-SIX

MOLLY SAT in her office at her desk, Malek across from her in one of the two chairs on the other side. She had been expecting him at some point, waiting and biding her time for the conversation to begin. He looked as pristine as always, aloof and full of himself.

Malek had always managed to give off that air even if it wasn't who he truly was. She'd known that for years when he'd trained her. Molly stared back at him, lost in her thoughts, and he let her be, the silence a welcome change to what her life normally was. She finally smiled at him and shook her head.

"Do you remember when I first came to train with you?"

"Like it was yesterday." Malek folded his hands in his lap. "You were so young."

"So very young and obnoxiously annoying."

Malek smiled, a blush rising to his cheeks. "Not so full of yourself, but you were particularly stubborn when it came to learning. At least from me. You took to Reina quite well."

Humming, Molly leaned back into her chair with a pen between her fingers as she slid it one long end to the other. Staring out into the room, she didn't see her books or her couch or her office. She saw herself showing up within the fold for the first time ever. She'd gotten news of her match through her father and had gone to begin her training. She'd barely been twelve.

"I was so young."

"Yes, you were. We all were when we started our training."

"Father had taught me well enough. I never understood why I couldn't stay with him to train."

"It's not how the fold works."

"I know, but as you well know, Malek, I do often think rules are made to be broken."

"Oh, I'm aware." He grinned at her. "You were always breaking the rules in my house."

"Your house had stupid rules."

Malek laughed and stared at her. She flushed, looking back at him. Coming around the desk, Molly leaned against the front of it as she stared at him.

"You know, Faye and I had a discussion the other day about you."

"I imagine you've had a host of discussions about me."

"Well, yes, to be honest. She likes you."

"As do you."

Molly's lips thinned. "I like who you used to be, Malek, but you never used to keep secrets from me either."

"You used to be part of the fold. That gave you the privilege of information. You chose to leave, and with that comes the loss of certain privileges."

"I'm aware."

Malek remained seated, staring up at her, his gaze raking up and down her body. "Is this about the other night?"

"You'll have to be a little more specific than that."

"You were telling me something."

Molly sighed. "The first time I gave myself to you I was so young."

"Yes, you were, younger than most."

Cutting her gaze to him, Molly clenched her jaw. "You were persuasive."

"I did you no harm."

"You didn't. Not then at least."

"Molly, if I ever hurt you, please tell me."

Sighing, Molly pulled her lower lip between her teeth. "I was fifteen."

"You were of age."

"Hardly. I was old enough to make a decision within the confines of decisions already made for me. I watched Pearl make her own decisions, live life as she wanted it to. I watched her magic grow in leaps and bounds, in ways my own magic was confined. I lived that way for years with you. Years of being held back all for the sake of the fold."

Malek stood up, moving close to her. He pressed a hand to her neck, gaining her attention, his thumb under her chin as she stared up at him. "Where are you going with this? I most certainly did not hold you back. I gave you everything I had in spite of what the fold wanted."

"You were held back, thus so was I."

"Watch your step. You may not be a part of the fold any longer, but I am. I respect our traditions as vehemently as you spurn them."

Molly dashed her tongue against her lips, turning to stare directly into his eyes. "You used to. I don't suppose you do so much anymore."

"What is that supposed to mean?"

"Why are you here, Malek? If you truly respected tradition, you would leave me alone and ignore me like the rest of them."

"You are still one of us. You are still a part of us." Malek dipped his head, crashing their lips together.

Molly sucked in a breath, her hands coming up around his neck to hold on as their tongues dueled for control. She scraped her nails against the back of his head, down his spine and up again. Malek covered her breast with his hand as he nipped at her lip and down her neck, stopping as he ran into the cloth covering her chest.

"I was never a full part of the fold," Molly whispered.

"You were, damn it. I made sure of that." Malek shook his head at her before resting his forehead against hers. "You were."

"I wasn't. I always resisted because of Pearl, because of what my father had taught me."

"He taught you to love, and that was greater than anything I could teach you." Malek once again bent down to touch their lips together, but this time it was far sweeter than before when it had been all heat. Pulling away, he smiled and straightened his back. "I'm here to rekindle what we once had, nothing more."

"You want me to join the fold again."

"That would be preferable, but not necessary. Molly, I do love you. I have for centuries. What I want is to fulfill our match, whether it is in the fold or not. I want to be with you, to carry on our lines, to learn from each other. I may have trained you for decades, but it is clear to me you have learned far more than I ever taught. You have more magic than I have seen one witch hold. You would rival Reina and Corbin and you are half their age."

Molly swallowed. He still hadn't figured it out, which was

good, but she wasn't about to tell him either why she had so much magic or how Pearl had done it. Her lips parted as she stared at him. "I don't think I'll be joining with you."

"Molly—"

"No. I don't want to be matched. You know that."

"But we are forever matched, whether you want to admit that or not."

Shaking her head, she crossed her arms. "No. You may choose to believe that, but I do not. Let the fold match you with someone else."

"There is no one else!" His voice boomed through her office, causing Molly to tense in immediate response.

"There has to be."

"No. We are a dying race, Molly. Maybe not witches, but our fold is dying. Without you it will be impossible to continue."

"I don't believe that." Molly stood, her hands at her sides as if she were preparing to battle. "The fold has survived for centuries with these traditions. They will continue if that's what they want."

"A child hasn't been born into the fold in two hundred years. Not since Tess."

Molly froze. "Why not?"

"There's no one left."

"This isn't because of the vampires. Two hundred years is not seventy-five. You can't blame this on their genocide."

"We're not."

"Then what happened?"

Malek shook his head. "I have no idea. But no child has been born to us since Tess was born."

"And you want me to return to break this curse?"

"To try at least. Molly, what would happen if we were to die out?"

"Maybe the awful traditions the fold has continued would also die." She stared at him in defiance. "I won't return with you. I have made my bed."

"With Faye?" he scoffed. "She's a nice kid, but she's just that, a kid."

Molly's lips pressed together and pulled tight. "She knows more of this world than you would think."

"She's a child."

"And how is that any different than you and me?"

"We are of the same bloodline!"

"We still need a vampire, and she is the only one left."

"Not the only one." Malek didn't dare look at her.

Molly cocked her head to the side. "What do you mean?"

"There is one more. Faye's father. Don't think that when she showed up on my doorstep all those months about that I ignored who—or rather what—she was. How she came into existence. I needed to know."

"Did you find him?"

"Your old school friend?"

"Yes."

"I know you hid him. I know you. You're a master at hiding, not just Tainted but yourself. I know you hid him through the war, protected him."

"Do you know where he is?" Anger surged into Molly's chest, her eyes widening in panic. If Faye were to know, she would be gone in an instant to find and kill Marcellus.

"No." Malek walked closer to her, gripping her hands. "I don't know where he is, but I can find out, if that is what you'd like."

"Hardly. I'd rather him be dead."

"Odd, since you saved him for years."

Molly stared directly into Malek's pale blue eyes. "He was my best friend, but even some betrayals cannot be forgiven."

"Noted."

"Speaking of betrayal, how shall we break the binding on your magic?"

"If you won't return to the fold with me, I fear this is how I shall be for the rest of my life."

"We shall see. Come with me."

"Where are we going?"

"We're going to test your abilities and see if we can push the boundaries of the binding." Molly grabbed his hand and walked toward the door. Malek dutifully followed. As soon as she reached the base of the stairs, Molly called for Faye, meeting her in the garage. The three of them climbed into one of the vans, Faye driving as Molly sat in the passenger side. It was a short ride, but Molly was tired of answers being skirted. She was ready to confront Malek head-on.

Faye parked at Lamek's final resting place. The sun was setting outside, and those in the area were slim. No one walked under bridges that time of night in that neighborhood without taking a great risk. Stepping out of the van, Faye cracked her knuckles as she leaned against it, pressing one foot behind her to hold herself up as she stared at Lamek.

He didn't move. He wouldn't while Molly was there unless Faye coaxed him out. Both she and Molly knew that. He hated Molly, and considering the last few times Molly had been there she'd tortured him, there was no reason for him to trust her. Well, he'd be in for quite the surprise when Molly released him.

Faye knew what her role was supposed to be. They'd talked it out in enough detail, and she trusted Molly to back her up when she deviated from the plan. Faye let out a sigh and turned to face the two of them, who stared at her with wise curiosity.

"Molly said you were going to free him."

"I...what?" Malek's eyes widened in surprise as he turned to look at Molly.

"Free him," Faye repeated. "She said you'd do it, that she can't bring herself to do it. So do it already. He's suffered enough."

Turning to face her friend, Faye made her face take on a long and sorrowful look. She probably should have brought him some heroin because she had a feeling freeing him from the prison of torture he'd been confined in for decades was going to be just as painful, if not more painful, than staying in it. At least it would be short term.

"I...I can't," Malek whispered. Then he turned to Molly. "You know I can't."

"What do you mean you can't? You're this all-powerful witch, Malek. Release him. You don't need her permission."

"I don't have the magic, Faye." He paled.

She knew she was close to having him. "So what the hell good are you to me? If you don't have magic you can't even initiate the bond. You can't do that, you get nothing from me. So why are you here?"

"I want to bring Molly back into the fold."

"Bullshit!" Faye spat. She flung her hand out at him. "If you wanted her in the fold, you would have shown up centuries ago or you never would have let her go in the first place. Why the hell are you here? I'm tired of dancing around this."

His lips quivered as his gaze shifted from Faye to Molly. Molly stared back at Faye, her face full of fake-shock, but she said nothing and didn't interfere.

"Stop lying!" Faye roared. "If there's anything I hate, it's a liar."

"As if Molly hasn't lied to you."

Faye snorted, then she stepped forward quickly, pressing Malek's back into the van and holding her forearm against his throat. "She has never lied to me. Kept information, yes, but never outright lied. If you have no magic, I could kill you here in two seconds and you couldn't do a damn thing. I could bleed you dry, but you taste disgusting, so I won't be doing that."

"I—I tasted bad?"

"Like rotten flesh."

Malek paled and turned to Molly a look of guilt on his face, fear as he took in deep breaths.

"Dear Lord, Malek. You didn't." Molly stepped closer, her hand on Faye's shoulder, easing her away.

"I didn't mean to harm you."

"Why would you do something that awful?"

"I needed you back in the fold."

"For what?" Molly's voice echoed with pain and hurt.

Faye kept her position between the two of them, protecting Molly in case Malek tried anything, though she was more afraid in that moment of Molly's anger getting the best of her like it often did.

"It was the only way."

"What the hell are the two of you talking about?" Faye interjected.

Molly gripped Faye's hand, squeezed tight. "The fold is conniving, Faye. If Malek made them a promise and they saw he didn't fulfill it, they would do this as punishment. Even with the despair they're in, they care more about rules and traditions than they do one of their own."

"It's not me they care about," Malek shot back. "They want you."

"So you offered me? You had no right!" Molly's temper rose, and Faye tried to hold it back as best she could, still standing between her and Malek.

"When Faye arrived, asking for my help, they saw an opportunity. Did you really think they would cleanse your body and expect nothing in return?"

"No, I don't suppose I did." Molly, calmed, stepped closer to Malek and pressed a finger into his chest. "And I suppose they sent you because they feel this is your mistake, that you never should have granted me the pardon."

The look he gave Molly told both of them she was correct. Faye sighed. "These rules are fucking stupid and this gives me a headache."

Molly snorted and threw her hand up in the air. "Why didn't

you tell me?"

"Because I wasn't allowed."

She spun on him. "You have never been much of a rule follower, Malek, not on the little things."

"And see where that's gotten me? Here. Magic bound, banished from the fold until I accomplish what they want, no way to reverse this situation. Come back with me, Molly. Help me return order. It's time for new rules, new traditions. You and I can do that. We can save the fold."

Faye held Molly back as she darted forward. She stepped between them, both hands on Molly's shoulders, and their faces close. "Don't do it, Molly. You'll regret it in an instant."

Molly drew in a sharp breath. She glanced around Faye to Malek. "The fold should fall."

"There's war brewing."

"What the hell is this, dump everything into this moment to try and get her to go back with you?" Faye rolled her eyes. "Grow up, Malek. You of all people should know you don't make Molly do anything."

"You can." He stared straight into Faye's eyes.

Faye raised an eyebrow at him. She was about to speak, but Molly cut her off. "Their antiquated system can die with them."

"If it dies with them, so does my magic."

"Then so be it."

"You can't believe that." Malek pushed away from the van, and once again, Faye made sure to keep herself between the two of them. "Magic is my life. You know that as well as I do. Molly, help me. Please."

"You have never lied to me before."

"I'm not lying now."

"I don't trust you."

Faye held out a hand against Molly's belly to hold her in place. She had no idea what to say or how to calm the situation down. She was out of her element. Normally Molly was the peacekeeper.

"You're here to find out how I have so much power. They sent you here to figure out what I'd done to surpass them. I damn well nearly beat them, didn't I?"

"Yes. They want you back."

"To find out how many of their precious rules I've broken. Well, I'm not afraid of the fold, not like you are."

"I'm not afraid of them. I trust them with my life."

"They *are* your life. They're not mine."

Malek stepped closer, and Faye pushed Molly back, but Molly stepped around her. Faye wasn't sure she wanted to let them get that close with the way the conversation was going, but she maintained, no one could make Molly do anything.

"They're not my life," Malek's voice was soft, endearing. "You are my life. You always have been."

Faye narrowed her gaze as Malek cupped Molly's cheek, her stomach twisting.

"I promise you I have never wanted anything except the best for you."

"I'm not a child, anymore. I know what this world holds. I know more of it than you."

"You do," Malek admitted. "And I would like to share that. I want to be with you and no one else. I want our match to succeed, whether within the fold or without."

Molly sucked in a breath. Faye's chest hurt from the amount of tension she held within it. She couldn't dare herself to look at Molly again. Stepping away from them, she walked across the road to her friend and pressed a hand to his large finger. She needed a minute, or a week, or hell, a year.

CHAPTER THIRTY-SEVEN

MOLLY DIDN'T miss Faye walking away. Immediately, she stepped back from Malek and turned toward Faye, following her across the street. Night had fallen in the midst of their conversation. Malek remained by the van, thankfully. Molly did something she never thought she would. She wrapped her arms around Faye's middle from behind and buried her face in Faye's shoulder.

"Talk to me."

"No."

"Faye."

"No, Molly. You got what you wanted."

Molly drew in a deep breath and let it out slowly. "No, I didn't. Here."

Taking Faye's hand in her own, Molly pulled Faye away from Lamek, walking backward as Faye came with her. She held out her hand for Malek to join them. As soon as he stood next to her, Molly pressed a kiss to Faye's cheek.

"I promised you I would release him, and I will hold to that promise."

Faye nodded, though she still didn't look Molly in the eye, which worried her. Ignoring the pressing weight on her chest, Molly focused her mind.

Closing her eyes, Molly called on her magic, the tingles that swam in her body constantly picked up speed. She organized them, tracked them, placed them exactly where she wanted and needed them to go. Opening her eyes, Molly stared at the troll in front of her. She called in a fog, one that would cover everything until she was done. It filtered in, hiding them from sight.

Faye squeezed her hand tightly, and Molly released the spell she had been building. Her magic flowed through her into Faye on one side, using Faye's love for Lamek to intensify. It pulsed. It heated. It surrounded them.

The lightning came from out of nowhere, smashing down against Lamek's hand. The stone cracked. Molly held her ground, her body glowing as her magic increased. She focused on the anger and the pain she had once felt. That moment, that terrible moment when she'd held her sister broken and dead in her arms. Her dark eyes so very much like her own wide open, staring at nothing, her short gray hair cropped against her head.

Tears streamed down her cheeks, falling freely to the sidewalk below as the next lash of lightning came down and cracked the stone around Lamek's hand away. Molly drew in a sharp breath as pain lashed through her chest, the same pain she had felt that fateful day almost thirty years before, the pain she had given to Lamek in the physical. Pearl had been her life, her partner in everything she had accomplished, and life without her had been uneven.

Another lightning strike, this time on Lamek's arm. He cried out in surprise, his head moving to come alive. Molly stared at him and felt Faye step forward, but she tugged Faye back, keeping her there. She needed her, whether Faye saw that or not, she needed Faye in her life more than anyone else.

Lamek shouted at Molly, telling her to stop, but she didn't listen. She focused on the lightning, dragging it down to him as rapidly as she could, wanting to make the process as short as possible. He didn't deserve any more pain. Faye had been right. Joel had been right. She'd frozen him in place, tortured him so she didn't have to feel it to herself. Pearl was her everything. Her big sister. The one who was her leader.

That had been what the fold had been so worried about, that the two of them were too close, that they shared too much. They'd attempted to separate them, and it had only drawn them tighter together. Their father had died for it, to protect their bond, and Molly wouldn't let that memory, her sister's memory go to waste.

Gasping, she drew down one more bolt of lightning, this one bigger than any of the others. It crashed right into Lamek's chest, breaking the stone from around his middle until it tumbled to the ground below. Molly didn't stop there. She pushed him down, sent him back to his family, to his kind. He sunk below the surface as she created a magical path to the trolls under the city, and she closed it after him.

The last thing she wanted to do was talk to him, to admit she was wrong to the very person who she still firmly believed wronged her. As tears continued to flood her eyes, she built the stone back up, sealing it together as if Lamek still lived under the thin veneer.

When she finished the spell, Molly let her magic fall into place within her. She turned to Faye, cupping her cheek and bringing their mouths together. Faye wiped the tears from her eyes and nipped at Molly's lips with her long teeth, exchanging energy for energy as Molly kept their bond in place.

Pulling back, Molly stared into Faye's slate-gray eyes, eyes she had known nearly her entire life even though Faye hadn't been born yet. When she turned to Malek, he stared at her with awe.

"How did you do that and remain standing now?"

Molly kept Faye's hand clasped in hers, ready to make a confession to him she hadn't told anyone in thirty plus years. "You spoke to me once of blood magic."

"You didn't—"

"Pearl and I spent years researching. We dabbled, we tested. Blood magic is not the evil the fold has made it out to be. It is wonderfully refreshing and freeing."

"Molly—"

"The night Pearl died? She shared her magic with me. I am now her and me combined, joint together. There is no undoing the spell since she is dead, there is no use denying the magic I contain."

"You mean you've got all her magic?" Faye asked.

"Yes," Molly reiterated. "Malek knows the importance of that and the threat of it to the fold."

"I knew you'd done something, but this?"

"Because of the cleansing?"

"Yes. You took everything in us to hold you. Without Faye there we wouldn't have managed."

"Then it's a good thing I had her on my side, and you."

Malek's cheeks were still pale as he stared at her in shock.

"This is why I can't return to the fold, Malek. You must understand."

"They will bind you."

"Yes."

"How could you?"

Molly stepped away from him, keeping Faye's hand in hers. "The choice wasn't mine. Believe me when I say I would love to go back thirty years and make a different decision."

"You still can. If you've dabbled in blood magic, then you should know you can."

Molly parted her lips. "I may know how to and can do it, but to what end? What would I change?"

"Everything you have wanted." He moved in closer to her, taking their joint hands in his. "Everything for us. Think of what you could change."

"I won't do it." Molly reached up and cupped his cheek. "It's not worth it. Malek, you are free to stay until you choose to return to the fold but know my answer will not change. This is my home."

Molly walked away with Faye's hand in hers. She had hoped her meaning was clear, not only to Malek but to Faye. They'd skirted around exclamations of love, talks of the future. They'd stayed rooted in the present for far too long. They would need to talk, eventually, about the past and the future, but until they had the time, she hoped Faye understood her meaning.

Faye flopped onto the couch in the game room, her leg brushing against Ben's as she let out a huge sigh. She closed her eyes and tried to morph her body into the cushions, but it was fruitless. Ben stared at her with an odd look on his face, and she shook her head at him. She didn't want to talk about it, or maybe she did and that as why she'd sought him out.

"What's wrong?"

"Nothing," she shot back.

"Faye, what's wrong?"

"Have you ever been to the arctic?"

Ben shook his head slowly. "What does the arctic have to do with what's wrong?"

"Nothing." Faye popped her eyes open to stare at him. He did look concerned. Maybe she should try to mimic someone who was happier with what was going on so she wouldn't have to worry everyone. "I was thinking about going up there."

"What the hell for?"

She smirked. "There's a mythological creature and I want to see if it's real."

"What kind of creature? The last time we went on the hunt for a mythological creature we came up empty handed, well, short-handed."

Chuckling, Faye agreed. "Yeah, that was a wild ride. This is a creature I've known about for a while, and I don't think we'll end up like last time, though I'm not sure we'll come home with one either."

"What is it?"

"Ijiraq."

"I'm sorry, what?" Ben's eyes widened. "What the hell is that?"

Faye shifted to sit up more fully. "It's a shifting creature. Lives in the arctic. Can shift into any form it chooses. Doesn't this sound a little familiar?"

Ben's gaze shifted down to the ground.

"I want you to fully embrace this side of you if you're going to do this. There's no shame in what you are or who you are."

"Right back at you."

Faye's heart clenched. "Touché. I was thinking the other day that we could go on the hunt for the ijiraq and test a lot of your skills in the process. Who knows, if they are real, then they might like you better than me."

"We're both shifters of sort."

"Truth." Faye smiled. "So what do you say?"

"Tell me more about it before I agree. I don't exactly want to freeze my ass off for a theory."

Laughing, Faye pulled up her phone and showed him a crude drawing that had been made in the middle of the last century. It looked kind of like a mix between a ram, bigfoot, and human. The hair on it was long, its eyes wide, curled horns on the side of its head.

"That thing is ugly."

"In this form, yeah, but they can look like anything, remember? Just like you. Except these ones, in theory, always have red eyes."

"That's not like me."

"I know, but maybe it's your long-lost cousin or something."

"Have you talked to Molly about this yet?"

"No." Faye flushed. She hadn't wanted to talk to Molly about anything yet. She needed more time to work through everything, all the information that had been dumped on her in the last couple days was too much. "She's been too busy with the idiots who took the drugs."

"You're one of those idiots."

"Yeah, but it won't kill me."

"You don't know that. And you didn't know that when you took it the first time."

Faye pressed her lips tightly together. He was right. She just didn't want to admit it. "What do you say? Want to go?"

"Maybe. I'll think about it."

"I need an answer, Ben. I'm leaving next week."

"You're serious?"

"Yeah. I'm coming back, don't worry. I want to go find this thing, see if it's real or not."

"Why so interested in myth suddenly?"

Faye sighed. "I've always loved myth. Even growing up. Hell, I am a myth. I wanted to know more about me, and really until I found Molly, I didn't know anything about vampires. They were still a myth even though I had been introduced into the world of Tainted."

"I hear you on that. All right, if she says yes, I'll go."

"Yes!" Faye grinned. "Perfect. I'll set it all up."

"You going to tell me what's wrong?"

"Nope." Faye pushed to stand up, but he gripped her wrist and dragged her back down. "Fine."

"Good."

"I don't know what to do with Molly, and you hate hearing about our problems."

"That's because all you two are is a problem."

Faye cut him a sharp look. "If you don't want to hear it, I can leave."

"No, I'm sorry. What is it?"

Sighing, Faye rubbed a hand through her hair and tried to morph into the couch again. "Something she said to Malek."

"What?"

"Something about coming home. I don't know. It's been bugging me."

"Coming home?" Ben pulled a funny face, his eyes squinting as he stared at her.

"Yeah. It was...intense under the bridge."

"How's Lamek?"

"Don't know. I haven't gone to see him yet. Kind of scared to go back down there after the last two times. Though, maybe if I go alone, they won't try to kill anyone."

"Probably. They like you."

"We'll see. When we were under the bridge...there was a lot of shit that came out."

"Of Lamek?"

"No!" Faye laughed. "About Molly. I'm not sure how I feel

about it all, that's it."

"But you're staying at the house."

"Yes, Ben, I'm staying at the house. I'm not leaving. I promise you."

"Good." He patted her leg. "Then I figure everything else with work itself out. You and Molly kind of always run circles around each other trying to catch one another and never seem to get there. You will, eventually, I think anyway, but for now that's what it's going to be."

"When did you become wise, Benny-boy?"

"Don't call me that."

Laughing hard, Faye stood up this time, stepping away so Ben couldn't pull her back down. "I'll talk to Molly about the ijiraq."

"Sure, but can we name it something else that I have chance in hell of pronouncing?"

"Nope." Grinning, Faye walked out of the game room and into the hall. She'd done what she'd gone there to do, convince him to fully embrace his shifter self and find a way to get a break from their boss. Molly confused her too much, and she needed the space.

She would make all the plans, book all the flights, get everything ready before she went to talk to Molly. That way Molly would be less likely to say no, and she could go even without permission. She would anyway, whether Molly approved it all or not. Call it a vacation, she would enjoy her time. Hopefully Ben would come even if Molly said no.

Faye walked through the hall toward her room when Malek popped out of Molly's and pinned her with a look that sent shivers down her spine. Faye eyed him up and down, trying to figure out what he was up to. They'd found out more information as to why he was there, though she still wasn't convinced it was all of it, and neither was Molly.

Malek walked right up to her, grabbing her by the back of the neck, tilting her head, and crashing their mouths together. Faye groaned as he shoved her into the wall, his hands against her sides, moving up and down, teasing her breasts. Faye nipped at his lip, closed her eyes, and waited for him to slow down. When he pressed his lips near her ear, she shivered.

"I'll be staying here for some time. We can explore this more."

"Oh good." Faye said the words on a breath. "Here I thought once was the only time we'd get. I'm not biting you, though. Sorry, but that was something I don't want to experience again, at least until you're done with whatever pissing match you've had with the fold."

Malek chuckled, the sound low in his throat. "Hopefully that will be ended soon enough."

"Oh? Do you have plans?"

"Not yet, but Molly is smart. She'll help me figure something out."

"That she is. Now, if you don't mind..." Faye slipped from his grasp and walked backward down the hall toward her own room. "...I've really got some work to catch up on."

"You work?"

She shrugged. "Guess you can train a vampire."

Chapter Thirty-Eight

Faye waited until Molly left her bedroom. She'd made all the arrangements for her and Ben to leave in four days to head up to the arctic to chase down the ijiraq or at least some signs of it and gathered the information to make her case for Molly.

As she stepped into Molly's office, she couldn't help but wonder if Malek had been leaving Molly's bedroom for a very specific reason, one Faye had actually called her out on. Pushing the thought to the side, Faye plopped down into the chair across from Molly's desk and stared up at her lover, the one consistent lover she'd had for four years which was the longest she'd ever spent in any kind of relationship, not that she'd call what she and Molly had a relationship, but she didn't have a better term for it.

"Your thoughts are loud, Faye."

"Are they?" Intentionally, Faye raked her gaze up and down Molly's body—at least what she could see of it. Her breasts were pushed up in the shirt she wore, enough cleavage that there was very little left to Faye's imagination. Goosebumps sprouted against Molly's skin on her chest and arms, and Faye was satisfied with the reaction she'd gotten.

"You are insatiable lately."

"I think it's more you who are." Faye crossed her arms and leaned into the chair, lifting her knee against the edge of Molly's desk. She wasn't there for a quick fuck, though she'd never deny one if Molly wanted it. She was there to talk about going to the arctic. Molly didn't need to know it was because she needed a break from the house itself.

"Cheeky." Molly's cheeks flushed. "What was it you wanted to discuss?"

"I want to go on a trip to the arctic."

Molly froze. "No."

"Come on. What's the worst that could happen?"

"You of all people should know better than to ask that question, especially where you are involved."

Faye narrowed her gaze. "What's that supposed to mean?"

"You know what it means. No mission ever goes smoothly. There's nothing there, anyway."

"There is." Faye pouted. "You haven't even bothered to listen to what."

Molly drew in a deep breath, settled the papers down, and gave Faye her full attention. "Then, pray tell, what is in the arctic that has grasped your attention so viscerally?"

"Why are you talking like that? Whatever. There's a creature there you might be interested in, but I know Ben is interested, and I thought since he's exploring his shifter side, it might be a good chance for him to learn about some of his history and to explore some of what he can do."

"The ijiraq?"

Faye glared. "How did you know that?"

"I know a lot of things." The corner of Molly's lips quirked up. "I have searched for the ijiraq a few times before."

"And I assume you have found nothing."

"You assume correct."

Faye nodded. "Doesn't mean we won't find anything."

"Also correct."

"So can we go?"

"You and Benjamin?"

"Yes. Just us." Faye rubbed her sweaty palms against her jeans to try and calm herself. She didn't know why she was so worked up over requesting a mission, except she'd never actually requested one before. She'd either just left to go on one or did as she was told.

"Faye, don't take this question the wrong way, but you do intend to come back, don't you?"

"Why does everyone think I'm going to up and leave?"

Molly gave her a soft smile, but Faye didn't see it reach her eyes. Instead of answering, Molly stood up and came around to Faye. Grabbing her by the hand, she led her out onto the parapet, the breeze gathering up the curls of Molly's hair and moving them across her shoulder as she stared out at the busy city surrounding them.

"You have a tendency to leave when things are uncomfortable."

"My life is uncomfortable." Faye leaned over the railing, making sure she didn't touch Molly. They still hadn't really talked about what had happened at the bridge, and she wasn't sure she was ready for that conversation, but that was definitely where this was headed.

"You've not had an easy life. I think anyone can attest to that."

Faye's eyebrows rose and fell, but she still refused to look at Molly. Molly's hand landed on her arm, and Faye turned to stare up into those dark eyes that so easily consumed her.

"You didn't answer my question."

"I am planning on coming back here, yes."

Molly released a breath, all her muscles relaxing as she stood next to Faye. "Good."

"Did you really think I'd leave?"

"I don't know what you're thinking."

"Didn't you just say I thought loudly?"

"About sex, yes. Anything else and you are a mystery sometimes. I can anticipate some of your responses, your moods, but when it comes to us...you are a mystery."

Faye's lips parted. She straightened her back and gripped the railing tightly, her knuckles turning white as she leaned into it. She could jump, and she'd survive. It'd hurt like fuck, but she could do it. It wouldn't prove any point other than she was reckless, which they both already knew.

"I'm not a mystery." Faye spun around and leaned against the railing. "I'm not. I'm the last-born vampire. I'm young and wild. I have no concept of what it's like to go through life without being a murderer. I thrive on blood, other people's life source is my life source. I can't self-sustain, ever. You can. You have no concept of what it's like to have to rely on someone else in order to survive."

"You're right." Molly touched Faye's hand lightly. "You're right, I have no idea. We might have a bond, but that only goes so far. We may thrive together, but I can survive without you."

"Exactly." Faye moved to shift, but Molly stepped in front of her.

"The difference, Faye, is I don't want to survive without you."

That uncomfortable niggling feeling that had been struggling to burst in the pit of her stomach twisted hard and grew bigger. Faye once again leaned against the railing, taking on the persona of being unfazed, of being unmoved by Molly's words.

"Look at me."

Faye's gaze locked on Molly's.

"I'm asking you not to leave me."

"I hear you."

"Will you stay?"

She didn't want to answer. Everything in her body told her not to, to run and hide, to jump over the railing and race in the other direction. Faye did the one and only thing she could think of, the only way to get out of confirming what Molly wanted, because yes, she may be the only one who could convince Molly to do something according to Malek, but it really was the opposite. Molly was the only one who could convince her to stay.

Cupping Molly's cheek, Faye dragged her closer, their mouths feverishly moving together. Molly moaned when Faye broke her skin, the iron tang of her blood filling both their senses as it reached their tastebuds. Molly initiated the bond immediately. Faye pushed, walking Molly back until she was held tightly between the wall of the house and Faye's body.

Remaining as quiet as she could, Faye pulled up Molly's skirt with a free hand and slid her fingers inside her, hard, forceful, firm. Curling her fingers, she jerked her wrist exactly like she knew Molly liked it. Molly's head hit the wall as her eyelids fluttered shut. Her hips rocked in time with Faye's movements.

Faye's nose brushed against Molly's neck, her pulse point. As her blood moved swiftly through her veins, she couldn't help but catch the scent. Arousal. Sweet with a hint of spice. Faye leaned in even more to Molly's form, using the wall to give her the perfect counterbalance. As Molly's muscles clenched hard against her, her orgasm ripping waves through the both of them, Faye sunk her teeth into Molly's jaw on the side of her cheek.

The blood wasn't plenty, but as the sweet notes hit the center of her tongue, she groaned and swallowed it down happily. Energy burst along with the tingles in her body already working in overdrive. She closed her eyes, pulling her mouth away after she swiped her tongue along the injury. Removing her hand from Molly, she brought her fingers to her lips and sucked them clean.

"Are you coming home?"

Faye swallowed, the moment suddenly connecting for her. Kissing Molly sweetly, she pulled away and nodded. "This time, yes."

"That's all I can ask for."

Faye kissed her again before stepping away and through the parapet doors. She walked out of the office, ready to finalize her plans with Ben for their upcoming trip. Whatever had just happened, it had been good, and she'd managed to sidestep the real question Molly was asking just in time.

Molly sat on the couch in her office with a whiskey in her fingers as she read over a book with the mythical ijiraq in it. She hadn't studied up on it in decades, not since she and Pearl and gone on the hunt before Faye would have been born.

She was surprised when her friend came into the room and shut the door behind him. He grunted at her before sitting next to her on the couch, taking up well over half of it with his giant body. Molly cocked her head at him, not moving an inch from the position he had found her in. The air in the room was tense, and she worried she knew exactly what conversation was coming.

"How are our guests?"

"Most have recovered."

"Without the need of magic, I see."

He nodded. "Time for the drug to leave their system. You gave them that."

"I wish I'd known sooner."

"Me as well."

Molly sipped at her whiskey, the alcohol burning as it slid down her throat. It was her third glass that night, and she should probably have stuck to wine, but the call of a good stiff drink after her conversation with Faye that afternoon had been too much.

"Will you have your report in soon?"

"Yes."

They lapsed into silence. Molly finished her drink and shifted to set it down. The book slipped, but she caught it, settling it next to her empty glass on the table. The night air came in on a breeze from the still open parapet doors. She hadn't had the heart to close them after her tryst with Faye that afternoon.

"Amachon, my friend, what's weighing on your mind?"

"I'm going home."

She sucked against the back of her teeth. "When will you return?"

He shook his head, his golden eyes tearing up. "I won't."

Tears immediately sprung to her own eyes, and she pressed a hand to the top of his large one. Her lips quivered as the tears stung, warmly flooding down her cheeks. Molly drew in a deep breath, and let it out on a shuddering sigh.

"I knew someone was leaving. I didn't suspect you, my oldest friend."

"I'm old."

She brushed away the tears as they fell. "Hardly an infant to me."

He chuckled but shook his head. "I'm nearing old age, and I can't do something like this again."

Molly reached up to turn his face to hers. "I fear I will never see you alive again, my friend."

He didn't answer her. Instead, he pressed their foreheads together and closed his eyes. Molly mimicked the move, drawing in a deep breath, her heart shattering into a thousand pieces. She hadn't expected this. She'd known at some point he would want to leave, but after thirty years together—she'd hoped he'd stay.

"Home?"

"I miss it."

She swallowed. "I understand that call."

"I knew you would. I'm too old to keep up with you any longer."

"Hardly." She sniffed, tears still slipping down her cheeks. "Whatever shall I do without you?"

"You will learn to survive."

Molly let out a half-sob, half-laugh. "I suppose you're right."

Taking the risk, Molly leaned forward and wrapped her arms around his neck, pulling him in for a hug. She didn't want to let go. Tears ran from her eyes and onto his shoulder, his shirt damp with the salty drops. He held her tightly, running a hand up and down her spine in a soothing motion. She stayed there as long as she could stand it before pulling away.

"How dare you leave me?"

"Not leaving." He grunted at her, his chin rising each time he did it. His large hand reached up and pressed to the center of her chest. "Always here."

"You're the only one here who knew her."

"I only knew her because you wanted me to."

"You are irreplaceable."

"The decision is made."

Nodding her understanding, Molly touched the back of his hand again. "When do you leave?"

"Tomorrow."

"Amachon." Molly stared at him, surprised. "You couldn't wait any longer?"

"I'm old. I'm tired. I have watched too many patients die from this drug. I can't do it anymore."

"Running from your problems?"

He shook his head once slowly. "Running toward the solution."

"Who will replace you at the clinic?"

"I have set up a temporary hire for now. You will have to find a new medic as you find time."

"Oh Amachon. You're breaking my heart."

"I know." He lifted her hand, kissed her palm gently, and stood up. He walked out of her office without a glance back.

Molly pushed the tears off her cheeks before standing herself and refilling her glass. She knocked it back in one fell swoop before settling the glass down. Shutting the doors to the parapet, Molly stared at her empty office.

It was so representative of her life. Full one moment and empty the next. Lust. Knowledge. Pain. Loneliness. What she would give to be able to age with the rest of them. Instead her blood haunted her, the same blood Faye lusted after and survived on was her own undoing.

When her door opened again, she was surprised. Malek stepped through it, his eyes instantly taking in her form and his face changing from curiosity to understanding. He shut the door behind him. Malek held his arms open, and Molly gladly walked straight into the embrace. She wrapped herself into him, holding tight as sobs tore through her.

He shushed her. He kissed her head. He held on tight as she let the emotions run through her one after the other. Amachon had been her closest friend for thirty years, since Pearl had died, how was she to survive without him, how was she to go on without knowing he was right there to back her up.

Malek asked no questions as he comforted her. He would know exactly what she was feeling, exactly what ran through her, this intense loneliness they were both cursed to live with. When he kissed her temple, she turned her chin up to capture his lips. When he cupped her cheek, she stepped impossibly closer to him. When he tried to pull away, she dragged him back in. She wasn't going to let go of the one person who had been her lifelong constant.

The door opening again did surprise her, and she jerked back, wiping her lips as Faye walked through, worry written all over her face. "He just told me. I had...I had to make sure you were okay."

Molly smiled, tears once more falling fresh onto her cheeks. Faye's hand remained on the doorknob like she was going to run, but Molly couldn't let her. Walking briskly, she grabbed Faye's hand and fell into her like she had Malek. Holding out her hand, she reached for Malek, knowing he would come. Molly had no words. As soon as his fingers clenched hers, his arm came around her and Faye, she knew she was right where she needed to be. Home.

About the Author

Adrian J. Smith has been publishing since 2013 but has been writing nearly her entire life. With a focus on women loving women fiction, AJ jumps genres from action-packed police procedurals to the seedier life of vampires and witches to sweet romances with a May-December twist. She loves writing and reading about women in the midst of the ordinariness of life. Two of her novels, *For by Grace* and *Memoir in the Making,* received honorable mentions with the Rainbow Awards.

AJ currently lives in Cheyenne, WY, although she moves often and has lived all over the United States. She loves to travel to different countries and places. She currently plays the roles of author, wife, and mother to two rambunctious toddlers, occasional handy-woman. Connect with her on Facebook, Twitter, or her blog.

www.ingramcontent.com/pod-product-compliance
Lightning Source LLC
Chambersburg PA
CBHW052027220726
48293CB00015B/415